A MATTER

OF

DEGREE

Colin Andrews

COLIN M. ANDREWS

Matador
5 Weir Road
Kibworth Beauchamp
Leicester LE8 0LQ, UK
Tel: (+44) 116 279 2299
Fax: (+44) 116 279 2277
Email: books@troubador.co.uk
Web: www.troubador.co.uk/matador

All characters appearing in this work are fictitious. Any resemblance to real
persons, living or dead, is purely coincidental.

ISBN 978 1848766 952

British Library Cataloguing in Publication Data.
A catalogue record for this book is available from the British Library.

Typeset in 10pt Aldine401 BT Roman by Troubador Publishing Ltd, Leicester, UK
Printed and bound in the UK by TJ International, Padstow, Cornwall

Matador is an imprint of Troubador Publishing Ltd

To my wife, Sonja, and to my son, Gareth.

CHAPTER ONE

Thomas and friends

I stood on the top of the station steps, looking over the small square and car park. Three buses nudged forward like inquisitive cattle towards the group of people, mostly in my age group, already waiting under the single shelter. I hoisted up my rucksack, took one large suitcase in each hand and made my way to join them.

"Share a taxi?"

I barely registered the voice. I didn't recognise any of the destinations displayed on the buses, and I was considering whether to take pot luck with them and hope for the best.

Someone tapped my shoulder. "Care to share a taxi? I presume you are bound for Thomas Hall?"

I turned, and recognised the athletic profile of one of my erstwhile travelling companions on the train from Shrewsbury. Not that we'd spoken. In fact, along with the other occupants of the compartment, there'd been pretty much mutual lack of interest and I'd watched the unfamiliar landscape flow past the window for most of the journey.

"Er, yes, I'd be pleased to. Thanks."

An old saloon with a self-adhesive sticker proclaiming 'Tax' with a droopy 'i' pulled forward from the single dedicated parking bay.

"How did you know where I was going?" I asked, almost as an afterthought.

"Elementary, if I may borrow a phrase," he said. "You look as if you are new to this metropolis, you have the innocent look of a fresher straight from school and, thirdly, the labels on your luggage clearly state your destination."

I wasn't sure about the innocent bit, but I was grateful not to be humping around heavy cases to an uncertain destination by public transport.

"I'm Gerald Simpson, by the way," he said, offering me his hand as we settled down on the worn leather seats, and the taxi lurched off.

"Robert Kiddecott," I said, returning the gesture. "You don't look like a student yourself," I added, judging by his light grey suit and highly polished shoes. "More like a successful sales executive." My polo sweater, jeans and trainers spoke for themselves.

"Thanks very much!" he laughed. "That's what my father had in mind for me, but I couldn't settle down. I'm what you might call a mature student, in my final year of the teaching degree course here in Tencastle."

"Why didn't you introduce yourself on the train? I would have been glad of some background to this place."

"Oh, I prefer to observe people and their expressions, and hypothesise over their background and lifestyles. I'd guess you're Southern Counties, probably from Devon?"

"Yes I am." My irritation at being an unwitting guinea pig for his amateur psychoanalysis must have shown in my voice.

"Okay, don't take offence! No harm meant!"

"Well, suppose you tell me about Tencastle."

The taxi pulled up at traffic lights, and indicated a left turn. Gerald leaned forward and spoke to the driver, "Aren't we going a little out of our way for Thomas Hall?"

The driver glanced quickly in his mirror, "Roadworks along by the park. Quicker to go the other side of the river."

"I trust the detour won't cost more than the direct route?"

The driver muttered something unintelligible and executed a sharp right turn as the lights changed, to the consternation of a learner driver behind.

"Bloody peasant!" Gerald breathed out. "Anyway, what was I saying?"

"About Tencastle," I prompted.

"Oh yes! Well, as you'll discover, it's not a bad place. It rather lives on its former glories as a second-rate spa town. Before that it was quite a successful centre for the wool trade and they even dug a canal to link the town to the Lower Tene. By the time it was finished, however, the trade had passed its peak."

"So was the canal ever used?"

"Only for a few years, until the railway made it redundant."

The taxi pulled up behind a short queue of vehicles held up by temporary lights.

"It's surprising that a small place like this can support a university," I commented.

"Oh, the town's quite proud of its academic tradition, but they're very conservative here – with a small 'c' of course – these Welshmen would never admit to having voted for Heath's government. Very puritan and chapel, too. No boozing on Sundays – not unless you know where to go! They even wanted to put a fig leaf on Goliath."

"Goliath?"

"Sorry, of course, you won't know. Goliath's our famous athlete perched in the altogether on his pedestal opposite the Town Hall. It's rumoured he has an erection every time a virgin passes by."

"Who on earth put him there in the first place?"

"Dedicated to one John William Thomas. Apparently he was a local-born philanthropist who made the civic fathers an offer they couldn't refuse. He wanted to be remembered as the all-round sportsman but they say he was actually short and fat but very, very rich."

"And would that be the same Thomas as in Thomas Hall?"

"That's right!"

The old saloon left the commercial area of the town and began to climb a gentle escarpment, bathed in the late afternoon sun. Middle-class suburbia had crept inexorably up the slope, but a strip of meadow separated the last well-proportioned semi from a belt of woodland. From its midst protruded a white concrete structure topped by a dome which seemed to glow pink in the sun reflected from its windows.

"John Thomas," Gerald pointed out.

Obviously. "What's the hemisphere on the top?"

"An observatory, would you believe?"

The taxi turned into a tree-lined drive and drew up in front of an imposing brick-built mansion.

"Here's where we part," said Gerald.

"But what about you? Don't you live here too?"

"Used to, last year. I've got a flat now just over the hill."

Gerald helped me with my cases from the boot. The driver remained resolutely in his cab.

"How much do I owe you for the taxi?" I asked, reaching for my wallet in my back pocket.

"Oh, that's okay. Have this one on me."

"Are you sure? Thanks!" I wasn't inclined to turn down his offer.

"No problem! Look out for the girls now!"

"What do you mean? I thought Thomas Hall was single sex."

"It is. But you can always wave to them from the observatory. They won't see you, of course."

The taxi pulled away in a cloud of acrid exhaust fumes.

I suppose that Thomas Hall might once have been an imposing private residence, with landscaped gardens and a commanding view over the Tene valley. Its former grandeur, however, had been somewhat

3

diminished by a stark if functional two-storey red brick extension to the main house, whilst beyond the shrubbery bordering the lawns a rectangular, dome-capped white tower rose up from the outline of a modern concrete building. The oval forecourt was bustling with activity, as private cars and the occasional taxi jostled for access, spilling out the new inmates of Thomas Hall, together with luggage and assorted paraphernalia, essential or otherwise, for three months' survival until the end of term.

The reception area presented a scene bordering on chaotic, as students, many still gripping their cases, jostled to reach the notice boards covered in typed lists. A fair number of mums and dads were also trying to say loving farewells to their precious sons, no doubt with well-meant exhortations to avoid the evils of drugs, sex and booze. My parents, who rarely travelled further than Exeter in any case, had decided that my independence started at our farm gate, and as for the evils of sex and so on, what they – or I – didn't know about, they weren't inclined to worry over.

A small queue had already grown in front of a small window beneath a sign stating 'Reception – please ring'. I parked my luggage in a few square inches of spare space by a plinth bearing a bronze bonce – J.T. again, I guessed – and joined the half dozen or so bodies in front of me.

As we shuffled forward, I could see a head of well-coiffured brunette hair behind the reception window. Its owner barely looked up, as she checked the sheets of paper on her desk and, mechanically, passed a key and sheet of paper to each student.

My turn next for the automaton.

"Name?"

"Kiddecott."

"How do you spell that?"

A flippant reply came out unthinkingly. "T…H…A…T."

She rapidly scanned her lists, and stopped abruptly. For the first time her head jerked up and her eyes fixed me with an affronted stare.

"Very funny!" she snapped. "Don't waste my time!" Her head went back down again.

"Sorry, I just wanted to see your face. It would look quite nice with a smile." She was actually young and quite pretty.

Her head jerked up again quickly, and I thought I could just detect a slight thawing of her manner, before her pencil once more began its traverse.

"F wing 106. Keys." She thrust them into my hands, without the information sheet other students had been given.

There were, however, plenty of spares abandoned in the foyer – a map of Thomas Hall, meal times, house rules and so on.

F wing, I discovered, was in the new block, not in the tower itself but in a two-storey spur which branched off from the central lobby. A burly, bespectacled old buffer with an official-looking peaked cap emerged from a small office just inside the entrance.

"Can I help you, sir?"

"Yes, thanks, I've been allocated to F106."

"One moment," he said, and consulted a clipboard. "You'll be Mr Kiddecott?"

"That's correct."

"Right, sir, your room's down this corridor, ground floor, third on the left," he said, pointing to the double glass fire doors on the left of the foyer. "I'm Perry," he added, "one of the porters on this block."

Perry the Porter. Christian name or surname? I wondered.

"… responsible for security, and keep an eye on things," he continued. "If I'm not here then young Astleyson probably will be. Anything you need, just ask us."

"Okay, thanks."

Cell F106 – for first impressions were definitely claustrophobic, and not helped at all by the outlook onto a six-foot ivy-clad wall overhung by trees from beyond – was one of ten presumably similar study bedrooms set on either side of a surprisingly broad corridor. I dumped my bags, and went in search of vital facilities. I found them near the double doors from the foyer – three water closets, three shower cubicles, one bath, a separate urinal, and a small kitchen-cum-utility room, the latter spartanly equipped with a toaster, twin electric ring, electric kettle and a washing machine which had seen better days. I was thankful that the fees for Thomas Hall included half board, plus Sunday lunch.

Beyond the double doors, a staircase led to the first floor. I went up, just out of interest, to find, not unexpectedly, a clone of the ground floor. I completed my quick tour of inspection by returning down a staircase at the far end of the corridor, beyond which a further room lay on each floor. On the door of the upper room, a nameplate stated 'Dr. Cruikshanks', while below was the room of a Dr. Ambersham.

Second impressions, on returning to my room, were more favourable. While swinging a cat was a certain non-starter, the space had been utilised to the best advantage; a good-sized but simple desk with three drawers either side, bookshelves above, a padded upright chair, small armchair, built-in bed with storage drawers below and more shelves above, and a wardrobe unit with double sliding doors. One half of this was conventional hanging and shelf space, while the other half revealed a small washbasin, mirror and shaving point. Space had been left above the unit to put suitcases or other bulky items.

I'd hardly begun to unpack when I heard a tap on my door. I opened it to a thin worried-looking youth dressed in pale cream, sharply-creased trousers and matching blazer. His bow tie looked even more incongruous, and I half expected to see a straw boater in his hand.

"Yes?"

His prominent Adam's apple bobbed up and down agitatedly. "Has your room got one?"

"Er, one what?" I asked, confused.

"One of these!" He flourished a red leather bound book.

"Thoughts of Chairman Mao?" I ventured.

"Certainly not!" He sounded personally insulted. "God's truth! I am appalled that the college has not seen fit to provide every student with the comfort and protection of the Lord."

Hellfire and brimstone, didn't he trust in Perry and Astleywhatsit for his protection and comfort? "To be honest, I haven't looked yet," I said, meekly but truthfully.

"Here, you can have mine!" He obviously hadn't heard what I'd said. "I intend to take this up with the Warden!"

He thrust the tome into my hand, and strode off down the corridor, head bobbing forward and back like a hungry chicken.

"Thanks!" I said, gobsmacked, to an empty corridor.

I set about making the room feel more like home. It didn't take long for every available surface to be covered with an assortment of personal effects; order would come later, perhaps. The house rules vetoed any attachment of posters and such like to the walls except on the ridiculously small cork pin board by the desk, but, judging by the number of small discolourations and slight flaking of emulsion, the rules had obviously been ignored by at least one previous occupant. I'd also come prepared.

When I made my way over to the refectory for supper, Perry Porter was patiently listening to an animated monologue from Bow-Tie. He'd acquired another little red book to wave.

Next morning, I set off at a brisk pace, following a group of students who looked as if they knew where they were going. The rudimentary map sent to freshers was a masterpiece of abstract art. Thomas Hall was, according to the college literature, optimistically described as being situated only fifteen minutes' walk from the college. Ten minutes later, and still in my estimate barely half way to town, I fell in beside a stocky, red-headed lad who'd been just in front of me checking into Hall the previous night.

"Hi, are you new to Tencastle?" I said by way of a mundane opener.

"Yeah. I suppose this is the right way?" he replied, tentatively, in a strong Black Country accent.

"Depends what you're looking for. Salvation?" I said lightly, remembering Bow-Tie.

He laughed. "I'll settle for registration for now."

We walked on in silence for a hundred yards or so, before he added, "You know, I think you're probably the first other student I've really spoken to since I arrived at Hall yesterday."

"Me too." I didn't count Bow-Tie, since my input had been minimal. "It's a bit daunting, coming to the back of beyond," I said, conversationally.

"Yeah, and Tencastle isn't exactly a large town, is it?"

We could see the extent of its territory spread out below us, and beyond to where the silver strip of the Tene emerged from a narrower valley into the broad hill-bounded natural amphitheatre in which the town nestled.

"It's quite large compared to my part of the world," I said. "But not to somewhere like Birmingham. You're from that area, I guess."

"You guessed right. Brian Cheeke," he introduced himself. "Though my friends call me Rud."

"Rud?"

"Yeah, short for Ruddy."

"I'm Rob, Robert Kiddecott, from Devon."

"So what made you choose this academic backwater?"

"It chose me, sort of. It was the only place to offer me an unconditional place based on my A levels."

"Your predicted grades, you mean?"

"No, I'd already got them. I'd been earmarked at school as a likely Oxbridge candidate, but my results, well, they fell rather short of my school's expectations. They'd as good as accused me of idling away my last six months."

"Why didn't you resit them?"

"I didn't fancy another year as a superannuated schoolboy." I had briefly considered this option, but decided I wasn't really that academically committed. "No, I've had a year off earning a bit of cash, and reassessing my future. I thought I'd give teaching a go. What about you?"

"Believe it or not," said Rud, "Tencastle was my first choice."

"Why?" It seemed a legitimate question. The college was no more than a minnow in the world of academia, though, by all accounts, it was

7

fiercely proud of its independence within the University of Wales.

"I've always wanted to be a teacher, and I wanted to be out in the country, away from the city, near hills and mountains. And I wanted flexibility in the combination of specialist subjects. Tencastle seemed to fit the bill."

We arrived at the main college building, a rambling red brick structure situated in a park, on the banks of the River Tene.

"See you later," said Rud. "I've got a couple of things I need to do in town first. Like find a bank!"

During the college terms the population of Tencastle, just under four thousand, must have risen by at least a quarter with all its students. A good proportion of them were gathered in the foyer of the main, or rather, only college building, other than the student hostels and the various administrative offices I'd noticed scattered amongst the Victorian buildings in the vicinity.

The entrance hall had something of the atmosphere of a Christmas market – a melée of bodies, a multitude of stalls, and a hubbub of chatter punctuated by the cry of a stallholder promoting whatever he had to offer. Most of the student clientele seemed to be carrying plastic bags bearing Tencastle's academic crest. To one side of the hall, a timid sign above an archway advertised 'Registration'. This led into a smaller assembly area which evidently doubled as a drama studio – black drapes, gantries for lighting, and a moveable deck of banked bench seats. In front of a low stage, arranged in a semi circle, were a number of tables each bearing a faculty label: Science, Art, Humanities, Languages, Mathematics, and General. As a prospective student teacher specialising in Chemistry and Geography, I faced the dilemma of whether to register as a scientist or a human. The latter queue was shorter, and behind the desk was a face that I recognised, with a nameplate, Deirdre Beinyon, that I didn't.

After yesterday, I decided to be ultra polite when I reached the head of the queue. "Good morning, Miss Beinyon," I said as she looked up for her next customer.

"Oh, you're not THAT student again!" But she did smile. "And it's Mrs Beinyon, actually."

I knew a put down when I heard one, but I replied, "They keep you busy here, then?"

"It's all my job," she explained, her voice more friendly. "I work for administration, but in practice I'm almost full-time secretary for Dr Nightingale – the Warden of Thomas Hall, you know. But at busy times I register students wherever and whenever they need to be registered. And help look after their needs," she added.

Which particular needs she didn't say. Probably not the same as mine. "Anyhow, what are you in for? Kiddecott, isn't it?"

She'd have made a good hospital receptionist, too, but at least my name had registered.

Clutching my newly issued college library card, I rejoined the student throng in the foyer. As I edged along by the first stall one of the plastic goody bags was thrust into my hand by a hirsute character almost completely smothered by an outsize olive green sweater. His tin badge carried the ambiguous exhortation, 'Up the Union!'.

The carrier bag, whatever its original contents, was a godsend to stow the host of handouts from every stand; free pocket diary and biro from Bookwell's, the official college bookshop and stationers, a menu and free meal voucher from the town's only Chinese take-away, and all manner of temptations from all the main high street banks to manage one's overdraft, even though only two of them actually had a physical presence in Tencastle. Endsleigh were keen to insure everything up to my eyeballs, and another college franchise would have me suitably attired in tie and scarf, the latter in green with thin black stripes. I couldn't quite remember how I acquired the large white helium balloon proclaiming 'Spirits arise!' – Paranormal Society, or from one of the God squads that were touting for members. I caught a glimpse of Bow-Tie somewhere amongst them.

One display caught my eye. 'Bejesus!' screamed the banner, the word flanked by hairy faces of indeterminate prophets.

"What denomination do your represent?" I inquired curiously, of one who might have been the model for the banner's illustration.

"The lowest common one, probably," he smirked, sharing a secret joke with his petite female companion who sported the biggest nose stud I'd ever seen, like an opalescent wart.

She saw my puzzled look. "We're not actually a religious group. We're a Celtic music appreciation society."

"Really?"

"Irish music, particularly," she added, helpfully. "Though it helps with Student Union funding if we have a wider appeal."

Naturally. "So why 'Bejesus'?"

"Ah, well, that was the favourite expression of the founder. He was Irish."

"Of course." I gestured to the hairy blokes. "And what about the prophets?"

"They're two members of The Dubliners, the group's inspiration, you might say." She handed me a leaflet. "Would you like to join?" she asked hopefully. "It's free."

9

Well, that was an incentive, since most of the other societies seemed to be extracting money before you could sign on the dotted line. "I'll think about it," I replied.

I could see by the disappointment on her face that she knew I meant no.

Leaving the main college, a few minutes' walk took me from the park to the Students' Union, a functional building which looked as if it had once been two separate four-storey terraced houses. These were situated in a cul-de-sac just off the main street.

It was over four hours since I'd tackled the cooked breakfast of rubberised egg and crisp of bacon bloodied with tinned tomatoes. I tossed up whether to settle for a baguette in the bustling coffee bar adjacent to the entrance lobby or to go for something more substantial. My appetite won.

The refectory, signposted boldly, like the other facilities, in Welsh with optician's chart bottom line translation in English, was found along a corridor, past the wall-to-wall notice boards mostly given over to various sporting activities. Cafeteria style, it offered a surprisingly good choice of main meals and desserts at affordable prices. I settled for beef curry, and looked for a spare seat, since all the tables were already at least partly occupied.

Rud would have stood out in a crowd anywhere with his red mop. So too would his companion, some six-foot-three of solid ebony with shoulder-length straight black hair. He was just easing himself into one of the three vacant chairs.

"Hi, Rud, mind if I join you?"

"Be my guest. Rob, this is Jacob, he's on my corridor in Hall."

"Hiya, Rob." Jacob offered me his hand, "Jacob's for formal occasions. Most times Jake will do."

The accent in the deep rich voice was difficult to place; mainly London or definitely the South-East with a slight American inflexion. His confident manner positively flowed with vitality and his sardonic grin rarely left his face, as if he found all of life one big joke.

"And Mike Pattison, here, he's up in the Tower," said Rud, introducing me to a third member of the group, a slightly-built lad with sharp features and close-set eyes. Black stubble of a wannabe beard speckled his chin. The follicles seemed to have fallen on stony ground.

"Pleased to meet you," murmured Mike, in a tone which suggested he couldn't have cared less.

"I see you've been doing your shopping," said Jake, pointing to my carrier bag.

"Eh? Oh, that's just the freebies from registration. Haven't you been processed yet?"

"No, we'll pop up there this afternoon. We've been taking in the atmosphere of Tencastle."

"Yeah, car exhausts and bloody sheep droppings!" Rud chipped in. "Seems Wednesday is market day. Absolutely bloody heaving down the other end of town, and you can't get in the pubs for gold dust."

"'Scuse me, gotta be off," Mike grunted and rose abruptly, pushing his chair away.

"Cheerful bugger!" I commented, as Mike strode towards the door.

"Oh, he's okay," said Rud. "He's feeling a bit homesick, I think."

"What, after one day?"

"He was telling us earlier that it's the first time he's ever been away from home even for one night," Rud explained. "He's very shy. Finds it all a bit overwhelming, with all these strange people."

"Just as well he didn't go to London, then!" I added, not with much sympathy.

"That's where he comes from!" said Jake. "Same as me."

Must have led a bloody sheltered existence, I thought.

"Let's have a look at your spoils," suggested Rud. "No point in being lumbered with a lot of junk I don't need!"

I pushed the remains of my curry to one side and tipped the bag's contents onto the table. I'd managed to park my balloon on the railings of the Methodist chapel next door. Jake and Rud helped me sort through the bumf, though I made sure the useful items like the diary and biro returned to the bag. Apart from the bits and pieces I'd acquired from the stalls, we found a copy of the student newspaper, Llais y Castell, and a thin publication, 'Student's Guide to Tencastle'. Jake was thumbing through a more substantial booklet, 'Tencastle Union of Students'.

"Useful stuff, this," he declared. "Like where to go if you're pregnant …"

"I'll bear that in mind next time I'm in the club." I remarked.

"And look here, there's even a student folk club …"

"Are the two connected?" Rud chuckled.

"… must give it a try with my banjo," Jake continued, unfazed.

"You play a banjo?" I asked. I could manage two chords on my guitar – three on a good day.

"Never go anywhere without it!"

I looked around for the said instrument.

"Except today. Left it in my room."

Four young females approached the table with their meal trays. The adjacent table had just two spare places.

"Are these chairs free?" said one of them.

"No charge, for pretty girls," Jake grinned, flashing his white teeth.

I'm sure the poor girl would have blushed, but for her olive-brown complexion. Embarrassed, she stammered, "Th... thank you!"

Her tall blonde friend came to the rescue, "That's about the quickest chat-up line I've ever heard!" she said, disapprovingly.

"Sorry," said Jake, holding his hands up in apology. And then immediately negated its effect. "But I always tell the truth. You are all pretty."

The blonde certainly blushed. But Jake was right, all four were attractive, in different ways. The olive-skinned girl was slightly built, with dark, straight hair and deep brown eyes in a round face. She could have come from anywhere from the Mediterranean eastwards to Pakistan. Her blonde spokesperson easily topped six foot, slim, with slightly rounded shoulders and small breasts. Her blue eyes and petite freckled nose would have complemented a smile, had her lips not been still set straight. Of her other two companions, both were shorter by a head, one dark-eyed, with short cropped black hair, a baby-smooth complexion with just the hint of make-up, and a firm roundness of bosom. Strong Celtic blood I would have guessed. The fourth seemed quietly amused by the exchange. She was the only one with glasses, and her dark brown hair perfectly framed her oval features. Her figure was rather concealed by an amorphous pale green pullover, but she had shapely legs.

"We apologise for our friend here," said Rud. "Please do come and join us. We're not all lechers like him."

"I'm not ..." Jake began.

Blondie would have probably led the group elsewhere if there had been another table free.

"Please," implored Rud.

The sweater and spectacle girl decisively put her tray on the table, and pulled a chair round to face us. "Come on, Suzie, they're only human!" she said to Blondie.

Which seemed to imply that we were an inferior species. But her friends followed her lead.

"Sorry, Suzie, I got carried away," Jake looked contritely at the tall girl. "Must be the monastic life at Thomas Hall."

All one day of it, I thought.

"And, to you, as well!" Jake turned to the dark-skinned maid, with an expected introduction in his tone.

"No problem," she said, quite composed. "Suhindra. Sunny for short."

"Jake," he replied. He made to offer his hand, but withdrew it in case it was interpreted as another manifestation of forwardness.

"Rob," I chipped in. I chanced my hand, and was rewarded with a surprisingly firm grip from Sunny, and a damp limp one from Suzie.

"Rud," added Rud.

Sweater girl introduced herself as Linda, and her Celtic-looking friend as Bronwen.

Ice broken and honours restored we chatted for half an hour or so along well-trodden paths of conversation, like where we came from, what we were studying, and so on, until Rud reminded Jake that they still hadn't registered.

"Oh, Christ, no!" Jake exclaimed. "We'd better get a move on before they close! See you all!"

The girls gave him and Rud a polite wave. I was studying a leaflet I hadn't noticed before amongst my clutter.

"I see there's a freshers' dance on Friday night. Will you be there?" I said hopefully, but not obviously to any one of them in particular.

They looked at the leaflet I handed them.

"Would you like to come?" I pressed the invitation. Not that I was thinking of actually dating all four at once, but I was sure Jake and Rud would appreciate my magnanimity, "After all, there's safety in numbers!"

"Perhaps!" Linda smiled.

After I left them, I spent an hour or so poking around the shops in Tencastle, not with any definite purchases in mind. The market stalls in the square were being dismantled, amid an obstacle course of cardboard boxes, empty and full. The pens at the livestock market nearer the station were still damp from being washed down with disinfectant, the smell of which still hung on the autumn air. Only a couple of farm lorries remained.

It was late afternoon, then, before I started to make my way back up to Thomas Hall. Pleasantly elated from the day's activities, I felt that I could have done a lot worse than Tencastle.

Unlike the morning, very few students were on my route at this time. Some distance ahead of me I glimpsed a figure I thought I recognised but I was over half way home before I drew level.

"Hello, again, Mrs Beinyon."

She turned towards me. "Seems I can't get away from you, doesn't it?" Her gentle, lyrical Welsh accent softened any implied reproach.

"I'm sorry, Mrs Beinyon, for being silly last night." I was, too.

"Don't you worry about it. I'd had a long day and I was a bit stressed out." She sighed and added, "It did give a bit of light relief, on reflection. I'll have to pay more attention to people, in future, won't I?"

She almost sounded self-critical.

"Please, not on account of me, Mrs Beinyon."

"Deirdre. Most students call me Deirdre when they get to know me. How did your day go?"

"Very well, thanks! I think I'll like Tencastle."

"Most do." Her tone had a touch of wistfulness.

"Have you always lived here?"

"No, only when I got married. I come from the Gower."

"Does your husband work at the University?"

"Did. We're divorced."

Oops. "I'm sorry."

"No need to be," her voice hardened. "He was a right bastard, pestering any young piece that caught his eye at college, barely out of our honeymoon, taking it out on me whenever he got drunk."

"He physically attacked you?" I was appalled that anyone would even think of striking her.

"You could say that! Fortunately, he went too far with a student one day, and she complained to the college authorities. More complaints came out during the investigation and he was kicked out. I didn't go with him!"

"You didn't go back to Gower?"

"No reason to. Parents were dead, no other family, to speak of. And I had some friends here. Anyway, I mustn't bore you with my woes! You're nearly back at Hall."

"Aren't you going there too?"

"No, I've finished for the day. I'm off home to put my feet up."

Impulsively I said, "May I walk on with you?"

She looked at me quizzically. "I know my way. Do you know yours?"

Ouch!

"But thanks anyway. You're very sweet."

I floated in on cloud nine.

CHAPTER TWO

Bronwen

Tencastle believed in easing their new students gently into the system, in that no lectures were scheduled to begin until the Monday after the first full weekend in residence. Like me, most freshers had arrived on the previous Tuesday. After registration, the rest of the week offered an overview of the B.Ed course, a meeting with a personally assigned tutor, and informal 'familiarisation seminars'.

We had been advised that all the tomes specified on our reading list could be purchased at Bookwells, the official and indeed only academic bookseller in Tencastle. When I arrived at the premises the cramped space inside was already full but a large notice in the window listed many of the standard textbooks together with their price. I stood perusing the list, and making rough calculations as to how much of my grant I'd have to part with.

"Depressing, isn't it?"

I recognised Jake's voice, and turned.

"They'll rip you off, you know."

"Probably, but I haven't got much choice, have I?"

"I wouldn't say that. Follow me."

Intrigued, I obeyed. Jake checked the name of a side street a few hundred yards further on, beyond the main shopping area, and turned into it, then stopped outside a nondescript terraced property with a faded wooden sign above the door. Through the grubby window I could see the range of paraphernalia one might expect to find in a run-down bric-a-brac shop. A young female came out with a heavily laden carrier bag.

I regarded Jake with concern. "Doesn't look much like a bookshop to me."

"You're right but I'm sure this is the place!"

A bell clattered in the bowels of the shop when we entered the door. A thin bearded fellow about our own age emerged from a back room. "Textbooks?" he asked, correctly surmising that we weren't in the market for brass candlesticks or kilner jars.

"I saw your advert in the students' paper," said Jake.

Obviously I'd missed it. I'd only really scanned the broadsheet, not actually read it, let alone taken in every last detail.

"Good. Would you like to come through?"

Unlike the cluttered and dusty décor of the main shop, the rear parlour was bright and tidy, with newish pine book shelving from floor to ceiling along two walls.

"I presume you've got a list?"

We both handed over a sheet of notepaper for his examination. He darted about, extracting a volume or two here and there from the various shelves, and assembling two sizeable stacks on the table in the middle of the room.

"I can do most of them for you, but there are one or two that are very recent publications, or I've already sold all my copies. I'm afraid you'll have to pay through the nose at Bookwell's for the rest."

The total bill came to a fraction of what I'd expected to pay.

"How come you can sell them so cheaply?" I asked.

"Recycling."

He saw my puzzled look.

"Will you want these after you've finished the course?" He pointed to my bundle.

"Probably not. Why?"

"I'll buy them back if they are still in good condition with no curry or coffee stains. I'll resell them. The textbooks have hardly changed since I was a student."

He didn't look old enough to be a graduate. "Do you really make a living from it?"

"Better than the antique business my uncle left me. I'm doing mail order as well now."

The bell signalled another potential customer. Jake and I gathered up our purchases.

"Remind me to buy you a drink tonight, Jake. You are coming to the Freshers' Dance?"

"Wouldn't miss it."

The upper refectory at the Union evidently doubled up as the function room for any event at which more than a handful of people were expected. For the Freshers' Dance the organisers had tried to give the plain utilitarian space a bit of atmosphere, removing the large folding tables and scattering a few hay bales around the sides. Coloured lights strung around the walls provided the only illumination, save for a couple of spotlights focussed on the makeshift stage which was nothing more than a platform of boards resting on further bales. A young rock group were tuning up – at least I assumed that the discordant twanging wasn't their first number.

We, that's to say Rud, Jake, and Dan Chater from my corridor, were among the early arrivals, and the clientele so far consisted largely of several clusters of male students, chatting amongst themselves and casting hopeful looks at the odd few groups of the opposite sex present.

"Nothing much happening yet," said Jake. "How about you buy me that beer, Rob."

No drinks were allowed in the dance hall. The bar, a recent addition to the Union facilities according to our handouts, was situated in a converted committee room along the corridor.

Apparently, so Jake told us – though where he'd got the information from so soon was anybody's guess – a combination of objections from the town's licensees (who feared loss of business) and the non-conformist God-squad (who believed no-one, and certainly not students, should be permitted to consume alcohol) had only recently been overcome by gentle but persistent pressure from elected union officers. It was not a place for a quiet drink, however, and bony elbows were a distinct advantage in getting served before closing time. Jake had no problem.

"Have you a strategy for tonight?" Rud asked, to no one of us in particular.

"What do you mean?" said Dan.

"Well, you know, hooking up with a willing female."

"For what purpose?" asked Jake, innocently.

"What do you think? Obvious, isn't it?"

"Perhaps we don't all have sex on our mind like you, Rud," I said.

"Sex? Who said anything about sex? Intelligent conversation, of course."

"Yeah? Like Freud, you mean?"

"Yeah!" Rud paused. "Who's Freud?"

We heard the band start up in earnest, loudly. God knows what the decibel level was like in the hall, but we were all prepared to risk our eardrums regardless. Just inside the hall, Suzie stood out head and shoulders above her companions, the same girls as yesterday. Several students were already gyrating on the dance floor.

Rud nudged me, "Split them up?"

I nodded.

Rud made a bee-line for Linda. Whatever his chat-line was, it worked, and he'd separated her from the pack as efficiently as a sheep-dog cutting out one of the flock. The rest of us huddled in a group, not talking, for the electric noise booming out of the speakers made conversation impossible. Gradually we eased into pairs, Suzie with Dan, Jake with Sunny, and myself very happy to get closer to Bronwen.

The group were obviously influenced by the Rolling Stones, and covered two of their numbers in the first four offerings. Their overweight lead singer strutted and pranced around the stage, more like a boulder than a Stone and distinctly unsexy in his posing.

Bronwen and I rolled our eyes at the opening bars of *I Can't Get No Satisfaction*.

"Here we go again!" I mouthed.

While Mick Jagger might have got away safely with the energetic gyrations, the unsecured boards weren't up to the pounding they were suffering, and the front plank tilted over the edge of the bales, tipping the singer heavily into the arms of a hairy hulk showing off some novel footwork to his waif-like companion. The bass player and guitarist, facing the drummer in a frenzied riff, remained blissfully unaware of their partner's misfortune until the drummer's eyes returned from contemplating his navel and he brought the music to a crashing halt.

"What the f...?" came loud and clear. Fatty Jagger and Hairy Hunk extricated themselves up from the tangle in which they had fallen, and squared up to each other, mouthing obscenities, neither getting satisfaction of any kind. A couple of stewards rushed over, with the unenviable task of calming things down and getting, hopefully, the show on the road again.

"Shall we take a break?" I asked Bronwen. "Coffee or alcohol?"

"Coffee would be fine."

Unfortunately, with an unscheduled lull in proceedings, many other students had the same idea, and the coffee bar heaved with bodies.

"Um, not much chance of a quiet drink, I'm afraid. If any."

"No problem, Rob ... it is Rob, isn't it?"

I nodded.

"There's a little café I know just a couple of minutes' walk, if that's okay with you?"

"Fine with me."

We made our way through the throng to the main door. Bronwen made no objection when I took her hand as she began to lead the way to the café, which was in fact only a couple of hundred yards along Castle Street.

I brought two coffees to the plain but functional wooden table by the window. "Do you come from Tencastle, Bronwen? You're obviously Welsh!"

She laughed, "You can tell? No, I live over on the coast, near New Quay."

"I thought Newquay was in Cornwall."

"That's the well-known resort. We've got our own secret one. Actually, it's still a popular holiday spot for those in the know."

"But you are familiar with Tencastle?"

"Yes, my aunt lives here. It's one of the reasons I chose it because I could stay with her rather than going into Abercrombie Hall. What about you, Rob?"

I gave her an account of how I came to land up in deepest Wales.

"So, remind me, what's your particular area of study?"

"Well, a bit of Geography, but mainly Chemistry."

"Really?" Her eyes lit up. "I'm doing science, too, so we'll be seeing each other in College."

"I look forward to that." I wasn't just making polite conversation. Bronwen acknowledged with a smile that was difficult to read.

"Shall we head back to the dance?"

Bronwen shrugged. "I'm not really bothered that much. They're okay, but I prefer the real thing. Shall we have another coffee? On me, this time."

"I'm happy in present company."

That smile again.

"Did you know the other girls before this week?"

"No, not at all, we just, well, bumped into each other at registration and got chatting. It's a bit scary when you get to a strange place and don't know anybody. At least I knew the town, but I'm the only one here from New Quay as far as I know."

We made the second coffee last nearly an hour.

"I think I'd better be getting back, Rob. Thanks for a very pleasant evening."

"My pleasure. Bronwen. May I see you back to your lodgings?" I trusted I could find my way back to Thomas Hall.

Again she smiled. "If you would like … if it's not out of your way."

We set out, strolling in the opposite direction to Hall, past the main college building and over the river to where there was a short cul-de-sac of a dozen or so neat semi-detached houses. She hadn't objected when I first took her hand, but I felt her tense as we approached the last dwelling. I made a tentative approach to kiss her goodnight.

She pulled back, "Please, Rob, I'd prefer … I'm not ready for that."

"A kiss?" I was a little taken back after the friendly evening we'd enjoyed. It wasn't as if I was asking to roll her in bed.

19

"My aunt is very strict."

I wasn't intending to kiss her aunt. "No problem. Thanks for your company anyway. See you in college?"

She nodded, skipped up the path to the front door, then turned and waved me goodbye.

Ah, well.

Fortunately I have a reasonably good sense of direction, and given a small place like Tencastle I found my way to familiar surroundings with ease.

Perry the Porter was leaning on the door frame of his cubby hole. "Just in time, Mr Kiddecott, you wouldn't want to be locked out, would you?"

Jake was already at breakfast next morning, talking to a swarthy looking guy with long black crinkly hair sticking out as if he'd been permanently connected to a Van der Graaf generator. With equally hirsute face he could have easily auditioned for the Wild Man of Borneo.

"Hi Rob! Have a successful evening?" He gave me a knowing wink.

"Very pleasant. You?"

"Okay." He sounded non-committal. "Meet Benji – he's my neighbour on the corridor."

"Hi there, man!" Benji waved a dessert spoon in greeting.

"He's an artist."

I'd never have guessed.

Rud emerged from the servery and came over. Advantage or otherwise, Jake was easy to pick out in a crowd.

"Morning, guys."

"You sound bright and breezy," I said. "Stimulating conversation?"

"Eh?" The penny dropped. "Oh, you mean Kissy? Yes indeed. A meeting of like minds you might say." Rud saw our puzzled look. "Linda's friends call her Kissy."

I suspected Freud might have had some comments on their mental intercourse.

"Hey, man," said Benji. "That's so weird!"

We looked at him.

"What is?" said Rud.

"Over there!" He gestured towards the refectory entrance. "That guy. Who, for God's sake, would wear a bow-tie to breakfast?"

"That would be Joseph Carpenter," I said, even before I looked. "He's on my wing."

"Weird, man!" Benji repeated.

Joseph was agitatedly scanning the room, looking, I suspected, to bend someone's ear about the latest affront to Christianity.

"'Scuse me, see you later," I said, having no desire to be the target of whatever might have triggered his indignation this time.

I was soon to find out. He cut off my escape via the other door into the corridor

"Highly improper! On the Sabbath too!"

"What is?"

"This!" He thrust a card into my hand. The neatly typed note invited him to join Dr Ambersham in his apartment for sherry that Sunday afternoon at three o'clock.

"What's the problem?"

"Alcohol! The temptation of the Devil! And on the Lord's own day!"

I was devilishly tempted most days. "You'll not be going, I take it?"

"I shall not!" Joseph's nostrils flared in anger, real or simulated I couldn't tell. "Have you been invited?"

"I don't know. I haven't checked my pigeon hole."

"It was pushed under my door. Most irregular!"

I doubted that the method of delivery would have made any difference to Joseph's attendance or otherwise. I left him to his imprecations.

Under my door, sure enough, there was a similar card. I thought it was a nice gesture by the academic who was, I presumed, in loco parentis, or whatever was supposed to pass for the supervision of free-minded students at Thomas Hall. The invitation didn't give any indication as to whether formal attire was expected. I hoped not, since my only suit, which I'd outgrown anyway, was at home.

My choice of smart casual still made me feel distinctly overdressed for the occasion. My fellow students, in jeans and sweaters, were in accord with Dr Ambersham, in light brown cords and open-necked patterned shirt. Although the slight streaks of white in his full head of straw coloured hair suggested his age to be probably early forties, one could see how his smooth boyish complexion and slight build had inspired the nickname 'Babycham' that I'd already heard. His large rimless glasses and innocent kind of grin whenever speaking in his mild-mannered tone put me in mind of parish priest rather than college lecturer.

A couple of the other students I had already met, Dan Chater, for example and Dennis Sparks, who occupied the next room to mine. Sparkle, he had declared, was his common appellation, a contradiction I'd thought for one who always looked half asleep. My other immediate neighbour was Dicky Swift, tousled-haired, jug-eared and rather tubby. The tall slim bespectacled lad who could have easily passed for a banker or solicitor introduced himself as Tom Merchant, an English student. Two, I'm sure, had Celtic blood, both square-faced with dark hair and brown eyes, but only the shorter, less stocky one was Welsh, with a name, Huw Parry-Evans, to suit. Neil Tredinnick, built like a six-foot rugby prop, hailed from Cornwall.

Dr Ambersham looked at his watch, "We have apologies from Mr MacDowell, who was here last year, and also from Mr Carpenter, so we are just waiting for Mr Petrovsky."

MacDowell must have been the surly red-headed Scot I'd bumped into once. That's what living on thistles and porridge does for your character, I thought.

"Come in!" said Dr Ambersham, at the tentative knock on his door.

"Hi! Sorry if I've kept you waiting!" said the lanky late arrival with a thin face, scrawny neck and large beaky nose. His light coloured, greasy hair spread over the shoulders of his denim jacket. "I'm Ivan."

Dr Ambersham poured out generous measures of sherry from a cut-glass decanter. Personally I'd have preferred a beer. The good doctor did his best to stimulate conversation but with a group of students who hardly knew each other and were rather ill at ease in the contrived gathering, the focus stayed on stilted exchanges of information about background and interests. None, apart from Ivan, was a science specialist, and he was into Biology. Dicky and Huw intended to go into the primary sector. I never did discover the current interest of Sparkle, a former law student from North Wales, and thus a couple of years older than the rest of us.

"Now gentlemen, I need to come to one of the reasons, other than social, for inviting you here this afternoon. Though I am sure you are all responsible adults," he paused for the polite chuckle, "it is my responsibility to oversee your welfare during your residence at Thomas Hall. Should you have any issues or problems, academically, emotionally or socially that you would wish to talk over other than with your peers, I am here to listen, and where appropriate offer advice. Whether you take my advice is another matter."

Another chuckle. "You may also be aware that we normally expect all our residents to be in Hall by eleven thirty at night. Should you require a late pass then in theory you should ask me in advance. In practice, however, there will be a sheet with the porter on which you can sign out. Please remember to sign back in again when you return, gentlemen. The door will be locked but a porter is on duty all night. I will check the sheets regularly, and may well ask for an explanation if any one of you should make a habit of returning in the early hours. I do have the authority to 'gate' you for persistent abuse of the rules."

He paused. "And I'm sure I don't need to remind you gentlemen that it is against the rules to have a female visitor in your room between the hours of eight at night and ten in the morning. You are in any case required to sign in any visitor to your room, except of course other Thomas residents."

He looked around. A few knitted brows absorbed the implications of his pronouncements.

"Any questions, gentlemen?"

There weren't any, at least none that we wished to share.

"Well, then, gentlemen, may I wish you a pleasant time and success with your studies at Tencastle."

We shuffled out.

"Laid it on a bit thick, didn't he?" said Dan. His bushy eyebrows seemed to be knitted in thought, making his face seem quite serious, though I found him very easy going.

"Only if you're a night owl and randy," I said.

Considering how we had parted, I was a little apprehensive about how Bronwen would react on our inevitable contact again at the first chemistry seminar. There was no way one could hide in anonymity in a small establishment like Tencastle, where the groups for subject specialisms were small, sometimes not even getting into double figures.

Bronwen acknowledged my wave, however, as I took the only spare stool at the opposite end of the rear workbench. The others were, for the time being, strangers.

Our lecturer surveyed the ten new faces seated before him. "Good morning, ladies and gentlemen, and welcome to this crucible of learning."

Dead-pan delivery, so we shuffled on our stools, uncertain whether we were supposed to laugh or take him seriously. He saw our reaction.

"Relax, now, please! First of all, I'd like you all to introduce yourselves, and give a little background on how you came to be here in Tencastle. I'll start with myself. I'm John Tudor Evans. For the last seven years I've been responsible for instructing students in the noble art of chemistry and alchemy. Now, shall we start at the back?" He looked at me.

Taken unawares, I stumbled through the appropriate curriculum vitae.

When we'd all finished he asked us to write down all the names we'd heard, and one point of detail each person had mentioned.

I would be surprised if any of the others remembered half of what I had said. I usually had great difficulty remembering even a couple of names at mass introductions so I was quite chuffed that I managed four for certain, Bronwen of course, and Kitty Westsomething for her purring voice and leopard spot slacks. Liz Burke was strangely proportioned; nearly six foot tall, her upper body was quite slender but she was stout and as solid as a tree trunk from the waist down. Trevor Brewer was light of frame, with a stubbly beard, a ring in each ear and black greasy hair. Another four names I recalled but not necessarily their respective owners, and the other one I lost completely. The key facts I fared less well on.

"Well now, I'd be prepared to bet that none of you scored one hundred percent. How many of you excluded your own name and mine from the list?"

We all put our hands up, sheepishly.

"Shall we see how much you did take in?"

I found some consolation that, apart from the one bloke whose name I couldn't recall, our performance was generally pretty mediocre.

"I'd like to make two important points from your collective amnesia. As new teachers, you will be put in front of a group, not of ten, but at least two dozen, probably more, strange faces in each class you meet. They will pick up your name instantly. It will help to gain their respect, not to mention your handling of discipline, if you make a very conscious effort to learn their names quickly. Would you agree, Trevor?"

"Yes sir."

"John, please. I like to keep it informal. Kitty? Bronwen?" He went faultlessly through the whole group.

"I'm not a miracle memory man. As each name is given, repeat it to yourself, and latch it on to some simple mnemonic." He paused for breath. "Second point, as you've so ably demonstrated, you cannot assume because you've given a piece of information once that everyone – anyone, perhaps – will have heard, understood, and stored that fact for later recall, particularly when your average kid has got half his mind focussed on last night's television. Anything you especially want your charges to remember will need to be repeated, preferably in a number of different guises."

Pretty obvious, I suppose, when you thought about it, which I hadn't, hitherto.

"Nothing I've said so far is unique to my specialist subject," he continued. "You, ladies and gentlemen, are training to be performers, to a captive and indifferent, possibly hostile audience. How do you engage their attention, their interest, and leave them enthusiastically looking forward to the next episode?"

No one put their head above the parapet.

"No ideas? Now, you've all studied chemistry to 'A' level, so you are familiar with the subject matter. The main part of my job therefore is to teach you the tricks of the trade, as it were, to present the material in a way which will inspire the children ..." John was getting quite passionate. "... conjure up for them the desire to explore the mysteries of science!"

"He'll be handing out the black cloaks and pointy hats, soon," Trevor whispered to me.

"I have excellent hearing, too, Trevor. Would you care to address your colleagues?"

Trevor coughed nervously, "I don't really see myself as a man of magic figure you're describing. I'm not the extrovert, or mystical type."

"Nor do you need to be, my friend. Build confidence in yourself and your subject, give great thought to how best to put over a particular concept, and remember you're not supposed to be a walking, talking textbook. No need for a magic wand, just bring it alive!"

I thought of the pensionable old cretin who'd taught me at school. With one foot in the grave himself he was totally past breathing life into anything.

"The other hat I wear – apart from the pointy one, Trevor – is as the person tasked with extending your knowledge of your subject a little way beyond its current horizon. Obviously it will be unnecessary and inappropriate to venture as far as honours degree chemistry, but it is highly probable that many of you will aspire to sixth form teaching. The trend for advanced techniques and theory to filter down into the school syllabus is bound to continue, so, for example, we shall be looking at basic quantum theory, gas chromatography, NMR spectroscopy and ESP."

He paused, ostensibly to look at his watch. If he expected a hand or two to go up he wasn't disappointed.

"Excuse me, sir ... er, John, what is ESP?" This from Kitty.

"Extra-sensory perception. To you, having eyes in the back of your head, to make sure young Willy's not pickling himself in sulphuric acid!"

With that, he suggested that we take a break, before he got us involved in some group work.

"Quite a character, isn't he?" said Bronwen, as she welcomed me to join her at her table. "I don't think his lectures are going to be dull."

"You're right!" I put an Eccles cake onto my saucer and sipped my coffee. I decided to go for a direct approach. "Listen, Bronwen, I was wondering if you would like to come to the cinema with me tomorrow evening, if you're not doing anything else, that is."

God, she had a beautiful smile.

"Um, I'm not sure, Rob." She flicked some imaginary hair out of her eyes. "It wasn't my aunt, you know."

"Sorry?"

"Friday, when you walked me home. My aunt wasn't the reason I held back. I did enjoy your company, Rob, you're quite fun and easy to talk to …"

"But?"

"I'm … I'm going steady with someone back home. We're almost engaged … and I don't really want to get emotionally involved at college so soon."

"Next week, perhaps?"

She laughed. "You're incorrigible! What I'm saying, Rob, is let's just be good friends."

"Okay, I'll go with that. I'm sorry if I've seemed a bit forward, but you are … a very attractive girl."

She took it in good spirit, without even blushing. "Thank you. And you're very … understanding?"

I wasn't prepared to give up on my plans completely. "Tell you what, why don't we make it a foursome or so at the pictures? You know, with Kissy or Suzie, and Rud? We can all walk you home so you and your aunt won't feel threatened."

"I'll ask them."

I hoped John Tudor Evans had no more memory games lined up for us that day. Most of my brain cells were otherwise engaged.

Although I'd brought up the idea of a group visit to the cinema, Jake's enthusiasm for supporting live music had tipped the balance in favour of the folk club. Bronwen probably thought that there was safety in numbers, and anyway, the club was considerably cheaper.

The folk club had been well supported, perhaps for that reason, or possibly just curiosity from other freshers keen to sample all the few pleasures Tencastle could offer by way of entertainment. And it wasn't bad, if you were content with a succession of guitar-wielding folksy students heavily influenced by Bob Dylan, Tom Paxton and Joan Baez. I had listened entranced at the crystal clear voice of a dishy young girl who sang an unaccompanied song in Welsh, but the show stopper, by popular acclaim was a bearded trio who had only got together, so they said, a couple of hours earlier. They hadn't got round to thinking of a name for their group, so the MC introduced them as Peter, Paul and Hairy.

At the end of the evening, we didn't even get as far as auntie's door, however, as Bronwen promptly accepted an offer by Kissy and Sunny to walk back with her, leaving Jake and myself, and Rud, who'd come along at the last minute, to tackle the long drag back up to Thomas Hall.

"Interesting evening, Jake. Thanks for asking us along," I said.

"Dragged us, more like," said Rud, who'd been with me at supper when Jake had turned on his persuasive charm.

"You'd bugger all else to do!" Jake protested, and adjusted the banjo slung over his shoulder. "Not much atmosphere in that refectory," he continued. "Not even any straw bales, and no chance of lubricating my tonsils until the break. It needs more …"

"Booze?" Rud suggested helpfully.

"No, well, yes, that too, but a more … er … inspiring aspect. Know what I mean?"

We didn't.

"There would be a great aspect from the top of that tower." I said. Its dome was just visible above the tree line.

"What's its purpose?" asked Jake.

"I'm surprised you don't know already." He seemed to know most things about Tencastle considering the short time we'd been there. "It was supposed to be an observatory."

Jake digested the information. "And it's not used?"

"I'm not sure. I don't think so."

"Interesting."

I had intended, in fact, to satisfy my curiosity earlier over the throwaway remark Gerald Simpson had made in the taxi on my first day.

"Perry," I said next morning, seeing him standing by the lift instead of in his usual cubby hole. "Is it true there's an observatory on the top of the tower?"

"Well, yes, Mr Kiddecott. But, there again, no."

Confused, I waited for him to elaborate.

"Our former Vice-Chancellor's idea. He was into astronomy. When new student accommodation was proposed here at Thomas he managed to talk the architects into capping the tower with a dome."

"So what happened?"

"He died before it was completed and the College ran out of money."

"How long ago was this?"

"I've been here since this block opened, three years ago now."

"What is it used for?"

"Nothing really, just storage of junk, I suppose."

"That seems a dreadful waste, just left like that for so long! Do you ever go up there?"

"No reason to. And, Mr Kiddecott, it is out of bounds to students!"

Jake collared me as I emerged from a late Sunday breakfast with Dicky Swift and Dan.

"Ah, I was hoping I'd catch you. You remember what you said a couple of weeks ago?"

"Unlikely. What about?"

"The disused observatory. I thought we could have a look at it."

"It's out of bounds."

"I'll pretend you didn't tell me that." Jake turned to my companions. "You didn't hear him say anything about it being out of bounds, did you?"

They looked at me, unsure of whether to be drawn into the conspiracy, and stayed silent. Which Jake took as tacit agreement.

"Okay, then, no time like the present."

"Jake, I'm not going up there with you."

"Don't have to. I need someone to keep watch, but if either of you two care to join me? Just a peep, that's all."

I didn't like it, and said so, but Jake with a bee in his bonnet generated a momentum which was impossible to resist.

Astleyson, Perry's assistant, had his feet up on the small table in the office, reading the Sunday papers. He nodded to us as we came in. One of the windows gave him a good view of the lobby and lift doors – if he cared to look.

"Stairs?" said Jake.

"We could take the lift to the 6th floor bedrooms," Dicky suggested.

"I'll stay here and keep watch," I volunteered.

"How are you going to warn us if anyone comes, like the Warden?" asked Dan

I hadn't thought of that. "Dunno. I'll try to create a distraction." Whatever.

The three of them piled into the lift. I watched the numbers above the doors light up sequentially, stopping at six. A couple of minutes later, the ascending arrow came on again, and number seven became illuminated. Mike Pattison and a group of other students I didn't know entered the lobby and pressed for the lift. I kept my eyes on the floor indicator – down, up to three, five, down to four, and ground floor zero again, the doors opening to disgorge two fellows in running gear.

I watched and waited, feeling quite exposed in the lobby, for over twenty minutes, a long time just trying to appear casual. Nobody else came or went. I heard the lift machinery in action again. Astleyson must have finished his paper, for he put it aside, stretched, and glanced out. I saw his brow furrow when he noticed me still hanging around.

I hurried over. "Excuse me, I was supposed to meet a friend here from town. I wonder if I've missed him and he's already gone up."

"What's he look like? Is he from Thomas?"

"Um, er, no, he's second year. About my height, brown hair, and he's probably wearing a ... er ... baseball cap and ..."

Astleyson turned back into his office to look at the visitors' signing-in book. "Only one person this morning, about half an hour ago, a Roger Temple?"

"That's him!" I said, not knowing him from Adam.

"Visiting T204."

"Thanks!" I took the stairs to the first floor, not wanting to draw attention to the lift in case level 7 lit up.

I hadn't a clue where Jake and co. had got to. As I couldn't really return and wait in the lobby without attracting attention, I summoned the lift and rode to level six to see if they'd obtained access to the dome from that floor. It was deserted, but I noticed a padlocked door to what was obviously the continuation of the stairway. As I turned back towards the lift, uncertain whether to stay, attempt to go up or return to the ground floor, I heard a drumming of fists on wood, and Dicky's voice calling frantically "Is anyone there? Is anyone there?"

"What's happened?" I feared one of them had been injured.

"Rob? Is that you? Oh thank God! We're trapped!"

"What do you mean?"

"We can't get the lift to come back up to this floor."

"Right, hang on, I'll try from here."

I had to recall the lift from the ground floor again. The button for level 7 and the printed sign next to it were both covered with black tape. The button responded to my touch, however, the lift ascending without a problem. The doors opened onto a concrete floor strewn with various builders' debris. Without thinking I began to step out.

"Rob! Stay where you are!" Jake yelled. "If the doors close again we'll all be stuck here."

I beat a hasty retreat into the cabin. The doors started to close and I put my foot in the gap, jabbing the 'open' button at the same time. They folded back allowing my friends to scramble in.

"Thanks, Rob," said Jake, with obvious relief. "Christ, I thought we were going to be abandoned there like an oubliette."

"That's a dungeon not a skyscraper," said Dicky, pedantically.

"Bugger all difference if no-one knows you're there."

"But an oub ... "

Dicky's point of semantics was ignored as we emerged at ground level, and headed for fresh air.

"Sorry, you've just missed Mr Temple," said Astleyson, popping his head out as we passed his office. "I asked him to wait for you but he didn't want to know."

"Thanks."

"Who's Temple?" asked Jake.

"No idea," I said.

"Let's take a walk," Jake's tone carried more of an instruction than invitation.

We headed towards the town, in the absence of any other sense of direction.

"Well, what did you find?" I asked, unable to contain my curiosity.

"Quite a lot. Well, you saw for yourself that the only way up was in the lift, and all the junk by the doors we had to climb over."

"Not something I'd want to do every day," Dicky added.

"Along the short corridor from the lift, broad stone steps lead up to the dome proper. It's a fantastic place, with a view half way across Wales in every direction, but just a concrete floor littered with all kinds timber, bags of cement, cable and so on. It's almost as if the workmen were told one day that they weren't getting paid, and just upped and left."

"Might even be the case," I said, remembering what Perry had told me.

"Problem was when we wanted to come down there was no way to call the lift. There was a just a gap where the button should have been and a couple of loose wires."

"You could have tried touching the wires together," I suggested.

"And risk fusing the whole bloody show. Use your brain!" said Jake. A bit unkindly I thought, since if it weren't for me he'd have still been there. Mind you he did have a point.

Jake fell silent, but you could almost hear the wheels turning in his head. In any normal place our arrival in town would have coincided with opening time, but even the Union bar remained firmly closed on the Sabbath. We made do with coffee.

"I've been thinking," said Jake.

"Really! You surprise us!" Dan laid on the sarcasm.

"With a bit of work that dome would make a fantastic recreational area, far better than the piddling little communal lounge we've got at present. My aunt's front parlour is bigger!"

"Yes … but,"

"TV lounge, pool tables, gymnasium even," Jake continued enthusiastically.

"Roof top swimming pool?"

"Perhaps not, Dicky, but there's lots of possibilities!"

"One problem, Jake," I said.

"What's that?"

"Money. Who's going to pay for it?"

"Yes, there is that to consider." Jake pondered. "But you do agree it could be done?"

"Possible, I suppose, but improbable."

"Then, Rob, we must make sure that it comes to pass!"

I wasn't so keen on the implications of the 'we'.

CHAPTER THREE

Sandra

"Where are they sending you, Jake?" I asked, leaning over his shoulder to get a better look at the notice board.

"Pwllgoch Primary," he replied, then spotted my name. "And you've drawn Abergwnwyn, wherever that is," he added.

"About 20 miles or so into the wilderness, I think." I'd seen the name as a dot on the map. "But trust you to get a cushy number!" Pwllgoch was a moderate size village about seven miles from Tencastle. It still had a pub and a post office. More importantly, it was the next station down the line.

Within just a month or so of enrolment Tencastle directed us fairly gently into the first experience of our intended career with two and a half days a week at the chalk face over a four week period either before or after the Christmas break. Even so, it was not uncommon for a couple of students each year to pack their bags and scurry back home after just a few days in front of real live kids. Regardless of the age level of the children we eventually wanted to teach, the first teaching practice for all students was in a local primary school. However, since Tencastle itself only boasted two primary schools (three if you counted a small independent Welsh medium establishment) a 'local' placement therefore could mean anything within a thirty mile radius, in a remote school with perhaps two full time teachers, or fewer. To overcome the paucity of public transport, three college minibuses ran a carefully planned shuttle service into the sticks for trainee teachers. There was always the possibility of bed and breakfast on the job, so to speak, but few accepted the extra cost or disruption to their social life.

"You're in schedule B though, Rob," Jake commented.

"Is that good?"

"Well, at least you get to recover after the weekend. I'm in A, which means cold dark Monday mornings until Christmas." It also meant that he had to rise early three mornings a week against my two.

Staggering the TP (Teaching Practice) was the only realistic way that the college could place all its students, and even so, as we had been firmly briefed, it relied heavily on the goodwill of the head teachers. The students were allocated to the different schedules largely on account of their subject preferences, the specialist seminars and lectures being arranged to coincide with in-college days so that lecturers were then free to visit their charges in schools during the other part of the week.

"I guess we'll not be seeing each other much over the next month."

"I don't see why not," said Jake. "We've still got the evenings free, haven't we?"

"Lesson plans, marking, self-assessments," I volunteered.

His look suggested what I could do with the lesson plans, etcetera.

As it happened I didn't see Jake at all during the first week of TP. To get students to the furthest flung settlements in good time for registration, the college transport began its run at the ungodly hour of seven-thirty in the morning. Jake, on the other hand, travelling by train, could have at least an extra half-hour in bed!

The only consolation to our inconvenience was that we were picked up from Thomas Hall. Being in Group B, my stint began on Wednesday afternoon, so I had a leisurely departure at 11.30 a.m. on the first day. It seemed the minibuses did three full round trips on the midweek change over, returning at lunchtime with the Group A students.

I didn't know the other fellow waiting by the main entrance, but there was no mistaking his athletic dark-haired companion.

"Hi Neil!"

"Hello there, Rob. Didn't know you were on the jaunt too." Although Neil Tredinnick's room was just along the corridor from mine, our paths rarely crossed socially. He was into languages, including his native Cornish, probably, when he wasn't playing rugby.

One of the old green-and-gold Volkswagen minibuses with the college crest chugged up the drive. The three of us clambered aboard and took the seats at the back.

"By the way, this is Charles. Seems we're both at the same school."

"Hi Charlie," I said.

"It's Charles, not Charlie," he answered stuffily. He sat straight backed, incongruously dressed in a grey suit and tie. His conventionally short cut fair hair was already receding either side of the crown. With small rimless glasses and thin-lipped straight face he really looked a bundle of fun.

"Sorry." I turned to Neil again, "So where are you bound?"

"Tenbridge Mount Primary. New school, I believe."

I vaguely remember reading something about Tenbridge in the Guardian. "Isn't that where they had the landslide?"

"Yeah, a couple of years ago. A scree slope rolled into town and took half of the school with it. Fortunately it was during the Christmas holidays, so the school was empty. Could have been another Aberfan otherwise."

"So is this the first term for the new school?"

"I imagine so. I don't really know much about it."

One could say the same for any of the schools we had been farmed out to. Location, name of head teacher, transport times, strictly on a need-to-know basis.

The minibus pulled up outside Abercrombie Hall where three female students were waiting. Suzie, of course, I'd met on my first day and I'd passed the time of day with Liz Burke in my science group, but the other tall girl was a stranger. Outside the Union we picked up our last passenger, Trevor Brewer, whose scuffed leather jacket was very much in keeping with the generally unkempt appearance he'd presented in the seminars.

Apart from establishing where each of us would be based, we didn't chat much as the minibus headed northwards along the valley of the Tene. Beyond the village of Llanbeddrod, where Liz alighted, the valley narrowed considerably until we reached Tenbridge, a market town only slightly smaller than Tencastle. Built largely on the hillside between the confluence of the Greater Tene and its tributary, the White Tene, Tenbridge showed extensive evidence of quarrying on its neighbouring slopes, and screes of waste were still visible where they posed no obvious threat to the community. Across the valley, some distance from the town centre, the single track railway left the small station and followed the main valley north-eastwards.

We turned westwards, however, the minibus struggling against the 1 in 5 incline as the B road began to twist and climb out of the valley of the White Tene. It had taken us about twenty minutes so far. Another ten minutes took us over the watershed and down into the village of Ffynnon Cross where we dropped off Suzie outside a small whitewashed stone building. The road then followed the contours along the shores of Lake Dynad, a reservoir supplying water to the Midlands. The hamlet of Pentredynad clung to the banks of the lake at its western extremity. It hardly looked big enough to support a viable primary school but several outlying farms probably managed to raise enough children to keep the school going. I wondered what they would make of Trevor, who didn't seem a country type.

The road descended from the rugged and often barren uplands through conifer plantations into a broad and green valley. Apart from the driver my sole travelling companion was the tall girl who had hardly said a word during the journey.

"Spectacular scenery isn't it," I said conversationally.

"Yes. I suppose so." She sounded quite nervous. I couldn't quite place the accent. Definitely not southern, though.

"Are you feeling all right?"

"Yes … well, I'm not sure. I'm not used to all this open space. It seems awfully isolated."

"Where do you come from?"

"Nottingham. I'm used to having people around, not trees and rocks." She took a deep breath. and exhaled slowly. "I'm sorry," she said, "I'm Sophie, Sophie Brasier."

"Robert Kiddecott," I said, giving her my hand. "I'm from Devon. More or less grew up in the country."

"I suppose you get used to it."

"One can get used to anything. Hopefully you'll get to like it as well!"

Our transport came into a built-up area, the first speed limit signs and street lights we'd seen since leaving Tenbridge. Larger than a village, Abergwnwyn didn't qualify as the smallest town in Wales but it made Tencastle look like a metropolis. Its situation on the junction with a secondary north-south route through the Cambrians had obviously given it some advantage as a trading centre. My destination was a low, but two-storey stone building separated by iron railings from a muddy and uneven football pitch, just off the single street of small shops that comprised the town centre.

"Good luck," I said to Sophie. "See you later!"

"You too!"

I was surprised to see Joseph Carpenter standing at the school gates, obviously from the flushed look on his face very worked up about something. I thought he would have wanted to wait for the minibus to return from Llannerch, the last outpost.

He barely let me alight before climbing on to the bus. "Heathen!" he muttered, whether as his greeting to me or in reference to someone else.

The greeting from the headmaster could not have been warmer.

"Gwyndaf Davies," he said, shaking my hand. "Welcome to Abergwnwyn! Come and meet the staff."

He led me in through the entrance porch into a small lobby from which, through an open door on the left, I could see a hall-cum-gymnasium. Ahead was a tiny unmanned reception office and a flight of stairs with a thinning carpet.

"Tell me, Robert – or are you a Bob? Are you religious?"

I considered what answer he wanted to hear, but decided to opt for the truth, "Not particularly. And Rob's fine."

"Thank God for that!" he declared. "Young Joseph there would have had all the sheep in church reciting the psalms on bended knees! And he's only been with us two days," he added.

The Head's thin rimless half-glasses, thinning grey hair which would once have been blond, his pinched thin nose and windswept red-veined cheeks, all gave him a rather serious look which I soon found concealed a wicked dry sense of humour. Of moderate height and build, I would have put him in his mid-fifties.

At the top of the stairs, the door sign on the left read 'R.Gwyndaf Davies, M.A., J.P., Headmaster'. The right door led into a generously proportioned cupboard a.k.a. the staffroom. A well-rounded, buxom middle-aged woman was mopping up Banda duplicator fluid with a paper towel.

"Penny, meet Robert Kiddecott! Penny Little, my deputy, dogsbody and guardian of my sanity."

Penny's face creased into a laugh. "Pleased to meet you!"

"And you can dispense with your rosary!" the Head added. "At least until Monday!"

"How many staff do you have here?" I asked him.

"Apart from us you mean? Well, there's Mrs Callander, our secretary and cook, and old William, the caretaker."

"No other teachers?"

"No. We've only fifty children on the books, so strictly speaking we are over-staffed."

"You do get Nia Edwards coming in for half a day, Gwyn, to cover your admin time," Penny chipped in.

"That's true, and she often helps out as an unpaid classroom assistant. Which reminds me, she'll cover for me for an hour while we have a chat as to how we can best help each other for the next couple of weeks or so."

"See you later," said Penny, gathering up a pile of books as a bell rang below. A large handbell, judging by the sound.

At his request I followed Gwyndaf Davies into his office, of similar dimensions to the staff room. My room at Thomas Hall was spacious by comparison.

"Now, young man, what can you offer us?"

"Well, sir …"

"Oh forget the sir, I'm Gwyn to adults and Mr Davies to the kids."

"Okay, thanks. Science – chemistry – is my main subject with geography back up."

"Pretty basic science at this level," said Gwyn, rubbing his chin. "Apart from nature studies."

"The birds and the bees?"

"No, I think we can pretend to cherish their innocence for a little longer." He thought for a moment. "How's your history?"

I subscribed to the Henry Ford philosophy. "So-so," I exaggerated.

"Music?"

"Two or three chords on a guitar."

"Wonderful! You can help Penny's Rhyme and Rhythm session with the younger children on Thursdays. And see what you can do about the Battle of Hastings. That will be Friday next week."

I hope he wasn't expecting me to change the course of history.

"Now the children in my class are older, so if you can come up with some simple science experiments that don't require any equipment, I'm sure they would find it fun. That should keep you busy for the time being and we'll sort out the rest of your programme tomorrow. Now I suggest you spend the couple of days this week with Penny and myself on observation to get the feel of the school. You'll be happy to help with some playground duties?"

It wasn't so much a question as a fait accompli.

"You'll be welcome to sit in on the Welsh language lessons. Be good for you to learn some proper pronunciation. Many of the children here are Welsh speaking in any case and the others seem to enjoy it – even the few English immigrants. We had one or two of the parents kicking up a bit of a fuss, but there's nothing they could about it, if they want to live here." A thought came to him. "By the way, Robert, have you had any lunch?"

"No, not yet, but I've brought a packed lunch with me."

"No need in future. Gwen Callander produces the best school dinners you'll ever wish to taste. But take your time now, then come down and I'll introduce you to the kids."

The kids seemed quite unfazed by my appearance. They'd probably got used to a succession of trainee teachers as young as some of their older brothers and sisters. I sat in on Penny's arithmetic lesson in one of the two small classrooms which led off the main hall and, at her invitation, helped some of the children with their sums.

I hardly noticed the time passing and the bell at the end of day caught me by surprise. Well-trained, the children collected their coats and bags and waited in an orderly line for the word to leave. I followed them out to where a group of parents had gathered at the gate. One slim but well proportioned young blonde woman caught my eye and smiled at me. By the time the minibus arrived some ten minutes or so later, the playground was deserted.

Sophie seemed much more relaxed than on the outward journey.

"How did your day go?" I asked

"Oh fine, just fine. The Headmistress fussed over me like a mother hen – actually she did pretty much the same with the kids too. I think it's going to be all right."

As we picked up each of the rest of our group along the way much the same question was repeated and generally favourable first impressions were related, even from Charles, though he remained doggedly monosyllabic in his responses. Only Liz seemed a little put out, and this, I guessed, through having to hang around for nearly three quarters of an hour after the end of the school day for her transport.

The next couple of days were a doddle, apart from the shock of the seven-thirty departure. I was truly impressed by Penny and Gwyn as they guided their young charges almost effortlessly through activity after purposeful activity, with scarcely a voice raised in admonition. Nor had the Head been joking about the skill of Gwen Callander in the kitchen, for with seconds each day of custard-covered spotted dick or apple and blackberry pie to follow the shepherd's pie or liver and bacon, my waistline would have been in serious danger of expansion given a prolonged teaching practice.

It would have been difficult not to notice the attractive blonde among the morning and afternoon gathering of mothers at the school gates. On Friday, she was right by the entrance when I arrived.

"Hi," she said.

"Good morning," I replied politely.

"Are you a student teacher?"

"Yes. Does it show?"

"You're so young and …" She must have detected my embarrassment. Other mums were probably within earshot. "I'm sorry, I didn't mean to say …"

Her bright blue eyes looked at me apologetically. I didn't know quite what she did mean so I kept on safe ground. "You've got a child at this school?"

"Yes, the little girl over there." She pointed to where a curly-headed blonde girl of about nine or ten years old was playing tag with two friends. Too old I thought to have a mother who could have easily passed for a teenager.

"I can see the likeness."

"I'm sure you'll like my little Fanny."

I was keen to impress Gwyn and Penny with my potential classroom skills when I next returned to Abergynwyn. I'd already got some ideas for the science experiments, if I could persuade Mrs Callander to help with one or two ingredients. As for the rhyme and rhythm, I'd seen Penny's previous session and reckoned I could busk it. But I desperately required some extra information.

"I need to pick your brains," I said to Dicky, when he eventually answered my knocking on his door. He was the history buff.

"You're welcome," he replied, and invited me in. "As long as you leave me a few cells in case I need them myself."

"What do you know about the Battle of Hastings?"

"Ten sixty-six and all that, you mean? Well, in a nutshell Harold was thrashed by William and his Norman army. Ended up with an eyeful of arrow."

"Is that all?" It wasn't more than I already knew.

"What else do you want?"

"Enough for half an hour's lesson. That bit's not going to last more than half a minute!"

"Well you'll have to pad it out. Try some action replays, you know, that sort of thing."

I didn't know and told him so.

"Sorry! Don't get in a huff! Here, I can lend you this." He thrust a dog-eared textbook into my hand. It could have been a 1066 original edition.

"Thanks."

The rest of my Saturday was lost in the annals of time, until pangs of hunger reminded me I'd missed out on lunch completely.

It seemed that many students were also missing out on dinner, for the refectory was almost empty. Jake, of course, stood out immediately. I hadn't seen him since the previous weekend. He was poking the shrivelled sausage and watery mash unenthusiastically. I wondered if Thomas Hall could be persuaded to head-hunt Mrs Callander.

"Everything okay?" I asked.

"Terrified," Jake grinned at me. "Absolutely terrified!"

"What do you mean?"

"The kids! They were scared shitless."

"What did you do to them?"

"That's the thing, I didn't! Just walked in and smiled. And waited for the headmaster to introduce me. He'd just stopped outside to tell a boy off for running in the corridor."

Jake's smile was a winner with female contemporaries, but flashing white teeth from six foot plus of solid ebony might not have had the same effect on tiny tots.

"So what happened?"

"Well, the headmaster comes in and sees all these weenies cowering at their desks. He gestures to me to just stay back where I was, and goes around the class talking quietly to several of the children and nodding his head at their replies."

"Go on!"

"He returns to the front and invites me to stand next to him. He perches on the edge of his desk and addresses the class: 'How many of you live on a farm?' About two-thirds of the hands shoot up. 'And do you all know what a sheep looks like?' And all the hands go up. 'What colour are sheep? Yes?' He points to a boy in the front. 'White, Mr King,' Another boy puts his hand up. 'Some of them are black,' the boy says. 'Are there any other differences?' asks Mr King."

"What did they say?"

"Well, they all thought about it and one little girl calls out 'The black ones are more cuddly' and giggles, and soon her classmates are all joining in. 'Thank you, children,' says the Head. 'Now it's no different with people. Mr Moses here is no different to you or I. His skin is a different colour to most of us here, but he's the same as us otherwise – all part of one big human family.'"

"That was it, then?"

"Yes, the children were fine." Jake paused, "It's the first time I've ever been called the black sheep of the family."

"And are you?"

"Am I what?" Jake asked, puzzled.

"More cuddly!"

Joseph Carpenter again looked out of sorts when we swapped over the next Wednesday lunchtime.

Gwyndaf Davies also looked uncharacteristically harassed. "I'm sorry to say so, but I shan't be sorry to see the back of your friend Joseph. He behaves like a missionary trying to convert a tribe of jungle bunnies, if you'll pardon the expression. We're not a blessed Sunday School, for God's sake, we're an ordinary primary school trying to give a balanced education and a respect for people of all cultures." He let out a sigh of exasperation. "I don't want to condemn the fellow, or put in an adverse report, but, honestly, he'd try the patience of Job!"

"I'll have a quiet word with him," I suggested. Not that I thought I would make much impression on our zealot, who'd probably marked my card already for the fires of hell.

I spent most of that afternoon helping Penny with preparations for the school nativity play. I also tried my tutor's technique for learning the names of the children when I faced them for real through Thursday's science lesson. With limited success, I might add, though curly-headed Fanny I had no problem in remembering.

"My little Fanny thinks you're wonderful," the dishy blonde mum buttonholed me on Friday morning. She always seemed to be by the gate whenever I arrived or departed, and never with her daughter in tow.

"Oh, I don't think so, Mrs ...er?"

"Hughes, Sandra Hughes. My friends call me Sandy." She flashed a dazzling smile at me which left no doubt that I was included in this circle. "She was telling me that you'd given them all sweeties."

"Yes, that's correct. But all in the interests of science."

I'd handed out broken pieces of acid drops in twists of paper, along with another twist containing bicarbonate of soda. I'd had to have sharp words with little Miss Hughes for trying to nick her friend's sweet.

"Really?" Her blue eyes registered amazement. "I wish you'd been my science teacher. We had some useless short-sighted old fossil."

"It was just to give them some idea of acids."

"Aren't they dangerous?"

"Not all by any means. Look, I'm sorry, I must dash. I've got some things to get ready for another lesson."

"Perhaps you can tell me more another time."

Perhaps. I had a feeling she might want to move the subject on from getting blackberry juice to change colour with stomach powder and vinegar. Meanwhile, I had an epic battle to organise.

Although Dicky hadn't exactly been a mine of information about Harold and William, he'd given me the germ of an idea. Jake, too, had vaguely recalled someone reciting a humorous monologue about the subject at the folk club, and had managed to acquire a scribbled copy for me. From Dicky's textbook, I'd gleaned just about enough background information to set the scene.

I divided the class into Saxons and Normans, got them to choose who would play King Harold and William the Conqueror, and set them to work making up paper swords and such like, and a crown for Harold.

Penny had baulked at the thought of a pitched battle in the classroom, but suggested the hall as an alternative. The Saxons therefore took the high ground – a low dais at one end from where Gwyn usually conducted morning assembly – and we found a rocking horse from the nursery on which to install Harold 'On his horse with his hawk in his hand'.

I recited a few verses, in my role as U.N. Observer-cum-umpire, and the two armies threw some paper spears at each other, all landing safely in no-man's-land. I declared a stalemate so far and suggested a change of tactics; the Normans would gather their spears and pretend to run away, and the Saxons, thinking they had won, would charge down from the safety of the hill.

After the carnage, where newspaper and little Saxons lay scattered all over the battlefield, William the Conqueror placed a symbolic rubber-suction arrow on Harold's forehead and took his crown.

Roll over Cecil B DeMille!

When all the bodies had been properly resuscitated with orange juice elixir, we had a full debriefing, in which all the children were keen to make a contribution with questions and ideas for alternative strategies. I thought they would make a reasonable job of recreating the Bayeux tapestry in next week's lesson.

"Can you spare a minute?"

Joseph Carpenter looked surprised to see me. I doubt that he got many visitors to his room.

"Er ... yes ... of course! Please come in."

He moved a bible and a couple of religious tracts from the small armchair. "Take a seat," he offered. A large 'Jesus saves' poster completely covered his notice board. His desk was dominated by a large gilt crucifix.

"So what's the problem?" he asked.

"No problem really. Just wanted to compare notes with you about Abergwnwyn."

His brow furrowed, "That den of iniquity!"

I waited for him to elaborate but he seemed unwilling to do so.

"I find the staff there very friendly and the children co-operative."

"Heathens the lot of them!" He shot a dark look at me in disagreement. "Why?"

"The morning assembly is a travesty! A short garbled prayer – if you're lucky! No hymns! No worship of Our Father. No attempt to give thanks for His gracious bounty at lunchtime! And diluting the whole meaning and joy of Christmas by comparisons with other so-called religions!"

Joseph was more than warming to his rhetoric – he was becoming overheated. I was beginning to think that my intention of a quiet chat was not such a good idea after all.

"Your faith means a lot to you, doesn't it?" I said contemplatively.

"Of course! I am a servant of the Lord. He has chosen me to spread the true Word." Joseph spread his hands. The gesture was worthy of the Archbishop of Canterbury.

"Does He tell you how to spread the Word?"

"What do you mean?" Joseph bristled.

"You say God has chosen you, but do you have any discretion in how you promote his message to mankind?" I hoped my choice of words would be accepted by Joseph.

"I'm not sure what you're getting at."

"People can be brought round to change their views in more than one way, wouldn't you agree?"

"I suppose so," Joseph acknowledged guardedly. "But what's this got to do with Abergwnwyn?"

"You've been pretty stressed out both Wednesdays when we changed over, and Gwyn Davies was really worked up this week."

"So what's this to you? The man's a moron!"

"I think you are judging him too harshly. I honestly don't think it would take much more for him, reluctantly, to ask for your teaching practice to be terminated."

"You're not serious!"

"Sorry, but I am. At very least you could find that his report would be, shall we say, unhelpful to your career."

"I see." From the set of his jaw Joseph was barely controlling his anger. "And what's this to you? Did he put you up to this?"

"No, not all." Well, not exactly. "I just don't like to see conflict and tension – particularly if it can be avoided."

"So what do you think I should do?" said Joseph sarcastically. "I have no intention of forsaking God's work."

"I wouldn't expect you to, but, as I was saying earlier, there is more than one way…"

"Yes, yes," snapped Joseph. "There's no need to repeat yourself."

"If you'll just bear with me a moment, Joseph. Just suppose I were a life insurance salesman."

"I hardly think…"

I held up my hand. "Just suppose. Now if I were phoning you up, buttonholing you at every available opportunity, rubbishing the work of competitors, invading your personal space all the time, you'd soon get pretty fed up with it, even though you might accept life insurance was worth having."

"I'm sure I would. But it's in extremely bad taste and blasphemous to denigrate the Kingdom of God and trivialise my testament to His great works as little more than the efforts of a salesman!"

"That's the point! I'm not! The message may be very important, but the means of its delivery may not be the most effective."

"I see. Are you saying I'm at fault?" Still prickly, Joseph did seem to be giving some consideration to my argument. At least he was calmer.

"Fault is too strong a word."

"So what do you suggest I do?"

"Your faith in God is strong." He nodded. I waved my hand towards the crucifix. "Why not ask for His assistance?"

Joseph contemplated the icon in deep thought for a few moments. "Yes, I will do that," he said. He turned to me, in puzzlement and asked, "Tell me, Rob, why are you trying to help me?"

"As I said, I don't like conflict. I didn't want to stand back and possibly see a colleague kicked out."

"But you're not a committed Christian? I didn't think you even believed in God?"

"I'm not into organised religion, if that's what you mean. I don't like the way it seems to discriminate against women, or sexuality, or whatever. I suppose I do believe in a God, but not as some old gentleman floating on a cloud."

Joseph frowned. "You are something of an enigma, Rob. You talked to me as if you firmly believed in my faith, yet you deny the presence of God."

"I firmly respect that your faith and God is real to you. I can't myself see the reason why you, or millions of other intelligent people, for that matter, believe in God as you all evidently do."

"That's an honest view. There's hope yet for your salvation." I think Joseph meant it seriously.

"Tell me, Joseph, – without wanting to cause offence."

"Yes?"

"Do you think God has got a sense of humour?"

Joseph's nostrils flared. "Of course not!"

"Why do you say that?"

"It's … it's … sacreligious! Scandalous!" Joseph was clearly upset with my question. I had a feeling it was something he'd never considered.

"Just wondered. It seems odd to me that there are people who claim God has told them to do something and others who claim he has told them the complete opposite, like when opposing armies go into battle each claiming they have God on their side."

Temporarily Joseph was speechless.

"God works in mysterious ways," he murmured, as I took my leave.

By the third week, we were beginning to feel like old hands, and the minibus trip was a lively forum for the exchange of experiences from school life – the flashes of inspiration and depths of frustration, the gaffes, caricatures of the staff, the moments of enlightenment on innocent faces, the little tow-rags who should have been strangled at birth. I felt a little sorry for Liz, who, I discovered, was having a difficult time with a domineering headmistress and a teacher who'd have difficulty in keeping a class of waxworks under control. While she seemed reluctant to join the general banter, she would talk quietly with me whenever we sat next to each other. I did wonder how the kids coped with her strong West Country accent.

"What's the purest thing you know?" asked Trevor, apropos of nothing.

"Chastity?" This from Charles.

"Why?" enquired Neil.

"Water?" I suggested before we got into deep philosophy.

"Yes," Trevor came back at once. "That's the answer I was looking for from the kids!"

"So what did they come up with?" I asked.

"I bet it wasn't chastity," Neil murmured.

"No."

"What then?"

"A new born lamb!" Trevor declared.

A brief silence before we all collapsed in laughter. Actually it wasn't so daft when you thought about it, though I bet Joseph would have had a hey day with the Lamb of God and such like.

Talking of whom, Joseph positively radiated beatitude when I alighted at Abergwnwyn.

"God bless you!" he beamed at me, and climbed on to the minibus, where, even before it had pulled away, he had engaged Sophie in animated discussion.

Thus exalted and gobsmacked, I threaded my way across the playground between groups of youngsters in gnat-like motion. At the staffroom stairs Gwyn was chatting with a pert slip of a woman in a dark green skirt and matching jacket. Mid-forties, I would guess.

"Oh hello, Robert, I don't think you've met Nia. She covers for me on my admin and golfing days," he chuckled.

"Hi."

"Robert's our other student this term. He operates on a much more earthly plane than Holy Joe."

Nia smiled at the reference, and excused herself to round up the kids for afternoon school. Gwyn took me by the arm and led me up to his office.

"By the way, Robert, what the devil did you say to Joseph?"

"Er, not a lot, nothing, really," I replied modestly. "Why?"

"He's been like a man transformed today."

"How do you mean?"

"Co-operative, relaxed, not acting as if you'd shoved a crucifix up his backside. He's asked if he can help with morning assembly, and has discussed with Penny some promising ideas for the Nativity Play. I can't believe he's the same person as the arrogant bible-basher last week." Gwyn looked at me curiously. "Are you sure you didn't have a hand in it?"

"Probably divine intervention," I said diplomatically, but I don't think he believed me.

I'm not sure how long Gwyn had intended to spend with me but by the time we'd finished going through my teaching schedule for the remaining time at Abergwnwyn, half the afternoon had gone.

"One more thing," he said in parting, "did I tell you that your tutor is coming in tomorrow?"

Strangely, Sandra Hughes was not in her usual position by the gate when I left on Wednesday. Come to think of it, I hadn't seen her daughter either.

Not so the next morning; there was no way she was going to let me get through the school gate with my guitar case unnoticed.

"Good morning, Mr Kiddecott – or may I call you Robert? It is Robert, isn't it?"

"If you like. Yes," I replied neutrally, though God knows how she found out my Christian name. I'm sure Gwyn and Penny wouldn't have told her.

"You must be so talented – a scientist and a musician."

"Hardly a musician – a few chords at best." Just about enough to follow *Away In A Manger*, provided Penny thumped the piano hard enough to drown my mistakes.

"I'm sure you are being so modest. I've got a little instrument at home but it hasn't been played much recently. Do you give lessons?" Her voice managed to convey enough genuine interest.

"I'm not very good. I could teach you all I know in five minutes."

"Really?"

The way her blue eyes lit up from within their mascara'd eyelashes would have charmed the Muse in any man. Alas, not me, for Gwyn was already ringing the bell.

"Sorry, I've got to be going." The consequences of King Harold's demise had to be addressed.

In the aftermath of the battle, the tapestry was taking shape. In her attic, Penny had found an old roll of brown hessian-effect wallpaper which was now pinned up like a giant frieze almost all the way round two sides of the classroom. I divided the class into four task-forces, each with their own scene to illustrate. Each group, on Penny's recommendation, included children with a range of skills – signwriters, artists, production line workers to mass-produce simple origami soldiers, and such like. The landscape painters set to work on the wallpaper creating green fields and sea, soon to be populated by the opposing armies, their horses and ships. I had to explain, tactfully to one young lad who was mad on aeroplanes why it would not be appropriate to fill the sky with Messerschmidts. I promised him a key role in the Battle of Britain in the future.

Amidst the bustle of purposeful industry, gluepots, paint pots and snippets of coloured card, John Tudor Evans had slipped into the classroom. I'd been far too involved to notice, trying to get 'Arold's 'awk looking less like a budgerigar, and requesting an amendment to the 'William the Conker' banner from a bemused young boy – my own fault, I suppose, in likening the fearful spiked iron ball and chain to the humble horse-chestnut seed. It was only when I called the class to order, to begin my summing up and praise their efforts, that I caught sight of my tutor leaning by the door at the back. He was stroking his nine-o'clock shadow with a wry grin on his face.

"Well done, young man," he said, after the children had filed out for their afternoon break. "That was most entertaining." He examined the nearly completed tapestry with interest. "Tell me, as a history novice, why the Saxon soldiers all have beards while William's men are clean shaven?"

"It's the only way I could think of for the kids to distinguish between the two armies."

"Potential there for a Gillette commercial!" he chuckled.

I wondered what he'd make of my next production in which Kiddecott kids the kiddies in converting water into wine. I set up my specially prepared 'empty' clear wine bottles suitably rinsed with caustic soda or phenolphthalein, pulled out my dowel-rod 'magic wand' and donned a pointy wizard's hat I'd prepared earlier from scrap cartridge paper. I asked for an assistant – choosing Fanny Hughes from the thirty hands that shot up – and asked her to half fill one of the bottles with cold water from the tap.

"Who knows the magic word?" I asked.

"Izzy Wizzy!" a Sooty fan suggested.

"Hey presto!" a freckled faced little girl in an oversized blue dress declared, her friends nodding in agreement.

"Sardines!" a plump cherubic boy at the front called out. Sardines?

"No, silly, it's abadabra…. abaca…" the little girl's voice tailed off.

We settled for the conventional imprecation, and, with a loud cry of 'abacadabra!' I poured the water from one bottle into the other, producing an instant change to a vivid red liquid, a tad too rosé for most palates. The kids gawped open mouthed, their astonishment complete as I poured the 'wine' into a milk bottle previously rinsed with acid and the colour disappeared.

"You're all too young to drink wine," I said. "Best turn it back into water!"

Far be it for me to reveal the magician's secrets, but I did remind them that last week blackberry juice went one colour in acid and another colour in stomach powder. With a plentiful supply of vinegar and washing soda, plastic cups, and assorted coloured fruit and vegetable extracts, I asked the children to see what colour changes they could get.

"But remember," I cautioned. "Don't drink anything. I've put a spell on it to make it taste really nasty!"

With all the liquid testing – well most of it, at least – confined to the plastic trays from the canteen, the floors and desks didn't get too damp, and I insisted that everyone washed their hands thoroughly at the end. One or two kids may have gone home smelling slightly pickled, though.

John Tudor Evans spent ten minutes or so after the lesson, discussed the afternoon's session with me, and imparted some timely advice on safety issues, like warning the children against trying similar experiments at home.

"They're very impressionable at his age, you know. We don't want dads complaining of adulterated wine, or mums with chemical chaos in the kitchen."

"True," I agreed.

"What are you planning to hit them with next week?"

"It will involve a lemon, a few coins and a torch bulb," I confided.

"I'm with you. And I suspect our departmental reserves of magnesium ribbon will also be several centimetres shorter, am I right?"

"Probably. And I'd be grateful for the loan of a voltmeter."

"No problem!"

By the time we'd finished and I'd gathered up my guitar and other bits and pieces, my transport was already pulling up at the gates. Sophie was looking very happy.

A sunbeam day all round.

"Are you busy?"

"Preparing tomorrow's lessons, actually," I said to Jake. "But come in, anyway."

He moved my bag to one side and flopped down on the bed.

"Coffee?"

"If you're making one."

I opened my study door and looked out into the corridor. "Kettle!" I bawled.

Tom Merchant appeared from the end room. "Sorry, I forgot."

"No problem." The lone communal kettle had a habit of disappearing into one room or another. It would have been easier to bring my own, but strictly speaking, that wasn't allowed.

"Right," I said later when we both clutched a steaming mug. "What brings you over here so late?"

"I've had an idea."

Bang goes my lesson preparation, I thought.

"Actually, more than just thinking, I've made progress."

"On what?"

"The dome."

"I'm sorry?"

"The dome ... the observatory, you know. I went to see Dr Nightingale, and he's not averse to our idea in principle."

"Really? What about the cost?"

"He did raise the question. He agreed, however, to put the matter before the college authorities if we came up with more detailed proposals."

"'We' meaning 'you', I trust."

"I thought you'd want to be involved." Jake sounded a little disappointed at my lukewarm response.

"Ideas, perhaps, if you are serious." I saw his expression. "Is there something else you're not telling me?"

"Well ... I did hint that we might be prepared to do some fundraising, and help with the refurbishment."

"Bloody hell, Jake, we're penniless students, not flaming bankers or builders, how can we possibly..."

"You'll help then?"

No sun on Friday morning.. It was pissing down so hard that I was soaked just running from the entrance of Thomas Hall to the minibus. The surface water made driving hazardous with visibility made worse by the fine spray spewing out behind each vehicle and the slow journey became even more frustrating when the road was blocked before Tenbridge by a milk tanker and a tractor having become intimately entwined. It was possible to reach Tenbridge by a minor road which wound through several isolated farms and homesteads, a route not normally recommended, even less so when congested by much of the light commuter traffic that usually travelled the main road.

Damp and disgruntled, it was well past ten o'clock when I arrived at Abergwnwyn. I had barely enough time to gather my thoughts let alone all the miscellaneous materials I needed for the consumer survey I'd planned to conduct with Gwyn's class after morning break.

Following a hearty helping of Gwen's herby bangers and mash and treacle sponge with custard, I'd mellowed somewhat by the afternoon, and was feeling more than a little soporific. Somehow I floated through the afternoon, body and mind not quite in harmony, and the end of school bell came none too soon.

Sandra Hughes was waiting by the gate, looking quite agitated.

"Oh, Robert, I didn't see you this morning. I was worried that you might be ill."

"I was late. We had to take a detour to avoid an accident."

"Oh, I'm so glad. That you're not ill I mean."

"Thanks." Though I couldn't see why my health was her concern.

"I wanted to ask you something. Would you mind?"

"I don't know, until you ask," I replied, wondering what she'd got in mind.

"Silly me," she said deprecatingly. "Look, I'm having a few friends round next Thursday. For a musical evening. I'd be ever so pleased if you could come."

"It's kind of you to ask …"

"Oh, and bring your guitar!" she added enthusiastically.

"Well, it would be difficult, I'm afraid. There's the problem of my transport back to Tencastle."

"I could run you back."

"Thanks, but I couldn't possibly expect you to do that, it's over forty miles round trip!"

"You could stay over, then. There's a spare bed."

"What about your husband?"

"Oh, he won't mind!"

I was indeed quite tempted – apart from Sandra being very easy on the eye – by the idea of a jam session with some other musicians. "Are you sure it won't be putting you to too much trouble?"

"Not at all! And join us for a bit of supper too."

"Okay, then, yes. Thanks very much. I'll look forward to that!"

I could have sworn she blew me a kiss as the minibus pulled away.

"New girlfriend?" asked Sophie wickedly.

"No way. One of the parents."

"Uh-huh."

"So how was your day?" I asked, changing the subject.

"Oh, so-so," she replied. "Apart from the fact that I missed all my first lesson which I had taken ages to prepare. We were so late that Simon, the driver, stayed up at Llannerch all day, rather than risk another delay."

"Good idea." Inspired, actually, for the main road had only just been reopened when we got to Tenbridge.

Among the student fraternity, the festive season was being condensed into the one remaining full weekend before the Christmas vacation. Both in the Union building, which had sprouted an eight-foot fir tree in the foyer, and in Thomas Hall, which could only run to a balding imitation evergreen in a plastic pot, garish posters from almost all the societies exhorted us, in essence, to get pissed. I expected there would be more than a few sore heads on Sunday morning.

I found Jake had also entered the Christmas spirit.

"Bit optimistic, aren't you?" I remarked, observing the single sprig of mistletoe dangling from his usual string of desiccating tea bags.

"What do you mean?"

"Well, how many pretty girls do you think you're going to entice into your room?"

"Oh, I see!" he grinned. "You never know! Be prepared like a good boy scout! Actually, it's a souvenir from school," he added.

"Really?"

"From the staffroom party yesterday. There's this gorgeous young probationer ..."

"And?"

"And nothing! She just kissed me under the mistletoe."

"Why?"

"Why not? It is Christmas, you know. Anyhow, I'd just done my party piece."

Which raised all sorts of possibilities, as far as Jake was concerned. I hesitated to ask.

"You won't guess," Jake whispered conspiritorially.

"Probably not," I conceded.

"Give you a clue – a nursery rhyme."

That would not have been foremost in my suggestions. I thought a moment. "Not … not Baa Baa Black Sheep?"

He managed to grin sheepishly in confirmation. "Don't laugh! It seemed appropriate, given my introduction to the school."

"Yes, I remember," I chuckled. "So how have you been getting on with the kids?"

"Oh, fine. They're really quite sweet, though I still think they look on me as some kind of exotic animal from the zoo."

"Jacobus Moseii – the only one in captivity," I chortled.

"Fancy a quiet drink?" said Jake, changing the subject.

"You'll be lucky! All the pubs in town will be heaving with students tonight."

"No problem. I've found a little country pub about a mile up the road towards the next village, if you don't mind a walk, that is."

To be honest, I'd not ventured up hill beyond Thomas Hall. I'd assumed that the road serviced a few private houses and then, well, sort of ended.

"Sounds good!" I agreed.

It was one of those crystal clear winter nights with the sky full of twinkling stars and a guarantee of a heavy frost by morning – quite romantic, given appropriate circumstances.

"By the way," I said, as we walked beyond the wooded hilltop and descended through open fields beyond, "the reason I dropped by tonight was to ask if you'd mind running through a few songs on banjo with me on guitar."

"Why the sudden interest?" Jake asked.

"I've been invited to take part in a musical evening at school, and I'd like to get a bit of practice on my three chord trick."

"That's fine. Tomorrow afternoon okay? What exactly had you got in mind?"

"I don't know really. It's not actually at school. One of the parents invited me round to a party with some friends and asked me to bring my guitar."

"Is she pretty?"

"Well, er …"

"And out of his knapsack he drew a fine fiddle," Jake crooned.

"It's not …"

"And he played her such a merry tune!" he taunted.

The darkness spared my blushes. "It's not like that at all, she's …" I searched for the right words. "She's a married woman – she's got a young daughter!"

"Are you sure?"

"Of course! I've seen – I've taught – her daughter."

"But have you seen her husband?"

I hadn't. Come to think of it I hadn't noticed Sandra's wedding ring, but then that wasn't really my business, despite what Jake was obviously insinuating. Arrival at the pub gave a welcome break to the course of the conversation.

The Blacksmith's Arms, flanked by a couple of similarly constructed whitewashed cottages, was the epitome of the good old English pub, or Welsh, in this instance. The substantial heavy wooden door opened into a vestibule with a small serving hatch facing the entrance and doors left and right labelled saloon and bar respectively. We opened the door on the right and were greeted with a blast of hot, smoky air. The bar was heaving with probably half the rugby forwards in Wales, all talking loudly.

"Saloon?" I said to Jake.

Thankfully, this was much more civilised with a lower decibel count and a welcoming open fire. Though well patronised by couples mainly of middle-age and upwards and a small hen group, there were still a few vacant chairs around a couple of converted treadle sewing machine tables and a deep two-seater chintzy sofa beneath the window.

"Mine's a pint of that Crew stuff," said Jake, pointing to a hand pump half obscured by the Carling icon beyond the inevitable array of Hancocks taps. I wasn't aware that I'd offered to get the first round, but Jake had already flopped down in the sofa.

The handwritten label that Jake had spotted identified the brew as 'Cwrw D…' something, the rest illegible where inks had run and the cardboard oval had become frayed. The barmaid seemed a little surprised when I asked for a pint, but drew me off a sleever of ale as dark as Guinness without the froth.

"Make that two," I said.

"Hey, that's not bad," declared Jake, quaffing nearly half the glass in one pull.

I supped tentatively, to savour the taste, which was full bodied and malty, quite sweet but with a lingering hoppy finish. "Mmm, yes, it's certainly got more bite than Hancock's Best."

"I don't know how they can get away with calling it 'best'," Jake mused, the liquid level falling rapidly. "I hate to think what their worst is like!"

Our discussion of the merits of ale continued all through the second pint, pretty well oblivious of anything else going on around us, and I had just returned to the sofa with another refill when I noticed for the first time a couple at the table just across from us on the other side of the fireplace.

"That girl, she seems familiar," I said, interrupting his discourse on banana beer.

"What?" Jake peered across the brim of his glass. "Looks as if she's pretty familiar with him!"

True, they were holding hands across the table though I couldn't see their faces as they had their backs to me. I had a feeling I'd seen them both before. My curiosity got the better of me.

"Gotta take a leak," I said. The gents was on the other side of the room.

Coming back I could see them clearly. I wasn't intending to intrude, but as I was about to pass their table, she looked up.

"Why, hallo there, Robert."

"Hi, Deidre."

"I don't think you know my friend," she said pleasantly. "Robert, this is…"

"We have met," her friend interrupted. Rather rudely, I thought. "Master Kiddecott, the young student dairy-fresh from Devon." Gerald Simpson seemed far less agreeable than when we'd shared a train and taxi. I'd probably spoiled his sweet courtship patter.

"Nice to have met you again," I mumbled, feeling it was anything but, and edged away towards the sofa. If he'd have been on his own I might have retorted differently but I didn't want to make a scene in front of Deirdre. More than my humbled ego, I still felt a little sorry for her.

"Who was that?" asked Jake, as I slumped back into the sofa.

"Deidre Beinyon. You probably saw her when you checked in to Thomas Hall."

"Can't say as I noticed. Who's her boyfriend?"

"Some postgraduate prat I guess," I lied. In truth I felt embarrassed by Gerald's put-down.

"Do I detect a touch of jealousy?"

I didn't feel in conversational mode any longer, and anyway, we must have almost exhausted our verbal good beer guide. We sat contemplating infinity until our glasses were showing empty.

"Another one?" asked Jake.

"Not for me. My head's getting a bit woozy. How about we make tracks?"

"Fine by me."

The chill night air hit us like a slap in the face after the warm fug of the pub. The road to Tencastle looked much steeper and darker than on the way out, and we plodded none too steadily back up towards the dark woods on the skyline. I suspected that the beer must have been one of those high strength winter warmers, for we seemed to lurch into each other frequently.

The cold was also having a dire effect on my bladder. "Catch you up in a mo," I called to Jake who at that moment was trying, not very successfully, to keep to the dotted line in the middle of the road just ahead of me.

Meadows still bordered the road as we'd not yet reached the wood. I ambled to one side and, unzipping my fly, stepped on to the verge. Or, at least, where the verge should have been. My foot briefly touched grass several inches below expected ground level, and I tumbled unceremoniously down a grassy bank to the edge of the field below. Winded, and disorientated, but otherwise still in on piece, I sat amongst the thistles gazing at the stars, for how long, I don't know. But when I came to my senses and scrambled back up the bank, the road was deserted.

"Jake!" I called. "Jake! Where are you?"

No reply.

"Jake!" I yelled in consternation.

A thought struck me. Perhaps he'd come to grief like me. I tentatively approached the other side of the road, and peered down.

"Jake? Are you there?"

No Jake.

"Bugger!" My concern gave way to annoyance that he'd just gone off and left me. Christ, I could have been injured and perished in the cold! With that sobering thought I strode off up the road and into the woods, determined to give Jake a piece of my mind when I caught up with him.

Now I'm not normally of a nervous disposition but there can be something quite unsettling walking alone through a pitch-black wood at the dead of night. I definitely felt another presence, and, slackening my pace briefly, I was sure I heard the rustling of a creature moving amongst the trees. I wondered if they still had wolves in Wales. Whatever it was, it must have been a fair size, for there came more crashing of undergrowth and the snapping of twigs, and the monster lurched out onto the road no more than two yards in front of me.

"Jake!" I exclaimed.

"Where the hell have you been?" he demanded frostily.

"I might well ask you the same question!" I breathed deeply, "Going off and leaving me!"

"What do you mean? You were right behind me, and when I looked round, you weren't there!"

"When?"

"When what?"

"When did you look round?"

"A few minutes ago, just after we got to the woods, of course!"

"When you got to the woods, you mean. I'd stopped for a leak and fell into a ditch."

"Well, you might have let me know," Jake said, huffily.

"Next time I intend to go arse over tit, I'll ask your permission! Anyway what were you doing in the woods? Chasing rabbits?"

"I was looking for you, if you must know. You don't sound very grateful!"

"And what on earth would I be doing in the woods, you great pillock!"

"Chasing bunnies?" Jake suggested, calmly.

It was impossible to be angry with Jake for long.

There was certainly a buzz of the festive spirit in the air as we boarded the minibus on Wednesday morning, in no small part due to the approaching Christmas holiday, and to the fact we'd survived our first teaching practice so far. Neil was sporting a Santa hat and Trevor had acquired a sprig of mistletoe, which, once he'd used its charms, generously invited Neil and me to do likewise, with Sophie, Liz and Suzie all consenting graciously.

"Where's Charles got to?" I asked. Not that I could have imagined him joining in the fun.

"Probably chucked it in," Suzie offered.

"Could well be," Neil said. "He wasn't in school last Friday, and he was getting a hell of a lot of stick from the kids."

Strange, I hadn't even noticed his absence until just then.

Sandy was waiting at the school gate, evidently looking out for me. "Oh Robert, I'm so glad you're here today," she said with a great sigh of relief. "You haven't forgotten about tomorrow, have you?"

As if I could. I was quite looking forward to the occasion, a decent meal, pleasant company and an opportunity to play along with some other musicians who I was sure would be better than I. "I'll be there, don't worry." A rather important point entered my mind. "By the way, where exactly is 'there'? I don't know your address!"

"Of course! How silly of me! It's number eight, Llanishen Terrace. If you go just past the Drovers Arms in the main street there's a narrow lane on the left. I'm the last stone cottage in the terrace on the right. You can't miss it."

"And what time shall I come?"

"Shall we say five thirty?" She flashed me a smile one could die for. "Don't be late!"

Most of the school day seemed fairly mundane after the bright beginnings. My planned science experiments went by the board, replaced by further rehearsals for the Nativity Play and Carol Service. It's myth that all the Welsh can sing; several of the little darlings were seriously tone deaf, and always those with the loudest voice. Mind you, I had always been told to stand at the back of the class during singing lessons at my junior school. I liked to think my voice had matured since. Perhaps I might even be prepared to contribute a song at Sandy's soiree, if asked.

"No need to pick me up tonight," I said to Simon the driver when we arrived at Abergwnwyn the following morning, "I'm staying here overnight. And I won't be at Thomas Hall tomorrow morning either," I added superfluously.

"Something interesting?" asked Sophie.

"Musical evening," I replied.

"Have fun!"

"Thanks! See you Friday afternoon!"

I'd meant to have a word with Gwyn Davies earlier about staying on in school for a while in the afternoon before going to Sandra's. The prospect of mooching around Abergwnwyn for an hour or so wasn't particularly attractive.

"Well, I suppose so," said Gwyn, stroking his chin. "Although Penny and I will be gone by four today, and William is usually finished and locked up by four-thirty. Tell you what, if you don't mind checking all the doors and windows before you go, you could lock up."

"What about the key?"

"I'll speak with William. He's got a spare, and you will be here tomorrow, won't you?"

"I don't think I've got any choice about that!"

"What are you up to then, young Robert, if you don't mind me asking?"

"I've been invited to supper and a musical evening."

"Lucky you!" He gave my news further thought. "Anyone I know?"

"Mrs Hughes – little Fanny's mother."

"Really!" Gwyn's eyebrows shot up. "I didn't know our madam governess was musical, did you, Penny?" This to his deputy who had just entered the staffroom.

"Only to play a tune on men's heartstrings, I'd guess," responded Penny, uncharacteristically bitchy.

Governess? Heartstrings? My puzzlement was clear.

"She's on the board of governors," explained Gwyn.

"And spends all her time making eyes at the male members," Penny added.

"Anyway, never you worry yourself, Robert. A musical evening, you say?"

"Yes, she's asked some other musician friends round for a jam session."

"Well have a good evening then." Gwyn grinned wryly, "And take care!"

Strangely, Sandra was not lying in wait for me on Thursday morning. No doubt she was busy preparing for the dinner party.

Joseph had worked wonders with the children in preparing them for the Nativity Play, which went miraculously smoothly, and even when the Angel Gabriel's wings slipped around the said cherub's bottom the audience of parents in the pews managed to disguise their titters with discrete coughing. I didn't see Sandra amongst the congregation.

In the old, high vaulted stone church the singing, too, was transformed into a quite moving experience. Supplemented by a congregation of mature adult voices and by Penny's prowess on the organ, any stray off-key notes from the children were rendered undetectable except to the keenest ear.

After the service, I was tail-end-Charlie chivvying on the stragglers in the crocodile of kids along the main street back to the school. Chatting with the excitement of the season, they seemed completely oblivious to the bitter easterly wind. The bright wintry sun had given way to dull cloud, with rain or sleet due later. I only hoped that the forecasters weren't yet talking of a white Christmas – I didn't fancy getting stranded, snowed-up in Tencastle, let alone in Abergwnwyn. Still, on a brighter prospect, we had Christmas dinner to look forward to back at the school. I'd asked why it wasn't held on the last day of term, which seemed likely to be rather an anti-climax.

"Practicality, young man," Gwyn had replied. "There's always so much turkey left over that there's enough for a salad, and it makes for far less clearing up and far less waste."

I did wonder if I was going to be able to do justice to whatever Sandra was cooking up for the evening.

It seemed strange having the school to myself, after Gwyn, Penny and the kids had gone; spiritless and stark, all the gaiety and vibrancy dissipated into the cold dark winter evening. I'd not got anything particular to do, no lesson preparation for the next day, so I got my guitar out and strummed a few chords – the few that I knew, that is. Perhaps a little practice might help me to at least hold my own with Sandra's friends; impressing them was a little too much to hope for.

William popped his head round the staffroom door. "I'll be going now, Mr Kiddecott. There's no need to check the windows and other doors." He handed me a Yale key and an iron key attached to a large wooden tag. "Just make sure you turn off the lights and lock the main door when you leave."

"Thanks very much! I'll do that! I'll be gone myself in half an hour in any case."

I lost interest in perfecting my guitar technique after just a few minutes, and whiled away a few more aimlessly browsing the notices on job vacancies, control of head lice, and the odd teachers' union bulletin. I'd planned on just dropping in to the village minimarket for a bottle of plonk on my way to my dinner date, but I thought I could spin out a little time with window shopping rather than twiddling my thumbs.

The door key was not designed to be carried around by shoppers, and was far too bulky to stuff in my pocket. My light rucksack was already nearly bursting with my overnight things, toiletries and a change of clothes, but seemed a better bet than my new soft cover guitar case. Anyway, I wasn't going to need the key until the morning.

The predicted rain had not yet arrived but the icy wind wickedly cut through to exposed skin, and I was grateful to get some protection in the main street. Though undoubtedly small, Abergwnwyn did serve as the main source of provisions for the population scattered over many square miles of Welsh wilderness, and, as well as a minimarket and off-license, it also sported a chemist, newsagents with a post office counter, a butcher-cum-greengrocer with plucked turkeys dangling their wattles into the topmost branches of tub-sized Christmas trees, and Owen Owen Jones who stocked everything else to keep a rural community functioning. Lloyds Bank – more of a twig than a branch – opened two days a week in a squat stone single-storey building shared with a solicitors' office, which also exhibited estate agent's particulars for a couple of terraced cottages, a barn conversion and a disused mill – the original one-stop property shop! The bakery, the shelves almost bare apart from a couple of doughnuts and mystery pies, had a few tables for morning coffee and afternoon tea, but was on the point of closing, otherwise I could have been tempted, just to get warm. The pub, probably an old coaching inn despite the sign in the window saying 'no coaches', was not yet open. I couldn't imagine that they would have been overwhelmed by passing trade at this time of year, if ever. A garage with just two pumps – diesel or petrol – formed the last bastion of civilisation at the northern end of the main street. And the community did get a travelling library and fish and chip van once a fortnight – not together, I must add.

All this I gleaned in twenty minutes of wandering up and down the main street. I must have stood out like a sore thumb – a dropout from a rock band or suchlike. Just as well I didn't have a beard and long hair, else the locals might well have been making phone calls.

The church clock had not long chimed the quarter, but I thought Sandra would excuse me arriving a few minutes early. Clutching my purchase of Spar premium house red, I turned up the narrow lane by the pub. Unlit itself, a diffuse light from the main street was just sufficient to reach dimly to the end of the row of terraced cottages, all of which opened directly on the road, with not even a pavement in between.

The last cottage offered a choice of a plastic bell or a cast iron knocker in the shape of a lion's head on the stout rustic door. Discreetly I pressed the bell, which elicited no response. A gentle rap of leo's bonce soon produced the sound of footsteps hurrying down stairs.

"Sorry," said Sandra, breathlessly. "I was upstairs changing into something more casual."

Well, if the lilac and pink low-cut shoulder strap dress was casual wear, her best social costume must be something again. She looked quite stunning.

"Come on in, Robert, don't just stand there!"

"Thanks." I stepped in to the living room, cosy and warm from a wood-burning stove set into the fireplace. "Here, I've brought a bottle for dinner," I offered the wine, hoping she wasn't too discerning.

"Oh that really is sweet of you, Robert!" Her eyes sparkled as if I'd bought her diamonds. "You shouldn't have bothered, really. Let me take your coat!"

I unhitched my rucksack, and Sandra hung my parka next to her beige leather coat, the only other garment on the pegs beside the front door. A narrow staircase against the outside wall led straight upstairs.

"Would you like a coffee or tea? You must be frozen! Or perhaps something stronger?"

"Coffee would be fine, thank you, Mrs Hu… Sandra." My fingers were still feeling the chill from humping my guitar case without gloves.

"Have a seat and make yourself at home, then. I won't be a minute." With that, Sandra disappeared through the door next to the stairs.

I took a black leather armchair next to a similarly upholstered two-seater sofa, the two arranged in an arc around an oval glass-topped coffee table in front of the woodburner. A small television sat on an occasional table in the corner between the fireplace and another door, which I assumed led to a dining room. There was certainly no dining table, nor any space for one in the present room, cosy and compact as it was. Indeed the only other furniture of size was a flat-pack style tall cabinet, glass fronted above and black ebony effect below, between the kitchen and the other inner door, and a low two-shelf bookcase by the stairwell. Remarkably free of evidence of a lively ten-year old girl.

Sandra returned with two steaming mugs decorated with sheep in silly situations – the sort of thing you'd find along with kiss-me-quick hats in Llandudno. Still, the welcome coffee was genuine even if the containers were kitsch.

"What have you done with Fanny this evening?" I asked, as Sandra made herself comfortable on the sofa, one leg crossed over her knee to show a generous share of thigh.

"Oh she's with her Da."

"Right! Um…"

Sandra answered my unspoken question, "We don't live together. Fanny is with Terry most of the time."

"Are you, er, divorced? I'm sorry, I don't mean to pry."

"That's okay. No, we never actually got married, just sort of became close friends. Still are, I suppose, though that's probably because we've never lived together," she added, wistfully.

A number of questions about her relationship entered my head, too personal to pursue, but one seemed on safe ground. "Fanny has your surname, though?"

"Yes – but Terry and I are both Hughes, though not by marriage!"

I ventured a further thought. "Are Terry and Fanny joining us for dinner?"

Sandra cocked her head to one side and smiled wryly, "I don't think that would be a very good idea, do you?"

Not my place to reason why. "So it will be just a few other friends then?"

Sandra paused before replying, "Just a couple, I think." She placed her mug on the coffee table then sat up, clasping her hands round her knees, and changed the subject. "Anyway, enough about me, tell me about yourself."

"Not a lot to tell, really. I come from a Devon farming family."

"Brothers and sisters?"

"One of each. David's a few years' older and is taking on more of the running of the farm. Rachel is doing her A levels."

"Girlfriend?"

Who's getting personal, now? "Not really. Lots of female friends and I enjoy their company, but no-one steady."

"Do you enjoy my company, Rob?"

The telephone trilling in another room saved me from concocting a reply that was honest without encouraging more familiarity. I was getting distinctly uneasy about the reason for Sandra's invitation, and it wasn't my guitar skills!

She popped her head from round the kitchen door where she had gone to answer the phone.

"Dinner's almost ready, Rob. Would you be a dear and open the wine? There's a corkscrew on the dining room table."

"Sure!" I assumed, correctly, that the dining room was through the only other door from the lounge. Cosy it certainly was, with a large oval table that barely left space for the four dining chairs and dark wooden dresser at the far end. Only two places had been set. I queried this with Sandra.

"Oh, yes, sorry! One friend cried off with a stinking cold and that call was from the other couple. Their car has broken down," came the voice from the kitchen. "I hope you've got a good appetite."

Charitably, Sandra might have been psychic, but I very much doubted it. I felt rather like a fish that had been played, caught and hauled in hook, line and sinker. But the aromas from the kitchen were most appealing, and I was hungry, despite Gwen's massive lunch.

Throughout the meal Sandra made absolutely no further come-on advances or innuendo whatsoever. Indeed, it was one of the most pleasant evenings I have ever spent in female company, her culinary skills matching her undeniably attractive appearance and personality. Through the parsnip and apple soup, the steak and ale casserole, and fresh fruit salad, on which we dined at great leisure, our conversation ranged far and wide, over childhood anecdotes (she was brought up in Cardigan) through swapping of West Country and Welsh folk legends, to our respective literary and musical preferences, only occasionally putting the world to right in any kind of political context. The red plonk, finally exhausted, gave way to a ruby port Sandra discovered in the dresser, to accompany some Caerphilly cheese – not that I could have eaten a morsel more! By the time Sandra suggested we adjourn to the lounge for coffee, I was feeling quite relaxed and mellow, and forgot that earlier I had had any reason to question her motives.

"That was superb, Sandra," I said, genuinely. "Can I help with the washing up?" I offered honourably.

"I think that can wait till morning," she smiled.

I didn't push the matter.

It seemed quite natural to share the sofa, even to lounge there sipping coffee with my free arm casually resting around her shoulders.

"Rob?"

"Mmm?"

"You brought your guitar, didn't you?"

"Yes, you asked me to."

"Would you like to play me some tunes?"

"If you like. I'm not very good, though."

My alcohol consumption, while not improving what little technique I had, certainly fortified my confidence and extended my repertoire as I attempted to croon *We Shall Not Be Moved* and *Careless Love*, with extended pauses at each chord change. Nevertheless, Sandra clapped appreciatively, boosting my ego no end.

"Didn't you say that you played the guitar as well?" I remembered after a dodgy encore of *I Never Will Marry*.

"I've had a go once or twice. Not as good as you by a long way!"

"Here, give it a try!"

She took the instrument I offered, and held it, pensively. "Can you show me some chords? I've quite forgotten them."

I reached behind her, first of all placing my fingers on a simple G chord, then lifted her hand to the fingerboard to the same position, trying modestly to avoid looking down her cleavage. She strummed gently producing just a muffled sound. She took my left hand and placed it over her breast. I could feel her nipples harden. She laid the guitar aside and moved my hand inside her bra to the rounded softness of her right breast.

"Sandra, I ..." was all I managed to say before she rolled over to me on the sofa and clamped her mouth against mine, her tongue probing deeply. Taken by surprise, my groin reacted instinctively, as her hand began to work up to my crotch. Gently I pushed her away as she came up.

"Sandra, no, I'd rather ..."

"Don't you find me attractive?" Her look was more puzzled than hurt.

"Yes, I do. Genuinely. I just don't think that it's right, that we should, well, er ..."

"Well what?"

"Be having a … a sexual relationship. Student teacher and school governor …" All sort of conflicting thoughts, and, yes, desires, were clamouring for attention in my confused mind.

"I see." She said softly, though I'm not sure she did. Then, "Would you like me to show you to your room?"

Just like that, cordial, business-like, as if proposing the next item on the agenda.

"I think that might be best, if you don't mind," I replied. "I'm afraid I didn't bring a sleeping bag."

"That won't be necessary. Just give me a moment or two and I'll get it ready. If you want to use the bathroom, there's one under the stairs."

I was relieved that I was back in control of events, and Sandra didn't seem to be offended.

"Would you like to come up, Rob?"

Upstairs there were just two rooms, the door ajar to the further one. Inside with the sheets turned back on a double bed, Sandra was lying naked, pink nipples erect from perfectly formed milk-white breasts, and blond curls over her pubic area.

My eyes popped as my jaw dropped. "Sandra, I don't think … I can't …" And I turned and rushed downstairs, grabbed my parka and rucksack and opened the front door. I'm no prude, and certainly not averse to dalliance, but it didn't feel right to be seduced by a mother of one of my pupils. God knows what kinds of sanctions could be imposed to the detriment of my teaching career if it became known that I was shagging a school governor! What if she claimed I tried to rape her? I might just as well have been hung for a sheep as a lamb! These and other emotional and probably irrational thoughts sped through my brain in the few seconds it took me to leave Sandra's cottage.

The cold realisation of my actions hit me with the driving rain and bitter wind. Not least of which was that instead of a warm bed with or without Sandra (we could have probably agreed an honourable compromise) I was now stuck outdoors on a winter night with nowhere to go. I turned and knocked on the door. I thought I could hear crying.

"Sandra! I'm sorry! Please let me in again!"

"Go away, you bastard!"

That sounded pretty uncompromising. Upper curtains from the neighbouring house were beginning to twitch. 'You stupid, stupid bugger, Kiddecott!' I thought, 'What price your principles?'

In the warmth of the cottage, the evening had passed quickly, and a glance at my watch showed it was just past 11 o'clock. I wandered dejectedly down the street past The Drovers, which had already closed its doors, even if by any remote chance they would have done bed and breakfast at such short notice.

I remembered that I had the school key in my rucksack. Well, at least I could get out of the cold, and kip down in the staff room till morning. If the school building had felt lifeless when I had locked up earlier, it now seemed gaunt, dark and foreboding. With hardly any light, I fumbled with the key for several minutes, making enough noise to wake the dead, before the door finally yielded. I wondered about switching the light on, but unwilling to attract any more attention, I felt my way up the stairs to the staff room. Which felt as cold as an iceberg! Obviously the heating was on some timer mechanism, and not designed to cater for a stupid, reluctant Casanova. Somewhere, I recall, there was a blanket stowed for emergency care of sick kids. I chanced a flick of the light and found it behind a pile of rounders bats. Kids, though are considerable smaller than me, so I had a choice between keeping either my upper or lower half warm. I opted for the latter and kept my pullover on.

Despite the discomfort of a hard, cold floor, I suppose I must have dropped off to sleep, but I woke with a start when a torch beam played across the staffroom window and I could hear voices outside. I tried to remember whether I had locked the door from the inside. Eventually, footsteps died away and I heard a car door slam and the vehicle drive away. Any sleep I got for the rest of the night was fitful, as every strange noise and rustle, of which the wind created plenty, became the cause of speculation about intruders.

I had no idea what time William would be round to open up the school, but I reckoned I was pretty safe until seven o'clock. I didn't want to be caught napping, so to speak. I'd have to kill about an hour around somewhere before putting in a respectably early appearance at school again. Trying to be as unobtrusive as possible, I let myself out into the dark morning, and re-locked the door, then moved out into the lane, unobserved I hoped, just before the postman arrived on his bike. I realised that I had left my rucksack in the staffroom, and, of more concern, my guitar at Sandra's cottage. The former I could talk my way out of but the latter was a different matter. I considered swallowing my pride and calling on Sandra but I wasn't sure I could cope with either rejection or ravishing, and I thought it unlikely she'd invite me in for breakfast like nothing had happened. Still undecided, I wandered down the main street, where, fortunately, the newsagents' was already open to sort the morning papers. I felt as conspicuous as an Eskimo in the Sahara as I tried to spin out the selection of a newspaper, a couple of Mars Bars and a Coke as long as possible, hoping that the proprietor wasn't an inquisitive sort. Thankfully, he was still working on the paper rounds, and restricted himself to a brief 'Up early today then, young sir?' when I paid for my wares, to which I replied casually, "Long journey back to the city". Any city, away from Abergwnwyn.

Gwyn was already in his office, opening the post, when I rolled up just before 8 o'clock.

"My, my, you're an early bird, Robert! Couldn't you sleep?"

"I didn't get much to be honest," I said truthfully. "Strange surroundings."

Gwyn gave a knowing wink which implied he knew what Sandra and I might have been up to – would have been up to if she'd had her way, and could have been up to if I'd had any sense. I didn't feel it necessary to correct his assumptions.

"Do you usually get in this early?" I asked

"Not normally on the last day of term, but we had a report of intruders – not that there's much to steal! Someone saw a light on around midnight and called the police. Took them an age to come out from Tenbridge. Didn't find anything but they rang me this morning and asked me to check if there was anything missing or damaged. By the way, you left your rucksack here last night!"

"Yes, I realised that, but I managed without it. One thing though, I left my guitar at Mrs Hughes' house. I doubt if I'll have time to pop round there today before I leave and I'm not sure that she'll be bringing Fanny to school today."

Gwyn gave me an old-fashioned look. "No problem, I'll sort it out."

I was very apprehensive about showing my face outside the school that morning, in case Sandra appeared. Apprehensive too, about any possible repercussions. I was worried about whether I'd ever see my guitar again.

It was with great relief when the children dispersed after lunch, and I was able to join Gwyn, Penny, Nia, William and Gwen in the staffroom for a glass of sherry and mince pies before my minibus arrived. There too was my guitar, and Gwyn insisted that I give them all a quick song before I departed.

I managed to conceal a small pink perfumed envelope which dropped out of the guitar case among a few other Christmas cards I'd received from the kids. On the minibus, I opened it with some trepidation. A small card showed a robin perched on a harp, and inside the briefest of notes:

'*Sorry. Love, Sandy*'

I must have appeared quite emotional.

"Fan mail?" asked Sophie, leaning across the seat.

"Sort of," I replied.

CHAPTER FOUR

Eisteddfod

January had come and gone, cold, wet and windy throughout. I counted myself fortunate that my stint of teaching was over at least until my final year. I'd awaited my TP report with trepidation, unsure about any influence Sandra might have on the outcome. I needn't have worried. I passed with flying colours, with no reference to the aborted dalliance.

Jake was in buoyant form, having also received a glowing report.

"Eisteddfod next week," he said, apropos of nothing.

"So?" I replied, between spoonfuls of cornflakes.

"It's the inter-college eisteddfod next week. At Aberystwyth." His eyes suddenly found the toast crumbs interesting as he added, "I've put our names down."

My cornflakes remained suspended before my open mouth. "You've what!"

"Entered us for the eisteddfod." Now that he definitely had my attention, he became full of enthusiasm for his latest scheme. "Be a great weekend away and nothing to pay!"

"We don't speak Welsh," I pointed out.

"No problem, we don't have to. I've put our names down for foreign folk song …"

"So what do we do, recite *Frère Jacques*?" I objected. My French was only marginally better than my non-existent Welsh.

"No, no, no! We'll do an old Minstrel song, like *Oh Susanna*. Me on the banjo and you on, er, guitar … or something!" Obviously he'd got it all worked out.

"But that's not foreign."

"It is to the Welsh. English is their foreign language."

I couldn't help feeling that there was a flaw in his logic somewhere, but as usual with Jake, one tended to get swept along with him.

"And Dilly's going!" He added by way of a clincher.

That, or rather, she, was an attraction. Dilys Morgan was a pretty little dark-eyed Welsh girl who had been along to the folk club a few times since our return to Tencastle after the Christmas break. She always had a sparkle in her eye, and an infectious chuckle, not to mention a most captivating smile. Though I rarely saw her around college I had managed to engineer the odd conversation with her, and I was feeling good about my chances of a date. She didn't seem to have any fellow hanging on her arm. I didn't think to ask how Jake knew Dilly's plans.

That same evening, Jake was keen to get down to rehearsals, having taken the lack of outright rejection on my part as positive acquiescence. Of his proficiency on the banjo I had no doubt, but what my contribution to the performance was to be I was far less certain. Anyhow, I took my guitar and three chords along to his room in the main block.

"Tea?"

Dodging the usual line of used bags strung out to dry across the room, I declined. Jake plucked a shrivelled orange sachet from the line and dropped it into a mug of boiling water.

"Rose hip. Good for digestion."

Perhaps. I took his word for it.

"Right, now down to business." Jake picked up his banjo, "I thought we'd try a medley. *Oh Susannah* for starters, going in to *Campdown Ladies*. You know them?" He dashed out a short burst, with impressive (to me) frayling style, as he called it.

"Not personally. What do you want me to do?"

"Play the guitar, of course! I've written out the chords."

"Okay, I'll give it a go."

There were only three chords, but it would be an exaggeration to call me a guitarist. With no alcohol and pretty girl to boost my confidence my chord changes tended to follow about half a bar behind Jake. Eventually I managed to keep more or less in time with him. Until he suggested I join in singing the chorus as well.

"No way!" I protested. "My brain's in overload already!"

Jake reluctantly recognised my limitations. He re-attached the soggy tea bag to the string, his brow furrowed as he considered the problem. Not for long. His eyes lit up.

"Bones!" he exclaimed.

"Sorry?"

"You could play bones! You know, like castanets. You click them."

He grabbed a short plastic ruler and a biro from his desk, shoved them between his fingers and attempted a demonstration. Not with much success.

"And I suppose I dance a fandango?" I commented sarcastically. "Forget it!"

"No, wait a minute," yelled Jake and dashed out of the room.

I picked up the guitar and tried to get more co-ordination into my chord changes. It seemed the only option. A few minutes later, Jake burst into the room again, breathless.

"Here we are! Not bones. Spoons."

I could see that. Four dessert spoons, presumably from the dining hall. Jake took one pair in his right hand, and rattled away, tapping them against his other hand and on his thigh. Quite clever, really, particularly when he clattered them down the fingers of his left hand.

"Now you try!" Jake thrust the other pair towards me.

He showed me how to hold the spoons, and how to produce the various effects. Surprisingly, I picked it up quite easily, even to the extent that I could produce a reasonably percussive accompaniment to Jake's banjo. The singing, however, I left to another night.

Over the next couple of days we polished rather than perfected our act, and, on the Thursday evening before the eisteddfod trip, we tried it out on the folk club audience. No one walked out and they clapped quite enthusiastically, I thought, which boosted our confidence considerably. Dilly, I noted, wasn't there.

"By the way, Jake," I said, as we walked back to Thomas Hall. "What are the arrangements for tomorrow? You know, like travel and accommodation?"

"Coach from Union four o'clock tomorrow afternoon, I think."

I would have preferred more certain knowledge. "And digs?"

"Bring a sleeping bag. Dai Howells, the eisteddfod sec, told me we could probably kip down in their Students' Union. You have got a bag, I suppose?" he added.

"Yes, that's no problem."

It was no surprise that Powell's Pleasure Tours had been booked for the trip since they had the virtual monopoly of coach business within a twenty-five mile radius of Tencastle. School runs, rugby club fixtures, Sunday school outings were all grist to Powell's mill. They even mentioned continental tours on their promotional leaflets, though nobody knew of anyone who had actually been abroad with them. Even the 'luxury class' flagship of their ageing fleet wasn't one you would recommend for extended journeys, and students evidently didn't come into the luxury class of clients.

While the driver puzzled on how to get two large harps into the charabanc's rather small boot along with other assorted luggage and instruments, Dai Howells was checking off names on his list.

"Kiddecott, Robert," I volunteered.

He scanned his papers. "Who?"

"Kiddecott," I repeated.

"Sorry, you're not here. What are you down for?"

"Foreign folk song." Jake hadn't yet arrived, but I had a thought. "Try Moses," I suggested.

Dai checked his list again. He turned over the last sheet, and found an old envelope. "Ah yes, Moses Minstrels, two of you?"

"Yes," I said, hoping Jake was going to turn up. I didn't fancy doing a solo.

Unlike the four main colleges in Wales, at Cardiff, Swansea, Bangor and Aberystwyth, who would no doubt turn out in force for the eisteddfod, Tencastle's contingent was much more modest; a couple of harpists, three poets (or bards, as they preferred to be known), a Welsh folk dance group and a choir – and, incongruously, Moses Minstrels, of course. Barely one coach load!

It was getting on for four-thirty. Jake was still missing, and I was beginning to get worried, the fact that I had secured a seat behind Dilly being only a small consolation. I saw Huw from my corridor scramble on with a large box and take a seat behind the driver. Dai, standing at the front, looked at his watch, and at his band of eisteddfod hopefuls. One of the harps had been manoeuvred into the aisle in front of the rear seat.

"Just a few quick domestic details before we set off, then," he began. "You'll all be given a programme showing where and when the preliminary rounds for the various events will be, and of course, we'll see you all at the final winners' concert in the evening, won't we?"

The polite laughter suggested that a finalist's appearance was an unlikely event for any of them.

"Tonight there's food and fraternising with the opposition in the Union. Other meals there too. We leave Aber at eleven o'clock sharp tomorrow after the concert. You've already been given your sleeping arrangements. Any questions?"

I was about to ask for confirmation of our sleeping arrangements when Jake appeared up the steps of the coach, much to my relief. Dai tapped his watch and looked at Jake reproachfully.

"All here, now. Let's be off then," Dai said to the driver.

Jake stowed his rucksack and banjo, sans case but wrapped in a large plastic bag as a concession to wet weather, in the luggage rack, and settled down next to me.

"Where on earth have you been?" I said accusingly.

"What's the problem, I'm here by four thirty?"

"You told me four o'clock!"

"Did I?" Jake seemed completely unfazed. "Must have made a mistake."

On reflection I should have sat in front of Dilly. I could have then propped myself up in the seat and taken in her charms whilst chatting full frontal. Fortunately, Jake had opted for the window seat and, uncharacteristically, had drifted into pensive slumber. I caught the attention of Dilly's left ear as she turned to offer a Polo to an extremely buxom girl across the aisle. "Hi, Dilly, remember me? We met at the folk club."

She showed just a hint of puzzlement on her brow before a sparkle of her gorgeous brown eyes and a smile I'd die for. She didn't prop herself up to go face to face with my charms, though.

"Rob, isn't it?" A pencilled eyebrow rose quizzically. "I didn't know you were in to Welsh culture?"

"I've had Welsh blood somewhere along the line." I didn't mention it was mostly from the nose of a Welsh lad who ran into my forehead on the school rugby field.

"So what are you entered for?"

"International folk song. With Jake here." I jerked a thumb at my sleeping partner.

"Really! That's great! I'd love to hear you!" She could make a fellow feel great, even if it was only polite conversation.

"You should have been at the club yesterday. Star turn!" I exaggerated just a little.

She giggled. "Sorry about that, I had to practise. Perhaps I'll see you at the winners' concert?"

It was my turn to laugh. "Some chance! But what about you? What were you practising for?"

"I'm with the Tencastle Welsh Folk Dance Group."

"So do you wear one of those black pointy hats?"

"No, and I don't fly on a broomstick either!"

"I'm sorry, I didn't mean ..."

"No, that's okay, only joking." She was still smiling. "Those hats are more for the tourist image, but we do have our traditional style costume. I've been dancing since I was a kid."

"This won't be your first time to an eisteddfod then?"

"First time to the inter-college eisteddfod. This is my first year at Tencastle."

"Likewise. And is it your first time to Aberystwyth?" I reflected briefly that this sounded like a variation on the 'do you come here often' chat line.

"Hardly," she chuckled. "I was born there. It's my home!"

"Perhaps you can give me a personal guided tour of the town?"

"Perhaps."

The girl beside her called her attention to some feature of the fast darkening landscape and they chatted away in Welsh for the best part of the journey. However, when the coach drew up outside the Students' Union building in Aberystwyth an hour later, I still had designs on pressing my luck with Dilly. She took my hand as I chivalrously helped her down the steps from the coach, but almost immediately, with a quick thanks, she ran into the arms of a young man standing by a sports car opposite. Did I feel a touch of jealousy?

Although it was still early evening and the Cardiff and Bangor contingents had not yet arrived, the Union building was already heaving with humanity. We'd been allocated a room where we could leave all our gear, but Jake refused to be parted from his banjo. He probably even took it to bed with him!

If joining the bun fight for supper of bean soup, burgers and Welsh cakes was difficult, getting within six feet of the bar for a pint proved well nigh impossible.

"How about we paint the town?" suggested Jake, whose banjo at least guaranteed him a little more elbow room. "And perhaps a quick run through our repertoire?"

"Fine by me," I replied, wondering if a single song could legitimately constitute a repertoire.

Aberystwyth would never qualify as the night-life capital of Wales but it took us a while to find the only pub without a decibel-enhanced jukebox. The publican eyed us dubiously when we ordered our pints, and when Jake attempted a few introductory bars on the banjo, the landlord told him in no uncertain terms where to put his instrument! His customers never even got to hear our repertoire.

"Bloody heathen!" complained Jake. "Doesn't appreciate good music!"

Maybe.

The deserted shelter on the promenade seemed to be the only place where we could practise without causing a disturbance. Fortunately, for late February, it was unseasonably mild.

"Here, put this on," said Jake, handing me what looked like a small round pill box.

"What is it?"

"Black grease paint."

"No way!"

"Oh come on, Rob, we have to look the part," urged Jake.

"You already do!" I wasn't happy. "How about you do the black and I'll do the white minstrel bit!"

"No, no, we've got to do it properly. It comes off easily."

I thought about retorting that he'd never had to try, but restrained myself to one valid objection. "This is only a rehearsal, it's dark, so what the hell does it matter?"

"It's just to get in the right mood," Jake persisted.

The mood I was in didn't match that sought by Jake, but then one never wins an argument with him. I relented.

"How do we, sorry, how do I get it off?"

"Students' Union bog!"

Jake volunteered to plaster my face, and applied the grease quite liberally until he was satisfied with the effect. I was glad I didn't have a mirror. We tried our number through a few times until I was able to play spoons and join in the chorus simultaneously, our only audience a few passing seagulls. They didn't applaud, but didn't crap on us either, so they must have enjoyed it.

We were, it must be said, feeling quite confident in our minstrelsy as we started to find our way back to the Union building along a side street which Jake swore was a short cut. I felt much less confident about the appearance of the five skinheaded youths who staggered into our path from a pub doorway.

"Well, boyos," sneered the leader of the group. "What have we here, a pair of coons?" Heavily tattooed and dressed in grubby singlet and jeans, the belt of which was largely hidden by his overhanging belly, he poked a finger at Jake. "We don't like niggers here!"

Jake was unfazed. "We're minstrels. On our way to a fancy dress party," he explained calmly, handing his banjo to me. I wondered what sort of defensive weapon it would make.

"Hear that!" guffawed Fat Gut, turning to his cronies. "F——ing minstrels, my arse! F——ing nig-nogs!"

"Look, it's only grease paint." Jake demonstrated by drawing his finger across my cheek, leaving a white streak.

Fat Gut belched loudly and drew closer.

"Hey, would you like us to sing for you?" Jake launched into an Al Jolson impression of *Mammy* and made to put his arm round Fat Gut's shoulders.

"F—— off, you f——ing poofter!"

The other guys smirked.

"A million miles for one of your smiles…"

"F—- OFF!"

"Maybe he fancies you," called one of the gang.

"You shut your bleedin' trap!" bellowed Fat Gut, rounding on his mates.

"Mammy's getting angry," Jake crooned to me in a loud aside.

Fat Gut wheeled angrily to face his tormentor with an expression totally devoid of motherly love, and made to swing a beefy fist.

"Aw, leave them be, Tom, they're pissed as assholes!" A lanky youth with bad acne caught Fat Gut's arm. "There's other real wogs down by the take-away. Why waste time with these third rate fairies!"

Jake began to draw himself up to his full six foot. "Are you suggesting …"

"For Chrissake, Jake, knock it off," I hissed, "and let's get the hell out of here!"

With contemptuous sneers, Fat Gut and co. turned and slouched off up the street. Feeling considerably paler than my current complexion showed I suggested we should find another route back to the Union.

By the time we had reached there, however, most of the student population of Wales seemed to have crammed into the Union building, which was being shaken to its foundations by raucous songs epicentred in the bar. All in Welsh, of course, and some fine harmonies were evident, although some singers seemed intent on finding a note that no one else was using.

I had more urgent things to attend to, like restoring my normal appearance, which, due to a lack of soap, paper towels, and hot water in the gents, was not quite as easy as Jake had suggested. When I eventually emerged, feeling like a coal miner after a pit bath, the crowds were beginning to thin out, time evidently having been called at the bar. More to the point, the rest of the Tencastle contingent seemed to have already dissolved into the night. Obviously they had been billeted elsewhere.

"Looks as if we'll have the room to ourselves, then," said Jake as he wriggled into his sleeping bag onto the floor between Tencastle's harps and other paraphernalia.

"Suits me," I replied, trying to find my own piece of vacant floor. Actually it was quite cosy, and quite peaceful after the remnants of the revellers had left. Peaceful for at least five minutes.

"We've got visitors," observed Jake and nodded towards the doorway, which had just been filled by an officious looking gentleman with a moustache.

"What do think you're up to?" said Whiskers, in a tone which didn't bode well for us.

"We were trying to get some sleep," replied Jake, in an affected posh accent.

"Not on my floor you don't!"

Jake opened his mouth to comment, probably about public servants serving the public but I cut in with a more reasonable approach. "We were told it would be okay to kip down here."

"Well I'm telling you it's not okay!"

"But ... we've no-where else to go!" I tried to appeal to his better nature, failing miserably.

"Not my problem, so clear off before I throw you out!"

The Porter looked pretty serious about his threat.

Jake looked at me and shrugged, "I guess we'd better pick up our beds and walk."

Clutching partly-rolled sleeping bags, rucksacks and banjo, we emerged into the deserted street. The door was firmly closed and bolted behind us. A chill breeze had sprung up off the sea.

"What the bloody hell do we do now?" I felt Jake should have the answer – it had been his idea.

"Sleep on the beach?" Jake offered, tentatively.

"In this wind? And you bet the tide's coming in!"

A Mini screeched to a halt in front of us, and a bespectacled, bearded and balding driver yelled out, "Are you the two I'm supposed to be putting up for the night at my place?"

We didn't wait to consider whether anyone else was likely to be sleep walking the street.

"That's us!" called Jake, trailing his sleeping bag down the stone steps of the Union.

There were already two other bodies apart from the driver, which made for unavoidable intimacy.

"Beats me how some people manage to have sex in a Mini," observed Jake.

'My place' was a reasonably-sized study bedroom with en-suite facilities in Ty Coch Student Residence, though I guessed the driver was a cut above your average student to warrant such luxury. Unless, of course, Aberystwyth was more generous to its students. It certainly seemed more liberal than Tencastle in its attitude to mixed-sex accommodation, for I'd heard several female voices in the corridor.

Three sleeping bags, as yet unoccupied were already spread out on the floor, and there was just about room for ours as well. The driver had disappeared and Jake was taking a shower while I was temporarily exposed between drying off and dressing for bed.

A knock came on the door, and, before I could reply, a girl in a flimsy nightdress entered.

"Adieu kerrima?" I think that's what she said.

A recently discarded sock was closest to hand as I tried to show some modesty. "Er … je non parlez ne …um … non suis Gauloise," I stuttered. Languages were never my strong point.

"Oh, you're English! Sorry, I was wanting Ceri."

Christ, but she was pretty, and nothing to hide!

"Will I do?" I said hopefully, and I realised that is wasn't only my hopes that were rising.

She briefly lowered her eyes and grinned, "Another time perhaps." And then with a flash of pearly white teeth she was gone.

"What's this, the latest fashion – knitted condoms?" said Jake as he emerged from the shower.

My sock slid listlessly to the floor.

I must have been pretty shattered because I slept soundly until my presence became a serious obstacle to the mass of humanity that wanted to invade my floor space. Two more sleeping bags had joined those of the previous night and there seemed to be a forest of hairy legs around me.

Jake wandered in munching a round of toast and dropped a few crumbs in my hair.

"Where did you get that?" I asked, wriggling out of my cocoon.

"Help yourself in the kitchen." Jake waved his toast vaguely in the direction of the door.

I dragged on some clothes and shuffled out into the corridor. From a doorway a few yards away came the smell of coffee and a buzz of chatter. A little larger than our Tencastle equivalent at Thomas Hall, the kitchen still held about twice the number of people it was designed for, and the toaster and kettle were working overtime. Although no-one seemed to be in charge, there was some semblance of a production line in operation to satiate the appetite and slake the thirst of all comers. No sign of the nightie girl, I rued.

Our driver from last night appeared in the doorway, and called out something in Welsh, then yelled, "Ten minutes!" and, in case there were any other foreign nationals present, held up both hands with all digits spread out. The other occupants showed a certain degree of urgency, so I downed my coffee in one gulp and hurried back to the bedroom.

"Ten minutes!" I called to Jake.

"What for?" asked Jake from the bathroom.

"I dunno, but everyone's a lot more animated out there!"

"Okay, best get our gear together, just in case."

Two fellows and a girl breezed in and started gathering up the sleeping bags. We collected our belongings and emerged into the corridor. We hadn't a clue where we were supposed to be going or what we were supposed to be doing.

"When in doubt, go with the flow," suggested Jake.

The 'flow', or rather a steady trickle of students, led us out to a driveway in front of a large, modern student residence which commanded an imposing view of the old town way below us. We hadn't even noticed the elevated position of our 'digs' last night!

A bearded gent with a clipboard was ushering students onto a coach. We joined the short queue and Beard just looked at us briefly, ticked something on his sheet, and waved us on board. There was absolutely no sign of any other members of the Tencastle crowd.

"Do you think he knew us?" I asked.

"Doubt it," replied Jake. "Probably more concerned with numbers than names."

I had the wicked thought that we may have displaced some key members of the Aberystwyth competition. On the other hand we might have just joined their cultural exchange to Outer Mongolia!

Dai Howells was handing out some leaflets to our Tencastle team mates as we disembarked outside the Students' Union. He gave us a puzzled look as we joined the group and gave us one of the handouts.

"Wondered where you two had got to," he commented, passing us a leaflet. "Here's the details of times and venues for the various competitive events, and the winner's showcase concert. "Remember," he said, addressing the whole group, "the coach leaves 11 o'clock sharp from here. Don't miss it." He looked pointedly at us. "It's a bloody long walk home!"

I had the feeling that we had been expected someplace else last night.

Jake was studying the leaflet intently. I, on the other hand, was trying to catch Dilly's attention, resplendent as she was in red tunic and dress, with lacy trimmings and a kind of white woven shawl about her shoulders. Sadly she seemed to be involved in a discussion with a lanky youth with red waistcoat, black breeches and long green socks. Possibly her dancing partner, the lucky bugger.

"It's all in Welsh!" Jake exclaimed. He'd probably said something else to me as well.

"Sorry, what is?"

"This bloody programme!"

"Well, that's not surprising, is it?"

"But how are we supposed to know where we're performing?"

Dilly, along with the others had begun to move off towards a large quaint old building just down the road.

"Here, let me look!" I grabbed the leaflet and flipped through it. Among the unintelligible text, the words 'international folk song' appeared bracketed and in italics.

"11.15 am room G23, in there," I said, confidently, pointing towards the building into which the Tencastle stragglers, ourselves excepted, were already disappearing.

Jake, for once was amazed, "How did you work that out?"

It's not often I get one up on Jake. "Easy," I said, showing him the entry in the leaflet. "That's obviously our event, the time is self evident, the last column is obviously the room, and everybody seems to be headed towards that same building."

"Obviously," conceded Jake.

We had about an hour to kill before our scheduled spot, a quarter of which we spent deliberating whether to use it sightseeing, rehearsing, or to find a warm cafe. By mutual disagreement we did none of these but ambled towards the rehearsal building.

"Might as well black up and ogle the opposition," Jake grunted.

Or put the fear of God into them.

Inside the old college building, an enormous staircase curved up to the first floor from each side of the cavernous entrance hall. Incongruously, beneath the balcony a wooden trestle table supported a steaming urn, a caterer's tin of Nescafe, a jumble of plastic cups and a nest of tea bags in various stages of hydration. Back at Tencastle, Jake would have had them strung up to dry in no time. A flip chart on an easel helpfully showed the location of the various competitive events.

After a black coffee and a blacking-up session in the bog, we climbed the right hand staircase and made our way along a high-vaulted corridor in search of room G23. If there was any logic to the room numbering it wasn't immediately apparent. From what was evidently a library came the swell of male voice choir, and further along, the mellifluous ripple of a harp wafted through the ether. Up another flight of stairs, quite ordinary by comparison, we came to a garret disguised as a small seminar room.

The 'opposition', such as it was, had already arrived; a young girl who looked barely into her teens rather than nearly out of them, a beefy blond fellow with a battered accordion, and a lanky long-haired couple, probably one of each sex, though it was difficult to tell beneath their broad-brimmed hats dangling with corks. Their other props consisted of a sheet of metal and a long, thick bamboo cane. We quietly took a couple of vacant seats in the small semicircle of chairs, with just a nod to our competitors. We might have been in the waiting room of a doctor's surgery, such was the sombre atmosphere.

"I feel as if I'm waiting for an interview with the headmaster for being a naughty boy," murmured Jake.

"And we're six of the best?" I replied quietly, my eyes indicating the rest of us in the room.

Jake chuckled, which helped to break the tension for all of us, just as the door opened to admit a new trio – presumably our judges, as they clearly weren't of student age. They took their seats in silence behind a small table, facing us, but then the leader, a stocky, grey-suited man with a shiny bald pate conferred with his colleagues either side, a buxom middle-aged woman with brushed-back dark brown hair, and a tall bearded gent with straggly thinning hair and a fisherman's heavy sweater. They lifted the table to one side, and placed their chairs at the end of our semicircle.

"Good morning, ladies and gentlemen," said Egghead, "I trust you will prefer the more informal seating arrangement. We would like you to feel you are performing to all of us as the audience, rather than appearing at an interview."

We all laughed politely.

"Now, unless you have any objections otherwise, we'll ask you to perform alphabetically in college order, that is," he paused to consult a sheet of paper. "Bangor, Cardiff, Swansea and Tencastle."

No one objected. I wondered what had happened to the home team.

The young girl was first to go, and she appeared quite nervous, as she launched into an unaccompanied ballad in some strange modal key. She had a voice like liquid honey and put the full gamut of facial and tonal expressions into the song, which was, regrettably, exceedingly depressing with more deaths than an Agatha Christie novel. When she was finished, she gave a little bow, and the room was for an instant totally silent.

"Bravo!" called Jake, and began to clap. We all joined in the applause, not only out of politeness. She could certainly sing!

I think we were all grateful for Jake for breaking the ice, and the next act, the Aussie pair from Cardiff, were visibly more relaxed. What they lacked in vocal finesse they made up for with energy as they wobbled their wobble-board and made rude noises on their didgeridoodah in a spirited cover of Rolf Harris's *Tie My Kangaroo Down*.

Swansea kept closest to the international idea with the only rendering in a language other than English. The blond beefcake tried to generate some gemutlichkeit with a German drinking song at full volume on both voice and squeezebox. Shame he'd forgotten his lederhosen, but we applauded all the same.

"And, now, if you please, the Moses Minstrels from Tencastle!"

The big moment. Jake limbered up with some impressive frayling on the banjo as he launched into a completely unscripted introduction, in an exaggerated southern states American accent. "Yo, me an' mah buddy, we're gonna sing yuh a li'l ole number fro' mah ol' home. Take it away, Homer buddy!"

Homer? My cue, I guessed, and I rattled away with the spoons as Jake built up momentum on the banjo. For the next few minutes I was completely immersed in working the spoons, trilling them over my fingers, hammering them on my knee and clacking them on various other parts of my anatomy for good measure. I'm sure though that Jake had sung more verses than we'd ever rehearsed by the time we reached the agreed repeat chorus for the finale – a last chord, and sudden break.

The audience, small as it was, clapped enthusiastically. Jake gave a sweeping bow, and walked off, still frayling on the banjo. I followed suit with a clatter of spoons.

"Thank you very much, ladies and gentlemen for your entertainment," said Egghead. He sounded as if he really meant it. "The adjudication will be posted in the entrance hall by two o'clock this afternoon. First and second placed performers should make themselves available for the winners' concert, which starts promptly at three p.m.. You'll need to check with the M.C. to find what time you're on."

"So what now?" I asked.

"Drink?" suggested Jake.

"Sounds good to me!"

"Hey, come and join us, and we'll get a session going." The kangaroo crew offered a general invitation to all. "There's a great little pub we know just around the corner."

We didn't need our arms twisting, though the young Bangor girl politely declined. We trooped off after the Aussie singers in search of the pub.

Jake looked rather worried as we approached the chosen hostelry. "Recognise this?" he said. "It's the one we got chucked out of last night. Some chance of a session!"

Anyway, we followed the others in. There were only a couple of locals drinking at the bar, and the snug was empty. No sign, either, of yesterday's sourpuss barman, but a rather dishy young brunette with Barbara Windsor boobs.

"Okay if we have a jam session in the back?" This from the didgeridoo player.

"Sure, Iewan, go ahead," the barmaid replied. "Up for the eisteddfod, is it?"

"That's it. Just had the prelims, and results aren't for an hour or so. Can you pull us all a pint of best?" Iewan turned to us, "That okay with you lads?"

No dissenting comments were heard. Jake looked at me with raised eyebrow.

We all settled in the snug, and Jake related to Iewan our reception in this very same pub the previous evening, and added, "You seem to be known to the barmaid."

"I ought to, she's my aunt."

"And what about Grumpy?" I asked.

"Oh, he's um a sort of, er … an honorary great uncle."

It didn't seem politic to enquire further as Aunty brought a tray of foaming pints over to us. Jake was already tuning the banjo to the accordion of Kristian, the lad from Swansea; he apparently had a German father. Iewan's friend, Glyn – he was male, despite appearances- produced a mouth organ, and pretty soon we were working away through a cosmopolitan selection of tunes and songs that we all more or less half knew, not that uncertainty of melody or lyrics inhibited us in any way. I don't remember anyone actually ordering any more beer, but our glasses never seemed to be empty, though not for the want of trying.

Aunty (Aunt Rose, it was, we learnt) eventually interrupted us, "Time, lads, it's well past time." Then added, "I'd be quite happy for you to sing here all day, but I expect you'll be wanting to get to the concert!"

Which by my watch had already started five minutes earlier.

Ten minutes or so later, after family farewells and reluctant acceptance of our attempt to pay for any of the beer, we emerged into the fresh February air. Iewan was all for a curry, but I thought it fair to remind him that one of us might, possibly, be imminently required to perform at the winner's concert.

"Oh, don't worry! They'll be ages yet. They always are!"

Glyn and I volunteered to go back to check the adjudication list, while the rest of them headed for an Indian take-away and promised to save us some.

We found them again in the foyer of the cinema which had been requisitioned by the University for the day. Jake was licking his fingers clean of curry sauce. His white lip paint had become streaked with brown.

"Well?"

"Well, what?" I answered, innocently.

"You know bloody well what!"

"Oh, the results you mean?" I said, prolonging the moment of disclosure.

"Pillock!"

"Fourth place, Abertawe." I pretended to consult the back of a crumpled envelope. Jake glared at me impatiently. "That's Swansea, by the way. Third place, Cardiff."

Glyn hadn't seemed too surprised or disappointed, for that matter. "Sorry," I said to Iewan, who shrugged.

"Not to worry, it's a great time anyhow. Wouldn't have missed it."

"Second place, Bangor."

Jake's chicken leg hung suspended before his open mouth, as realisation dawned.

"And first place, the Moses Minstrels!" I punched the air, smiling.

"You're joking!" cried Jake, mouth agape even more.

"I kid you not! We've won for Tencastle!"

For a few seconds Jake still couldn't take it in. Then he beamed, and grabbed me with a bear hug, chicken leg dripping curry sauce down the back of my neck. "Bloody hell, Rob, I don't believe it! We won? I never even thought we'd ... bloody hell!"

I'd rarely seen him so emotional. After a few more bloody hells, his mind turned to practical matters.

"So that means we'll be on stage, doesn't it?"

I nodded agreement.

"Christ, we could be on any time! What was that we were told about the M.C.? I don't remember! We'd better find out right away! Here, hold this!"

He handed me his banjo and a foil container with a handful of fried rice and the remains of an indeterminate brown goo in which a few flakes of poppadom were half submerged. I realised that I hadn't eaten since breakfast.

Inside the auditorium, the concert was indeed under way. At least, there was a fellow on stage giving some kind of recitation to a harp accompaniment while in the wings hovered a beanpole of a bloke with straggly ginger hair, huge horn-rimmed spectacles, and a clipboard. He peered anxiously out over the banks of tiered seats which were barely one-quarter occupied. The audience for the most part appeared to be giving little attention to the performance, and there was a considerable ebb and flow of bodies in the aisles. Blocks of seats had evidently been allocated to each college, with banners suspended from the roof emblazoned with the college crest and name, Caerdydd and Abertawe holding prime position at the front. Tencastle merited only a modest sign mounted on a pole to the rear of the side stalls. Jake and I were currently the only occupants.

The act finished, to exuberant whoops and yells from a band of supporters in the Bangor sector and a muted, polite applause from a few people elsewhere. Beanpole the M.C. sauntered centre stage and began jabbering away in Welsh until drowned out by an encore of celebration by Bangor students. The M.C. tried again and managed to make himself heard once more above the buzz of chatter which persisted.

"Any idea where he's got to in the programme?" I whispered to Jake, whose information mission had yielded a printed leaflet with a running order. All in Welsh, of course.

"I dunno," he replied. "But all items up to 5.30 p.m. seem to have very similar wording. There's something else, and then at 6.30 p.m. it's got here 'dawns', could be their attempt at 'dance'."

"And we're on when?" I asked, just to double check on what he'd told me earlier.

"The words 'International Folk Song' are listed here at 7.30 p.m.," he said, authoritatively. He'd obviously picked up my tips on interpretation of notices in an alien language.

"Okay. I don't fancy hanging around for another couple of hours of this recitation stuff. Even if I could understand it."

"Me neither," agreed Jake. "What say we head for the Students' Union and get some grub and a pint. I didn't get much lunch," he added pointedly.

Neither did I. The remains of his take-away didn't really count.

The auditorium was considerably fuller by the time we returned, though the scene was pretty chaotic. Beanpole was looking stressed as he tried to bring the audience to order. Rousing cheers from the Swansea block were soon drowned out by Cardiff's patriotic yell of 'Ar Daff', to which, Bangor and the host college obviously felt obliged to respond in kind. Tencastle's contingent provided virtually the only area of calm. Even if we'd had a college anthem we would have made little impression against our giant rivals.

Honour satisfied, the noise dropped to a level at which Beanpole was able to introduce the next act.

"Not more bloody harps!" groaned Jake. "They must have signed up the whole bloody Heavenly host!"

I spotted a fellow with a clipboard making his way up the main aisle, apparently searching for something or somebody.

"Hang on, Jake, be right back!" I eased myself out from the row of seats. "Hi, we're the winners of the International Folk Song section. Can you tell us when we're supposed to be on?"

"And you are?" he said.

"Moses Minstrels. From Tencastle."

He consulted his clipboard. "From Tencastle? That's a change." He seemed genuinely pleased as well as surprised.

"Well, you were supposed to be on at 7.30 but we're running a bit late. Come backstage at 8 o'clock, and we should be almost ready," he said, optimistically.

"Okay, thanks!"

"Well?" asked Jake, as I returned to my seat.

"Half an hour, or so."

The auditorium erupted into another bout of partisan support. The sight of yet another harp being manhandled onto the stage did nothing to raise Jake's spirits, but stirrings in the meagre ranks of our fellow Tencastle supporters made me sit up.

"There's Dilly!" I exclaimed, poking Jake in the ribs.

Indeed, Dilly looked positively radiant at the head of the Tencastle Welsh Folk Dance team.

I'm no expert on the intricacies of dance, but to me their performance was perfect. I was on my feet even before they'd finished, and as they took their bow, I led the yelling and applause from our back corner. We made ourselves heard, for the body of the hall was strangely muted, and I could have sworn that Dilly blew a kiss in my direction.

"Second place, that's pretty good!" commented a Tencastle guy behind me.

I was oblivious to the first placed team. Jake and I were already heading for the performers' staircase to prepare for our own showpiece.

There were still a couple of acts in front of us, a quartet singing a jolly little Welsh song to guitar accompaniment, and a trio doing acapella harmonies, also in Welsh.

"Nervous?" whispered Jake.

That would be an understatement. Butterflies were breeding in my stomach and my bladder was beginning to signal its need for relief.

Performing in front of friends or a few people at the preliminaries was one thing, being in the spotlight in front of several hundred fired-up students was quite another.

Beanpole managed to get the audience settled fairly quickly, but then waited for another couple of minutes while a group of somewhat inebriated Morris dancers in Bangor colours capered down one aisle and up the other.

Banjo frayling away before we even left the wings, Jake quickly strode over to the mike and went into an even longer 'Homer, mah ol' buddy' routine, calling me on to join him. We hadn't rehearsed that – it just happened. My butterflies flew away as we launched into the song, spoons rattling furiously to keep pace – just – with Jake's dynamic banjo. I'll say this for him, he's one hell of a showman, and when he burst into an unscripted fancy finger-picking style banjo break complete with tuning-peg tweaking, I wasn't the only one who was gobsmacked. Back on course, even our supposed finale wasn't enough for him.

"One more time!" he yelled into the mike, hoisting the banjo high above his head. Two more verses and choruses with the whole assembly stamping their feet and clapping in time, and the applause after the final chord was deafening, standing ovation and all. Beanpole had to bring us back for a second curtain call to quell the uproar.

"I need a drink!" Jake gasped, sweat pouring off him.

The student union bar was, unlike last night, almost deserted and relatively quiet apart from a scrum of rugby types telling bawdy jokes. We'd made our escape from the stage door of the hall, both of one mind as to our immediate course of action.

"We did it!" said Jake, flopped out against the bench seat and gazing contentedly at his half-empty glass.

"I think we can say that," I agreed, from a similar pose. "You caught me on the hop with your improvisations though. What was that you were doing on the banjo?"

"Oh, just a bit of Scruggs style," he said dismissively. "After Earl Scruggs, an American country and western banjo player," he added, catching my raised eyebrow.

Another pint later, we deliberated, briefly, on whether to return to the concert.

"No, I've had enough culture for one day," Jake declared. "Let's relax until coach time."

I wasn't inclined to disagree.

We were feeling pleasantly mellow, slightly soporific, and half pissed when the barman called time.

"Time for us to join our merry band," I said, yawning, and slinging my rucksack over my shoulder.

We were quite unprepared for the reception which met us outside. Powell's coach was decorated with the Tencastle banner from the concert hall, and Tencastle scarves hung at every window. And the Tencastle party were all gathered around the Union steps.

"Here they come!" yelled someone. A great cheer went up "Moses! Moses! Moses for Tencastle!" and we were lifted bodily and chaired on our supporters' shoulders even, hazardously from my viewpoint, on to the coach. Scarcely had I got my feet to the floor when Dilly planted a juicy kiss full on my lips, and gave me an enormous hug.

"Brilliant, Rob, brilliant! You were brilliant. I'm so happy!"

I didn't get a chance to put in a word for Jake or commend her own performance, before she kissed me again. Fame has its attractions.

Dai was almost ecstatic, taking the microphone hardly before we'd settled in our seats. "Guys … ladies and gents! Never have we had such a good eisteddfod! Our choir – second place! Our dance team – wonderful! All of you! But, for the first time ever, a first place! Guys … I give you … the Moses Minstrels!"

Through thunderous applause, stamping of feet, and cheering we had no choice but to take our bow at the front of the coach.

"Give it us again! Give us some more," they yelled.

They weren't going to let us off quietly. Jake, as usual, rose to the occasion and after our prizewinning number, he led off into a whole range of songs with me tapping along beside him, joining in on vocals where I thought I knew the words. No matter! The whole coach load of students were singing their guts out with us all the way back to Tencastle.

The euphoria in the Students' Union lasted for at least a week – the student newspaper ran headlines which made us feel like pop stars, and there was even talk of an eisteddfod celebrity celebration concert.

Jake and I, however, couldn't have sung another note – we'd lost our voices somewhere on the coach, and could only communicate in croaky whispers for several days.

CHAPTER FIVE

Charlie

With the preparations and aftermath of the eisteddfod, I'd done precious little academic study for nearly three weeks. Particularly in the aftermath. I blamed Jake for exposing me to Aberystwyth's sea breezes in February, for not only had I lost my voice, but I'd developed a streaming cold that had threatened to turn into bronchitis. It had even kept me confined to bed for two days, and scuppered immediate plans to press my advantage with Dilly while my fame lasted. When I'd eventually recovered, I'd gone along to the next folk dance group meeting in hopeful anticipation of impressing her with my interest in Welsh culture. She'd greeted me warmly enough, with a hug and a kiss, then quickly returned to the company of her dance partner from the eisteddfod. The instructor, a middle-aged slightly portly man with a florid countenance, had done his best to involve me, but, with no unpartnered females, I'd felt like a spare John Thomas at a honeymoon. Besides which, my brain had enough problems conveying dance instructions to my legs in English, let alone in Welsh, which everyone present except me had spoken fluently.

Disheartened, with no immediate prospects that I could see for a relationship, dance or otherwise, with Dilly, I planned to devote all of the weekend getting back into the rhythm of work. By Saturday evening I was even beginning to feel motivated enough to continue for another couple of hours after supper.

"Phone, Rob!" called the disembodied voice, following closely after the tympanum of knuckles on the door.

"Damn!" I exhaled, and then louder. "Okay, be with you directly."

"Damn!" I muttered again, laying aside a well-chewed pencil, irritated at the interruption.

Reluctantly, I heaved my body out of the study chair and made my way along the corridor and up to the lobby to where the telephone receiver hung limply from beneath the Perspex canopy adjacent to the lift.

"Kiddecott here," I said, disinterestedly.

"Christ, Rob, you do take a hell of a time," came the spirited reply.

Puzzled, my brain quickly scanned my store of female voiceprints, and made a tentative, if unexpected match.

"Charlie? Is that you, Charlie?"

"Of course it's me you thickhead, who did you expect?"

I could have thought of several possible answers, but none so unlikely. "Sorry, I didn't recognise you at first. You're not, er, one of my usual …"

"I'm not what?"

"You're not, er, I mean…" Floundering, I opted for truth and safety. "I wasn't expecting you. Er … where are you calling from anyway?"

"Here, of course!"

"Where's here?"

"Tencastle, you bloody idiot! I've just arrived!"

"Arrived? What, here in Tencastle? I mean, how? Er, why?"

I detected exasperation in the audible exhalation of breath.

"I must say, Rob, you don't seem all that pleased to welcome a poor simple country girl to your big metropolis," she replied, with more than a hint of reproach in her tone.

The thought of my cousin Charlotte being either poor or simple brought a smile to my face, despite wondering what the hell she was doing in Tencastle at eight o'clock on a Saturday evening in March. The last time I had seen her was a few months earlier, at Aunt Ethel's funeral. Even the black hat and gloves required by protocol had not hidden the vivacious spirit and lively mind that lay not so far below the serene and sun-tanned complexion. I couldn't help thinking that the freckled-faced little tomboy I had played with many a time on my Uncle's farm during holidays had matured into a feisty and very attractive young woman.

"Sorry again, I'm still a little surprised to hear from you."

"Oh, Robert Kiddecott, you can't tell me that you've forgotten already! You did invite me down to stay with you and I did write to let you know I was coming."

Charlie sounded rather hurt. Wheels in my mind were beginning to turn. At the funeral supper, whilst grannies and granddads, aunts and uncles, and a parlour full of obscure relations had prattled away over the gossip of half a century, I'd spent quite a bit of time chatting with Charlie, establishing childhood rapport and all that, after several years of going our own ways, or rather, in the direction our respective parents had decided. After our early primary schooling in neighbouring villages, Charlie had spent the rest of her formative years away at a moderately well-known public school, her parents always having felt that they were a cut above the rest of the family. I'd gone through the adequate but undemanding machinery of the local comprehensive, from which, despite earlier promise, I'd arrived at Tencastle. She was two years younger than me, nearly the same age as my sister. I remember she'd said something about going on to Art College after her A levels.

I vaguely remembered offering to show her what university life was like, and I may have even suggested I would be happy for her to share my pad on a long weekend. Delighted I would have been, too, but it was just one of those friendly casual invitations which even if she had accepted at the time I wouldn't have imagined she would have taken seriously. Besides which I didn't even have a 'pad' then! Or now.

And I certainly hadn't had any letter from her.

"Are you still there? I've just put my last change in." Charlie's voice brought me back to the present.

"Er, yes, I'll be pleased to see you."

"You don't sound too sure." Charlie's voice showed a hint of concern, "It will be all right won't it? You did say I could stay at your place, and I don't mind sleeping on the floor."

Hell, what could I say? "Um, I ...er, well, yes, but there is a slight problem."

"You haven't got a girl with you, have you, Robert?" Charlie suggested suspiciously.

"No, of course not!" I denied vehemently, wishing that the problem were that simple. College rules were quite specific about two members of the opposite sex sharing the same building, let alone the same room, in the halls of residence.

"But there is a slight problem – I can't really explain over the phone." I didn't think that the lobby was the best place to make illicit plans. "Don't worry, I'll meet you in town and sort it out there. Where are you now?" I added almost as an afterthought.

"By the large roundabout near a park. I hitched from home and got a lift right to the town centre. Are you sure it'll be all right?"

"Not at all ... I mean, yes, it's okay." I hoped I sounded more convincing than I felt, "It's just a question of, er, making up a spare bed. Look, just give me a few minutes, and I'll meet you in town at, say, 9 p.m.. That's about three quarters of an hour. Walk along by the park until you come to the statue of the naked man with the very large ... er, well, you can't miss him!"

In an emergency, which, in my book, this clearly was, I can usually remain cool headed. By the time I set out for town fifteen minutes later, I'd come up with a plan that, technically at least, circumvented the prudish college regulations forbidding even the opportunity for heterosexual relationships within its walls after dark. It was fortunate that my room was on the ground floor, on the blind side of the porter's lodge, and, whilst my window was still too high for direct access by all except a dedicated athlete, the two tree stumps below the window of the neighbouring room provided a convenient – and not infrequently used – unconventional means of entry for late night revellers and the like who wished to avoid 'signing in'. And Dicky Swift, resident of number 104, owed me a favour.

"You come from the country, Rob, you'll stand in for me, won't you?" he'd said. "It's only a debate, a piece of cake for someone like you."

And in all innocence, I'd agreed, though how the hell Dicky had got involved in the first place I didn't enquire. It had been clear from the start of the January meeting of the Debating Society, however, that 'The House' clearly did not believe that 'Fox Hunting is a Necessary Form of Conservation' and were in no mood to be swayed by even the most rational of arguments to the contrary. By the end of the evening, having been hounded by a baying pack of very vocal students, I'd felt more than a little sympathy for the fox at the end of his tether. Dicky very definitely owed me big time for his timely attack of laryngitis.

I saw her as I crossed the road from the Town Hall and Museum which overlooked the north side of Tencastle's Town Park. The green corduroy jeans and thick Aran-style button up cardigan, most necessary in the cool of a March evening, disguised to a casual observer the femininity of their wearer.

"Charlie!"

At my call, she turned towards me. "Hi, there, Rob! What was all the mystery on the phone?" Her bright blue eyes and mischievous smile held no trace of the earlier sharpness of tone. The traces of her childhood freckles were still there, high up on her cheeks. I wondered how one should greet an attractive female cousin. A warm embrace? Shake hands? In the event Charlie took the initiative and kissed me firmly on both cheeks.

"Good to see you again, Charlie!" I meant it. "Sorry about the phone, but you sort of caught me by surprise." I took her rucksack from her.

"I wonder if he's ever been caught by surprise?"

"Who? Oh, you mean Goliath!" I said, glancing up at the generously endowed statue. "I doubt it. He's supposed to get an erection every time a virgin passes by. He's not had one yet."

Charlie laughed, "What kind of wicked city have you brought me to?"

We relaxed into the easy uninhibited banter of friends. "Seems you brought yourself, more likely. Have you eaten?"

"Only a coffee."

"So what's it to be, champagne and caviar, or fish and chips?"

We opted for the student budget menu.

I gazed earnestly into the depths of my expresso. Shrivelled remnants of batter and half-cremated chips lay bloodied with tomato sauce on the polystyrene plates, sad survivors of culinary carnage at Ffion's Fish Fantasia.

"You mean that you expect me to sleep in a dormitory full of randy students." Charlie's amused expression mellowed the indignation in her voice. Or was it anticipation?

"No, it's not like that! As I explained, you'll have your own room. Or, rather, mine."

"And I'm not sleeping with you!" Charlie's eyes suggested that the randy students might have been a better option. "Anyway, it's illegal, isn't it?" she added by way of afterthought.

"You don't have to!" I had other notions of illegality which I didn't want to go into, and, with the tone of an exasperated schoolmaster explaining simple arithmetic to a remedial infant, elaborated, "I've arranged to sleep on the floor in Dicky Swift's room."

"Won't Dicky mind?"

"No, it's all arranged. He owes me a favour."

Dicky had, or course, minded. "Why the hell," Dicky had demanded earlier in the evening, "can't you sleep on your own floor, if you've got someone staying with you?"

"My cousin snores," I'd replied, and I'd pressed him to honour his outstanding obligation over the fox hunting debate.

We crept along the narrow, hummocky strip that ran between the hostel wall and a high privet hedge bordering the road, avoiding the Porter's lodge and the Warden's flat. Fortunately, we'd not had any rain recently, and the ground was dry underfoot. Last autumn's carpet of fallen oak leaves from the trees overhanging from the road formed a soft cushion beneath our feet. Dicky's horizontally-pivoted window was about six feet above ground level, but the two large tree stumps beneath his window, left by the building contractors almost as if to encourage night-time revellers, allowed reasonably easy access to those with a certain degree of agility. Indeed most residents of 'Queer Street', as Dr Cruikshanks' corridor above was known, preferred this means of entry to seeking the rarely granted late pass. Even Babycham's students were occasional users.

"Bloody hell!"

Dicky had noticed his visitor. With his attention hitherto directed to heaving my rather bulky form through his window where Charlie had passed with relative ease a couple of minutes earlier, Dicky scarcely believed his eyes.

"Bloody hell, Rob, he's … she's a girl! You didn't say, you randy bugger!"

"You never asked. Anyway, let me introduce my cousin, Charlotte – Charlie."

"Bloody hell!" Dicky's tone suggested he was viewing his visitor in a different light – and liked what he saw. "Are you sure she's your cousin?" He asked with a touch of envy and suspicion. "Bloody hell!"

"I'm afraid Dicky's not much of a conversationalist, but he does have his good points."

"Really!" Charlie's eyes opened wide in mock surprise, "Pleased to meet you, Dicky."

In more conventional circumstances, being introduced to a most attractive female, Dicky would have probably kissed her, but with me as her chaperon, he made to offer his hand, looked at it, withdrew it limply and settled for another, 'Bloody hell'.

Charlie giggled, and Dicky recovered his composure.

"Oh, I'm sorry! I'm Dicky Swift. You're welcome." Dicky settled for a handshake after all. "It's not every day Rob brings a maid in through my window."

"How does he usually bring them in, then?" asked Charlie wickedly.

I changed the subject quickly. "Thanks for your help, we couldn't have had Charlie walking the streets of Tencastle all night, could we?"

Dicky thought about this, but kept silent.

"Now, I'll take Charlie next door to my room and get her settled in. I'll be back again shortly."

Dicky's eyebrows registered cynicism.

"Thanks, Dicky, you're a poppet!" Charlie planted a kiss full square on Dicky's mouth, and edged quickly out of the door as I gave the all clear.

"Anytime," murmured Dicky.

The tapping at the edge of my consciousness grew more persistent. I yawned and stretched to overcome the stiffness brought on by enforced encampment on an unyielding floor. The tapping was soon joined by an urgent whisper.

"Rob, are you awake? Robert, for Christ's sake!"

Fully awake in an instant, I quickly grasped the situation and sprang up to unlatch Dicky's door. Dicky, as was his habit before nine o'clock on any morning, remained lifeless save for the regular rise and fall of the bedclothes which all but smothered him.

"Charlie! Keep your voice down – and get back to your room!"

More out of concern lest my cousin should be discovered than from annoyance at being roused from my sleep at seven on a Sunday morning, my voice probably came out more irritably than intended. Charlie looked ready to make an equally sharp retort, but catching the flick of my head towards my study bedroom, she deferred and retreated.

"Look, just hang on a tick, will you, while I get some clothes on – and you too!" I added, noting that her light coat barely concealed the flimsiness of her nightdress.

"I hope you don't intend to keep me prisoner in your room for the whole weekend, Rob," Charlie declared when I joined her a few minutes later. Her voice had lost some of the impatience but nevertheless conveyed concern over her situation. "I am going to have to find a loo, and … I could do with a shower."

"Er, right. That, er, could be a problem."

"What do you mean?" she demanded.

"Okay, it's not a problem, just keep calm!" I didn't want to risk her throwing a tantrum. "But we can't have you wandering around these corridors half naked, or dressed, for that matter at this time in the morning!"

"That's all very well, but I've got to … well, you know. Can't you chaperon me?"

I must admit that, faced with the more pressing problem last night, I hadn't given much thought – actually, to be honest, no thought at all – to such mundane matters. Whilst wash basins and shaver points were standard in all the student rooms, showers, bathroom, and WCs were situated, along with rudimentary laundry and kitchen facilities, at the end of each corridor for communal use by all ten students on the wing. At the opposite end was Dr. Ambersham's small self-contained flat, which had its own separate access from outside, so that it was virtually unknown for him to be encountered in the student corridor.

"Surely you don't want me to hold your hand in the shower?" I asked.

"Trust you to think of that! No, I don't, but you'd better do something to protect your reputation and my innocence – or vice versa."

I thought for a moment. I didn't really fancy loitering outside the bog on sentry watch. People could get the wrong idea.

"Okay, then, here's what we'll do. Put on my long coat and hat and I'll check it's all clear. It's most unlikely anybody else will be up yet. When you've finished just open and close the door two or three times, and the light will flash at the end of the corridor. When it's on we know the loo's besetzt – same for the shower."

"Be what?"

"Occupied. It's German," I added helpfully. One of the few words I had remembered from school.

"I don't care what nationality it is, I'm bursting for a pee!"

I must have taken rather longer than I thought in clearing the last traces of my night's sojourn from Dicky's floor, and although I had glanced out from time to time, the toilet light was flickering furiously as I returned to my room with an armful of blankets. Throwing them unceremoniously just inside the door, I hurried along the corridor and knocked on the WC door.

"It's okay, you can come out now. I saw you flashing and there's no one about."

"What the fook are you on about, laddie?" The WC door was flung open and I was confronted by the considerably heavy and considerably hairy frame of Rusty MacDowell, the generally uncommunicative Scot from 101, nearest to the amenities suite. The sound of the toilet flushing barely masked the explosive chortles from the shower room.

Red-faced, I mumbled lamely, "Sorry, Rusty, I was expecting, er, someone else."

The shaggy red raised eyebrow said everything. Rusty lumbered back to his room, with an audible mutter, "Bent boogger!"

A gentle knock from inside the shower reminded me that Charlie had yet to be rescued. She seemed to be recovering from a coughing fit.

"Gee, Rob, you do have a way with words!"

I obliged with another choice selection.

With us back in the safety of my room, I took a few deep breaths to regain my composure. Refreshed, Charlie had a large smirk on her face.

"Well now, Sir Galahad, what's for breakfast?"

Food being a subject dear to my heart, this was something I had already considered. Being Sunday, no one – Rusty MacDowell excepted – was likely to rise early, and no cleaners would come in to service the room. Indeed, breakfast in Hall was served an hour later than usual, from 8.45 to 9.45. Although guests could be signed in for evening meals, this facility was not normally extended to women and never at breakfast. I wasn't troubled about missing official breakfast, which on Sundays consisted of toast and boiled eggs – always rock hard, but hot before nine o'clock, stone cold afterwards.

"How do boiled eggs, beans and cream crackers grab you? And coffee of course."

"Perfect! I'd grab anything at the moment. I'm famished!" Charlie had always been known for her healthy appetite, in spite of which she still retained a remarkably slim figure.

"Right then, hang on and I'll be back in a moment."

The shared kitchen facilities were basic, to say the least; a fridge, toaster and a single ring electric hob with a faulty thermostat. Very few students had ever produced a snack in the ideal state between refrigeration and incineration. Theoretically the kitchen was also the home of an old electric kettle, which was much more likely to be found in one of the study bedrooms since all of us in the corridor were inclined to borrow it for a brew up in our respective rooms. Fortunately for my breakfast plans, it was in its proper place.

I returned bearing the electric kettle, two eggs and half a tin of baked beans.

"Where did you rustle those up from?" asked Charlie, curiously.

"Communal kettle, Dicky's eggs and beans."

"That's very good of him."

"He doesn't know! He won't surface till lunchtime, and I'll pay him back on Monday."

Charlie regarded the prospective repast dubiously, "I'm not sure I fancy raw eggs and cold baked beans"

"No problem, we'll use the kettle."

Charlie looked at me quizzically.

"We put the tin in the kettle of water to heat it up, and then when the beans are cooked we put water in the tin and the eggs in the water. Q.E.D."

Charlie was still unconvinced, "I think I'd prefer the coffee first, if you don't mind."

"As you like," I said cheerfully, and set about the culinary task with more enthusiasm than expertise.

Charlie, no doubt feeling that her stomach would be more likely to accept what was offered if she were to remain unaware of the finer details of its preparation, busied herself for several minutes brushing her sleek, shoulder-length auburn hair and applying a modest degree of make up with skilful ease.

I cleared some desk space between my well-used Principles of Chemical Analysis and the sleeve of a Tom Paxton album that Jake had lent me.

"Would you care to take your seat, Madam?" I bowed low, and with a flourish of my hand-towel doubling as an oven glove, I placed a blue plastic tray stacked with a brightly congealed mass of beans and cream crackers onto yesterday's Sun. A coiled wire pencil rack served as an egg cup.

"I'm sorry I don't have any plates or cutlery – we'll have to eat off the lid of my biscuit box and share the coffee spoon."

"I hope we don't have to keep the eggshells as coffee cups." Charlie tucked in. "Not quite Egon Ronay, but it tastes better than it looks."

"Egon Ronay doesn't have to cook in a kettle!" I retorted. "Which reminds me, better return it before it's missed," I added.

"So what's the plan for the rest of the day?" I asked as we finished our coffee.

"I'm in your hands. I'd like to see the sights of Tencastle."

"That won't take long!"

"And then I'll hitch down to Swansea to see a school friend who moved there last year."

"Does she know you're coming?"

"Of course! Why do you ask?" Charlie had failed to detect the hint of sarcasm in my voice.

"Just wondered. Okay then, we'll get cleared up here and then wander on down into town." I looked at the breakfast debris. "If you wash up, I'll wipe."

"Typical male chauvinist, but I applaud your ingenuity!" Charlie dumped the mugs, biscuit box lid and coffee spoon into the washbasin. "Any washing up liquid?"

"Sorry. Try my shaving foam."

"And use your razor to scrape off the egg?"

Charlie ducked as the towel-cum-ovenglove flew in her direction.

I must have polished the mug several times before Charlie broke in, "Penny for your thoughts, Rob?"

"Sorry. I was thinking of the best way of getting you out of here."

"Not through Dicky's window I hope."

"No, through mine." I caught the disapproving frown and rushed to explain," Look, we'll lower you out of my window. You then go round to the Porter's Lodge, sign in and ask for me."

"Isn't that a bit pointless? I want to leave, not get trapped in here again."

"It's alright, it's after ten and we're allowed female visitors until eight. They trust us not to have sex during daylight hours apparently. If you've signed in, you can officially sign out and leave. That way, if anyone has seen you on site this morning, I've got a sort of alibi."

"An alibi means you were elsewhere."

"Well, I was, sort of. I wasn't in my room!"

Charlie shrugged and obviously saw no profit in arguing with my semantics.

Her egress, though not without its tricky moments, was accomplished without injury to person or pride, and a few minutes later, Charlie, now an official visitor, knocked on my door.

"Hey, Rob, what a place! I wasn't able to see much of it last night. Tell me what's the structure on the top of the tower?"

"Shortly to be our new common room, but it was originally intended to be an observatory."

"Wow! Can we go up there?"

"Shouldn't be a problem. We let the Porter know if we want to work up there." Since Jake and I – no, just Jake really, since he'd done all the planning and talking – had surprisingly got the Warden's agreement to develop the dome as a student recreation facility, all of us on Jake's official working party had been allowed more or less free access.

"Probably best if you go on up to the sixth floor while I get the key. I don't want him getting too inquisitive if you're hanging around."

There was still a lot of work to do, but the dozen of us that Jake had roped in to his 'Dome Project Committee' had already transformed the area from its state just three months earlier. All the debris had been cleared and all the woodwork given fresh paint over the bare primer. We were fortunate that central heating radiators were already in place, if hitherto unused. We'd manhandled a few chairs up there, mainly to lounge around in and admire the view when we took a break from our voluntary labours. The College had agreed to cough up the cash for carpets and basic furnishings and the Union, too, were prepared to chip in.

Charlie was impressed. "This is fantastic! You could hold functions up here and charge people a fortune."

"I don't think I'll mention that idea to my friend Jake just yet. He's got more than enough ideas to keep him going already." Like a coffee bar or even a booze license.

Charlie would have stayed there much longer just soaking in the panorama. I tactfully suggested that we should make our way into town and get some proper food.

"I think I'd better carry your rucksack," I suggested. "It might look a bit odd if you walk out with luggage you didn't have when you arrived half an hour ago."

Charlie signed the visitors' book again, and we walked through the grounds to the main entrance. I noticed the Warden strolling along the lower path, apparently examining the herbaceous borders.

"Just as well you're legit," I said. "There's Dr. Nightingale, the Warden, on the prowl. He's got eyes like a hawk. He's bound to check the book."

Charlie pondered the avian contradiction, and looked at the portly, dark-suited, bespectacled gentleman walking, hands behind his back, on a parallel track.

"He looks quite a sweetie."

"Not the word us students would immediately think of. Basically he's a pompous, old fashioned dinosaur. Took a degree in something obscure, like oceanography, and got washed up here twenty years ago. Keeps budgerigars. Rumour is, he has them fried for breakfast." All the more surprising, really, that he agreed to Jake's project, I thought.

Charlie giggled.

I was feeling quite pleased with myself as I returned to Thomas Hall. After the initial panic of the previous night, which I felt I'd handled quite brilliantly, I'd really enjoyed showing Charlie around Tencastle, which when you looked at it (and I'd never really bothered before, not as a tourist, so to speak), was quite an attractive town. In the park, bordered by the impressive Victorian facades of the town hall, museum and college buildings, the trees were just coming into leaf and the extensive display of daffodils glistened, wax-like, in the spring sunshine. Inexpensive lunch at the Students' Union, followed by window shopping (the shops closed, of course) along the main street and a stroll by the banks of the Tene in the easy company of my cousin had made for a perfect day. Feeling rather protective towards her, I'd persuaded her to take one of the only two Sunday trains to Swansea instead of hitching, and to ring up her friend beforehand to check that she really was expected. All things considered, Charlie's visit had gone ahead very smoothly, and we'd parted in high spirits, determined to keep in regular contact.

Rusty MacDowell, however, was not happy. Wielding a kettle in one hand and a mug of evil-looking liquid in the other, Rusty was sounding off at Dicky, cornered by his door.

"What stoopid fooker would put tomato sauce in the bloody kettle!" he ranted. "Just taste this coffee – it's more like bloody soup!" Rusty, to prove his point, took a large swig, went to swallow, and spat it out onto the floor. "Aw, fooking hell, there's bloody bones in it!"

Dicky regarded the white flakes amongst the reddish brown patch on the floor suspiciously. He caught sight of me holding back by the entrance lobby, and flashed an accusing glance but kept silent. Rusty dived back into his room and I heard the tap running and the sound of gargling, as I sidled past towards my room. I thrust an IOU for two eggs and a tin of beans into Dicky's hands.

My euphoria soon evaporated on Monday morning. In my pigeon hole next to the dining room I noticed a lone small brown envelope with my name typed on it. Intrigued, I opened it at once, rather than leaving it until after breakfast. The message was brief and terse:

Please make an appointment with my secretary to see me at your earliest convenience.

It was signed by Dr. Nightingale.

I suddenly lost my appetite.

"Good morning, what can I do for you?" Deirdre Beinyon looked up from her desk. "Gosh, Robert, you don't look well! Touch of flu is it?" she added with concern.

I didn't feel well – a tight knot in my stomach, as my imagination ran wild with speculation as to what manner of sanctions could actually be imposed on me for having a female in my room overnight. I had little doubt as to the reason for my summons, and I had decided to get it over with there and then rather than spending an anxious day in limbo.

'I'll be okay, thanks, Deidre," I said without conviction. "Seems Dr. Nightingale wants to see me."

"Oh, that's right. Do you want to go in now or after college?"

"May as well be now," I shrugged.

I had never been into to Dr. Nightingale's study before. The Warden sat behind an enormous mahogany desk with his back to a bay window with views over the lawns and drive in front of the original Thomas Hall building. A large cage with two budgerigars hung from a freestanding frame to one side of the window. Three more cages rested on a sideboard, coffee table and some kind of antique pedestal. The leather upholstered sofa looked uncomfortable, even more so than the two straight-backed wooden chairs arranged in front of the desk.

"Please take a seat, Mr. Kiddecott." Dr. Nightingale laid his fountain pen carefully by the blotter pad, and looked at me thoughtfully for what seemed like minutes. He rested his elbows on his desk and supported his double chin on his clasped hands.

"I'll come straight to the point. Did you have an unauthorised guest in your room over the weekend?"

I took a deep breath before replying. "Yes, sir." I tried to look contrite.

"Two nights?"

"No, sir, only Saturday."

"Any meals?"

"No, sir. We had a snack in my room for breakfast and went out for lunch."

"I see." The Warden sat back in his chair and appeared to be giving his replies a good deal of thought.

Here we go, I thought, … castrated, rusticated, cast out in the wilderness.

"…. the College regulations are quite specific on this matter, as you must know." Dr. Nightingale was summing up and about to pass sentence. "However, in view of your honest admission and the fact that you did not attempt to obtain food by deception, I am mindful to overlook your indiscretion on this occasion. But be in no doubt that the consequences of a further breach of regulations will be serious indeed!"

I looked up, scarcely believing my ears. Surely a female companion was not going to be ignored!

"I think, young man," continued Dr. Nightingale, taking a small white envelope from his drawer, "that you should tell your friend Charlie to take more care how he addresses his letters."

He? His letters? My confusion must have been obvious to see as I took the letter, addressed to 'Rob, Thomas Hall, Tencastle, Wales'. Inside, the single sheet of paper torn from a ring-bound notepad, was also economical in its message:

Hi, Rob,
Coming to Tencastle this weekend. OK to stay?
See you.
Charlie.

"We received this letter on Thursday," explained Dr. Nightingale. "And so we were alerted to the possibility of someone having unauthorised accommodation. Our student lists showed at least three dozen possible 'Robs'. As it happens you are the first to be interviewed, so you've saved us a considerable amount of time by admitting your involvement so quickly." Dr. Nightingale allowed himself the ghost of a smile as he continued, "Your friend, Charlie, I think he owes you a drink for the problems he's caused you."

"Thank you, sir!" A great weight had been lifted from my head, "Charlie's my cousin," I gabbled.

And thank God, I thought, that she wasn't christened Mary or Elizabeth!

CHAPTER SIX

The Party

It was one of those parties where I wasn't quite sure for what or for whom the celebration had been organised, or even whether I really should have been there.

Returning from a balmy Devon after the Easter break, it felt as if Tencastle was still clinging to winter, with daytime temperatures struggling in the chill wind to get anywhere near the seasonal average for early May. With a fault in the central heating in F wing, which left me either fried or frozen and a couple of dissertations to complete, the prospects for the weekend were decidedly unappealing. Until Rud came to the rescue.

"Anything planned for tomorrow?" he asked, taking a seat opposite me in the hall dining room.

"Not really," I replied as I picked small bones out of the fish pie.

"Fancy coming to a party?"

"Where to?"

"Watkyn Street, I think. I've got the address scribbled down somewhere."

"Never heard of it."

"I think it's one of those terraces beyond the market."

"And you've got an invite?"

"Yes. Well, sort of. A girl in my seminar group, she's got a friend whose current boyfriend shares a house with a couple of others. She mentioned it to me, 'Bring a bottle and friend,' she said. Interested?"

"Why not? There's bugger all else to do. Are you sure it'll be okay?"

"No problem."

Rud had no idea what time the party was supposed to start, but we thought it best to give it chance to get under way. There would be less likelihood of us not being accepted as bona fide guests. We wandered into the town around eight-thirty, and stopped off at the eight-till-late corner shop for a few cans of Heineken and a bottle of cheap plonk.

We eventually found Watkyn Street, the last of four identical cul-desacs leading off Canal Road beyond the market and almost in Pant Gorau. Of the dozen houses on each side of the street there was no doubt which one was hosting the party, even without the couple of balloons hanging out of the upstairs window. I hoped their neighbours weren't paid-up members of the Noise Abatement Society. The front door was ajar, fortunately, for I doubt if anyone would have heard the bell, even if it had worked. Our senses were simultaneously assaulted by throbbing high decibel heavy rock and a pungent cocktail of tobacco, alcohol and curry, not to mention the heat and sweat from a crush of bodies.

A lanky lad with a beard and glasses emerged from the throng. "Hi, You're Sal's friends?"

"Uh huh," replied Rud.

"Great, help yourself to a drink!" he said, relieving us of the booze.

"Who's Sal?" I asked Rud.

"Dunno."

With the thought of rescuing at least one Heineken apiece we jostled our way through the melée in Lanky's wake, trying to avoid being splashed with alcohol or stubbed by cigarettes. We gained a modicum of elbow room in the kitchen – 'compact and utilitarian' is how an estate agent would have described it, for which read 'small and basic'. Our eyes confirmed what our noses suspected to be the source of the curried atmosphere. Two large saucepans heavily stained with garish yellow and brown pungent goo were piled in the sink, which was infested with plump white maggot-like rice grains. A pedal bin overflowed with stained paper plates and plastic cutlery, several empty wine bottles littered the drainer, and a black bin liner was already half full of empty cans. Even so our modest contribution scarcely made an impression on the booze still available. I grabbed a Newcastle Brown.

"Recognise anyone?' I asked Rud, who'd broken off half the cork in a Mateus Rosé and was trying to extract the rest with a potato peeler.

"Damn it!" Bits of cork bobbed about in the wine just below the neck. "Sorry, what did you say?"

"Do you know anyone here?" I hadn't seen a single familiar face.

"Um, no, not yet."

A cracked ceramic mug with an embossed red dragon was the only vessel Rud had found in which to decant the wine. Even so, cork flotsam drifted onto to his upper lip at each swig.

The kitchen was as good a place as any to view the partygoers, for a succession of bodies extricated themselves from the mass to refuel or use the loo, beyond the kitchen. Propped around the doorway, we contented ourselves with drinking and ogling the girls, all of whom seemed accounted for. After a second Newcastle I'd taken charge of the Mateus bottle when something or someone must have caught Rud's attention.

"Better circulate," he mumbled, and edged his way towards the front lounge.

I started to follow, but saw he had latched on to a tall blonde with goofy teeth and pigtails. Well, two's company, so I thought I'd see what circulation could do for me. I drifted into the rear room, which was quieter but darker. On each side of the fireplace the only seats, a pair of large old fashioned armchairs, were both occupied, but from one a dumpy spiky-haired girl with an immodestly short mini-skirt was being helped to her feet by a weedy long-haired youth of indeterminate gender. Her companion, a tallish girl with straight shoulder length dark hair remained perched on the arm, sipping a glass of wine and looking rather dream-like at nothing in particular. Her low cut dress was supported by the thinnest of shoulder straps.

I took my chance. "Is your friend coming back?"

She shrugged, gave a non-committal wave of her hand and the ghost of a smile. I took it as an invitation to claim the vacated chair and lowered myself into its depths, gratefully, as I'd been on my feet all evening.

Perhaps it had a gammy leg or in protest at the extra burden, the chair tilted suddenly, tipping the girl, with a yelp, from its arm into mine, her glass of wine spilling onto my jeans. My left arm was pinned around her bare shoulders, and her face was just inches from mine, like two new lovers in a movie moments before their first exploratory kiss.

"I'm sorry..." we both started to say, and paused. She began to extricate herself from my involuntary embrace.

"My fault, I'm sorry," I began again. "That wasn't intentional ..."

"I've spilt wine all over you," she interrupted. She seemed genuinely concerned. "Here, let me help," she said, and dabbed at my crotch with a threadbare antimacassar from the back of the chair.

I'd never been aroused quite like that before. "Mmm, that's nice..."

"What? Oh!" The effect of her actions dawned, and she blushed, "I'm sorry ... just did it without thinking ..."

"Best way!" I grinned. "No, don't get up! It's not everyday a pretty girl falls into my arms!"

She was now sitting on the edge of the chair, which was almost big enough for two.

"Can I get you another drink?" I waved the Mateus Rosé bottle to which my free hand had been clinging.

She looked at me – her deep brown eyes in a longish face – and evidently liked what she saw. She slowly put her wine glass down, took the bottle from my hand and carefully placed it next to the glass, and fell back in my arms. Her mouth found mine, her tongue probing between my lips, and she pulled me close to her body until I could feel the softness of her breasts against my chest. I stroked the bare skin down the back of her dress. Coming up briefly for air from time to time, we continued to explore each other's mouths with renewed passion. Until my hand strayed too close up her thigh.

She gently removed my hand, and sat up "I think I'll have that drink now," she murmured.

I too pulled myself upright, for the first time since she'd dropped in on me, so to speak. Though we were still occupying the same seat and her arm was still around me, I had a feeling that the best of the action was over – for the time being.

"Did you come here with your friend?" I said, nodding towards the doorway where the chair's former occupant, was entwined on tip-toe with the long-haired Weed.

"Yes, we're both in Abercrombie Hall."

"First year?"

"Second. We're both doing history."

"You didn't fancy moving out into a pad like this, then?"

"Too much hassle. It's comfortable at 'Crombie."

"Are you a friend of Sal?"

"Who's Sal?"

"It's her party."

"Oh, is it?" she said, unconcerned. She took a sip of wine. "What about you? You don't live here do you?"

"Christ, no! I'd have known about this chair, otherwise, wouldn't I?"

She smiled and kissed me, just a peck, "Perhaps ... perhaps not."

"I'm at Thomas," I volunteered.

"Don't tell me you're there for a second year? I hear the food's pretty gross."

"Well, it wouldn't win any Michelin stars. No, I'm first year."

Such light as emanated from the low wattage bulb in the heavily shaded table lamp on a bookshelf flickered and died. The house was, briefly, eerily quiet as the ghetto blaster also expired.

"Sal, have you got any coins for the meter?" came a disembodied male voice from the hallway.

Someone flicked on a cigarette lighter and placed a Nitelight in a saucer on the mantlepiece.

"Romantic," I whispered, gently pulling her closer to me again.

She didn't resist, and rested her head on my shoulder.

"Just don't try getting into my knickers again," she murmured.

We nestled there in each other's arms, not speaking, for some time. I caressed her hair and shoulders, keeping my actions more or less honourable. Not sure I could say the same for my thoughts, though. By the even gentle rise and fall of her bosom, I guessed that she had drifted off to sleep.

I don't know how long I enjoyed the closeness of her company – I may have nodded off myself – but my contentment was broken by a loud voice calling, "… Williams, taxi for Mary Williams!"

My companion woke with a start, "Oh, God!" she exclaimed. "Is that the time?" She scrambled to her feet and brushed down her dress. "That's for me and Carys!"

I stood and took her hand, "Let me walk you back."

"Thanks for the offer, but I'd better go." The spiky-haired mini-skirted girl – Carys, I assumed – was already beckoning furiously.

"Mary," I ventured. "Can I see you again?"

"I'd like that," she said, kissed me, and made to follow Carys who'd already disappeared from view.

"Tuesday?" I called across the room.

Mary turned and nodded. "… 'Crombie" was all I caught of her parting comment as she waved goodbye.

The taxi call had prompted others to think about leaving, and the party was definitely winding down. I looked round for Rud but however his evening had turned out he was nowhere to be seen. I wished I'd asked to share the taxi as far as Abercrombie. As it was the long, cold and solo walk back to Thomas Hall in the small hours of Sunday morning sobered my mind and cooled my passions. Fortunately, I'd had the foresight to get a late pass so I didn't have the hassle of waking Dicky Swift to use his window.

I didn't see Rud on Sunday. Actually, I didn't see much of Sunday at all, sleeping a full ten hours till past midday. I hadn't bothered to rush up and face lunch in the refectory, and I'd made do with a couple of cream crackers and a Mars bar until teatime. I'd spent the afternoon stretched out on my bed, ostensibly reading about the history of education, with background Bach from some Jacques Loussier tapes that Jake had lent me. In practice I'd spent more time fantasising about my prospects for Tuesday evening.

"What happened to you?" I asked Rud when I eventually caught up with him on the way into College on Monday morning.

"Don't ask!" he replied, in a tone which clearly invited further questions.

"No joy?"

"Yeah, well, I thought I'd got it made, didn't I?"

"And?"

"Well, there was a local girl that I knew vaguely."

"Oh yes?" The goofy one, I supposed.

"And we were hitting it off fine. She invites me back to her place, so we walks all lovey-dovey like a bloody mile or so beyond Pant Gorau to this swanky house in the middle of bugger all. 'Parents away for the weekend', she says, so there we are in this bloody love nest..."

"What went wrong?"

"Her bloody parents! We'd just progressed to the master bedroom, you know, a bit of foreplay, helping each other undress and so on, when we hear the crunch of car tyres on gravel. Well, she leaps to her feet in a panic, grabs her bra and knickers, and yells for me to get out, get out. 'My Da,' she says, 'he'll kill you if he finds you here!' Christ I've never lost an erection so fast in my life! 'Hurry up!' she keeps yelling, and my clothes are half inside out, 'You must go down the back stairs, into the garden. Hurry!'"

"Why did her parents come back?"

"I don't bloody know and I didn't bloody well stop to ask them! She grabs the rest of my gear and hustles me downstairs and practically pushes me out through the back, just as I heard the key turning in the front door. 'Where do I go now?' I yelled in a loud whisper. 'Across the lawn,' she says, 'there's a gate in the rear wall. Now go!' And she slams the door in my face. Anyway, I scrambled on my shoes and coat, and edged around the lawn. It would have been just my luck to find the gate locked, or trigger a security light. I only hoped they didn't own a Doberman."

"But you got away okay?" I commiserated.

"Well, I didn't get shot or mauled, I suppose, but it was blacker than Jake's arsehole beyond the gate and I hadn't a bloody clue where I was! There was a rough track and I had a choice of heading uphill or down."

"Which did you choose?"

"Down, of course! Reckoned it would bring me to the main road along the river. Wrong choice, though."

"Why?"

"Brought me out about another mile beyond the house."

"Well, the other way might have led you halfway up the mountain." The hills around Tencastle were mostly densely wooded and rose to fifteen hundred feet in places.

"Suppose so," Rud conceded, "but it took me two bloody hours or more to walk back. And then I had to wake the bloody porter. Anyway, how did your evening go?"

I told him.

I couldn't wait for Tuesday evening to come. The lectures and seminars on Monday and Tuesday washed over me, their subject matter instantly forgotten. Such notes as I had made didn't seem to make a lot of sense when I came to review them. I'd kept a look out around college, especially in the vicinity of 'Crombie, hoping to catch a glimpse of Mary, but to no avail. I rushed through supper on Tuesday, smartened myself up and made my way back into town as quickly as possible. I'd no idea what time Mary would expect me, but I didn't want her to think I'd stood her up by being late.

As a sop to security, Abercrombie Hall had been fitted with the latest technology where you had to press four buttons in a particular sequence to gain access, or ring the bell for the Porter. Unless, like me, you found someone you knew just about to enter.

"Hi there, Rob," said Dilly. "What brings you here?"

"Chance of seeing you." I flannelled. I still had hopes of getting to know her better, especially if tonight didn't work out.

"Liar!" she laughed.

"I hoped I might see you at the Folk Club again." That at least was genuine.

"Sorry, they've changed the Welsh Folk Dance night, so it clashes."

"That's a shame."

"I'd be pleased to see you at the dance club again." Dilly sounded as if she really meant it.

"Two left feet, neither bilingual, I'm afraid." I said lightly. There was fat chance of prising her away from her present dance partner, I thought.

"Anyhow, Rob, who are you really here to see?" Dilly made to key in her access code.

"I'm supposed to be meeting Mary Williams here. Could I ask you to see if she's around?"

"Which one?"

"I'm sorry?"

"Which Mary Williams? I know two and I think there's at least another one."

Which one? I hadn't really got a good look at her, except her face at very close quarters, and then not standing up.

"Um, well, she's quite tall, and, er, straight dark hair down to her shoulders, … and brown eyes … I think. We only met briefly."

"Not your girlfriend, then?" Dilly teased.

"Hardly." Which was, I suppose, technically correct.

"You don't happen to know her room number I suppose?"

"No, I'm sorry."

"Okay, just wait here for a moment, I'll see what I can do. Is she expecting you?"

"I hope so." I then had a sinking feeling that I hadn't told Mary my name. "Tell her it's Rob, from the party." I hoped that she would make the connection.

Dilly looked at me quizzically then disappeared upstairs while I waited in the lobby.

The Porter, a Perry clone, came over to me.

"Good evening, sir," he said, formally. "How can I help you?"

"It's okay, I'm just waiting for a friend."

A few minutes later, a well-dressed young woman with elegant poise descended the broad curving staircase. She was a little taller than I remembered, and her features seemed more angular in the well-illuminated entrance hall, but she was undoubtedly a stunner. She smiled, and, wasting no time on formalities, led me into the Common Room. A couple of girls were curled up in two ancient armchairs, reading, three others were chatting away over a cup of coffee at an old bench table, and a small group were gathered around the television at the far end.

I introduced myself, just in case she'd forgotten my name, even assuming I had told her.

"You're the party man, right? I'm glad you could come."

We sat down side by side in a couple of more modern armless chairs in front of a coffee table strewn with a newspaper, a college prospectus, and a glossy glamour magazine.

She smiled at me, "Now I'd like to get involved as fully as possible…" Wow!

"…and I'm keen to start right away."

"I'm not sure that's …" I stammered. Not with a dozen onlookers.

"Oh, of course, you'll want to know a bit more about me, my credentials, and so on."

"Er, yes, well." I wasn't used to love in the fast lane. "Look, could we go somewhere, er, rather more private?"

She considered my request in a clinical sort of way, "Yes, of course. I expect you've got things you want to show me."

All in good time. "Where do you suggest?" I should have taken the initiative I suppose.

"Well, we could go to my room but it would give us barely an hour, and I expect you'll need longer than that, won't you."

True, I didn't intend to set a time limit.

"How about the Rivers Hotel across the road? It's fairly quiet there," she suggested.

I doubted if they rented rooms by the hour – and anyway I was damn sure I wouldn't be able to afford it. "Fine, but let me buy you a coffee."

"That would be nice – but decaffeinated of course. Much better, I'm sure you agree."

Frankly, I couldn't stand the stuff, but I wasn't going to upset her by saying so.

The Rivers was one of those old-fashioned hotels where alterations and extensions over many generations gave it a rather rambling appearance, further enhanced by the rampant ivy which clung to most of the front aspect. It boasted three stars from the AA, and advertised weekend fishing and walking breaks. During the week it was rarely full but boasted a comfortable lounge bar and restaurant open to non-residents. Only at the start and end of each term and during graduation week did the hostelry normally attract students when those with well-heeled and far-flung parents booked in for a night or two. Apparently it was also popular for wedding receptions, with a decent sized function room.

Apart from one old codger half asleep with his gin and tonic in front of an unseasonable blazing log fire, the bar was deserted.

I ordered two coffees and joined Mary in the leather covered bucket chairs in a window alcove.

"You know, Rob. May I call you Rob?"

I nodded.

"I'm surprised you don't have a case or something with you."

Why, for Christ's sake? "It's not necessary," I said, for want of any better response.

"You don't come prepared with literature or handouts?"

What on earth did she expect? Porno magazines and prophylactics? I felt I was getting in beyond my depth. "Not always appropriate for a first meeting," I said guardedly. I wondered how long we could fence around before she stripped naked and fell on me. She'd been pretty forthright so far. More so than Saturday night even.

"Although," I said conversationally. "This isn't actually our first meeting, is it?"

"What do you mean?" she said, puzzled.

"The other night."

"I've never met you before in my life!"

My turn to be puzzled – and bolder. "But surely you remember? You look a little different – even prettier than I recall."

"I don't know what you're talking about! You've got a bloody nerve, trying to get me on my own, and chatting me up. I thought you said you were from the party?"

There was no smile. In fact she looked considerably angry. I couldn't understand it – hot to ice cold in under a minute.

"I am – I was at the party in Watkyn Street last Saturday, and so were you. We talked, remember?"

Her face turned pale, "You're not from the Conservative Party?"

"No, should I be?" Heaven forbid.

"Oh my God!" she whispered, holding her hand over her face, which was blushing a deep shade of red. "I thought ... Oh my God! ... You thought ... Oh Christ!" Mary made to gather up her handbag, and began to stand just as the waiter brought our coffees.

She stood, taking several deep breaths, "I thought you were a representative from the Conservative Party! I'm sorry!" She looked as if she were going to burst into tears.

"At least stay and have the coffee. You look as if you need it." Me too, for that matter.

She stood, undecided, for a few moments. "Thanks, perhaps I will." She sat down again, and took a slow drink. "This is so silly. I'd written to the Conservative Party offering my help. Even though Heath scraped in at the general election, it seemed they could do with some help around here – and I thought ... well, you know." A thought occurred to her, "How did you know my name?"

"I was at a party and met a girl called Mary Williams. She said she lived at 'Crombie, and, well, we sort of made a provisional date."

Mary was beginning to grin. "But it wasn't me ... I wasn't there!"

"So it seems, but, well, it was quite dark at the party and I'd had a few drinks, and, we ... er ... weren't standing up, and ... I suppose I wasn't able to describe her very well, so when I called at 'Crombie..."

"You got me! And you thought ... And I thought ..." Mary collapsed in laughter, and I joined in.

"Christ, whatever did I say? Whatever must you have thought?"

"Well, I was taken back by your forwardness, I confess."

"And you're not a Conservative at all?"

"'Fraid not. I'm apolitical and agnostic," I didn't add amoral. I've got some values, but having got so far, I added, "Now we've cleared the air, so to speak, can I see you again, Mary? If you'd like to, that is."

She smiled and put her hand on mine on the table, "That's really sweet of you to ask, but I'm engaged already."

I noticed the diamond ring. Shame.

"Is your fiancé at Tencastle?"

"Good Lord, no, he's a banker in the City. A childhood sweetheart from back home."

No chance for a peasant farmer's son, then. Actually, that's unfair on my dad, he's well respected in our community. He almost made Justice of the Peace once, but definitely not a Tory.

"But what about the Mary Williams you really came to see?"

"Is she as attractive as you?"

"That's not for me to say, is it?"

"But do you know which of the other Mary Williams I want?"

"Well, if you say she's about my height, with dark hair, I guess she's the Chester girl, though I think her hair is really more auburn. I don't really know the other one, but she's short and blonde. Did you notice her accent?"

"Can't say as I did. It was dark."

"Look, Rob, why don't you come back over to 'Crombie and I'll see if I can find her."

I thought about it. I'd quite enjoyed the company of Mary-number-one, despite the misunderstanding, and I wasn't sure I wanted to start a chat-up of number-two with half the evening gone. However, perhaps she might be pining away, upset that I'd stood her up. Did I say a time? Oh, what the hell, number-one was a lost cause any rate.

"Would you?" I paid for the coffee. It was much more reasonable than I'd expected. We wandered back over to Abercrombie Hall, where Mary keyed in the access code.

"You'd better wait here by the door," she said. "All male visitors are expected to be off the premises by now, but Percy won't mind if he can keep an eye on you."

"Percy?"

"The Porter. Wait here a moment."

"Has he got a bro…" But she had already gone over to Percy in his little office just inside the second glass door from the lobby.

She seemed to be having quite a conversation with him. Mostly about me, I would guess, as they both turned their heads towards me on more than one occasion. I hoped she wasn't being too graphic in describing the circumstances of our meeting.

After a few minutes – though it seemed much longer – she returned, looking slightly puzzled.

"Are you sure your real name's Rob?"

"Of course!" I couldn't think what would have prompted that question. "Why?"

"Not Matt?"

"No, look, what's this all about?"

"You're not Matthew Rose?"

"No! I'm Robert Kiddecott. Always have been!"

"So this can't be for you then?" Mary showed me a lilac envelope. In petite looping script it was addressed to: *Mat. Rose (party)*.

The penny dropped. "That is for me, I think."

She raised an eyebrow.

"I don't think I told her my name, but I was carrying a bottle of Mateus Rosé. I offered her some. And as you know, I am the man from the party."

Mary smiled wryly, "You'd better have it then."

I took the letter, and kissed her hand.

"Goodnight, Rob. I hope you find your true love!"

With that, Mary slipped back into the foyer of Abercrombie Hall, and I took my leave. Beneath the street lamp outside, I carefully opened the envelope and removed a delicately perfumed notelet decorated with lilacs.

"Dear???? – I'm sorry I don't even know your name, but if you receive this you will have taken the trouble to find me. Because I had to leave so quickly I wasn't sure that you really wanted to see me again or even when. But I do remember the wine!

I couldn't bear the thought of you perhaps calling round in vain, thinking I was avoiding you, or that I didn't want to see you again, or that I thought of you as nothing more than a casual party encounter. In normal circumstances I would have liked to meet you again, but that may not be possible. My father was rushed into hospital on Sunday evening, and my mother is confined to a wheelchair. There is no one else to look after them, so I must go back home to Chester. I do not know how long I shall be away, or even if I shall be able to return to Tencastle.

I hope you will understand.

X X X Mary

PS Any letters to me at Abercrombie, room 156, will reach me eventually."

I resolved to write to her the moment I got back to Thomas Hall. What I was going to say I hadn't a clue.

CHAPTER SEVEN

Power Play

With the end of year examinations only a few weeks away, my best intentions were to spend at least two evenings a week on solid revision, and to forego earthly pleasures for a while. Not that I'd had any recently. As yet I'd received no reply to the difficult letter I'd eventually written to Mary offering my condolences and the vague hope of seeing her again. For any realistic chance I had of developing a relationship with her, however, Chester might just as well have been in the Antipodes.

I felt quite pleased with myself that on the first occasion of concentrated study I managed an almost uninterrupted four hour stint until midnight then crawled into bed, ready for a decent kip. By the small hours, the last mug of coffee had percolated to my bladder, and when I clambered back into bed after a trip down the corridor, I was in that state of heightened awareness between sleep and full wakefulness when even the ticking of a clock sounded like Big Ben and prevented easy drift into slumber. My wristwatch wasn't guilty, but I was aware of a low chuntering, like a monk reciting his catechisms sotto voce. The words were indistinct but persistent and seemed to be coming through the wall from Sparkle's room rather than from Dicky, my other immediate neighbour in F104.

I thumped on the wall to wake him, sure that I'd cure him of talking in his sleep, or, if he'd perhaps left a radio on, he'd realise and turn the bloody thing off. The murmurings stopped abruptly. The silence lasted for all of thirty seconds, then the low voice began again.

"For Christ's sake, Sparkle, turn the ruddy volume down!" I punctuated my plea with another hard rapping of the wall.

"Sorry!" came the weak reply.

Sparkle was all apologetic next morning when we met walking over for breakfast.

"What on earth were you doing? "I asked.

"Just revising."

"What, at three o'clock in the ruddy morning?

"Yes, I was going through some study notes. I find I remember things better if I read them out loud."

"Why can't you do that during the evening, like any normal person?"

"I find it difficult to concentrate then, with interruptions. You should try it sometime, it does work."

"I'll remember that when I practice my arias for the operatic society." Sparkle looked worried. "You're not serious?"

"No, I'm not," I said. "What were you working on, anyway?"

"The Merchant of Venice."

"Well if you are planning an encore tonight, the quality of my mercy might become sorely strained."

"Sorry, Rob, I promise I'll talk much more quietly on the other side of the room."

I doubted whether Tom, his other neighbour, would be more appreciative of a night-time soliloquy, even though English was his specialist subject. "Perhaps you should consider studying mime," I suggested.

I thought about Sparkle's revision technique during the day, and could see some merit in the idea, minus the verbal commentary. Just after supper, therefore, I turned in, having set my alarm for midnight.

I nodded off surprisingly quickly, I think. Until the sound like a moggy in distress shattered my dreams. I'd forgotten that Huw was in the habit of practising a couple of tunes on his bagpipes before his regular Welsh folk dance practice night. I couldn't really complain, and he rarely continued for more than ten minutes anyway.

I got my head down again. This time I doubt if I got even thirty winks before some prat knocked on my door.

"Who's there?"

"It's me, Jake!"

Anyone else I'd have told to bugger off. "Wait a minute."

"Hey, Rob, guess what I've found!" Jake waved a piece of notepaper at me, as he waltzed into my study.

"Map of buried treasure?"

"Don't be facetious!"

"Well, how am I supposed to know?" I said testily, as I sat down on the edge of my bed.

Jake noticed that I was in my pyjamas. "What's up, Rob, are you ill?"

"I was having an early night."

"What, at eight thirty? Must have been a bloody good night yesterday. Who was she?"

"Piss off. I was in all evening. Working, if you must know. Anyhow, what's so flaming important?"

"It can wait till morning if you'd prefer."

"Now you're here may as well get it of your chest." I flopped back on the bed.

"You won't believe this."

"I presume you are going to enlighten me?" A guessing game wasn't what I needed.

"We've been invited to perform."

I sat up. "You're joking! Where?"

"Not the London Palladium, I'm afraid, just the local old folks' home."

"Oh, right. Why do they want us?"

"Well, they haven't specifically asked for us. There's a note from the Eisteddfod Secretary wondering if we'd be interested. Seems someone contacted the Union, and Dai remembered our moment of fame."

"But we only did one song!"

"Yes, you have a point." Jake rubbed his chin in thought.

"I suppose Huw along my corridor might play a few tunes on his Welsh pipes," I said.

"Wonderful! And we could pad it out with some singalong stuff, you know, get the old fossils joining in."

I raised an eyebrow.

"Oh come on, Rob, they'll enjoy it. We might even get a bob or two out of it."

"I'd be happy to do it for free." I realised as soon as I opened my mouth I'd implicitly accepted the idea. "When is it?"

"Ten days time, so plenty of time to practice. I'll give them a ring."

It was a couple of days before I bumped into Jake again.

"All sorted!"

"What is?" I asked.

"Moses Minstrels ride again! Have we got Huw on board?"

To be honest, I'd rather put the old folks do to the back of my mind but I didn't admit that to Jake. "Mentioned it to him in passing."

"And?"

"He's thinking about it."

"Good. Get him to commit if you can." Jake paused for a moment. "It was quite strange, really, when I told them that we'd do it for free. That was what you wanted, wasn't it?"

"Well, yes, given our limited experience, but I wouldn't have refused payment if offered. What was strange?"

"The women said that the other gentleman had asked for a fiver."

"What other gentleman?"

"That's what I was wondering. Anyhow, she's happy for us to do it."

We didn't have to wait too long to find the mystery man. Rather, he found us next day in the college coffee bar, and his attitude was far from gentlemanly.

"What the hell do you think you're up to?" Mike Pattison was clearly angry. Not many people would have the gall to get in Jake's face in that manner, particularly if they were nearly a head shorter.

"What do you mean? And you can stop poking me in the chest!"

Mike stood back, but ranted on, "Poaching that gig. Deliberately undercutting."

"Do you mean the old folks' home? I was not aware that anyone else was interested until the woman told me someone else had asked a fiver for it."

"That invite came to the Folk Club!" Heads were turning towards the source of the raised voice. "You've no bloody right to butt in…"

"Just hold it there!" Jake too took umbrage. "For your information, Mike, I've every bloody right. My invite came from Dai Howells, the Eisteddfod Secretary."

"But I represent the official Union Folk Club! I insist you withdraw."

"I don't care if you represent the flaming Archbishop of Canterbury. We've agreed to do it."

I'd rarely seen Jake really worked up. I added my twopenn'orth. "Have you already got a group with a programme worked out?"

Mike turned to me, and snapped, "No, not yet."

"We have," said Jake, with sweet vitriol. "So we'll save you the trouble, won't we?"

"You can't…" Mike continued to protest.

"Sorry, chum, we can and we are!"

"You'll hear more of this!"

"I'm all ears!" Jake called after him as he flounced away.

Rud, who'd caught the tail end of the exchange, came over to us. "What's rattled his cage?"

"He seems to think the Folk Club's got exclusive performance rights," said Jake. "I didn't know he was into folk anyway, I don't remember ever seeing him at the Club."

"Doesn't surprise me. Mike's into committees in a big way," said Rud. "He doesn't really give a toss what it represents, as long as he can have his finger in the pie."

"Bit of a control freak, is he?" I asked.

"Pain in the ass, more like," Rud replied.

Putting the incident behind us, we spent every evening over the following days working on a coherent programme of music and song, since Jake had been a little economical with the truth with regard to our state of readiness.

With no elderly relatives to speak of, and several decades away from likely personal requirements, it was the first time I'd been in any care home for the elderly. Set in an old Victorian mansion on the outskirts of Tencastle, its rather foreboding exterior belied the bright and homely atmosphere inside, albeit with a faint antiseptic odour. The plan, originally, was for us to perform in the garden, but even in late May the evening breeze was distinctly chilly, and, mindful of the welfare of their charges, the matron decided to relocate the event to the communal lounge. One of the residents looked barely in touch with the world, vacant eyes staring at the ceiling from her wheelchair, and another appeared asleep, his head lolling against the winged chair back. Most, however, seemed genuinely pleased to see us, and gave a polite muted clap when we were introduced.

Jake, as usual, was on good form in his entertainer mode. We kept largely to songs like *Molly Malone* and our award-winning *Oh Susanna*, with which we expected our audience to be familiar. After our third piece, we handed over to Huw, to take us up to the tea break.

One wizened old fellow, who hitherto had sat head down and hands folded over his stomach, sat up sharply at the first grunts and wheezes from Huw's bagpipes. As he launched into a medley of tunes, which I assumed were traditional Welsh, the old boy's eyes lit up like candles, and, with surprising animation, he began gesticulating at the instrument and attempting to speak to his neighbour, an obese woman cocooned in a huge shawl.

"Huw's turned someone on," Jake commented to me.

One of the care assistants went over to calm the chap down, and stayed with him all through Huw's performance. At the break she came over to us.

"I hope you don't mind me asking, but I wonder whether you would be willing to let Mr Inman play on your pipes."

Huw was clearly apprehensive. "They are very expensive ... I'm not sure ..."

"I can assure you that they will be in safe hands."

Huw looked towards Mr Inman who nodded his head, his eyes fixed on the bagpipes. "Okay ... If you're sure," he said, uncertainly.

"Thank you so much." She wheeled the gent over and helped him adjust the air bag comfortably under his arm.

He inflated the bag and began to play, breathily at first, but then as smoothly and melodically as I have ever heard. Huw, in my opinion, was good, but this veteran made him sound like a novice by comparison, melodies flowing sweetly and effortlessly such that we were without exception spellbound, the atmosphere electric.

He continued, seemingly without pausing for breath, for a full ten minutes, and the applause at the end was worthy of a concert hall.

Huw went over to talk to him, and shook his hand.

"He can hear you, but he can't speak, I'm afraid. His vocal chords are damaged," said the assistant. "But you've really made his day."

"Where did he learn to play like that?"

"In his younger days, before the war, he was the champion piper at every eisteddfod in Wales. He's been with us many years now, ever since he lost his home in a fire. Lost his pipes and all his other belongings, too, I believe."

"That's so sad," said Huw. "Look, would it be okay for me to come in again from time to time to see him? I'd love to hear him play again. I'm sure he'll know a lot more tunes than I do."

"I'm sure he'd be delighted. Just ring up and check with Matron before you come."

We gave them a bit more singalong stuff after a cuppa, but it all seemed very tame by comparison.

"I wouldn't have missed that for anything!" Huw enthused, later, as we sat enjoying a beer in the Castle, courtesy of the fiver that the Matron had insisted on pressing into our hands, despite our token protestations.

"Me neither," said Jake. "Funny how things turn out. I wasn't really expecting the evening to be a great bundle of fun, more like a noble duty."

I reminded the pair of them that we hadn't booked a late pass at Thomas Hall, and that at the rate we were going, there wouldn't be time to sink another round.

"Good thinking," said Jake, and ordered three more pints.

I checked my pigeon hole in the array of personal mail-boxes next to the Hall refectory on the off chance that somebody loved me. My parents weren't keen letter writers, and even Charlie had given up after a couple of exchanges, correctly addressed. Nothing from Mary either.

The contents of the little folded note rapidly deflated the sense of well-being I'd woken up with. I looked in the refectory to see if Jake was taking an early breakfast, then, with no apparent sign, checked his pigeon hole where I was not surprised to find a similar missive.

"Hang on, hang on, no need to wake the flaming dead! I'm coming!" Jake bleary eyed and unshaven was not a pleasant sight. "What do you want at this godforsaken hour?"

I felt no guilt about disturbing his slumbers, merely returning the favour. "Have you seen this?" I waved the note.

"Of course I ruddy haven't!"

"Can I come in?" I went in anyway before he had chance to refuse. "Read it!"

His face, I'm sure, would have darkened if that had been possible. "The bloody cheek!" He screwed up the paper and threw it towards the waste bin, missing widely. He plumped down on the bed from which he'd risen only a short time before. He thought for a minute.

"Rob, do you fancy a trip to the Folk Club this evening?"

"You think we should?"

"I'm damned if I'm going to have some jumped-up little prat tell me what I can and can't do!"

"But it says we're banned."

"Like hell we are!" He saw I had doubts. "I'd appreciate your support in this, Rob."

"You've got it."

I was still an occasional supporter of the club, when I hadn't got anything else to do, or Jake dragged me along on a guest night for a 'must-see' artist. He was by far a more regular, and confident performer anyway. My interest in the club had waned somewhat when Dilly no longer put in an appearance, due to her dance practice night now coinciding. After my first abortive visit to the dance club I'd felt no inclination to play wallflower again.

The upstairs refectory was already over half full when the girl on the door took our money, with no problem. Mike, who had been chatting to a couple of singers with guitars, turned and spotted us before we'd got through the door. He rushed over, hand out, barring our way.

"You can't come in here, you're banned."

"Really?" said Jake, innocently. "Why?"

"We don't have to spell it out." Mike turned to the girl, "Give them their money back."

The poor thing was confused. The queue in the corridor was growing.

Jake refused to take the coins. "We? Who's we?"

"The Folk Club Committee!" Mike said sharply. From the assembled audience a few heads turned at his raised voice. "Now you can get out!" he yelled.

"If you can't show me proper reason or authority, then we've no intention of observing your so-called ban." With that, Jake strode past him, with me close behind.

Mike stood there fuming, and clenching his fist, but, short of physical restraint which even he must have recognised as unwise, there was nothing he could do. I heard a few jeers from the queue as Mike pushed angrily past them.

"We'll stay at the back," Jake whispered to me. "There will be more action yet, I'm sure."

"What can he do?"

"I've a pretty good idea. He'll not want to lose face so readily." Jake didn't elaborate.

Sure enough, the second club singer had just finished her opening song when I caught sight of Mike again, pointing at us for the benefit of the Union President by his side. I nudged Jake. The President caught our eye, and with a barely perceptible flick of his head, signalled us to join him.

Mike grinned smugly. "These are the trouble makers!" he sneered.

The President looked at him quizzically and addressed us. "Let's talk about this outside."

We moved to the half-empty coffee bar.

"Mr Pattison tells me you have been banned from the Folk Club, but you forced your way in."

"They did!"

"Please be quiet. I'd like to hear their side." He looked at Jake to respond.

"He says we have been banned but refuses to give a reason ..."

"It was a committee decision!" Mike interjected.

"I think it has more to do with his nose being put out of joint over the old folks' entertainment," Jake continued.

"I heard that was very successful. So what's the issue between you?"

"He was undermining my authority!" Mike complained.

"To my mind, you've got no authority whatsoever!" Jake recounted fully what had gone before, despite more attempted interruptions.

"That doesn't excuse the disruption when I tried to prevent them entering the clubroom!"

"I think you'll find, Mr President, that thirty odd witnesses in the room will confirm that any disruption came entirely from Mike Pattison."

"That's a lie!"

"Mr Pattison, that is quite enough, thank you," the President said firmly. "It seems to me that it's a storm in a teacup, of your own making. I strongly suggest that you stop playing petty politics and avoid using the smokescreen of a Union society to pursue any personal grievances. Not that I think you've got any except damage to an obviously inflated ego." He turned to Jake and me. "I can see no valid reason why you should be banned from the club, so go ahead, and enjoy the evening."

We needed no second bidding and stood to leave.

"Oh, Mr Moses, just a moment!" The President called us back. "I believe you're the leading light in the dome project. A marvellous initiative if I may say so. I'm looking forward to attending the official opening."

Mike Pattison sat looking black as thunder. He was nominally one of the volunteer working party, though no-one could recall him actually doing any work. He was pretty good, though, at telling anyone who was unable to escape his rantings what was wrong with the project, and how he would have done things differently, seeing as how he'd been just about to present a similar idea to the Warden when Jake upstaged him.

We made a point of going to the Folk Club for the remaining three weeks of term. Ever since he'd stormed off, cursing, after his presidential bollocking, Mike had not been seen around the Union, but had, we heard, tendered his resignation as club secretary. Talking to a few of our acquaintances, he'd dominated the proceedings, twisting the easy-going chairman and other timid committee members to follow his own agenda, in effect running it as his own personal fiefdom with little regard for the niceties of the club constitution. Bloody good riddance, I thought.

Unsurprisingly, Mike didn't bother to turn up at the end of term party for which Dr Nightingale had allowed us to open up the Dome. It was still on the conservative side of spartan, with décor limited to a few scrounged armchairs and well-worn rugs, but, no matter, we shared a considerable degree of pride in seeing the fruits of our hard labour. All that was lacking was female company, which had been strictly vetoed by the Warden, obviously concerned about the prospects of a drunken orgy. With no opportunity for sexual dalliance, alcoholic stupor seemed to be the main aim for most of the evening's guests, rather like a stag night with Jake, as the Dome project's initiator, receiving more attention and congratulations than if he'd actually been the groom.

Distinctly merry, but not rolling drunk, I stayed behind to help clear away some of the bottles and cans, then joined Jake and Dan in the now properly functioning lift down to the lobby.

"Seems a shame we'll miss out on this next year," Jake commented.

"What do you mean?" I asked.

"Well, I presume you won't be staying in Thomas Hall next year."

"Um …" I hadn't seriously given the matter any thought. "What will you do?"

"Get a place in town, I suppose. I don't want to cough up the extra twenty percent they screw out of second-year students who stay in Hall."

"Christ, I didn't know that!"

"It's in the small print somewhere in the fresher's brochure," Jake said. "Tell you what, why don't you and Dan join me?"

"You mean that?" said Dan. "I'd been wondering what to do about digs."

"I'm game," I said. "But we've only got a couple of days left before we're off home."

"No problem. I'll sort something out. Just leave me your home phone number and I'll get in touch."

I must have shown some doubt in my expression.

"Trust me," said Jake.

CHAPTER EIGHT

Jessica

She was older than me by a couple of years and she wasn't beautiful but almost from the start of my second year at Tencastle we spent a lot of time in each other's company.

It was Jake, of course, who was responsible.

At the end of June, when we'd all gone our separate ways, Jake had undertaken to sort out digs for us – that's to say, myself, Jake and Dan Chater. I'd heard nothing from him since, however, and with just a month of the summer vacation remaining, I was resigned to the prospect of another year in Thomas Hall.

My mother handed me the phone. "For you," she said.

"Rob, Jake here! I've got one!"

"One what?"

"Pad! Home! Our own digs!" There was no disguising his enthusiasm.

"Hey, that's really great!" I was genuinely excited as my fall-back option certainly didn't inspire me. But, returning to the practicalities, "Where is it?"

"You'll really like it."

"I'm sure I will." I had a feeling that Jake was holding something back. "Whereabouts in Tencastle is it?"

"It's very reasonable too, the rent shared between four of us is much less than any of us would have to pay in Hall."

That was good, but I knew Jake hadn't told me the downside.

"Where is it then, Pant Gorau?" That was the seedy, distinctly unfashionable area of Tencastle, behind the decrepit warehouses on the old canal.

"No, Penybont."

I couldn't bring it to mind.

"You still there, Rob?"

"Where the hell is Penybont?"

"Only a couple of miles out of town."

"Only a …!"

"And there is a bus."

"There had better be!" My brain didn't register the singular. But another thought struck me, "You said four of us would share. Who's the fourth?"

A slight pause, "Benji."

"The artist? Christ, you must be joking!"

"He's okay. Really. Dan's happy with it. See you in a few weeks. Bye!"

"But …" No use, I was talking to a dead phone.

"I knew you'd like it."

It was, indeed, an attractive cottage in an idyllic setting – assuming one's idyll was an old stone-built detached dwelling perched above a babbling brook in the middle of almost bugger all. The rest of the hamlet of Penybont consisted of a terrace of four or five small houses and a phone box on the other side of the stone bridge. A wooden nameplate which hung lopsidedly on chains from the porch identified our cottage as Ty Melin.

"How on earth did you find this place, Jake?" I asked.

"It's a long story." It would be with Jake. "But basically it belongs to a friend of a cousin once removed."

"In the family, then?"

"It was his holiday cottage, and he's off to Australia for two years. We're sort of, well, looking after it."

The cottage really was quite a chocolate box gem, I'll give credit to Jake, whose distant relative evidently had more faith in the stewardship of undergraduate tenants than was perhaps prudent. Though the well-equipped kitchen included a newish electric cooker, it also retained a Rayburn stove, almost certainly predating the modernisation. The small dining room overlooked the rather unkempt generous garden which sloped down to the stream, while the cosy lounge featured a large open fireplace with an enclosed wood-burning stove.

Upstairs, Benji had already installed himself in one of the two single rooms. "Perfect, man, just perfect!" he muttered, as he knelt on the floor, his fingers smearing strands of multi-coloured goo from various half-empty toothpaste tubes onto a large canvas. He glanced up, eyes aflame from his round, hirsute face under his distinctive shock of jet black hair.

"Got to capture the atmosphere! First impressions, man, know what I mean?"

I didn't but obviously his impressions were perceptibly different to mine.

Jake gave me a guided tour of the separate toilet facilities downstairs and the first floor bathroom.

"Benji's already staked his claim," I said to Jake, "so how do you envisage allocating the rest of the accommodation? I've no aversion to sharing a room, as long as it's not with pots of paint."

"Well, Dan's not here yet, so how about we give him the other single room?"

I had no problem with that suggestion, since it was, if anything smaller than my old room at Thomas Hall. And Dan was very easy-going.

"And I share with you?"

"Uh huh. Unless of course you want to covert the lounge into a fourth bedroom," Jake added tentatively.

Jake obviously had his eye on the master bedroom, with its en-suite facilities, and I could cope with sharing a room, even if it meant sacrificing personal privacy for superior accommodation. Fortunately, its previous occupants had preferred adjacent twin beds to a traditional double.

Jake and I spent the next couple of hours settling in and rearranging the furniture. Sharing a room with Jake was one thing, but I drew the line at waking up with his fizzog a foot away from mine. We set up the beds on opposite walls. After two hours, when we'd added our personal touch to our room, its hitherto immaculate appearance had taken on the image of the aftermath of a WI jumble sale. Benji, meanwhile, was still happily smearing paint.

Leaving the bedroom somewhere between chaos and a semblance of order, we began an inventory of the kitchen. Benji joined us, searching hopefully for a picture hook.

"When's Dan arriving?" I enquired. We'd taken the luxury of a taxi after meeting up, as per Jake's instructions, at the Station Cafe.

"Oh, he said he'd get the bus," replied Jake.

"Talking of buses," I began thoughtfully. "How often do they run?"

"There's one at 8.30 in the morning, back at midday, another at 2 o'clock, back at six. Except Sundays."

"And it's how far to town?"

"Two miles."

I raised an eyebrow.

"Well, probably nearer three-ish," he conceded.

"Are you intending that we forego all our earthly pleasures?"

"What do you mean?"

"Wine, women, etcetera. The last bus from town is six o'clock, and I suppose there's no pub within three miles. No anything, for that matter!"

Silence. Jake and Benji looked at each other.

"I hadn't thought of that," Jake eventually conceded.

That's the problem with these arty types – no consideration for practicalities. And my stomach reminded me of another practical matter.

"By the way have you bought any food?"

Another, longer silence, broken by a knock on the door. Dan arrived.

"Hi, fellas. Wow! What a place!" he enthused. "No neighbours – just great for parties."

"Have you brought any food?" we all cried in chorus.

Dan's enthusiasm bubble quickly burst. Our first evening feast together consisted of a small tin of sardines and three and a half stale cream crackers, presumably left by the previous occupants, washed down with a glass of vintage well water.

Four subdued and very hungry students waited by the bridge for the early morning bus into town. The previous evening we'd had a long and sober discussion – with no choice over the latter – about the pros and cons of country life. The cottage was without doubt exceptional accommodation for mere students, but the biggest 'con' we all agreed was commuting. We needed wheels. Actually Jake had found two, attached to a rusty bicycle frame in the garden shed, and he reckoned he could get it in working order with a few purchases from town. Dan thought he could 'borrow' his grandmother's moped, since her failing eyesight would, he declared, require someone to walk in front of it with a white stick. Benji was not the least bit concerned about transport; even in the cold light of morning he seemed to be transported to another plane of existence, probably still high on solvent from his acrylic paints. Pedal power, even with motorised assistance, had never appealed to me and shanks's pony was even less attractive.

In town, Jake, Dan and Benji left me to my thoughts and the remains of a large fry-up at the Station Cafe. The solution faced me as I sat, elbows on table and head in hands, staring out of the window at the morning bustle which passed for the rush hour in Tencastle.

Owain's Auto Emporium, on Station Road, was the only second-hand car dealer in Tencastle with a half-decent reputation for fair trading and the proprietor was rumoured to have a soft spot for students, especially if female. My summer job as a mushroom picker, together with a small windfall from a recently deceased aunt, had given me a limited amount of capital to save or squander as I saw fit. I had no illusions about the type of vehicle my resources would stretch to, and, looking at the price tags, for all the Amazing Special Offers, my choice in reality would have delighted Hobson; one Ford Popular, 1950's vintage, in black and pink livery.

It looked reasonably clean.

"Ideal first car, young sir!" This from Owain, presumably, who waddled towards me from his matchbox-size office. Well, he would say that, wouldn't he, I thought.

"It's been well looked after. Two lady owners, both known to me, and regularly serviced."

Owain's knowing wink made me wonder whether the service had been mechanical or biological.

"And the mileage?" I asked tentatively.

"Very low for its age. Only seventy-five thousand. There's still plenty of life in the old girl yet."

Another wink. Still on about his lady friends?

I'm not particularly knowledgeable about cars – tractors are more my forte – but I'd been with my father on occasions when he was looking for a second-hand car for mum. Trying to appear more confident than I felt, I looked at the tyres, and bent down to examine the underside. There wasn't anything hanging loose.

"It's a basic model, but a reliable work horse, I'd stake my reputation on that," declared Owain, who'd sensed that I hadn't got much choice or real knowledge, but needed reassurance.

"So it comes with a guarantee then?"

"Well … not exactly. Not one of those written things which exclude ninety-five percent of any faults, but you have my word that I'll fix any problem in the first two months without charge. Can't say fairer than that."

As I said, he did have a good reputation for fair trading.

"Here, why don't you take it for a little spin? You have got a full license, I assume?"

"Yes, over three years now."

My seventeenth birthday present from my parents had been a course of driving lessons and I'd passed first time after only three months. Apart from brief excursions in my mother's Beetle, back home, however, I hadn't driven since coming to Tencastle.

Owain encouraged me into the driver's seat, and gave me a quick run down on the controls. "Lights, indicators, dip switch, wiper – they all work, see! That's the choke, pull it out, dip the accelerator three times and try the starter!. Never fails!" Owain rummaged under the passenger seat. "And if it does, you've got a back up starter handle."

Much to my surprise, the old Ford spluttered on the first attempt then coughed to life and settled down into a contented chugga chugga, patiently waiting for further demands for action.

Clutch depressed I tested the gear lever, to Owain's instruction, "Three forward gears, down, across and up, down. Reverse up from first gear. Watch the clutch, it's a little fierce."

Owain wisely stood clear. I selected first gear, and gently worked the clutch and accelerator. The car leapt forward like a kangaroo and stalled. After a second failed attempt Owain, not to mention me, must have been having second thoughts, but the third time it moved obediently at a gentle pace across the forecourt.

"Just go down Station Road and back around the park," Owain called out. "And take care!" That comment was probably more out of concern for the car than for me.

Fortunately the traffic had thinned out, and apart from the occasional jerk, and one disconcerting grinding of gears, I made it safely back to Owain's Emporium. I was a little apprehensive, but I also experienced a great feeling of achievement and exhilaration – I could actually be a proud owner of a car!

But there were a few minor matters to sort out first.

"Well, what do you think?" beamed Owain.

"Yes, er, well, not too bad." I didn't want to sound too eager. "The gears seem to grind when I change down, though."

"Ah, that's because there's no synchromesh on bottom gear. You have to double declutch."

"Come again?"

"Double declutch. Same on all the old cars. You blip the clutch, change into neutral, blip it again and change down." Owain made it sound easy. I supposed I'd get the hang of it.

Decision time, then.

"Okay, I'm interested, but it's stretching my budget, and I've got to sort out insurance and road tax. How about £70?" I'd offered him £20 less than the asking price.

Owain looked pained, "I've got my budget to think about too, you know!" He thought again for a moment. "Tell you what, split the difference, and it does already have five months tax still on it."

"Fully serviced?"

"No problem."

"Agreed then!" And we shook hands.

Owain got down to the real business. "Now, if you'd like to come into my office and sign some papers and leave a deposit, you can sort out your insurance and the car will be all ready for you to pick up on Saturday. You've made a very good choice, young sir!"

I hoped so.

I didn't say a word to the others about the car for the rest of the week. Jake had strewn bike parts around the kitchen for two days but had managed to do a convincing restoration job. Dan was going home for the weekend and hoped to return with a moped, while Benji appeared and disappeared at will.

Benji was the only one at home when I parked my new acquisition on the hard standing beside the cottage.

"Hey, man! That's real cool! Would you like me to paint some flowers on it?"

"Thanks, Benji, I'll pass on that for now." He seemed disappointed that I wasn't more keen on his idea.

Jake returned from a cycle trip. "Visitors?" he asked, and then added, "Who on earth would drive a thing like that?"

I sprung to its defence, "It's mine. It's just a car!"

"Jess' a car," Jake mused. "Jessica! We'll call her Jessica!"

I had no say in naming my baby. Jessica it was.

"Rob, can I ask a favour?"

"You can ask, certainly. Depends what you've got in mind whether I agree." I was well used to Jake's innocently sounding comments leading to all manner of unexpected commitments.

"Would you be willing to run us all up to Thomas Hall on Friday evening?"

It was the first time Jake, or my other house mates for that matter, had formally asked for Jessica's services in the three weeks we'd been at the cottage, though I had given lifts at various times when our interests coincided. Generally the bicycle and moped had served Jake and Dan pretty well, and Benji seemed to rely on teleportation.

"Probably. Why, what's happening?"

"The opening."

"What opening?"

"Oh, come on, Rob, you can't have forgotten, after all the work we put into it!"

The penny dropped. "The observatory? But it was opened for use before the end of last term."

We had received barely a week of benefit for our labours, which had taken up hours of our spare time most weekends since the approval of Jake's ideas. Even so, the facilities were minimal, consisting of a few armchairs and a table tennis table. The view over Tencastle was something else!

"This is the official opening, by the Vice-Chancellor. The Union President and his whole Executive, all the bigwigs from town and college, the local newspaper, they will all be there."

"And us?"

"The humble workers – all of us at Thomas last year that contributed to the project."

A thought occurred to me. "It's not going to be a dressing up occasion, is it?"

"Why, what do want to dress up as?"

"Pillock! I mean formal wear, penguin suit etcetera."

"I believe it will be informal, like smart casual."

"You said all of us. What work did Benji do?" I'd never seen him doing any painting, as in decorating.

"He produced a few abstract canvases to cover the interior walls. Stars and heavenly bodies kind of thing, you know."

Any guess concerning Benji's masterpieces would probably have been wrong.

"Christ alive!" Jake could scarcely believe his eyes, "They must have coughed up some serious money for this!"

The stark recreational area we'd created on a shoestring budget out of a building site had undergone a remarkable transformation over the twelve week summer break. A coffee bar adjacent to the central stairwell now separated a recreational area, complete with pool table and table tennis, from a refurbished lounge area which gave the best views over the valley.

"You can even show off your disco skills," said Dan, indicating the uncarpeted oval in front of the armchairs and coffee tables set around the half circumference.

"That will be a great asset in an all-male hostel," I commented. "Unless the rules on female visitors are relaxed."

They were certainly relaxed for the present occasion, since the drinks and canapés were being offered by a quartet of attractive young girls whom I was pretty sure weren't students. Most of the other females were the wrong side of middle-aged and attached to the numerous dignitaries knocking back the free wine.

"What's up, Benji?" Jake asked. "You're not on the wagon are you?" Our artist in residence looked uncomfortable and downbeat.

"My paintings, man! They're not here!"

We looked round. No artwork on display whatsoever, not that there was any obvious display space.

"Perhaps they've not got round to putting them up yet," I offered, in feeble consolation.

"Took me bloody hours, man, to get the composition right!" Benji complained.

We caught sight of Rud and Dicky, two other key members of our dome task force. Rud was on form, chatting up one gorgeous blonde waitress, who kissed him surreptitiously and left a tray of nibbles on the table behind him.

"I suppose we'd better circulate," Jake said, and wandered off in the direction of the Union President.

"I've something else I need to circulate," said Dan, heading for the loos on the lift shaft corridor.

Benji was still lamenting his missing masterpieces.

Left to my own company, I scanned the assembly. The Thomas Hall students, for whose use the facility had been developed, seemed conspicuously under-represented at the bun fight. Just half a dozen or so of the current social committee were the only students in attendance other than ourselves and the Union executive, apart, possibly, from a black-haired girl who was standing alone, sipping nervously on her orange juice and looking totally dejected. I eased my way over to her.

"Hi," I said. "You don't seem to be enjoying the evening much."

She wrinkled her pert little nose. "Ugh, not much fun with this load of stuffed shirts!" She looked at me coyly and smiled. "You know, you're the first person I've spoken to this evening."

I couldn't believe it. The normal complement of testosterone-powered students would have been falling over themselves for the attention of this strikingly attractive young woman. Her shiny, sleek, dark hair, parted down the middle, hung partly over her thin, high-browed face. Delicate use of eye shadow and lipstick smoothed her rather sharp features. Her satin-shiny green dress clung closely to her slim body, curved in all the right places.

"Are you one of the students here in Thomas Hall?" she asked.

"Last year, but not now. I was one of the instigators of the dome project group." I exaggerated, slightly.

"Really? I thought it was a college initiative."

"They've carried out many improvements over the summer, but my friend, Jake, persuaded the Warden to let us make use of the dome. We did much of the work in our spare time."

"That's marvellous. I hadn't heard about anything like that!" Her eyes sparkled with interest. "Tell me, what's your name?"

"I'm Rob. And you?"

"Tania."

"I hope you don't mind me asking, Tania, but you're not a student, are you? I haven't seen you around college before and I'm sure I would have noticed."

She chuckled, her cheeks colouring briefly. "I am a student but not in Tencastle. I'm back home for a few days and got dragged along with the official party." She looked around the room. "God, what a bore!"

"I'm glad you came."

"Sorry, Rob, I didn't mean you! You're the one bright spot in the proceedings."

My turn to blush.

"Would you like to take a break from the tedium?" I suggested.

"What have you in mind?"

Quite a few things came to mind which I chose not to mention. "Breath of fresh air, perhaps? We'll not miss much here for a while."

We met Dan rushing back up the stairs. "Hey, Rob, I've found Benji's …" he began excitedly, before realising I'd got a girl on my arm, figuratively speaking. "Oh, sorry …"

"Tania, this is Dan, one of my housemates."

"Hi!" He seemed lost for further words.

"You were saying?"

"Oh, yes! Benji's paintings, I've found them!"

"He will be pleased."

"I'm not sure about that, they're hanging in the gents."

I laughed. "All of them?"

"I dunno, didn't look in the girls' room."

"Benji's also in our house," I said to Tania. "He's got aspirations of being a great artist. I wonder, could you have a quick look in the girls' room and see if there's any abstract art on the wall? Not graffiti."

She considered the unusual request, and smiled. "Sure."

Dan watched her as she clacked along the corridor in her high heels to the loo. "Hell, Rob, how did you pull that gorgeous creature?"

"Two lonely people at the party."

"I don't believe you! And you're leaving early?"

"We're just going for a breath of air."

"I don't believe that either, you randy sod! Don't leave us stranded here, will you? She can sit on my knee while you drive."

"Bugger off!"

Tania re-emerged. "One canvas. Dr. Who meets Picasso, right?"

"That sounds like Benji," Dan said. "I'll break the good news to him. See you later!"

Tania and I headed for the lift.

"Is it just the three of you in the house?"

"No, there's Jake, too. He's … er … quite a character."

"Sounds an interesting household. Where in Tencastle do you live?"

I told her. "Would you like to see it?

"I'd love to!" She became pensive. "But I've got to go back to Cambridge tomorrow."

I took a bold decision as we crossed the lobby. "No time like the present."

"What do you mean?"

"Well, I've got my car here. We could drive out to Penybont, have a quick look and be back again in half an hour, well before they finish all the speeches."

She paused, briefly, before replying, "Why not?"

Jessica seemed as pleased as I was to have female company, and purred contentedly all the way to the cottage.

"Wow, Rob, what an amazing place!" She wandered in awe through the ground floor rooms. "It's so … so romantic." She took my hand and pulled me close, her lips seeking mine.

I needed no further encouragement. We tumbled down on to the sofa in passionate embrace. She wrapped her arms around my shoulder and clamped her mouth firmly onto mine. I stroked her sleek black hair, my hands unable to explore further until I could free my arms. Coming up for air she released her hold, and we rolled over, side by side. My tentative caress of her bosom through her dress fired her up for more passionate French kissing. She then flopped back on the sofa, content for my hand to creep down over her stomach. Until she caught site of the clock above the fireplace. She struggled up, brushing down her dress.

"Rob, we must get back right away!"

"'S'not midnight. My car won't turn into a pumpkin," I said lazily.

"My father will turn apeshit if he finds I've done a runner !"

"Who is your father?"

"Dr. Cruikshanks." She saw my astonished look, "You didn't know?"

"I wouldn't have guessed," I said truthfully. "You don't talk like him," I added, ambiguously.

"Any deviation from the Queen's English is discouraged in a select ladies' college."

"You're staying with him at Thomas?"

"With all those randy students around? Good lord, no!"

I wasn't sure whether that included me. "So, where?"

"At my mother's house, in town. My parents are divorced. I'm fond of Dad, but I wouldn't want to live with him. He'd wrap me up in cotton wool, he's so possessive."

"Do you …"

"Look, can we get a move on? I don't want to upset him."

"Right."

We'd been away from Thomas Hall just under the hour in all, though it seemed much longer. Jessica flew. We rushed into the tower lobby, and fortunately found a waiting lift.

"Tania, is there any chance we could meet again?" I said hopefully.

"Faint chance I'm afraid, Rob. I'm usually only here during the vacations and not always then, and I presume you're back home. Wherever that is."

"Devon."

"I'm sorry, Rob." She kissed me again, just a peck, "But thanks for a great evening. Better than I ever imagined."

I felt much the same way. We made it to the assembly just as the Union President was winding up a vote of thanks.

"… and, finally, I'd like to give a special mention to a small group of Tencastle students without whom this marvellous facility might never have been developed. Jacob Moses and his team!"

Jake caught sight of me and signalled me to join him and the rest of the group in acknowledging the applause.

"The Vice-Chancellor looks as if he's swallowed a lemon," I whispered when I reached his side. "And Dr Nightingale's not too happy either."

"Not one bloody word of acknowledgement about our work from either of them," Jake grimaced. "Made out it was all their idea!"

"And they hung my paintings in the flaming bog, man!"

"Yeah, shame, that!" Dan said. "And the laundry bills, Benji."

"What do you mean?"

"When they piss their pants while standing there trying to make sense of your daubings."

"Aw, man, that's not fair!" Benji looked despondent.

"Cheer up, Benji, time for a beer," said Jake, then thought of the logistics. "That is, if Rob doesn't mind stopping off in town."

"He may have other plans," said Dan, suggestively. "This girl, she had …"

"She's safely restored to her father's side," I said.

"Virtue intact?"

"I don't know what you mean, Dan," I said innocently. "I'm sure she's as virtuous as when I first met her."

CHAPTER NINE

House Warming

I was surprised really at how quickly we established a routine at Ty Melin. The household chores seemed to get done without the need for a formal rota. Even Benji lent a hand, when it wasn't holding a paint brush.

At college, the second year was the one of greatest stability with regard to routine and social life, too. With no on-the-job teacher training in god-forsaken backwaters, we slipped into a regular weekly programme of lectures, seminars and, for me, practical sessions in the laboratory. Though the latter were more concerned with scientific accuracy and technique they still included helpful tips on ensuring that teacher demonstrations to a class of kids actually worked, or at least providing a convincing range of reasons if they didn't. Bronwen and I had long established an easy-going working partnership in the laboratory, but over the Summer, her finger had acquired a silver and sapphire engagement ring, to ward off other potential suitors. I felt some feelings of envy towards her fiancé.

I counted myself fortunate to have John Tudor Evans as tutor for my main subject. The Geography lecturer was okay, but she was nowhere near as inspiring as John or, for that matter, Dr. Ambersham, who surprisingly breathed life into the dry topic of educational philosophy, with witty asides, stimulating debate and a penchant for unorthodox illustrations of key issues. Unfortunately one couldn't say the same about Dr Cruikshanks. Dour and humourless and given to frequently · brushing back his shoulder-length greasy black-dyed hair, his speciality was supposed to be the history of education. It was probably not the most captivating topic at the best of times, but, delivered in a low monotone in a barely intelligible Scottish accent (he came from Kirkaldy, he told us in one of his many digressions) it was easy to drift off into a reverie, even forty winks. Dangerous, though, since he had a nasty habit of firing off a barbed question to anyone he perceived as being inattentive, and the unfortunate recipient usually fell foul of his caustic sarcasm. The female students were far more likely to be targeted.

"Bastard," said Sophie Brasier, as we left the college together after one particularly dreary Friday afternoon lecture. "He's the most mean-spirited, lousy, useless lecturer I've ever come across!"

"You don't like him, I gather." He'd put her down badly by implying she couldn't tell the difference between Queen Victoria and Elizabeth II.

"Does anyone? We're nearly five weeks into term and he's still droning on about the nineteenth century or his ruddy prodigy of a daughter!"

"I've met her. She's actually very nice." I felt no need to elaborate.

"Unbelievable with him for a father."

"Fancy a coffee?" I said, changing the subject.

Sophie heaved a deep sigh, "A whiskey would be better, but I'll settle for coffee."

Other than an old vending machine that dispensed three different flavours of tepid dishwater, refreshments in the main building were unavailable after half past three, so we wandered over to the Union. Since the first teaching practice minibus journeys, our social contact had been casual, although we had shared a number of lectures and seminars in common.

She had a preference for wearing loosely fitting jumpers which, given her height, concealed her figure. Today, however, she sported an open, though still long, knitted cardigan over a neat white cotton blouse, which, contrary to my impression that she was flat-chested, held small, but surprisingly pointed breasts. With short blonde hair which seemed to curl naturally, pale blue eyes over high cheekbones and a short, straight nose, she was quite attractive, face to face over the refectory table.

"Where are you living now? I presume you're not still at 'Crombie?"

"In that nunnery? No way! I share a small two-bedroom flat just off the top of Castle Street."

"Very handy. Do I know your flat mate?"

"Tamsin? Probably not. Even our paths don't cross much in college."

"Name doesn't ring any bells."

"And where do you live, Rob? I don't see you around the town much after college."

"That's because I'm out in the sticks, at Penybont. There's four of us in an old cottage."

"Sounds fun."

I wasn't sure whether she meant it truly or sarcastically. On an impulse, I said, "Come out and see it. Tell you what, we're having a housewarming party next weekend. Would you like to come?"

"Why not? I'd like that." She knitted her brows, "How do I get there?"

"We've not quite worked out all the logistics yet, but the principle is for people to get the last bus out on Friday, bring a sleeping bag, and get the bus back in to Tencastle on Saturday. Bring a bottle or two. We'll have some food laid on and bacon butties for breakfast. Bring Tamsin as well, if you like," I added.

When Jake had raised the idea of a party, we'd all been enthusiastic, but short of me running a shuttle service all bloody night, which I didn't fancy and said so forcibly, the only viable option of getting anyone to come, not to mention getting rid of them again, was to rely on public transport. Which inevitably meant overnighting from Friday to Saturday, since the Sabbath was a day of rest for Tencastle bus drivers. The guest list we'd first drawn up had looked extremely unbalanced in favour of our male friends ex Thomas Hall, so inclusion of any members of the fairer sex from amongst our acquaintances was to be encouraged.

"Tamsin's away next weekend, I think," said Sophie. "But that sounds like some marathon party!"

"Fireworks!" Jake announced.

"What about them?" I asked.

"We could have a firework display at our party."

"It's not Bonfire Night, man," said Benji.

"Don't put more ideas into his head, for Chrissake," I said.

"Close enough, though," said Dan, spilling coffee over his toast and marmalade. "Bugger!"

"Agreed then? Ask everybody to bring a box along to the housewarming?" said Jake. There was no point in arguing when Jake had already decided.

"While we're on the subject of housewarming," I said, "it's been getting decidedly chilly in here these last few evenings. Do you have any idea how to get the central heating to work?"

There were radiators in all of the rooms, bar the kitchen, but we'd enjoyed something of an Indian Summer since we'd been in the cottage. There'd been a suggestion of frost, however, on Jessica's windscreen that very morning.

"Presumably the Rayburn," said Jake.

"I did wonder about that," I said. "But I can't see any pipes coming from it." My parents' Aga back home provided all the hot water and heating, and gleamed with polished copper tubes from its body.

"Well, we can always try it out. Do you know how they work?"

"You put the coal or wood in and burn it," I said.

"I'd never have thought of that!" said Jake, sarcastically.

"Do we have any coal or wood?" Dan asked.

Jake looked at us and shrugged. He stood up and made for the back door. Dan and I followed.

To the rear of the cottage, accessed either from the kitchen or from a rough gravel patch just large enough to accommodate Jessica, there were a couple of small ramshackle outbuildings at the edge of the paved area. A lawn badly in need of attention sloped gently downwards to a few small trees and shrubs, beyond which an overgrown vegetable garden stretched down to the small stream. From the lumps of masonry scattered around its banks it was likely that some other building had formerly stood there. On the far side of the stream a thin tongue of meadow edged up the hillside to deciduous woodland, resplendent in the rich colours of autumn. I was tempted for one brief second to call Benji out to capture the scene on canvas.

"Few odd nuggets in here," Dan called from one of the outhouses.

"Gold?" said Jake hopefully.

"Black gold."

Further rummaging yielded a rusty saw, a wooden saw-horse with badly woodwormed legs, and a small pile of logs in one of the two bunkers built into the outhouse.

"I suppose we'll have to order some coal," said Jake.

"Anthracite is best for the Rayburn."

"If you say so, Rob." Jake's attention turned to the forest across the stream. "Plenty of wood there."

"It doesn't belong to us, man," Benji pointed out.

"Don't expect they'd miss a few fallen branches."

It still sounded dubious to me, but Jake said no more about it then.

We found a Tencastle coal merchant listed in the telephone directory, and Dan volunteered to call in there on Monday morning.

It was evident Jake wasn't planning on attending Sunday service. Not that any of us had a clue where the nearest church was anyway, even if we'd felt inclined to worship.

"Going to a tramps' ball?" I didn't know Jake even possessed such ragged old jeans and jacket.

"No, he's got a weekend job as a scarecrow," said Dan.

"Very funny. I'll need your help."

"What, to collect a penny for the guy?" Dan chortled.

"Foraging, you pillocks!"

"Come again?"

"Over in the wood, you know, gathering firewood."

"Now hang on, Jake, I'm not sure…"

"'S'all right, you and Dan can stay safe on this side, I'll do the dirty work."

"But…"

"Come on, we can't afford to buy wood as well as coal and still eat! See you by the stream in five minutes."

Benji suddenly discovered he had more urgent things to attend to.

"Right," Jake said to us, a few minutes later. "Here's the plan, I bring the wood to the stream here." He pointed upstream. "Float it down, you pull it out on your side."

"I don't fancy wading in," I said.

"Just hook it with the hoe and rake from the shed. Should be a doddle."

"But we can't burn the wood if it's sopping wet," Dan objected.

"It will soon dry out."

"In front of a fire?"

"Why not?" Jake had missed the sarcasm in my voice.

Dan had other concerns. "Are you going to wade across? The stream doesn't look that deep but I can't see the bottom."

"I wasn't school long-jump champion for nothing. Watch!"

Jake took a deep breath, pounded down the rough path, and launched himself into space. He easily made the far bank but as he landed, upper body slightly forward, his feet slipped backwards in the mud. He fell spread-eagled face down in a recently deposited cow pat. We hadn't noticed any beasts in the field yesterday.

I don't think Jake really appreciated our applause. Browned off probably described both his mood and appearance.

"Wait there!" he grunted, after rinsing his face in the stream. "I'll be back soon!"

"You going to jump back too? There's no livestock this side!" Dan added helpfully.

Jake made a rude gesture with his finger and strode up the meadow towards the wood.

"I don't think we'll be needed for half an hour or so," I said. "Shall we grab another coffee?"

In the event it must have been nearly an hour and a half later that we heard Jake yelling.

"Where the hell have you two been?"

"Sorry, we, er, got distracted," Dan said lamely. By the television, he refrained from mentioning.

Jake really had been busy. He'd assembled an impressive pile of lichen-covered branches on the far bank.

"Ready then?" Jake launched a two-foot section of broken limb. The current caught it, turned it lengthways parallel to the banks.

Try as we could, it slipped past our garden tools.

"Fat bloody use you are! Took me ages to drag that one down."

"Sorry."

The next item of driftwood was much easier, being multi-branched. In fact, we secured it with a piece of rope, and used it to trap the other flotsam. We became quite adept at retrieving the wood, and within an hour had transferred the stockpile into our garden. All except, that is, a log of substantial diameter which Jake had saved till last. He manhandled it upright to the edge of the stream, and, aiming for a small depression in our bank, let it fall.

The log fell across the stream with about a foot clear on either side, though not quite in the intended position. Jake stepped on the log, and teetered precariously, arms waving above his head to keep his balance.

"I think you'd be safer to crawl across," I called.

"Think you're right!" Jake replied.

Jake spread himself along the log, which was significantly narrower than his body, and used his hands and knees to edge himself forward up the slight incline. His head was within a few inches of our bank when the log rolled over, dunking Jake into the stream. Though his feet slipped off the log, he'd at least held on with his hands, and we were able to haul him, spluttering water and curses, onto dry land.

"Need a bloody shower to get all that dung and duckweed off me!" Jake shook himself like a shaggy dog, and dripped into the house.

"Hey, man," called Benji from the front door. "Just been down to the bridge. One of the cottages there has got logs for sale." He caught sight of Jake, "Man, are you all right?"

"No, I'm bloody not!"

My signal to Benji warned him not to say any more.

We really had no idea of how many would turn up. We'd decided against posting an open invitation on the Union notice board, but we had certainly mentioned it to a fair number of friends and acquaintances. The distance from town was, we expected, likely to be a limiting factor. Jessica had for a couple of days served as a delivery van, ensuring that we'd got in a reasonable supply of booze, bacon, bread and cheese, milk, coffee and a generous supply of plastic tableware. We'd fired up the Rayburn and when this failed to heat the radiators, we also got the wood-burning stove in the lounge in action. For some reason which we didn't understand we noticed after a while that the whole house had acquired a cosy warmth.

We were as ready as we could be. Peace before the invasion, which began with the arrival of the evening bus that normally carried just a handful of people. Today the stream of students clambering out with bedding, bottles and rucksacks seemed never ending, although, in truth, there were only a dozen or so in all. I was pleased to see Sophie amongst them, and gave her a welcoming hug, but holding back from a kiss as we didn't know each other that well, yet. Last year's F wing at Thomas was well represented with Dicky, Huw, Sparkle and, unexpectedly, Ivan Petrovsky with whom I'd had minimal contact in Hall. I wondered what on earth he'd got in his bulky and obviously weighty backpack. From the warm embrace he gave them, Dan had evidently maintained far more regular contact than I with Kissy and Suzie, who arrived with Bronwen. Now, Dilly I would still have been very happy to know better, but she still seemed to be with the same fellow from the Welsh Folk Dance group. One slightly older bloke I vaguely recognized, alas not his shapely companion, nor the other couple of girls.

A throaty roar of a diesel engine heralded more arrivals, some friends of Benji in an old Land Rover pick-up. All three were definitely the arty types, the male bearded and the girls bedecked with bangles, beads and body piercings. I knew by sight the one with a guitar from Folk Club. They were generous, though, with their offerings of four-pack lagers and a bottle of red wine. Benji took them up to his room to dump their stuff and show them his latest creations.

In the extended melée of introductions, getting a drink and chatting above a background of vintage Beatles (Jake's choice, not mine), I noticed one petite female who, after nearly a whole hour was isolated from the action, looking worried and chewing her nails.

"Hi," I said. "Are you okay? Can I get you a drink?"

"Oh … er, not just yet … thanks." She looked close to tears. "It's just … I don't know anyone here … he said he'd meet me on the bus, but he wasn't …"

"Who wasn't?"

"His name's Brian. Oh, I wish …"

I only knew one Brian. "Is he, er, sort of chunky, with red hair?"

"Yes." Her eyes brightened, "You know him?"

"That would be Rud, I think. We thought he'd be coming. I'm Rob, by the way, one of the hosts."

"Cathy."

"Are you new this year at college?"

Her face reddened, "I'm not at college. I work in the supermarket."

"Sorry, Cathy, I didn't mean to embarrass you. You're very welcome here, and …"

Above the hubbub, someone was hammering on the front door.

"Excuse me a moment."

Rud stood there, looking, well, ruddier than usual. "Bloody hell, Rob, what a bloody place to get to."

"What happened?"

"Missed the bus, didn't I? Decided to hitch, but no bloody cars about, were there? Ended up walking most of the bloody way. I'd arranged to meet someone, hadn't I?"

"I think there's someone here who's going to be pleased to see you." I relieved him of his bag of goodies and stood aside.

"Cathy!"

"Brian, oh thank Christ!"

I'm sure they spent the next twenty minutes at least in each other's arms without coming up for air. Until Jake gathered everyone's attention by ringing a large hand bell he'd got from God knows where.

"Boat race in five minutes!"

Everyone, myself included, looked puzzled, not sure that we'd heard correctly.

"And bring your fireworks with you, guys!"

There was a certain reluctance to leave the warm fug of the cottage for the chill clear air of a late October evening, but most of us eventually filtered out through the back door. Jake handed everyone a small paper plate as they passed. He'd already been busy. The path to the stream was lined with several night-light candles flickering in assorted small glass jars.

"Right, here's what we do. Put a firework on your plate. When the rocket goes off," he pointed to where a milk bottle had been wedged in a fork of an apple tree, "light it and launch it. Winner is the one whose boat goes furthest before the firework dies."

"What's the prize?" someone called.

"It's a surprise!" Jake replied promptly.

Those who hadn't already done so were invited to add any fireworks they'd brought to the old metal biscuit tin near the river bank, where Jake had also provided some long wax tapers to light them.

"Wouldn't it be better if we do it three at a time, with the winner of each heat going into the next round," I suggested. "We can't get everybody on the bank at the same time."

"Good idea, Rob. Hear that, everyone? Ladies first, shall we say?"

That wasn't actually an advantage, as it happened, for the first three girls each selected a 'Vesuvius' and placed the conical firework in the centre of the paper plate. Taper in hand they knelt on the bank, on a piece of old carpet Jake had thoughtfully supplied, and waited for the signal.

The whoosh of the rocket, when it came, took Kissy by surprise and she released her plate before lighting the touch paper. It drifted off into the far bank and capsized. The other two were slightly more successful but Dilly, over-eager, gave her plate a helping shove, swamping it with water so that no sooner had it erupted than her volcano was extinguished. That of the third girl displayed its full pyrotechnics while its vessel, caught it an eddy, described a gentle circle upstream before sinking gracefully where it had been launched. To mild protest Jake declared Dilly the winner as her craft had travelled the furthest downstream, by all of six inches.

The second team fared little better; although all fireworks were ignited, the round plates, lacking any streamlining, tended to drift to the banks and get trapped. Suzie unwittingly chose a banger and scuppered her vessel spectacularly.

Those following quickly grasped a few principles of marine engineering and bent their plates to give some semblance of a keel and bow. Multi-coloured sparks flying from their squat chimney, the paper boats generally now made it at least two or three metres downstream. Most of the dumpy fireworks had been expended by the penultimate heat of the first round, leaving only an assortment of taller Roman Candle varieties.

"That's not fair!" claimed Dicky. "They'll never stand up!"

His didn't. The little bit of molten wax from the tapers which Jake agreed could be used to hold the cardboard tubes upright gave way almost immediately, and his boat shot well ahead of the field as it spewed out a fiery exhaust. Suddenly jet propulsion technology caught on and the remaining three contestants beat all previous records handsomely.

The six heat winners, all with the benefit of experience, lined up for the 'semi-finals'. Cathy, already eliminated from the competition, jumped up and down in excitement on the bank, shrieking encouragement to Rud as he did battle with two of Benji's friends. All three of their craft were caught in the main current and made it past the end of our garden and into the bend, where those of Rud's rivals collided and sank.

Jake changed the rules for the climax of his regatta. Rud and Ivan, the other finalist, were both allowed two fireworks of a specific kind they hadn't used before, with the exception of a rocket. He also gave them a larger diameter plate and a length of 10 amp fuse wire to improve the stability of the boat in any way they wished. And since he'd run out of rockets anyway, the race would be started with a banger. Ivan opted for a steel-strengthened prow and a twin-cylinder power pack of Golden Rain. Rud, of an inventive mind and to impress his new girlfriend, chose Catherine Wheels. He secured them on a spindle of wire through the folded up sides of the plate and also fashioned a couple of wire mesh paddles.

Rud's device was quite ingenious and actually worked, except that he'd hung the Catherine Wheels the wrong way round so that the thrust tried to drive the little craft upstream, to groans of anguish from his supporters, who thought the battle over. Ivan's vessel had started well, but only one firework ignited, and, being off centre, it also created a turning effect. When, therefore, the second tube eventually fired, set alight by the dying exhaust of the first, the prow was already pointing back upstream and, with opposite torque, then headed straight for the bank. Meanwhile, Rud's entry, caught in midstream current, floated swiftly backwards downstream, the longer lasting Catherine Wheels still spinning furiously but ineffectively for several seconds after Ivan's boat had beached.

To a round of cheers and a kiss and hug from Cathy, Rud took a bow.

"And, now, to our worthy champion, in recognition of his matchless skill and daring, in this, the first festival of…"

"Get on with it, Jake, it's bloody brass monkeys out here!" Dan yelled.

"As I was saying, in this first festival of fire and water, I present Brian Cheeke with this medal …"

It looked suspiciously like a cocoa tin lid on a string.

"… and his prize!" Jake handed Rud a box of Ship brand safety matches.

We all gravitated to the lounge where the stove was giving out a homely warm glow. Most of us, anyway. I think Cathy had some other rewards in mind for Rud. We'd cleared out as much clutter as possible, so there was at least a few inches of floor space for those not fortunate enough to get a chair. I flopped next to Sophie on the sofa, and she didn't object when I put an arm around her shoulders. The girl with the guitar starting strumming softly.

"Give us one of your songs, Tess," Benji encouraged.

"Sure?"

"Yeah, man."

She rendered a passable cover of Dylan's *Blowin' in the Wind* in a sweet, but, for my register, rather high voice. But we all joined in regardless, and clapped politely when she finished. Jake fished out his banjo from behind the corner armchair, a general signal for other instruments to materialise, a penny whistle from Huw, and a small accordion from Ivan.

"Go on, Rob, get your guitar!" Jake said.

My guitar prowess was still very limited, and I was quite comfortable nestling up to Sophie. But others were joining in Jake's exhortations, so, reluctantly, I yielded.

"Back soon," I whispered to Sophie, and picked my way amongst bodies to the door.

I suppose I should have knocked, but one doesn't normally think about that before entering one's own room. I reached for the light switch automatically and a squeal came from behind Jake's bed. I caught a glimpse of flailing bare legs, grabbed my guitar case and beat a hasty retreat.

Downstairs, Ivan was amazing his audience with spirited high speed music on his box.

"That's incredible, man!" said Benji. "Where did you pick that up?"

"Oh, here and there," Ivan said, modestly. "Thought I ought to learn a tune or two from my ancestral homeland."

"Do you do that Russian sort of dancing as well? You know squatting on your heels?" Kissy asked.

"'Fraid not. I'm really very English. Just got a Russian name from my grandfather."

"Jeff can do something like it," Dilly spoke up, to our and her boyfriend's surprise. He'd probably even less claim to be Russian.

"Can you play a reel on your whistle?" Jeff asked Huw. "A lot slower than the last one, though."

Huw hummed a few bars. "Is this okay?" I guess he was more used to playing his bagpipes for dancing.

"Fine. Anyone got a broomstick?"

"We all came by bus," someone called out.

Next problem was clearing enough floor space. Two more bodies perched on the sofa.

Well, it didn't look Russian, that's for sure, but Jeff certainly had the dancing on one's haunches technique, along with a few other figures like hopping over the broomstick, clapping hands under his legs, and, unbelievably, jumping over the broomstick held between his linked hands.

Out of breath, he bowed to applause, loudest from Dilly and Bronwen.

"That's a Welsh dance. Can't let the Russkies have it all their own way, can we?" he said, winking at Ivan. "Anyone else want to try?"

Jake, for one, would never resist a challenge. He wasn't the only volunteer who collapsed backwards onto his bottom, legs in air, the rest of us collapsing in merriment.

After such an inspired start the music and singing continued unabated, hidden talents emerging. Bronwen gave a beautifully moving rendition in Welsh of a ballad, about a blackbird, she said. Sparkle, who couldn't sing two notes in tune, compensated with irreverent parodies of some well-known poems we'd all been subjected to at school. And Jake, of course with his banjo, which then jogged someone's memory that I was a wizard on the spoons – or so they said. As the midnight hour came and went, a more relaxed and soporific mood settled upon us, slow airs on the whistle from Huw, gentle guitar riffs and soothing soft ballads from Tess, whose repertoire seemed inexhaustible. Some people drifted sleepily into the dining room or upstairs to the room Jake and I shared, where they could, if they wished, stretch out their sleeping bags, now that Rud and Cathy had rejoined the party. She asked me for an alarm clock or wake up call as she was working next morning and had to catch the early bus.

"I'm pretty sure there will be plenty of activity," I said but lent her my travel alarm as a back up.

In an alcohol-generated state of comfortable contentment, I must have drifted off to sleep on the sofa. I awoke, briefly, a couple of hours or so later, to find Sophie still dozing in my arms and several other bodies sprawled around, the silence only broken by the whisper of even breathing punctuated by an occasional snore.

Next thing I knew someone was shaking my shoulder. "Wassup?" I grunted.

"Rob, can you help, Cathy's getting terribly upset 'cos she's done something to the loo. Dunno where Jake is."

"Gimme a sec, Rud." I rubbed my eyes. Sophie had somehow extricated herself earlier and had disappeared. Several bodies were still inactive but there were stirrings within the house in the grey light of dawn.

I guessed what had happened. The cistern in the en-suite upstairs was rather temperamental, and if you didn't catch the handle quite right it was inclined to get stuck, unflushed. Cathy was almost in tears, perched on the end of my bed (thankfully unused) with her head in her hands.

The bucket of water I'd grabbed from downstairs dealt with the flushing. The handle could only be reset by removing the top of the cistern and waggling things about. I knew one day we'd have to call in the plumber to fix it properly.

"All sorted. No need to worry," I said laying my hand on Cathy's shoulder. "Come and have some breakfast."

She nodded.

Downstairs, Sophie and Dan were already taking charge of the kitchen, the kettle steaming on the Rayburn hob to fill the array of coffee mugs set out on the table. Bacon sarnies were next on the agenda.

"A bright and beautiful morning to you all," Jake called out as he breezed in through the front door.

I can't understand how anyone could be so bloody cheerful after hardly any sleep. He was carrying a plastic bag from which he extracted a handful of soggy paper plates.

"Been down by the bridge. Thought I'd better fish these out of the river before the locals complain." He dumped them in the waste bin. "Everything under control? Gosh, that bacon smells good. Shall I give a reveille call?"

His entry would have woken the dead anyway, I thought.

"Bus goes in half an hour," he called loudly to no-one in particular. Mostly it fell on deaf, or rather dozing, ears.

Cathy and Rud, and the three I didn't know were the only passengers. For Dilly and Jeff it was a toss up between bus and bacon butty. No contest.

Various bodies stirred at odd times all through the morning. Bacon sandwiches were still on the menu for elevenses, and lunch, too, for the last to rise, Huw, Ivan and Tess, who, I'm told, had kept live music going well into the small hours. Benji's other friends had deserted Tess sometime during the morning, taking Dilly and Jeff with them in the Land Rover.

Considering the houseful we'd had, the debris wasn't half as bad as I'd expected. It wasn't our intention to expect any of our guests to help with the cleaning but the girls, with the exception of Tess, more or less took charge, directing Sparkle, Dicky, Dan and myself with great efficiency, so that we ended up doing the hardest work. We shooed last night's musicians like itinerant minstrels from one room to another with broom and Hoover, as they experimented and fervently discussed plans to become Tencastle's answer to the Fairport Convention.

For the survivors at lunchtime, Kissy and Bronwen raided the larder and rustled up a huge bowl of pasta and tomato sauce to supplement the bacon diet, and we made a successful attempt to avoid surplus beer packs being returned to the cash-and-carry.

"Would you like to stay for the afternoon?" I asked Sophie, as the deadline for the last bus drew nearer. "I can run you back later." One thing and another we hadn't really spent a lot of time together, awake at least.

"Thanks, Rob, but I don't really want to put you to the trouble."

"No trouble at all."

"You're very sweet, Rob."

Those words, I thought, were becoming the catchphrase for my unrequited love life. I waved goodbye to Sophie and reflected that we'd hardly got past first base, even though I'd slept with her, in a manner of speaking.

As I turned back to the cottage I remembered the plain white envelope which Dr Ambersham had given to me at the end of Friday's lecture. I'd stuffed it into my back pocket and forgotten about it during the whirlwind twenty four hours of the party.

"This is from Thomas Hall," he'd said. "I'm afraid we did not have your forwarding address, so the Warden asked if I could get it to you."

I'd no idea why Dr Nightingale should want to contact me. As far as I knew there weren't any unpaid bills and I certainly hadn't damaged any furniture or fittings in my old room. I slit open the envelope. Inside, a smaller one in pastel lilac bore handwriting that I recognised. Eagerly, I extracted its fragrantly scented notelet.

Dear Robert,

I was so delighted to receive your letter, and to know that you had received my note. I felt such a fool not even knowing your name.

I'm sorry I haven't replied sooner but it has been a difficult three months for me. My father did not come out of hospital. For thirty five years my parents had never been apart, and my mother has taken it very badly. It has affected her mind, and she keeps asking me when dad is coming home. She will be going into a nursing home soon, near to my aunt and uncle in Birkenhead. I'm not sure yet what's going to happen to our house.

Enough of my woes! On the bright side Tencastle have agreed that I can resume my course, probably next year. Will you still be there? I'm not sure I will be able to return earlier.

I hope you won't think it presumptuous, but if you would like to visit Chester, I'd be ever so happy to show you the city.

Please write.

Love,

Mary x x x

Wow!

Gobsmacked, I looked at her envelope again. Addressed to 'Robert Kiddecott, F106, Thomas Hall, Tencastle', it was postmarked 18th September – over a month ago! When I'd written to her back in June I'd unthinkingly assumed that my college address would remain the same. I wondered why it had taken so long for Hall to pass the letter on, and, indeed, why they had felt it necessary to open my private mail. It wasn't as if I could have been planning another unauthorised bed and breakfast.

I entered the cottage, grinning like a Cheshire cat.

"You look happy," said Jake. "Get the canary and the cream?"

CHAPTER TEN

Snowed Under

As the weather turned progressively colder through November, we discovered, after alternating between cosy warmth and arctic conditions in the bedrooms, that there was a very definite link between a fire in the lounge and hot radiators. Just as well, really, as winter drew ever closer.

"Hey, take a look at this!"

I opened one eye. "What?" I wasn't asleep, merely curled up cosily in bed, lamenting what might have been had Mary not called off my weekend visit to Chester at short notice. 'Unforeseen circumstances' she'd claimed, without elaboration. It had been a real downer, after our promising exchanges of letters over the previous month, ever since we had each other's correct address. There was some consolation in that I hadn't already bought a train ticket, having decided to put my trust in Jessica, and I had no reason to doubt that our reunion had been merely postponed.

"Incredible!" said Jake, pulling back the bedroom curtains fully.

My brain vaguely registered the grey light of morning. I crawled out of bed reluctantly and shuffled over to the window where Jake stood, mesmerised.

"Bloody hell!"

Where yesterday we could look out over the garden to the stream and woods, today the garden seat and shrubs were just vague shapes under the heavy blanket of snow, and the woods were hidden deep in the swirling whiteout.

"This wasn't forecast, was it?" I said. We'd had the occasional flurry over the weekend.

"They mentioned high winds and heavy showers for Sunday night, rain mostly."

Looking at the Siberian scene outside, I doubted if Tencastle itself had fared any better. Which brought another thought to my mind. "I think we'll be lucky to get into college today."

"Really?" The idea had obviously not occurred to Jake.

"You'd need a dog-sleigh, I reckon. No way Jessica could cope with this."

"Hmm."

I washed and dressed, leaving Jake still gazing at the snowscape.

Downstairs, I soon made a discovery. The electric kettle didn't work. Neither did the toaster. Nor the lights.

I swore under my breath. "Jake! We've got no electrics!"

He appeared at the top of the stairs, towel wrapped around his waist. "What do you mean?"

"Just that. No power, no electrics, nothing, zilch!"

"No TV?"

"No TV either."

"Shit! Could be the fuse."

"All of them?" I thought a moment. "Where's the fuse box anyway?"

"Dunno."

I had a look around in the kitchen and under the stairs while Jake made himself presentable, eventually finding the electricity meter in a cupboard in the front room. Not that it was much help, since there appeared to be no master trip switch.

Jake appraised the situation. "Suppose we'd better phone the power company."

I picked up the handset. "No tone," I said glumly.

"Wonder if our neighbours are off as well?"

I couldn't see that the information would actually help us, but I supposed it would do no harm to check that we weren't alone in our predicament.

"Coming, then?" Jake pulled on his parka, and the single pair of communal wellies.

We got as far as the front door. Some of the three-foot drift piled against it toppled onto the mat. We heaved the door closed again with difficulty. The situation wasn't quite as bad at the back, inasmuch as we could at least get out onto the patio. Round the side of the cottage a car-shaped snow sculpture sat where I'd parked Jessica. I hoped Owain had included antifreeze top-up in his service.

The snowfall was now much lighter, unlike the blizzard-like conditions earlier. The silence was quite erie. Nothing moved. No lights could be seen in the nearest cottage by the bridge. We returned to the warmth of the kitchen.

"Well, at least we've got means of heating and cooking!" I said. "We have got coal and wood, I suppose?"

Jake shrugged, "I think so. Expecting a coal delivery later this week, but there should be enough to last a few more days."

"Food?" I usually topped up our supplies on a Monday.

"We've plenty of cream crackers and sardines. Won't have any bread and milk though, unless we get out tomorrow."

I couldn't see that happening, not by car. "I don't suppose we've got any candles, either. An oil lamp would be nice, too."

"Couple of night lights left over from the party."

We pondered on our isolation from the rest of the world, which, looking on the bright side, could have been much worse if we'd been totally reliant on electricity.

There was the portable radio, though reception in the valley was unreliable, and I couldn't guarantee the state of the batteries since we usually plugged into the mains. Come to think of it, I'm not even sure it had any batteries.

Benji burst into the kitchen. "Man, have you seen the snow! It's up to the hedges! Must be five foot deep at least."

That, for Benji, was one hell of a long statement, even more remarkable for coming long before his usual appearance. It was not yet ten o'clock.

"Can't wait to get to work, man!"

I looked at Jake, to see if he also thought Benji had blown a fuse.

"Not much chance of that, Benji."

"What do you mean? Fantastic! – ice sculpture, snowmen …snow-women even!"

"What's the difference?" I asked.

"Snowballs," Jake murmured to me, "didn't you know?"

"I suppose you'll want to build an igloo as well," I said, with just a hint of sarcasm.

Benji took me seriously, "Great idea, man!"

"Watch out for polar bears," said Jake.

"You having me on?" Benji looked worried. I wonder what creatures inhabited his world. "Hey, why's the toaster not working?"

We explained, in plain non-scientific language.

I realised something else was missing from our community. "Anyone seen Dan this morning?"

"Still asleep?"

I doubted it. "He went into Tencastle on his moped yesterday teatime. Got a new girlfriend, I think. Anyone hear him come back?"

Jake shook his head.

A quick look upstairs confirmed that his bed hadn't been slept in.

"Christ, I hope he's all right!" I was more than a little concerned that he'd got caught out in the blizzard.

"Why not ring his girlfriend, man?"

I gave Benji a withering look. "One, I don't know his girl friend, two, the phone's not working."

"Oh, really?" He didn't seem at all bothered.

"We could send out a search party," Jake suggested.

I thought this idea was as impracticable as Benji's and said so.

Over the two or three months we'd been at the cottage, there had been a few occasions, at weekends, in particular, when all of us had been together all day, each doing his own thing. The prospect of being obliged to spend long hours, possibly days, together cooped up, with no escape, and, come evening, sitting in darkness with no television held little attraction. But, for the present, there were things to be done.

Jake commandeered the wellies again, so I had to make do with my walking boots.

"Hey guys, wait for me!" Benji called as we made for the back door.

We ignored him. We cleared the worst of the snow off the paving, brought a whole load of logs inside, with more stacked by the door, and filled the coal bucket. By which time, Benji had flattened a circular area where the lawn was supposed to be, and had begun to build a snowman and family. He abandoned this activity promptly when he saw us heading round the side, armed with shovel and tin tray.

"Will you cut blocks for our igloo, man?"

"Your igloo," Jake corrected. "We cut, you carry."

We found him an old panel of plywood in the shed. While we dug a path through the drifts Benji was as happy as an Eskimo carting roughly rectangular dollops of soft snow to the lawn and laying the foundations. Of building material there was no shortage, and it took us an hour of hard labour to clear a passage past Jessica and away from the front door. I was unsure whether to remove Jessica's virgin white mantle or leave it as insulation, since the cloud was breaking and I reckoned we were in for a clear, frosty night. I left her fully clad.

Jake and I found some packet soup to share for lunch, and generously left some for Benji, who continued industriously with his construction. Which, when it was finished, we were invited to admire.

It was recognisable as an igloo, just, if you used a bit of imagination. The conventional domed form had changed to a slightly concave conic structure, large enough, perhaps to house a pole cat or small husky. If they could have got inside, that is.

"Thought igloos were rounded," Jake commented.

"Oriental influence, man."

I didn't think the Inuits would be employing Chinese architects. "Shouldn't it have a door?" I asked, innocently.

"Ah, yes, I suppose so…" The idea obviously hadn't occurred to him. Still the snowman and his wife weren't complaining.

We caught the news headlines on Benji's pocket radio, which we persuaded him to share, for the common good. It told us nothing that we didn't already know or could guess; heavy snow falls and drifting over much of Wales, communities cut off, power and phone lines down, linesmen drafted in from other parts of the country, rescue services stretched to the limit, RAF and Naval helicopters, the SAS squadrons at Hereford cutting short their training exercises to help – the whole gamut of responses that are called upon whenever the weather springs one of its not uncommon surprises. No doubt some national tabloids would be blaming burning of fossil fuels and others forecasting a return to the ice age, whichever their respective editors thought would sell more papers.

Dining by candlelight may be okay in a posh restaurant with a pretty girl, but vegetable stew by single flickering night light with only your other male housemates for company didn't quite have the same appeal. We'd even had to amputate the nose from Benji's snowman as we were otherwise out of carrots. In humble dwellings in days of old, I'm sure that families occupied the long dark nights creatively, to produce a crop of babies in the early autumn. We didn't have that option. By eight o'clock, sitting just in the red glow of the wood stove at Jake's insistence to conserve the candle, conversation had been exhausted, telling ghost stories had quickly palled, and Jake's attempt to rouse a singalong with his banjo failed to strike a chord. By the light of the full moon we all retired to our beds at the earliest hour since we'd been in short trousers.

Next morning was Christmas-card idyllic – bright sun sparkling on crystal snow, undisturbed in the meadow and forest beyond our garden. There was even a plump robin puffing his chest out on an apple bough. But still no telephone or electricity. The radio reported restoration of services in the Aberystwyth and Carmarthen areas but for us that might well have been the moon. Our larder, too, would soon be competing with Mother Hubbard's. No bread, eggs or milk, one apple, half a banana and an onion, three tins, two without labels, and a few oddments of packet soups and pasta. Cream crackers we had aplenty. Even more seriously, we had no beer, having shared the last can of lager between us the previous evening.

"Well, what's it to be, guys?" Jake asked as we sat draining the weak tea from one bag. "Pull in our belts or set out for fresh supplies?"

"We could go hunting." Benji offered.

"What do you suggest? Cut a hole in the ice and catch a seal?" Jake teased.

"If the polar bears don't get there first," I added, and narrowly avoided the soggy teabag.

"You never take me seriously," Benji complained.

"That's not true," I fibbed.

"Only trying to be helpful, man!"

"Is there a shop closer than Tencastle itself?" Jake asked.

I tried to remember. One doesn't always notice these things when you're driving. "Not sure, Jake, but I think there's a newsagents and general store this side of the river. There's a few old houses and a one pump garage about half a mile from the bridge, or a mile from college."

"Decision, then, gentlemen," said Jake. "Do we go today or hold out for rescue tomorrow? Weather's clear today, tomorrow who knows? They may get a snowplough through, but guess this road won't be high priority. Rob?"

"Bugger all else to do, let's be positive."

"Benji?"

"Well, I had some more ideas for ice sculptures…"

"You could always open them to the public and make a few bob." No risk of another teabag projectile. Jake was guarding them like gold.

"Yeah, why not?"

"Not many tourists about, though," I added.

"Suppose not." Benji took himself seriously. "Okay, man, let's go for it. If only to get some some candles and do something useful, other than listen to you two rattling on."

"Like painting by moonlight?"

"Yeah." Sarcasm was lost on him.

"Next question. All of us, two of us or solo expedition?"

"No point in all of us going," I said.

"Two could carry more," A rare logical point from Benji.

"True. Draw lots or volunteer?"

No hands went up. Jake cut off three squares of paper from a notepad, scribbled something on each, folded them into an empty cereal bowl. Benji and I each pulled a piece out, and Jake opened the remaining chit.

"I go," he said.

Mine said stay. "It's you and Benji, then." In a way I was quite pleased with the outcome. I wasn't sure that Benji would be the best person to leave alone in the house – God knows what kind of artistic chaos he would have created in our absence – and I wasn't too keen either on trudging miles through the snow.

My suggestion of a shopping list was taken up, as was the pooling of such cash reserves as we had.

"Can I borrow your tennis racquet?"

"What on earth for, Jake?" And then the penny dropped, "Oh, no bloody way are you using my Slazenger for a snowshoe."

Last night's frost had given a hard crust to the snow, enough to bear an adult's weight without sinking in more than a couple of inches. Jake insisted on taking emergency supplies of a chocolate biscuit and a cream cracker with him.

"Well Captain Scott," I said to Jake, as the pair prepared to set out, "good luck!"

"Shackleton, if you don't mind. Scott didn't come back!"

At first I enjoyed the tranquillity. I made sure we had enough coal and wood in the house, cleaned the ashes out of the Rayburn and stove and scattered them over the paths we'd cleared. I cleared the snow from Jessica and debated whether to try starting her up.

The old girl was reluctant at first, giving barely a cough when I swung the handle. After a few more similar attempts she spluttered, backfired loudly and belched a cloud of pungent exhaust fumes – and died. One more swing and she was back to normal, ticking over with her normal chugga-chugga tone. I ran the engine for several minutes to warm her up – not that it did much for her interior as the heater was primitive and temperamental at the best of times.

These various tasks I found had kept me occupied for little more than an hour. Too soon, I thought, to expect the return of the expeditionary party, for whom I nevertheless began to feel some anxiety.

Faced with the snow drifts, we'd not got round to following up our intention to check the well-being of our neighbours, which I thus decided to do forthwith, if only to get some other human contact. Our paths had never crossed since we'd been at Ty Melin, though we had seen the odd person about.

The row of four terraced houses stretched along by the stream on the far side of the bridge, the end dwelling sideways on to the road and the others accessed by a broad track which led behind them. Wisps of smoke curled up into the clear air from three of the chimneys. Snow had been brushed off an old Morris Minor parked incongruously in front of a smart red Jaguar.

I tapped at the door of the first cottage. A shuffle of footsteps, and the top half of the door opened, a bald headed, wizened old man with hunched shoulders and white stubbly beard stood there puffing on a pipe. He looked at me warily, puzzled perhaps at having a young stranger calling.

"Hello," I said pleasantly. "I live just up the road. I was wondering, er, well … if you were all right here."

"No reason why we shouldn't be, young man."

"Er … well, our electricity and phone is cut off, and I … er, we're all right, but we thought, perhaps, we ought to check that you, er, were okay or, er, needed anything." I felt a bit of a fool, to be honest.

"That's nice of you to ask. We're always well prepared. It's not the first time we've been cut off since we've lived here." He decided that my visit was genuine and I wasn't on the scrounge. "Come on in, boyo, meet my good woman, now you're here."

"Thanks, but I don't mean …"

"Nonsense, come in to the warm." He opened the door fully, and I stepped into the warm fug of their parlour. "Bessie, this young man is from Ty Melin." A short plump woman with bright red-veined cheeks and a large green chequered apron looked up from the large mixing bowl in which she was kneading some dough.

"Come to check we're not suffering any hardship, would you know," he chuckled. "Sorry, I don't know your name."

"I'm Rob, Rob Kiddecott."

"Evan Jones." He held out his hand

"Pleased to meet you, Mr Jones."

"Oh, Evan, please, we don't stand on ceremony, here, do we Bessie?"

"Lord no." Her voice was surprisingly high pitched. "You'll not mind if I don't shake your hand."

Caked with flour as it was, I didn't mind.

"You'll have a cup of tea?" she said in a way which would have been churlish to decline.

I sat down on a padded dark wooden chair with arms and carved back. Bessie rinsed her hands at the enormous enamel sink then took down a half-gallon sized teapot from the dresser, scooped in ladles of tea and filled it from the enormous black kettle that stood steaming away on their solid fuel range.

"You're very warm and cosy in here," I said, conversationally.

"Oh, indeed we are," said Bessie. "Wouldn't be without my stove. No time for all these new fangled electric things."

"What about lighting?"

"Well, yes, we do have electric light, but before that came we made do very well with oil lamps," said Bessie.

"Still come in useful in times like this," Evan added. "But how are you managing?"

"Electricity is still off, but we have coal and wood for the Rayburn.

No oil lamps, though – we're making do with candles for the moment. My housemates have walked in to town today to stock up on a few things."

"How many of you up there?" asked Evan. "We see the odd coming and going, but, for students, you seem remarkably peaceful and quiet."

"Evan, don't be rude!"

"No offence, Mr … er, Evan. Apart from our little firework party the other night, we don't get many visitors, being this far from Tencastle."

"How did you end up out here, if you don't mind me asking?"

"The house belongs to a family friend of a housemate who's abroad for a couple of years. We're sort of looking after it." I'm sure he didn't want to hear the full saga. "How long have you lived here?"

"Nearly forty years now. I used to work in forestry before I retired."

"Still does, when he thinks I'm not looking," said Bessie.

"And what about the other cottages?"

"There's an old widower next door – lost his wife last year, a young couple at the end, though they're away at the moment – or can't get back, probably. And the other is a holiday home for some posh pair from London. I don't imagine they're enjoying being cooped up here anymore than we enjoy their company. Thankfully they rarely visit these days."

"You don't get on?"

"Too darn la-di-dah, and a couple of spoiled brats as well," said Evan with obvious feeling. "You know there used to be an old woollen mill up where you live," Evan continued, puffing clouds of fragrant tobacco smoke. Long gone, before my time, of course. These cottages were for the mill workers."

The odd chunks of masonry we'd found might well have been the remains of the foundations. I could imagine Jake wanting to do full scale excavations when – or if – I passed the information on to him. Thinking of Jake, I glanced at the old grandfather clock.

"I'd better be getting back. My friends should be home soon, and I don't want them sending out a search party for me!" I eased myself out of the chair.

"Okay, young man, nice meeting you – and you and your friends are welcome to pop in for a cup of tea and a chat." Evan rose to shake my hand again.

"Thank you. And you, too, Bessie, for the tea!"

With the sun shining on virgin snow on the hillsides it would have been a glorious day for skiing – if I'd felt so inclined, and, indeed, had all the necessary gear. Not that it was an activity in which I'd ever considered participating, but even so, I could imagine the appeal of being in a majestic white landscape amidst snow-covered peaks. Standing gazing back at the bridge, a well placed soggy snowball coldly interrupted my winter reverie, sending icy rivulets trickling down my back.

"You bastards!" I turned round to where Jake, Benji and Dan were lining up for another salvo. I hadn't heard them coming.

Any virgin snow outside our cottage was quickly violated in the ensuing furious fifteen minutes of snowball fight. Dan, to be fair, came over to my side to even the odds.

"Where have you been?" I asked, as we all retired indoors, dampened and exhausted.

"Staying in town with Wendy ..."

"Bloody typical!" Jake interrupted, "We're cut off in the wilderness, and he's playing around in a Wendy House!"

"Moron! As I was saying, I was intending to ride back, but Wendy didn't want me to risk it and offered ..."

"Lucky you!"

Dan threw Jake a murderous look, "... and suggested I stayed overnight. Wasn't much better next morning. I did try to ring, but couldn't get through."

"It's been off, like the power," I said.

On cue, in contradiction, the phone rang. Dan raised an eyebrow.

"For you," I said, handing the handset to him.

Trying not to eavesdrop too conspicuously, I turned to help Jake and Benji unpack their laden rucksacks. "Successful foraging?"

"Yes and no." Benji's reply was typically enigmatic.

"Well, no fresh milk or bread or fresh vegetables either," Jake explained, "but we've got various tinned stuff, some milk powder, margarine and flour..."

"Make our own bread, man!"

"Bought up all we could afford," said Jake. "Dan's got a few more things. We met him walking back, near the shop."

"Candles? Matches?" I asked.

"Matches, yes. Candles, well, all they had were a few fancy Christmas ones and a couple more night lights. They'll have to do."

I suppose it was better than sitting in complete blackout.

"That was Wendy," said Dan. As if we hadn't guessed. I didn't actually know anything about Wendy, not even her name, until a few minutes ago. It must have all come on rather sudden with her and Dan. "Just checking I got back okay. She's looking after my moped until the road's open again. Thought you said the phone wasn't working?"

"It wasn't, earlier."

"Perhaps the juice is on as well?"

I assumed that in Benji-speak meant electricity. Nothing from the light switch.

"What other goodies has Wendy given you?" Jake asked.

Dan missed the innuendo. "A homemade steak pie and some flapjacks, half a dozen eggs and a cabbage."

I was beginning to like Wendy. The steak pie wouldn't have been more than a snack for Desperate Dan, but was far more than our Daniel would manage. We offered to help him out.

"Pity Benji's vegetarian," I said. "Still, there's always cabbage soup."

"Aw, man, I could eat a horse right now."

We dined well that evening on pie, cabbage and pasta, with tinned peaches in evaporated milk to follow. Even the candles added to an atmosphere of warm camaraderie, now that we were reunited.

"Must offer our thanks to Wendy," Jake said, over coffee.

"Yes, when are we going to meet your girlfriend?" I asked.

"Wendy's not my girlfriend …"

"Then … Who?"

"She's her stepmother."

Dawn heralded another clear bright day, but any attractions, such as they may have been, of living in a winter wonderland were beginning to pall. Even Benji was out of creative ideas.

"Wonder how long we're going to be stuck here," he grunted. "Don't fancy trekking to Tencastle every day. "

"What were the conditions like in Tencastle?" I asked Dan.

"Nothing much moving on Monday and no power, but they'd pretty well cleared the main roads by yesterday, and Wendy said the lights had just come back on when she rang."

"Fancy some toast?" asked Jake.

"Sure, man!"

"Fine, but we haven't got any bread, remember?" I said.

"No problem, Rob, we'll make our own. Your idea, wasn't it, Benji?"

"Yeah!"

"Unleavened?" I asked. "Or did you buy any yeast?".

"What? Er…"

"You need yeast to make bread," I pointed out.

"Yes, yes! So you said! Let me think!" said Jake.

I personally would have settled for cooking up simple flour and water pancakes, but Jake was not one to take the straightforward option when a more complicated procedure could be devised.

"Yeast," he said, thoughtfully. "Beer and wine. Anything else got yeast in it?"

"Marmite?" suggested Dan.

"Yuk!" said Benji.

"The dregs from that old bottle of cabernet. Must be some yeast there. And that flagon of farm scrumpy you brought back with you, Rob, from Devon. Must be some live culture in that."

"Only culture they've got in Devon," said Dan.

"Pillock!"

"We'll add sugar to the dregs, keep it warm – and bingo!" Jake had a greater confidence in biotechnology than I had.

With a lack of suitable containers in which to decant the wine and cider we had no option but to consume them. It would have been a crying shame to pour it down the drain. Bread making had its attractions.

Faced with the lack of a suitable large bowl to take the two full bags of flour that Jake decided was necessary, he took advantage of our willingness, with nothing better to do, to lend a tipsy hand. "Right, whoever makes the best loaf, buys the first round – whenever we get to a pub again!"

"Do you mean the best loafer gets a pint from the rest?" Dan queried.

"Yeah, right!"

Two saucepans, one casserole dish and a fancy decorated fruit bowl were the only containers of suitable size available to us. Jake divided the flour out equally.

"Your own recipe, guys, use whatever you like as long as it's edible." Jake paused, "Any comments or questions?"

"We will need a hot oven," I said, remembering vaguely my mother's home baking.

We stoked up the Rayburn, and set to work.

None of us had any idea of the correct ratio of flour to water. I adopted the cautious approach of adding a little water at a time and mixing in the flour well to keep a stiff dough. Dan was absolutely plastered, literally – and probably alcoholically to boot – with an exceedingly gooey paste which he bulked out with a handful of Rice Krispies.

Jake attempted to remedy over-saturation by decanting the excess liquid into a tea cup and covered most of the kitchen table with grey sludge. On health and hygiene grounds I didn't dare look to see what he did to get his dough together again.

Benji, meanwhile, muttered something like, 'nut loaf, man' and was attacking half a packet of salted peanuts on a chopping board with a carving knife.

Jake had left the cider and wine dregs laced with a spoonful of sugar in the bottom of the Rayburn, hopefully to entice any stray yeast buds into fermentation. The brownish residue he presented us showed a few tentative bubbles.

I declined my share.

Being chemically inclined, I'd remembered another way of generating the carbon dioxide to make the loaf rise. Unfortunately, I couldn't find any baking powder or bicarbonate of soda in the larder, but upstairs I had some Andrews' Liver Salts which I was sure had basically the same ingredients.

"'Scuse me a mo," I said, and palming an egg cup, headed for the bathroom.

It was obvious that not all our loaves could be put in the oven at the same time, particularly as we only had one proper baking tray and a round cake tin, the latter being the only possible option for Jake's slop.

Benji's solid mass shared the oven, and kept its shape when eventually taken out. It did look, well, more or less bread shape and colour. Jake's bake, however, had set like concrete, and crumbs fractured all over the kitchen when he tried digging it out with a knife. Took him ages, too, cleaning the tin ready for Dan's dough.

I bided my time. I was pretty sure that I'd get a rapid rise once I added my secret ingredient, and so I wanted to get the advantage of a short blast in a high temperature oven. Doubtful of quite what residual flavour I might get from the Liver Salts, I surreptitiously added a teaspoonful of curry powder to my mix.

Lunch was an interesting experience. We all agreed that every one of us should sample all the products, and, hopefully, the bread winner would be acclaimed by mutual consent.

Even Jake was not prepared to risk his teeth on more than a tentative gnaw at his rock bread, but he was magnanimous in defeat. "Missing some vital ingredient I think," he said. Like yeast.

While Dan's was at least edible, if somewhat crunchy, rather like self-toasting sliced bread, Benji had, as befits an artist, created something quite unique. It would have been wrong to call it bread since any attempt to cut it caused the disintegration of the delicate matrix which held the large lumps of coarsely chopped peanuts into a pile of crumb. It was, however, quite tasty if you liked peanuts.

My acclaim as master baker was in no doubt from the moment the loaf emerged from the oven. It had exceeded all my expectations in the amount it had risen to form a rounded light brown dome, which, on slicing, revealed a very open texture of a golden yellow hue.

"Wow, man, how did you do that?"

"Family recipe, Benji," I lied glibly. "It's best served with cold meats, definitely not a bread and jam loaf."

"Will corned beef do?"

"Fine."

We tucked in with gusto. I must admit, it didn't taste half bad.

"Strange flavour," said Jake, into his third slice. "Slightly oriental touch, I think."

"What's the recipe called?" said Dan

"Indian liver bread."

"First I've heard of it. Nice though."

Two events later that day indicated that an end to our isolation from the outside world was in sight. During the afternoon, a tractor with a mechanical shovel appeared at the top of the hill, and by the time the light was beginning to fade, it had cleared a single track past our cottage and just over the bridge. In the evening electricity was restored. Our plight, or, rather, that of other remote communities in mid-Wales was still the main headline of the news. The forecast also indicated an end to the cold weather, with a warm front moving up from the South West.

The thaw, when it came, was sudden and dramatic. By morning the snow had all but disappeared except where the digger had piled it by the roadside and our placid frost-bound stream had become a raging torrent, already washing several feet over the bottom of our garden. After breakfast it started raining cats and dogs.

Toying with the idea of taking a trip into town for fresh supplies, I braved the deluge to check whether Jessica's access to the road was now clear. I was barely aware of anyone calling at first, but as soon as I looked down towards the bridge the danger facing our neighbours was all too plain. The terraced cottages were undoubtedly flooded, piles of dumped snow funnelling melt water and rain towards the already swollen river. On the far side of the bridge the road was virtually impassable with slushy ice floes on swirling water and on our side the carriageway was already flooded across its whole width to a depth of at least a foot. A small group of people, Evan amongst them, huddled on the bridge, a solitary umbrella giving little protection from the downpour. They waved and called when they saw me.

Acknowledging them with a raised hand, I dived inside.

"Jake, Dan, come quickly! There are people trapped by the river."

Dan wasn't fully dressed but Jake grabbed a coat and ran with me down the road.

"Evan," I shouted. "Are you all out of the houses?"

"Old man Jenkins won't leave. He's upstairs, but the water's getting deeper."

I could see Bessie, trying to comfort a young girl, and, presumably her mother. A tall fellow holding the hand of little boy looked back at the houses and then at us. They were all drenched.

Dan ran down to join us.

"Dan, best go back and ring 999. There's an elderly man trapped in his house, as well as those on the bridge."

"We need to do something now," said Jake.

"We're calling the emergency services," I called over. "But can you wade through?"

Evan looked at his wife, who gave a slight shake of her head.

"That water looks pretty deep to me," Jake whispered. "Rob, have you got a rope in your car?"

"Yes. What have you got in mind?"

"If you back Jessica down to the water's edge, and secure the rope to her, I'll take the other end through to those on the bridge and lead them back one at a time."

Jake saw that I had doubts. "Come on, the water must be less than waist deep at the moment, and the rope is just security in case anyone loses their footing. Unless you've got a better idea?"

I hadn't.

Dan re-appeared. "Benji's phoned, but they're, well, flooded with calls, but they'll be as quick as they can."

I outlined Jake's idea.

"I'll get Benji to stoke up the fires and dig out all the spare blankets. They're going to be pretty miserable and cold. I'll join you shortly."

I'd never untwined the yellow nylon tow-rope I'd thought prudent to buy soon after I acquired Jessica, in case Owain's guarantee of reliability was misfounded, but it looked long enough for Jake's plan. Jessica, after freezing and soaking since the weekend, took a bit of coaxing and cursing to fire up ready for action. I reversed the hundred yards or so downhill, and stopped with the back wheels inches from the water's edge. Jake found a secure point under the boot to attach the rope.

"Keep the engine running, and be prepared to edge forward gently if we have to pull anyone out."

Jake stripped off his jeans, looped the rope round his waist, and waded into the flood. He was soon knee deep, and it was obvious that he experienced a deceptively strong current as he neared the bridge itself where the water rose almost to his groin. Evan and the younger man took his arms to help him onto the tarmac of the bridge. No-one seemed too eager to make the first crossing back, but, with no option other than staying where they were soaking wet anyway, the man hoisted his daughter onto his shoulders and tied the rope around himself. Jake led the way, holding on to the rope tightly.

Dripping wet, the father leant against Jessica's door. "Thank you, thank you so much!" he said, with deep sighs of relief. Dan made to lead them both up to the cottage, but the father said gently to his daughter, "You go on with the young man, I'm going to wait and make sure Mummy and Timmy are all right."

Jake meanwhile had returned to the bridge, and was coaxing Bessie to the water's edge, amidst cries of, "Oh my goodness, oh my goodness!" Slowly she waded in guided by Jake. By the time she'd reached safety, the waters were lapping round Jessica's rear tyres. I moved the car forward as little as I could.

The mother took all of the efforts of Jake and Evan to persuade her to leave the bridge. Her son was crying and she herself was on the verge of hysteria. Jake volunteered to carry the little lad and to follow closely behind her, holding on to her safety harness of rope. She screamed when the icy water reached above her waist and, but for Jake's persistence, would have turned back. Tentatively she began to edge forward again, her breath coming in deep sobs. She was through the deepest part and on a rising slope when she tried to look back at her son behind her, and lost her footing.

"Hold on, HOLD ON!" yelled Jake, as he, too, struggled and failed to maintain his balance.

"Move Jessica!" Dan shouted, and then, "NO! Stay on the bridge!" In my mirror I caught a glimpse of Evan about to plunge in to help.

I could feel the extra pull on the car and carefully allowed Jessica to take the strain, balancing the accelerator and clutch, and edging forward inch by ever so slow inch.

Dan waded in to help the woman who was slowly being dragged to the water's edge "Stop, Rob, for God's sake STOP!" She lay there like a beached porpoise.

Her husband had rushed into the water to help his son, who, with Jake, had toppled over into the flooded stream. The boy clung on for dear life to Jake's coat, while Jake splashed and scrabbled around to regain his footing.

Dan helped the woman to her feet. Her shoulders were heaving with shock and shivering. "Let's get you all into the warm. Jake, take them back up and get dry yourself, I'll go and help the last one through. Rob, keep Jessica ready, just in case."

Jake, also shivering and dripping, was in no state to argue. He had already been in and out of the water for over half an hour before his total immersion.

My immediate concern was for Evan, who, being short of stature and with water levels still rising, might well have a real problem getting through. Dan, too, was much more slightly built than Jake. The only consolation was that it had stopped raining and the cloud base seemed higher.

Dan tapped on my window and pointed upwards. Jessica's clattering engine had masked the sound of an approaching helicopter. I got out and we both waved furiously to attract attention, though I think they'd already seen us, as they started circling back. Dan raised his right hand and waved his finger in the direction of the bridge, and tried to show with his left hand the water level up to his chin. It might have been an exaggeration, but it got the message across.

Hovering high above the bridge, a man was lowered and secured Evan, lifting him the few yards across the flood to where we stood. Stoically, he looked none the worse for his ordeal.

"You've got the others out?" asked his rescuer.

I nodded.

"Brave of you, but very risky."

"We weren't sure how soon help might come," Dan said.

"Well, you're okay now?"

Evan spoke up. "Mr Jenkins, my neighbour, he is still in his cottage. He's not very mobile and insisted on staying put."

"Okay. I can check on them, but I don't think I'll be able to get him out of there myself. May have to get the fire boys up here."

"What's it like in Tencastle?" I asked.

"River's burst its banks to the south, but no flooding in the town itself, as far as we can see. The roads are still passable with care. If the rain holds off, the next couple of hours should see things getting better."

"Thanks."

"Right, let's see about this other chap. And, well done, lads!"

Tempting as it was to watch the rest of their operation, the prospect of getting warm and dry again was far more appealing. Dan and Evan walked up while I got Jessica going.

The changing room of the Welsh rugby squad after hot showers couldn't have produced a more steamy atmosphere than that of our kitchen. Soggy garments airing over the chair backs by the Rayburn, and, elsewhere in the house, over every radiator. In the lounge the family foursome and Bessie huddled round the stove, wrapped in an assortment of blankets and jumpers. I recognised my old fairisle polo-necked sweater. Benji was doing a sterling job with mugs of hot soup and the left-overs of our homemade bread, and I encouraged him to keep the kettle on for Dan and I when we'd changed into dry clothes.

Warm and safe, everybody's spirits had perked up by the time Dan and I, Jake as well, came downstairs again. Benji even had the youngsters giggling over his antics with a puppet he'd made – I'd never really imagined him as a children's entertainer – while Bessie had taken charge of the refreshments.

"I don't know how Bruce and I can thank you enough." The young woman still looked pale and nervous, but was no longer tearful. Someone had liberally tended to her few abrasions with sticking plaster. "You all deserve a medal!"

"Indeed," said her husband. "Alice was terrified that Timmy was going to be swept way. I'm glad that Miranda was already in here." Strangely, he seemed almost ready to weep. "I don't even know your names, to thank you."

We introduced ourselves, with a brief potted history of our student status.

"What exactly happened this morning?" I asked.

"First thing we knew someone was hammering on our door," said Bruce.

Evan explained. "I'd got up early as usual and found water seeping through our front door. We're slightly higher than the other cottages so I guessed they would already be more badly affected. Outside, my old Morris was sitting in several inches of water and their car likewise." He turned to Bruce and Alice.

"We were going to drive back to London today," said Bruce, wistfully. "Supposed to have gone on Monday."

"I thought if we could get across to your house, we might be able to phone my Bessie's sister," Evan continued. "She's in Llanbeddrod."

"You haven't got a phone?"

"No need, with the box just by the bridge. No much use half full of water, now."

"Ours wasn't working," said Alice.

"So, we paddled out. It wasn't too bad, then just over our ankles, but when we got onto the bridge it looked so much worse on your side. That's when we saw you. Rob."

"What about the Mr Jenkins?"

"I had the devil's own job to rouse him – he's half deaf – but he was determined to sit it out. Stubborn as a mule, just like his wife."

"I presume you must have been flooded before in the years you've been there?" I said.

"Strange to say, we haven't. Been pretty close a few times, and we've certainly been snowed in before, but we've never seen anything like this." Evan paused. "The dumping of that snow, the rapid thaw and the heavy rain, it was all too much for the stream to cope with."

"What will you do now?"

"You mean, tonight, or the future?"

"Sorry, we aren't intending to turn you out in the cold again."

Actually, Dan had inadvertently raised the question of coping overnight with a houseload of bodies. Without any spare clothing.

"I realise that. No, if I can use your phone, I'll ask my sister-in-law to put us up for the night, and we'll go back to the cottage when the water's gone down, dry out, get on with things. I don't think we'll be moving until they carry us out in a box."

"No problem, you know the number?" I said.

"Excuse me, gentlemen, but could I also make a couple of calls?" Bruce said quietly, as Evan dialled. "We're very grateful for your hospitality, but I think it would be unfair to expect you to cope with all four of us overnight."

I had wondered.

"Your sister will be with us in about an hour," Evan said to his wife.

Bruce spent several minutes on the phone. From his expression it seemed things weren't going quite the way he required.

"Rob," he said, when he eventually put the phone down. "Could I impose on your goodwill and ask one more favour?"

"Uh huh," I replied, without committing myself.

"I've managed to get a room at the Rivers Hotel for the night, but I can't get through to the taxi firm, and they don't seem to have heard of car hire in Tencastle."

Which didn't surprise me. The likes of Hertz and Avis wouldn't know Tencastle from Timbuctoo, and the three taxis that serviced the town were probably themselves stranded or broken down.

"Would you be willing to run us into Tencastle?"

"If the road's okay, I don't mind. I'm afraid Jessica's no match in comfort for a Jag, though."

"Jessica? Oh, your car, you mean. I don't think we've got a lot of choice, have we?"

"What about your Jag?" asked Jake.

"Well, it's not going anywhere today. We'll get the train to London tomorrow and I'll pop down again next weekend to sort it out and clear up."

By the time we had all dried out and our refugees had reclaimed their clothes, the afternoon was drawing on. Evan and Bessie were the first to depart, sister arriving in a Land Rover every bit as ancient as its owner.

"What's the condition of the roads?" I asked. I suspected Jessica wouldn't enjoy swimming.

"Not too bad, a few large puddles across the road, but you'll manage," said his sister, looking at Jessica appreciatively. She probably appeared like a blithe young teenager in comparison to the Land Rover.

Perhaps to prove that she was as good as a Jaguar any day, Jessica was on her best behaviour. Started first time, and purred contentedly all the way to town, even splashed happily through puddles like a tomboy. It was fortunate that the kids were still small, otherwise Jessica would have needed elastic sides. Even so I think the family were glad when Jessica pulled up on the The Rivers forecourt, not in the least embarrassed to be seen in the company of a silver Mercedes and yellow Cadillac.

"I won't forget what you and your friends have done for us," said Bruce as he shook hands. The children solemnly did likewise.

Alice gave me a hug. "Thank you, from the bottom of my heart." Quite emotional, really.

CHAPTER ELEVEN

Ragtime

My pleasure at finding a belated Christmas card from Mary on our return to the cottage had soon dissipated in the discomfort of unrelenting, bitingly cold January north-easterlies. The unexpected £25 windfall in the form of a cheque from Bruce had also been effectively dissipated by the Ty Melin household on essentials, like food, fuel and beer.

Among the group of us gathered in the Union refectory over lunch, our banter was uncharacteristically muted and the usual avenues of conversation seemed too well-trodden. We were trying to stay in the warmth as long as possible before venturing back to the main college for the afternoon session. Dilly had already left before I'd made up my mind whether to be positive and ask her for a date or pursue romance at a distance with Mary.

Dan sauntered in, dumped his duffle coat on a chair and drew up another between Sunny and Sophie as Dicky Swift brought over more coffees.

"Hey, have you seen that Rag's been re-instated?" Dan said, waving the student broadsheet, Llais y Castell, which appeared more or less fortnightly in term time.

"I didn't know that Llais had been suspended," said Dicky, unenthusiastically.

"No, no, not the paper, you moron, Rag Week!"

"What's that?" I enquired innocently.

Dan seemed quite astonished at my ignorance. "You don't know? It's a fund-raising week when students do all sorts of daft things in the name of charity. Every college has one."

"Except Tencastle," observed Sunny.

"Yes, that's the point," replied Dan. "Seems we used to have one until a few years ago."

"So what happened?" I asked.

Dan scanned the paper. "It says here that Rag was banned by the college authorities under pressure from the Mayoress."

"Why?"

"Goliath had an erection."

Dan had our undivided attention.

"Go on!"

"Some boffin students had got massive sponsorship by proposing to fit Goliath with a prosthetic, operated by a sensor when anyone approached his plinth. Unfortunately the Lady Mayoress had chosen Goliath as a backdrop for a photo call with the local MP. Seems she got too close!"

"Made her day, did it?" chortled Dicky.

"Not exactly. Particularly when the caption *Mayoress meets the member for Tencastle* appeared in the local newspaper under a photo of Goliath's giant todger dwarfing the daffodils in Her Worshipful's hat"

"I take it she was not amused," I said.

"She went ballistic, apparently. Demanded that Students' Union be closed down and that the perpetrators of the prank be expelled forthwith, not to mention the threat of legal action against the Press. Fortunately, the MP was of a different political persuasion and also had a sense of humour. He managed to calm things down. But Rag was banned and the boffins forced to apologise, even though they raised a record sum."

"So why the change of heart?"

"Change of council, it says here," Dan continued. "Her Ladyship got unceremoniously dumped at the last election in favour of the Plaid Cymru candidate. He's a Tencastle alumnus."

"So when is this Rag all supposed to be happening," I asked, conversationally.

Dan scanned the paper again. "February. About five weeks time, just before the elections for President and the other Union bigwigs."

"That should liven things up a bit. They're usually so full of hot air it's a wonder that they don't blow away like a balloon," Dicky said cynically.

"I've been thinking," said Dan on the way back to the cottage.

"Well, that makes a change!"

"No, no, seriously. We ought to try and do something for Rag."

"Why?"

"Well, why not? It's all for a good cause." Dan in his more sober moments had the makings of a social conscience. "Besides, it should be a bit of fun."

"What have you got in mind?"

"Oh, I don't know. I hadn't got that far."

Dan's plans might have remained unconceived, not even stillborn, had I not opened my big mouth over supper.

It was one of those rare occasions where all four of us were not only in the cottage but actually sharing a mealtime together, courtesy of Jake, who'd been given as a Christmas present a book on budget cookery for students.

"Curry Tuesday!" he'd announced at the weekend. "I'm trying out a recipe for four."

The rest of us had exchanged expressions of concern.

"And you want us as guinea pigs?" I'd asked.

"Why can't you just divide the quantities by four?" Dan had suggested.

"Oh come on, guys, it's not every day you get an offer of free nosh. Besides, it's economy of scale – it's cheaper to buy in bulk than for one individual." Jake, as always, sounded convincing even if his logic was questionable. "And, Benji, it's vegetarian," he'd added.

Dan and I had clubbed together to buy a large bottle of cheap red plonk. Benji would probably have made decorative candles if he had thought of it.

Jake's culinary efforts were surprisingly good, and we were feeling pleasantly warm and mellow.

"What's the news from town, then?" asked Jake.

"Nothing much," said Dan. "Except Rag's been reinstated."

"Yes, and Dan's had an idea. Well almost, at least," I contributed.

"Oh," said Jake, with interest. "And what's that?"

"Dunno really," Dan shrugged. "Just thought it would be nice to do something for Rag."

"Why not do a Mummers' Play, man?"

Now for Benji to make any suggestion which didn't involve plastering something with oils and acrylics was a noteworthy event indeed.

"What's that?" The three of us said almost in unison.

"A Mummers' Play," he repeated, when our laughter had subsided. "You know, dress up in rags and tatters, like in disguise."

"Why?" I asked.

"We do it back home in Gloucestershire," he went on.

"Well that probably explains it," Dan commented in a loud aside, 'it' being left ambiguously undefined.

Benji warmed to his topic, undeterred. Must have been the wine.

"You must know the story of St George and The Dragon. That's what it's all about, man, ritual drama! Triumph of good over evil! Symbolic death and resurrection!"

Heady stuff for a fundraising event. I had a practical objection, however.

"I can't see the natives being too keen on their Welsh Dragon being slaughtered by an English Saint, even in the name of charity."

"It wasn't a Welsh dragon and St George wasn't English!" Benji protested animatedly.

"I think those points might just get overlooked. With an increase in support for Plaid Cymru, patriotism's quite rife at the moment."

"Why not make it King George?" Dan suggested. "Or, better still, St David – slaying the English Lion with a leek and a daffodil!"

"I think the locals might get uppity if we poked fun at their patron saint," I pointed out.

"Christ, Rob! You're really putting a dampener on the whole project, aren't you!"

Dan himself was getting uppity. I refrained from reminding him that all we had so far was a suggestion, not a project, and attempted to soothe any bruised egos. "I'm sorry, I was just playing the devil's advocate."

"That's it, that's it!" Some spark had obviously lit Jake's enthusiasm. He'd hitherto merely observed our exchanges.

We looked at him.

"That's IT!" he said again for emphasis. "The Devil's Advocate – we'll call the play the Devil's Advocate. It'll be a Mummers-in-Law Play!"

"Um, I don't see the connection ..." I began.

If he'd not been pacing the room, expanding his ideas, he might have noticed that we were less than enthusiastic about 'it'. But Jake was on a roll. "We'll rope in some others from the Drama Society or Folk Club!. We'll have to rehearse of course. Benji can write the script."

"Whoa, man! Hold your horses!" Benji broke in, "I'm a ruddy painter not a writer! I don't know one end of a pen from the other!"

But Jake was unstoppable. "No problem! Just give us some background and we'll do it," he said. "You can be our technical adviser, Benji, design and paint the sets and whatever. Brilliant idea! Brilliant, all of you!"

"Jake, there aren't any sets! It's done in the open air, pub car parks," Benji objected again, but less forcefully.

"Never mind! Paint the masks or costumes then!"

This idea seemed to make Benji happy. With memories of an earlier public performance, I put in my twopenn'orth before we got too far down the painting path.

"One thing, Jake, I'm not painting my face black again, or any other colour for that matter."

Misgivings we certainly had about Jake's proposals but, aided by a bottle of sherry which Benji had rescued from a party, we began to warm to the project, in principle at least. Jake suggested that I should be casting director and Dan in charge of publicity. I presumed he saw himself as executive director, producer and impresario-in-chief, but as we didn't have much of a clue otherwise as to what we were going to do, there didn't seem much sense in arguing over the credits.

First, however, we needed the dramatis personae and plot.

"Benji, you're the expert, how many different characters were there in your play?" I asked.

"Aw, hell, man, it was several years ago!" He buried his face in his hands, elbows on the table. "Let me see, there was St George, of course, a Turkish Knight, Father Christmas and, er, a prince of something …"

"Prince of Wales?" Jake suggested.

"Black Prince?" Dan contributed.

"Prince Charming?" I chipped in.

"That's Cinderella, you pillock!" Dan objected.

"No, no, at least I don't think so!" Benji scratched his head, his hand disappearing into the shock of black hair. "There was definitely a doctor … and, er, also a Valiant Soldier, Bold Captain, I think he was called, … or was it Big Slasher?"

"Piss artist, was he?" asked Dan, mockingly.

Benji glared at him.

"Is that all?" I enquired.

"Um, I'm not sure, man! Someone to wheedle money out of the crowd."

"Sounds the most vital role to me," said Dan.

"And the plot?" asked Jake.

"Oh, God, man, now you're asking! They all seemed to fight each other and the doctor brought us to life again with his magic potion. And they finished with a little dance using their swords."

I thought this seemed to be getting more and more complicated. Acting was one thing, sword dancing quite another.

"Can't you remember any of the dialogue?" prompted Jake.

"Not really, it was all supposed to be in rhyme. Sort of couplets, you know. They used to ad lib quite a lot, though."

"Well that certainly gives us scope for improvisation," Jake declared.

"Anything else?" I asked. There were barely enough bones even for a skeleton plot.

"I remember every character walked on with the line, 'In comes I.'"

"That's helpful," Dan said, with more than a hint of sarcasm.

We quizzed Benji further. He was quite positive about the costumes of paper ribbons, but otherwise he'd evidently already given us such usable information as he possessed. It didn't stop us tossing various ideas about until the early hours of the morning, however, and even though we'd got very little concrete down on paper, we felt we had already made a positive contribution to Rag.

I wasn't around the house very much over the following week, and whenever I saw Jake he seemed deep in thought and uncharacteristically uncommunicative. Neither Dan nor Benji brought up the topic of ragging or mumming at the occasional shared breakfast time, so I assumed that our ethereal drama had died a virtual death.

I should have known better. Eventually Jake collared me as soon as I'd tucked up Jessica for the night.

"We've got it!" he exclaimed, waving some sheets of paper at me.

"We have?"

"A working script! Already approved by Benji, so you can start casting right away!"

"Hmm." Right away I was far more interested in warmth, food and sleep.

"Now here's how it goes," Jake persisted, following me into the kitchen. "The Sharif of Nottingham wants his daughter to marry Pincer Wayles, and so does his mother, but he's queer and fancies the Valiant Soldier, and so does she, but he's supposed to be engaged to Candy-Ella, and his father's the Bald Captain. He's not happy with his son being compromised, and her father's got the hots for the Turkish Delight, and …"

"Whoa! Sheriff of Nottingham? Cinderella? Haven't you got your genres mixed?"

"It's all quite simple, really, you see, 'king George, he's …"

"The father of the Prince of Wales?"

"No, no, yes! And Candy-Ella."

"Hang on, hang on, Jake, my head hurts!" God, and I thought *Coronation Street* relationships were complicated. "Sounds more like a bloody pantomime!"

"That's the point, Rob!"

"It is?"

"Yes. Now, when Mother finds her son is slain she calls Doctor Huw and he …"

"Jake, just give me the script, and I'll look at it in the morning," I pleaded.

"But …"

"Tomorrow. I promise."

While I wasn't all that familiar with pantomimes and knew even less about Mummers' plays, Jake had done quite a good job in producing a workable script full of double entendre and corny puns. I was glad, however, that I'd stopped him from trying to explain the plot and the interpersonal relationships of the characters. Even with the full text it wasn't easy.

Jake had been hanging around all day, reluctant to ask me the obvious question but eager nevertheless to hear my verdict. By teatime he could contain himself no longer.

"Well?"

"Well what?"

"You know what! What do you think of it?"

"Yes, it's okay."

"Okay? Just okay?" Jake sounded most disappointed.

"Pretty good, Jake, to be honest!" I smiled. "Well done!"

Jake's face split into a wide grin, white teeth flashing, "Thought you'd like it. I spent some time tracing some traditional mumming texts, to try to get, well, a sort of feel for them. Including Benji's one from Gloucester."

"What part had you got in mind for yourself?" I asked.

"Oh, I thought I'd make a good Sharif. He's supposed to be of Turkish origin." Jake grabbed an onion-shaped lampshade which was waiting to be rehung, and slapped it on the top of his head. "Do I look Turkish?"

"Um…" There were several epithets that came to mind. Turkish wasn't one of them.

"And for my daughter, that's the Turkish Delight," he explained. "How about that ravishing young Pakistani girl, Sundra, or whatever her name is."

"Sunny," I said. "She's Iranian, I think."

"Near enough!"

A good choice actually. I could see her in the role, belly button bare and all. And Sunny, I was sure, would be up for it.

"Have you thought about the other parts?" I asked.

"Not really, though I think the battleaxe Mother Wayles should be a big fella in a frock."

"Ye…es." I wasn't sure I'd appreciate this part of my casting responsibility.

"And her son, Pincer, needs to be really camp. He moves mincingly, crab-like, hence his name."

"Right." More problems.

"Doctor Huw, now he ought to be Welsh." Jake thought for a moment and asked, "What part do you fancy?"

"None of those, thank you! If anything, I'll be the Valiant Soldier!" Who won his true love in the end.

Dan burst into the dining room, unstrapping his shiny white crash helmet. "Bloody perishing out there!" he complained. "Freeze the ba... What? What's up?" he asked, in consternation, seeing us staring at him.

"In comes I, the Bald Captain!" we both chanted simultaneously.

Surprisingly, finding enough volunteers to join our company of fools was much easier than I'd anticipated. We'd not put up any recruiting posters, and only mentioned the idea to a few friends, mostly in the Folk Club and the Drama Society, but word spread like wildfire. I was accosted on several occasions by strangers seeking an audition for our grand production.

What actual word had spread, however, was less clear, for it became obvious at the meeting which Jake arranged for all interested parties that there were more than a few misconceptions.

"No, I'm sorry, we're not attempting a dramatisation of the Mabinogion," explained Jake to one ardent Welshman. "Whatever the hell that is," I heard him mutter under his breath.

"I'm sure Shakespeare had little influence on this play," he replied to a seriously anorexic female who'd mistakenly thought Jake was playing Othello.

"I'm well aware that a pantomime in March would be unseasonable, thank you."

"I think your experience as lead soprano in Madame Butterfly might be misplaced in our little production," said Jake tactfully to a diva whose looks, let alone her voice, could have shattered a glass at forty paces.

As various illusions were dispelled, the assembly of nearly three dozen prospective thespians dwindled to single figures.

With only three weeks to go before Rag, the casting was finally completed. I had no problem in filling several roles from our circle of friends. Huw Parry-Evans and Dicky Swift, my former corridor mates in Thomas Hall, almost volunteered to play the Doctor and 'king George, while Kissy as the beautiful Candy-Ella and Sunny as the Turkish Delight were always going to be game for a laugh. Trevor Brewer was a surprise discovery – he'd obviously come out of his shell since his first teaching practice at Tencastle and gave us an entirely convincing performance as the gay Pincer Wayles. Jake's idea of a transvestite Mother Wayles proved beyond our collective powers of persuasion, however, and we were really struggling to find someone

177

even half suitable to fill the role, until Trevor came up with a suggestion.

"What about Liz Burke?" he'd said to me, at the end of a chemistry seminar.

I'd looked at Liz as she made her way to the laboratory door. Physically, she would be ideal for the part, with thighs like tree trunks and upper limbs to match. With a chest as flat as the Norfolk Broads, however, she'd need to borrow a D-cup bra and a couple of balloons.

"I wouldn't have thought it would be her scene," I'd said. "She always seems very quiet and reserved." Even on the minibus school run in our first term it had not been easy to draw her into conversation..

"I think you would be surprised." Trevor obviously knew her better. "Shall I ask her?"

Jake was adamant that we should all be properly rehearsed. He had persuaded the landlord of the Castle to let us use the back room gratis in exchange for the promise of consumption of large quantities of beer.

"Thank you all for coming," he addressed the first full meeting of the cast. "And especially to Liz, who has kindly stepped in at short notice."

Liz blushed.

"Now, we have a duty to the Rag, to our audience and to ourselves," Jake declared, pompously I thought. "We shall make this a Rag to remember!"

Not like Goliath I hoped.

"What about costumes?" asked Dicky Swift.

"Ah, yes..." Jake was caught unprepared, for a moment. "Yes, I was coming to that. What do you suggest, Benji?"

Benji had been sketching furiously on the back of an envelope and was equally unprepared. "Sorry, man?"

"What would your suggestions be about costumes?"

"Oh, definitely, man. I agree. Good idea!"

"How about we all make our own?" suggested Kissy.

"Thanks for that, Kissy, I think that's along the lines of what Benji was proposing." Jake would have made a good politician. "Use your imagination! Use your initiative!" he exhorted, as if he'd had the idea all the time, "We'll have a dress rehearsal in two week's time!"

Having topped up our glasses – the first of several refills during the evening – we got down to the serious business of reading the script. Not that serious was the appropriate word; for several characters it was the first time they'd seen the script, and Trevor and Huw soon discovered that laughing and drinking at the same time were incompatible. To Jake's consternation, ad-libbing as well as considered suggestions on changes to the dialogue blossomed as the evening and the beer consumption progressed.

"Blessed if I can remember now what I am supposed to be saying," Trevor grunted as we stumbled out of the pub at closing time.

"Just stick to the script," I said. I'm sure Jake would have approved.

The chill February air hit me with a sobering thought. I wasn't sober, nor was I reeling drunk, but I'd probably downed about four pints. And I'd brought Jessica, of course.

"Where did you leave the car?" asked Dan, emerging from the Castle, followed by Benji and Jake.

"By the park," I replied. "But there's a problem," I added quickly as the three of them began to head off. "I've had too much to drink."

That stopped them in their tracks. From their faces I could see that they relished the prospect of the three mile walk no more than I did.

"Aw, come on, man," said Benji. "There are never any coppers around Tencastle on a Monday night!"

"It's not your licence at risk!"

"Suppose you're not actually driving," mused Jake, obviously hatching a plan.

"There's no way any of you are going to drive!" I said, to forestall his scheming. "You're all as pissed as I am. Besides which, none of you have got a licence anyway!"

"No, no, that's not what I meant. If you've not got the engine on, you wouldn't actually be driving, would you?"

"Wouldn't I?" I wasn't sure the police would see it that way. Besides which, there was a more practical concern. "So how do we get Jessica to go? Pedal?"

"No, push."

We all looked at Jake as if he were mad.

"Aren't you forgetting there's a bloody great one-in-five hill between here and Penybont!" yelled Dan, incredulously.

"No, listen! We pretend Jessica's broken down, we push her to the edge of Tencastle – that's all fairly level – to just beyond the street lights. Then Rob drives the extra couple of miles. Should be pretty deserted on that road by now – and Rob will have had a chance to sober up."

I couldn't quite put my finger on the flaw in Jake's argument.

"Unless, of course, you all prefer to walk all the way," he added.

We didn't. Nor did we see any coppers.

The next two weeks were filled with frenzied activity. Three more rehearsals, in a spare room at the Union rather than the pub, produced a more or less generally agreed script. At the cottage, almost every surface and chair was covered with polystyrene, cardboard and cloth, like a Blue Peter set before they'd finished the-one-we-made-earlier. Benji had commandeered the fruit bowl and saucepans for papier maché props and I was concerned that the red stain on the table cloth was more likely to be paint than ketchup. We got some very strange looks from the rinsed hair brigade when Jake and I purchased two black dresses, and a D-cup bra from the Chapel jumble sale.

By the Monday of Rag Week, following a chaotic dress rehearsal – Kissy and Sunny were late, so their parts were read by Jake, with some inevitable conflicts of role identification – we were ready as we were ever likely to be.

Our first public performance, or rather, the first non-private show, was to the unsuspecting students at the Folk Club. Whilst the reception wasn't exactly rapturous, it was spirited, with unsolicited audience participation; wolf whistles for Sunny, with bare bejewelled midriff, calls of "Behind You!" for Liz's pantomime dame tussle with 'king George and the Sharif of Nottingham and, "Where's your Tardis?" on the line 'In comes I, Doctor Huw'.

All of which gave us confidence for the big day.

We planned for three or four performances around the town, starting in the market square. One would have thought that nine bizarrely attired characters wielding wooden swords and chanting strange dialogue would have created some kind of stir amongst the market folk, but the indifference was mind-boggling. Little green men from Mars could have landed without the locals even batting an eyelid. Only the sheep gave us their considered attention – and they were a captive audience, so to speak.

Somewhat deflated, we ambled up to the shopping precinct in Castle Street – a terrace of five shops with a double-width pavement frontage.

"Makes you wonder what would grab these peasants' attention," grumbled Dan through his helmet.

"Forty pence on their beer and fags," suggested Trevor.

"A crash in the price of mutton," Dicky contributed.

Perhaps because the venue was more intimate – or congested – we did at least manage to hold on to an audience of sorts; bemused shoppers looked on for as long as it took them to shuffle through the bottleneck we caused. The proprietor of Forget-Me-Nots, Tencastle's high-street antique shop, got quite agitated that we were driving away his customers, unfairly, I thought. I'm sure I saw at least two people take refuge in there when the collecting tin was passed around. Four pounds seven pence and ten centimes wasn't a generous bag for a morning's work.

"Time for a drink," declared Jake, and no one dissented. "We'll give it one last try at the Castle courtyard. Catch the lunchtime boozers."

With the bonus of an unseasonably mild and sunny day, several customers, including a couple of families and a portly red-faced gentleman in tweed jacket and hideous fairisle pullover, had taken their drinks and crisps outside to the half dozen trestle picnic tables around the courtyard and the pocket-handkerchief beer garden at the far end.

Having nothing better to do, I suppose, they looked on with mild interest as we made ready. But they raised a cheer when I made my imposing entrance with, "In comes I, the Valiant Soldier."

It was all we needed for us to give a performance of a lifetime. Each new character was greeted with applause, and our audience even laughed in the right places.

The play was well advanced when I laid out 'king George with a slashing blow of my silvery wooden sword, smeared with red for effect, and George bit into a sachet of fake blood, and died dramatically with at least two encores.

Liz, a.k.a. Mother Wayles, cried out, "Is there a doctor to be found to raise my husband from the ground?"

"In comes I, Doctor Huw."

"Doctor Who?"

"Huw, that's who."

"You Huw?" interjected the Sharif.

"What can you do, Huw?" asked Mother Wayles.

At which Huw spent several lines of dialogue establishing his skill and credentials, before the crucial question, from the grieving widow.

"And what is your fee?"

"My fee? Why, half a quid will meet my fee in Merthyr Tydfil. While those that live down in Carmarthen I'd only charge just one brass farthing. As for the folk in Abergavenny I'd be bound to ask a pretty penny. But for you fair maid I'll charge no fee, a kiss is all I ask of thee."

The wail of a police siren got louder and drowned out the next response, but Doctor Huw began to administer his mock potions to the prostrate George. The siren stopped as a two-tone car emblazoned with the legend 'Heddlu' drew up across the entrance to the yard, and two young coppers sprung out. I thought I could hear another siren in the distance.

"All right, get back!" commanded one officer, a tall, skinny individual, to no-one in particular as the other went to examine the body on the ground. The fake blood looked quite realistic. "Now what's going on here?"

Jake stepped forward. "It's okay. Officer, we can explain …"

"And your name is?" interrupted Skinny, taking a notebook from his breast pocket.

"Moses."

"And I'm the bloody Angel Gabriel! Now, Sambo, real name if you please!" Sarcastic bugger.

Jake rarely lost his temper, but he bridled at the officer's offensive tone, and held back his anger with difficulty. "I just told you, Moses, Jacob Moses." He fished into the back pocket of his jeans beneath the flowing robes, and pulled out a dog-eared student union card. "Here, if you don't believe me!"

Skinny took the card, glanced at it and handed it back with bad grace.

"We've had a report of a serious assault. Some bloke being set upon by a hooded gang." This from the other policeman who swaggered over to join his colleague. His thick black eyebrows joined together above his nose, and he appeared to be cultivating a Hitler moustache.

"Him?" exclaimed Jake, incredulously, pointing to 'king George. "But he's just been resurrected by the Doctor!"

And to prove it, Dicky staggered to his feet just as an ambulance screeched to a halt.

"We're doing a play for Rag, that's all," Jake explained. "Who reported us anyway?"

"Can't say," said Skinny, but his eyes flickered briefly to a third floor window in the house opposite the pub. I caught a glimpse of an old woman with glasses peeping through the curtain.

"Waste of time, Harry," said Hitler to the paramedic. "Just a load of students pratting about."

"We're not …" Jake begun to protest.

"Cool it, Jake!" I hissed.

But Hitler was determined to put in his two penn'orth. "We've a good mind to charge you for wasting police time."

"We're not! It's not our fault if some blind old biddy can't tell the difference between make-believe and murder!" Jake was getting really pissed off.

"Have you permission to perform here?" asked Skinny.

"I wasn't aware that we needed any! Anyhow it's private property."

"I think it would be best if you all moved on."

"Why?" Jake could be quite argumentative in the face of officialdom.

"Before we throw the book at you for obstruction, public disorder, you take your pick!"

And with that, Skinny and Hitler stomped off to their car and drove off.

Jake exhaled deeply. "Bloody typical! No bloody sense of humour and no bloody apology!"

No one seemed too keen on an encore, so we began to gather up our props and remove our costumes. We hadn't even got as far as passing the collecting tin around.

The fellow in tweed and pullover wheezed up to us. "Hey, guys," he called enthusiastically, in an American accent. "That was great! I don't know how you pulled off the police scene, but that was a touch of genius!"

We looked at each other in confusion.

"I'm putting on a drama festival next month at Ynysgwyn Manor, and I'd like you to take part. Add a bit of colour and tradition to the programme."

Tradition, would you believe it! This guy couldn't be serious. The Manor was well known as a very exclusive and very expensive country house and hotel up near Tenbridge. It was set in umpteen acres of forest and gardens on the banks of the river where the waters of the Tene were temporarily divided by a small white quartzite outcrop. Very picturesque, but not quite the place for students pratting about. Nevertheless...

The impresario took the bewilderment on our faces as indecision. "It's for charity, but we'll pay expenses and a modest fee."

"How modest?" Jake was quick to gather his wits.

"Oh, we could manage thirty pounds or so."

"Sixty," said Jake.

"Forty-five. Plus expenses of course."

"Done!"

We had to write in extra parts for the coppers and the walk-on paramedic, and twist a couple of arms, but the prospect of unlimited access to wine and canapés had a certain attraction. Tom Merchant and Suzie Wallace were quite leading lights in the Drama Society, and needed little persuasion to come along. They also had good access to costume props. Rud, too, was always game for a binge. We borrowed the Students' Union minibus and a volunteer driver, so that none of us would feel obliged to be restrained from the goodies promised. Personally, I would have probably settled for a pint of best bitter and a packet of peanuts.

Jake was really proud to see his name on the glossy programme. We didn't have the heart to point out the glaring inaccuracies in the first four lines. I was glad, for the sake of the audience, that there was some attempt to clarify the relationship of the characters.

Tencastle Students' Society
"The Devil's Advocate"
written & directed by Jacob Moses
A traditional mummers' play, incorporating the finest elements of pantomime

Cast (in order of appearance)

Bald Captain ……… *Daniel Chater*
Father of the Valiant Soldier.

Valiant Soldier ……… *Robert Kiddecott*
Engaged to Candy-Ella but tempted by the Turkish Delight. Also fancied by Pincer Wayles.

Sharif of Nottingham ……… *Jacob Moses*
Immigrant. Father of Turkish Delight. Would like daughter to marry Pincer Wayles & become one of the local gentry.

Turkish Delight ……… *Suhindra Rahman*
Young, pretty and flirty, fancies the Valiant Soldier.

Mother Wayles ……… *Elizabeth Burke*
Married to 'king George. Mother of Pincer Wales (on whom she dotes) and mother of Candy-Ella (whom she neglects). Domineering. Fancies Sharif.

'king George Wayles ……… *Richard Swift*
Lecherous drunken husband of above. Local gentry. Has hots for Turkish Delight.

Candy-Ella ……… *Linda Kesteven*
A sweet little thing, but shy. Engaged to Valiant Soldier.

Pincer Wayles ……… *Trevor Brewer*
Idle effeminate son of George & Mother Wayles. Fancies the Valiant Soldier.

Doctor Huw ……… *Huw Parry-Evans*
A Welsh quack.

First Police Officer ……… *Suzanne Wallace*
Second Police Officer ……… *Thomas Merchant*
Paramedic ……… *Brian Cheeke*

184

With tickets rumoured to start at £25 a head, I shuddered to think what the dinner-suited guests and their bejewelled partners would make of our production. However, taking it as seriously as possible, the audience tittered self-consciously and applauded politely when we took our bow, so they obviously must have appreciated it, if only as light relief after the first item, a long and depressing monologue involving a telephone ('Smooth Operator'). It probably put them in the right frame of mind for the final play, an abridged Hamlet with an all female cast.

The following week, Llais y Castell reported our contribution of forty nine pounds and seven pence to Rag funds. Jake had somehow managed to amass 'expenses' of fifteen quid. We dropped the ten centime coin into the donations box of the Methodist Church next to the Students' Union.

One evening in the week before the Easter break I returned to the cottage to find Jake lounging comfortably on the sofa, contemplating a half empty bottle of beer. Like a fool I'd said, without thinking, "Penny for your thoughts?"

"That Mummers' play was good fun." he replied.

"Yes … so?"

"We ought to get more involved in our traditions."

"Such as?" I said, warily. With Jake's ethnic mix, anything from voodoo to bull-fighting might have been included.

"Morris!" he declared.

"Sorry?"

"Morris dancing. You know, sticks and bells and hankies."

"So?" I'd caught a glimpse of some once down in Torbay. All beards and beer guts, as I remembered. And the drunken group at the eisteddfod.

"We could do it."

"Forget the 'we'! Anyway, you don't know anything about it."

His idea squashed, he took consolation in the rest of his pint.

"By the way," I said. "Don't forget that my parents are coming down over Easter. We'll need to tidy our room."

"Uh huh." He raised his bottle in acknowledgement. His mind was evidently still on other matters.

CHAPTER TWELVE

Greenfingers

My parents were among only a handful of passengers that alighted onto the single platform.

"Welcome to Tencastle!"

"Robert, so good to see you!" My mother enveloped me in a warm hug.

Dad went for a more formal handshake, "How are you keeping, son?"

"Fine, fine. Did you have a good journey?"

"Oh, lovely, dear, such lovely countryside. We stayed with your Aunt Lizzie last night. You remember her, she sends her love."

Aunty Liz lived in Wem, just north of Shrewsbury. During the long summer break from school, Mum used to whisk us away for a few days to stay with one of her four sisters, geographically scattered over most of the English counties, it seemed. Rural Shropshire was one of my favourites. As a family we didn't really have any other holidays as such, since Dad was unhappy to leave the farm for more than the occasional day trip to the seaside, or, of course, to an agricultural show. Nor was he happy with driving long distances. Long hours on his tractor were a different matter.

It came as no small surprise, therefore, when my parents had taken up my suggestion to come and stay at the cottage during the Easter vacation. Since we had to pay the rent even when we were not at college, there was no extra cost in accommodating them at Ty Melin.

I stowed their luggage onto Jessica's back seat temporarily. Juggling them around to make room for Mum could come later.

"If you're feeling peckish, how do you fancy a pub lunch before we go to the cottage? They do a good pint, too, in The Castle."

Mum deferred to my father, as she usually did on any important decisions. I was pretty sure he'd be ready for a beer, after having to sit on his bum doing nothing for the journey. He wasn't a great one for reading, other than the *Farmer's Weekly*.

"Lead on, lad!"

True to my expectations, the market square took his interest at once, and, as he stood sniffing the air, he was probably imagining how it would look filled with all the livestock pens and stalls.

"I'll bring you here tomorrow, Dad, for the market."

"I'd like that."

The Castle did wholesome though simple food, with generous portions of home-cooked, local produce, unlike those over-priced pretentious restaurants in grockle hot spots where artistic presentation rather than satiation of appetite was the raison d'etre.

"Are you going to show us the college?" my father asked, once comfortably fed and watered.

"Yes, sure, we'll wander back via the Union – that's where most of the student social activities take place – and then to the park. Be prepared to avert your eyes, Mum, when we get to Goliath," I said, tongue in cheek.

"Why?"

I told her.

"As a farmer's wife and mother of three, I don't think there's much I haven't seen in that department."

My parents' first impressions of Tencastle seemed favourable.

"Where's the castle?" asked Dad as we walked back to the car. "I presume it has got a castle?"

"Had, more like it," I said. "That's all that remains." I pointed across the park towards a raised mound with a few blocks of masonry poking through the grass.

They fell in love with the cottage at first sight. In the spring afternoon sunshine it certainly looked at its best. The only room designed to sleep two people, however, was the one Jake and I shared, which meant of course that some reorganisation had been necessary. It wasn't too difficult to move the single beds next to each other instead of their usual position on opposite walls. With Dan's agreement, I had arranged to use his room while he was away. I didn't fancy sleeping with half-finished plaster busts or picking my way through tubes of acrylics that invariably scattered the floor of Benji's room – or waking to face the giant garish murals created in his comic book period, one wet weekend in March.

Mum familiarised herself with the kitchen. Despite the culinary skills I'd acquired out of necessity I suspected it would be her domain for the duration of their visit. Meanwhile, I accompanied my father on an inspection of the grounds.

"We'll have to do something about this." It had needed only an instant to take in the generally neglected state of the garden.

"We were going to mow the lawn," I said.

"But you could grow your own vegetables! Marvellous soil," he said, "if we cleared all the weeds!"

"Dad, you're on holiday, remember?"

"Oh, nonsense, Robert, a little bit of useful recreation won't do us any harm."

He poked about in the shed, and came out with a grass rake, a rusty hoe and a leaky watering can – the sum total of our garden equipment, unless you included the old lawnmower and the wobbly wheelbarrow.

"Where's the nearest garden centre?"

"I don't know." I'd never seen one in Tencastle. "Why?"

"We can't do the job without proper tools." He saw the look of apprehension on my face. "Don't worry, I'll pay."

I racked my brains to think of a shop where these items might be available, never having been faced with any such request previously. Apart from a hardware shop – more pots and pans than plant care – no other place came to mind.

"Hello there, young Robert boyo. Saw the car outside and wondered if you needed more logs."

"Hi there, Evan, I think we're okay for the time being."

Since the flood Evan had kept us in wood for the fires and had refused to accept any payment. His erstwhile neighbours, Bruce and family, had put their holiday home on the market back in February, their enthusiasm for the country life obviously dampened.

I introduced Evan to my father.

"Tell me, do you know of any garden centres in this area? My father thinks I ought to get into horticulture."

"Good idea, too! "He thought for a moment. "There's nothing in Tencastle, nearest is on the main road just beyond Pwllgoch."

Dad looked delighted and would have set out there and then if I hadn't asked Evan in for a coffee.

"Just a quick one, then. Bessie will be wondering where I've got to!"

Mum and Dad established an instant rapport with Evan who within no time invited us all to join him and his wife for supper one evening.

The next morning we left Dad to spend an hour or so in his element at the market, while Mum and I poked around the shops, stocking up, so she said, on essentials. Enough to last me half the coming term.

I'd suggested taking pot luck for lunch in Pwllgoch, a place I knew only from Jake's limited description. The White Lion's beer was all sanitized keg fizz but the soup and crusty bread quite acceptable.

Not even the most severe myopic could have missed Green Willy's. A huge roadside billboard showing a hand with an extended forefinger in the form of a giant cucumber pointed to the entrance, through a wide trellised archway bearing the name of the centre and its proprietor, one W. J. Greenstreet. On one side of the single storied barn-like main store stretched a row of glass hothouses, while to the other side were arrays of benches with pots of all kinds of plants and shrubs. We joined the steady flow of people heading towards the retail unit, passing others returning to their vehicles with trolleys laden with the wherewithal to create their own piece of Eden.

The stack on Dad's trolley grew steadily, to my concern for Jessica's capacity, with a fork, rake, spade and seeds, together with flower pots and trays for their propagation. I even accepted a hefty bag of compost.

I drew the line at a self-assembly aluminium greenhouse. "Hang on, Dad, no way can I get that in the car even if you both walk back!" I was also concerned at the mounting cost. "I don't want you to spend a fortune. I'm only going to be at the cottage for another fifteen months."

"Don't you go worrying yourself, Robert." Undeterred, he sought out an assistant and quickly ascertained that the greenhouse could be delivered free of charge the next day. Which only prompted him to add a lightweight wheelbarrow and plastic watering can to his purchases.

Not to be outdone, my mother bought me a potted baby cactus. "Doesn't need much attention," she said, "just the occasional drop of water."

I christened it Spike.

Dad was all for getting our sleeves rolled up the moment we got back to the cottage. "We need to clear some ground, and get it levelled off ready to put up the greenhouse. Where would like it to go, Robert?"

I really didn't mind. "Wherever you think it would be best."

No sightseeing then tomorrow. At this rate I'd be lucky to get an opportunity to show my parents around the area at all, I thought.

We settled for a reasonably level gap between the edge of the lawn and the first of the fruit trees. Dad revelled in the role of foreman, supervising the digging, clearing and preparing foundations. I sweated buckets that afternoon and tried to convince myself that the hard labour was for my own future benefit. Mum kept the teapot busy and generally pottered around, contented as long as Dad was happy.

Green Willy's delivery service was most efficient. It must have been their first point of call, for they were knocking on the front door by nine o'clock, before I'd properly surfaced. I guessed Dad had been up and about for hours.

Erecting the greenhouse was a doddle, though not something I'd have been confident in tackling on my own, so well before lunchtime, we were standing back to admire our handiwork. I had to agree that it did add a sense of purpose to the garden.

"Thanks very much, Dad. I promise you, I will use it. Now, I'm going to insist that you both use the rest of your stay here to relax and do some sightseeing. There's a number of places I'd like to show you, and you may not be able to get up this way again while I'm still at college."

"But there's still work to do in the garden, Robert!"

"No, Dad, I insist. With the benefit of your advice I'm quite capable of tackling the rest by myself. I've got another week to myself before term starts."

"Well … if you think you can manage …"

"Oh, come on, Henry, give yourself and the boy a break. After all, you are on holiday."

Mum's gentle intervention and my suggestion of seeking out some pleasant country pubs tipped the balance. "All right, you two, I know when I'm beaten."

The road I travelled frequently by college minibus on my first teaching practice offered, I knew, the right balance of stunning scenery, the town of Tenbridge to wander round, and several suitable hostelries. I held back from venturing as far as Abergynwyn, not wishing to tempt fate by meeting Sandra and her little Fanny.

We even fitted in a day trip to Aberystwyth, which I was keen to explore in daylight, and an afternoon excursion to the Brecon Beacons.

In the days since I'd seen my parents safely on to the train, I enjoyed, for the first time, having the peace and tranquillity of Ty Melin to myself. I spent most of the time outdoors, firstly contemplating the work still to be done in the garden, over a bottle or two of cool beer, then tackling the job at a far more leisurely pace than would have suited my father. Once my back muscles had recovered from unaccustomed turning of clods of earth, I really felt quite chuffed about the progress I was making.

I also gave some thought to Tania. There was a reasonable chance that she would be in Tencastle during the Easter break, but I didn't know where her mother lived, and there was no way I was going to ask her father! Now …if her mother still kept her married name …if she was on the phone … if she wasn't ex-directory then … but what if … I mentally tossed around a few scenarios before checking the telephone directory. Prepared to hang up immediately if a Scottish male answered, I waited while the phone rang, several times.

"Vera Cruikshanks here." Definitely not Scottish.

"Oh, hello, is Tania at home by any chance?"

"Why, no, I'm afraid you've just missed her…"

Bugger!

"… but she will be back home again for a couple of days at the weekend."

"Oh, right!"

"Can I take a message and ask her to call you back?"

Hell, nothing ventured. "Would you, please?" I gave her the number.

"And who shall I say called?"

"Tell her, Rob, from … er …" I wasn't sure how specific to be. Though unlikely, I didn't want anything getting back to Dr Cruikshanks. "… from the cottage." I hoped that would be sufficient clue for Tania, if she'd forgotten my name. I didn't really have any high hopes that she'd call.

The phone went just as I'd finished moving my gear from Dan's room back to the master bedroom in preparation for use once again by Jake and myself.

"Is that Rob?" the soft voice enquired tentatively.

"Speaking."

"Hi, it's Tania Cruikshanks. My mother said you'd asked me to ring you?" She definitely sounded uncertain.

"Yes, I'm glad you called. It's Rob … you remember, from the Dome opening night."

"Rob! Yes, what a surprise! I hadn't made the connection!"

Obviously. "Listen, if you're free today, how do you fancy meeting up?"

She paused, "Um … I don't know."

"Do something in town," I said vaguely, then had an inspiration. "Or why not come back here and I'll show you the cottage in daylight?"

"I'm not sure…"

"I'll cook a meal as well," I persisted.

Another pause, before a decision. "Oh why not? I'd like that, Rob. Thanks."

"Shall we say 5 o'clock?"

"Where?"

"I'll meet you by Goliath."

"Goliath?"

"Sorry, you might not know. It's the Tencastle students' pet name for the John Thomas statue."

She chuckled. "I didn't know!"

She was, if anything, even more striking than the last time I'd seen her back in the autumn, even though her denim jeans and jacket were a tad more casual than her party dress.

"Hi, Tania!"

"Hi there, Rob." Promisingly, she followed her greeting with a peck of a kiss.

"You remember Jessica – my car – I expect?" I ushered her into the passenger seat, moving the goodies for supper into the back.

"Unforgettable." She didn't elaborate. "Tell me, how did you know how to contact me?"

"Aha," I said, tapping the side of my nose. "Intuition and detective work."

"Well, you were very lucky to find me in Tencastle. I've hardly been here since last October, and it's unlikely I'll be back again for some time."

Lucky indeed, I thought. "That's a shame. What keeps you so busy to avoid the delights of Tencastle?"

"Some delights," she laughed. "It's a pretty active scene in Cambridge. And next year I'll be in Spain and Portugal, as part of my degree."

"Costa del Sol?" I asked.

"No lazing on the beach for me! I'll be hours away from the coast. Valladolid. Do you know it?"

"Never heard of it."

Jessica drew up at the cottage.

"Go on in!" I said, unlocking the front door. "I've just got to get a few things from the car."

Tania was in the kitchen looking out over the garden. "Wow, this is amazing! I didn't see any of this last time! It's so … so beautiful."

"And so are you," I said, encircling her waist.

She turned and responded with a kiss, then, with arms round my neck, a long, passionate embrace.

I held her tightly. "Shall we …?" I nodded towards the stairs.

Another deep kiss. "Later," she promised. "Show me your estate before it gets dark," she added, gently breaking away from me.

I took her down to the stream, showing her the newly installed greenhouse and the results of my labours. The tour should have only taken a couple of minutes, but we made it last nearly an hour.

While hoping that Tania would be content with my culinary speciality of chilli con carne, I had also prepared for the possibility that she might be vegetarian. I needn't have worried. She wasn't fussy either over the cheap red plonk that was all my budget could run to. Just in case I had to drive her back that evening, I moderated my alcohol consumption, but the bottle still ended up empty.

I started to guide her over to the sofa.

"You didn't show me the whole house last time," she purred softly into my ear.

I didn't think she'd be interested in the single bedrooms. We fell upon my bed, clinging, rolling, caressing, kissing.

"Wait," she said, pulling herself up. She began to loosen her jeans. Her jacket she'd already discarded downstairs. We helped each other unbutton shirt and blouse, and embraced again, before falling back once more on the bed.

"Tania," I whispered, "I …"

I didn't finish. The creak of the front door, followed by a loud, "Anyone home? Rob? Are you there?" drowned not only my words, but in all probability the likelihood of enjoying Tania's charms.

"God knows what he's up to, Jake," I heard Dan say. "The car's outside."

I entertained several uncharitable thoughts about them for their untimely and completely unanticipated arrival.

"Tania," I said, "I'm really sorry, they weren't due back until tomorrow." I kissed her again. Her barely acknowledged response spoke volumes.

I heard Jake and Dan go out the back door, probably to check my whereabouts. Tania and I quickly made ourselves presentable and went downstairs.

"Oh, hi there … didn't realise you had company, Rob," Dan said conversationally. He seemed unaware that he'd almost given coitus interruptus a new meaning.

"You met Tania last year, at the Dome."

"Yes! Indeed," he said, recognition dawning.

"Rob invited me to have a look at the cottage," Tania said, recovering her grace and poise.

"Oh right!" said Dan, uncharacteristically for him devoid of all suspicion or innuendo. Though that might come later.

Jake breezed in. "No idea where he's … Oh, where did you spring from?"

"Might well ask you the same question," I said. "We … I mean … I wasn't expecting you."

Jake looked at me and then at Tania and raised an eyebrow in query.

"Tania, meet Jake. He's the one responsible for finding this cottage," I said. Responsible for most things I might have added.

"Hi Jake," Tania said, "I'm going to have to say goodbye, though. Rob was just going to run me back home."

I was? Well, I supposed it made sense. I wasn't going to get any more joy staying put.

"Right, guys, be back shortly," I said, more civilly than I felt.

I offered to drive Tania right back to her mother's house, but she suggested we stop by the park, and we walked the rest. She clung closely to me.

"I'm sorry again, Tania, about tonight. Truly."

"Mmm, I'm sorry too," she sighed. "But I've enjoyed being with you …" Her dark eyes glistened as she stroked my cheek.

"Is there … is there any chance we could meet again?" I said hopefully.

"I like you, Rob, truly … but realistically … I don't think it would work, do you?"

Realistically, I had to agree.

Jake and Dan were lounging around, chatting, when I returned to the cottage.

"Pretty maid, you've found yourself there," remarked Jake.

"Yes, and thanks to you two pillocks, probably now lost forever."

"What do you mean?" said Dan, surprised by my sharp tone.

"I was quite expecting her to stay the night until you two clodhoppers came barging in."

Dan looked at me open mouthed, then winked knowingly to Jake. "You randy bugger!"

"Anyway, what brought you back so soon?" I asked.

"Train and taxi," said Jake. Rather flippantly. "We got a cheap fare from London. Dan's been staying with me for a couple of days."

Dan was the first to notice the transformation. "Wow, Rob, you make Percy Thrower look like an amateur!" he said next morning.

"Dad's doing, mainly. Or design, should I say," thinking of who'd actually done most of the hard labour.

Jake was also impressed. Benji, too, when he turned up on Sunday afternoon.

"If you make a cock-up of teaching, you could turn to market gardening," Jake suggested.

"I don't think so. However, with a little help from you lot, we can enjoy our own fresh produce."

They chose to ignore the implications of the first part of the deal.

"Hey, man! We could have some chickens!"

"A cow, too, Benji, for fresh milk?" Jake suggested.

"Great idea, man! And a …" He paused. "What? What's so funny?"

One good thing about Benji is that he never took offence at us pulling his leg. Most of the time he wasn't even aware that we were trying to.

The following day I left the others to their own devices as I had a few things to attend to in Tencastle, even taking another trip to Green Willy's after lectures. With that and a chance meeting up with Rud, it had been past ten o'clock in the evening when I returned from the pub. I was more than ready to turn into bed.

Next morning I drew back the curtains, closed my eyes and stretched, to welcome in the bright sunshine of a new day. Jake had already padded off to the bathroom a few minutes earlier.

It didn't fully register at first glance. With a classic double take, I peered out of the window again to the garden below. I still didn't believe what my eyes were telling me.

"Jake!" His towel was pinned round his waist. "There's a cow in the garden!"

"Your imagination, Rob. It's probably Evan's dog."

"It's a bloody cow!"

"If you say so."

"I know a cow when I see one. Bloody hell, it's probably trampled all over the veg. I've planted!" And a heifer in a hothouse would be as bad as a bull in a china shop.

I hurriedly pulled on some clothes and rushed downstairs. Dan and Benji looked up from their toast as I dashed out of the back door.

I stopped, open-jawed, at the Jack-and-the-beanstalk vista. The greenhouse was filled with verdant foliage, huge bunches of purple fruits dripping from vines.

"Fast growing variety, was it?" asked Dan, standing behind me. "Even so, it is a bit early for grapes."

"Probably the fertiliser, man!"

"I believe he talks to them before tucking them up for the night," said Jake who had joined the spectators.

I looked at them, open mouthed. They grinned. I took a closer look at the greenhouse. Someone – no guesses – had been at work on the glass with a paintbrush. Inside the young seedlings I'd bought had undergone no miraculous growth. The brown cow beyond hadn't moved. Benji's cardboard creation really was most lifelike from a distance. Further down the path he'd reproduced a Magic Roundabout Brian, complete with simulated slime trail.

"You bastards!" I yelled at the trio collapsing with laughter on the patio.

CHAPTER THIRTEEN

Plain Capers

Jake waltzed in just as Dan and I were about to tackle the standard greasy fare of Ffion's Fish Fantasia we'd brought back from town.

"Looks good," he said, grabbing a couple of soggy chips from the newspaper tablecloth. "Not bad at all!" He looked at the greyish paste that Benji was plastering over a Ryvita. "Is that food or sculpture?"

Benji looked pained. "Hummus, man. Want some?" He held out a dollop on the end of a palette knife.

"No thanks, I'll stick with proper nosh." He reached for another handful of chips. Ffion's wouldn't win any Michelin awards but the portions were always very generous.

"You were right, you know, Rob," Jake said, licking his fingers.

"I was?"

"Yeah, about Morris dancing. I didn't know anything about it."

"Right." I wasn't sorry. Until now I'd given it no more thought and wrongly assumed he'd done likewise.

"But I do now!" he declared triumphantly.

"What do you mean?"

"I've been doing some research over Easter. Apparently, there's several different kinds of Morris, and one of them, would you believe, comes from the Welsh Borders!"

"They're miles away," Dan muttered. "So what?"

"…And here's the best bit," Jake jabbered enthusiastically. "They used to black their faces – like, disguise!"

"I'm not bloody well blacking my face again!" I protested, remembering the eisteddfod. "It's all right for you!"

"Not a problem. Anyway," he continued, undaunted. "They wore brightly coloured coats and hats and ribbons or flowers, and bashed each other with big sticks…"

"Cool, man! Psychedelic!"

I glared at Benji. With his endorsement Jake would be unstoppable. "Psychotic, more like it!"

I don't think Jake heard. If he did, it didn't stop him ranting on.

"Now you don't have to have a definite number, like other sorts, even three or four." He looked at us expectantly. I studied the remains of my battered fish intently. "And you remember the Castle? The landlord's happy for us to use the back room again on a Monday night if we buy a few pints."

"Hold on, Jake! Just hold on a moment!" I got his attention.

"What?"

"Before you have us all dressed up like circus clowns, there are a few things you seem to have forgotten."

"Such as?"

"Well firstly, you're making a big assumption that any of us share your enthusiasm for leaping about like dervishes."

"Yes, why on earth would anyone want to do it?" Dan had a valid point.

"Well," said Jake, "it's a traditional custom…"

"For whom?" Dan again.

"…and it's good exercise, and it's a good excuse to go to different pubs …"

"Why do we need an excuse?" Dan interrupted.

"Let me finish! And we could collect a few bob or two for our efforts. Apparently some out-of-work quarrymen went out dancing one Boxing Day to earn some cash …"

"That sounds a good reason to me, man." Benji chipped in.

I glared at him again.

"…and that's how it all started, really."

"What do you mean, all this Morris lark started from a few blokes on the dole pratting about?" Dan sounded incredulous.

"No, no no! It goes back centuries, but it seems some guy saw these men dancing, and spent the rest of his life collecting and teaching dances that had almost been forgotten."

"Poor bugger!" said Dan.

"And who do you think is going to teach the dances? I don't suppose that your guy is still alive?" I asked.

Jake furrowed his brow. "No, he died in 1924."

"Before he wrote the dances down?" I said hopefully.

"No, they're documented, mostly. Though the Welsh Border dances are very fragmentary." Jake went quiet for a minute, obviously considering a problem that hadn't entered his mind. "We could always make them up, I suppose?" he suggested.

"Bugger your traditional custom, then!" Dan observed.

"Ye…es, there is that," he conceded.

"And what about music?" I asked. "I suppose they did have musicians?"

"They must have. I'm sure I saw a photo with tambourines and a squeezebox."

"Which we don't have and don't play," I said.

"Jake could always play his banjo!" Dan grabbed a frying pan from the coffee table and made to strum it, singing out of tune "…*come from Aberystwyth with a banjo on my knee.*"

"Prat!" Jake wasn't amused. "I'll think of something before next Monday – that's our first practice."

Somehow along the line we all seemed to have been swept into Jake's designs for initiation into another folk custom. I wondered what prior commitments I could find for six days hence.

Jake reminded us on Sunday evening. "Tomorrow night at the Castle, lads!"

"What for?" I said innocently.

"You haven't forgotten!" He looked at us with some concern, "You will come, won't you?"

Dan and I looked at each other wryly. Benji appeared not to have heard.

"The first round's on me."

"That's bribery!" I protested.

"You must be desperate. You've never made such a rash offer before!" said Dan.

"Free beer, I'm on, man!" Benji's ears were obviously tuned to pick up important details.

"All agreed then?" asked Jake, in a way which didn't allow for dissent.

"What the hell, I suppose so," Dan capitulated. "If we're all going." He looked at me, expectantly.

I shrugged. "Bugger all on the telly."

Although nothing was said, I'm pretty certain Jake was counting on my acquiescence, not least for transport back to Penybont, since he'd not yet mended the puncture in his bike tyre. I had another thought, "What about music and instruction?"

"All sorted. You'll find out tomorrow."

Dan and I wandered in to the public bar of the Castle just after half past seven. Jake was already there, together with a group of other Tencastle students, several of whom I knew, Rud and Dicky Swift in particular. Huw Parry-Evans was clutching a large oblong wooden box, like a miniature coffin. Kissy and Sophie were the only females. No sign of Benji, though. We reminded Jake of his bribe, and he reluctantly drew his wallet from his pocket, shielding it from view from the others. Perhaps they'd come more cheaply.

"Okay, folks, one or two more to come, but let's make our way through!"

The function room, at the rear, had seen better times, but was at least functional for our purpose. About as long as a badminton court though not quite as wide, it sported a wooden floor, with a faded carpet and a few chairs at one end, and a token quadrant of a stage at the other. On one of the three small tables, Jake had laid out a dozen freshly sawn broomstick handles, while on another were a similar number of bootlaces strung with an assortment of budgerigar bells and garishly coloured plastic Christmas tree bells, plus a few other miscellaneous tintinabula. I'll say one thing for Jake, when he sets his mind to something, however outlandish, he's pretty imaginative in acquiring essential equipment and drumming up support.

A slightly-built, bespectacled, balding and bearded (naturally) man was studying notes on a sheet of paper and comparing them with a book set out on the third table.

As we entered he turned towards us, and I could see that the left sleeve of his jacket was tucked into the outside pocket.

His brow furrowed. "Oh, oh my!" he said to Jake, in a rich Welsh accent. "You didn't say there would be women present!"

"You didn't ask," said Jake, puzzled.

"Oh dear!"

"What's the problem?" asked Jake.

"Oh, dear. Well, it's … it's not … er, usual for women to dance Morris. I could get thrown out of the Ring."

"What ring?"

"The Morris Ring – it's the, er, national organisation for Men's Morris sides. They have a strict rule about not letting women dance."

"We can leave," said Kissy. "We don't want to cause problems."

"No way," Jake said to her. "It's everyone or no-one!" He turned to the worried man, "Look, Gron, we do appreciate you coming along. I believe you said that you hadn't actually been a member of any team for several years."

"That's correct."

"Then your former team can't be at risk of de-belling, or whatever they would call it, and anyway, who's going to know about it? We're only doing it for a bit of fun. What do you say?"

Gron scratched his head. "Well, I suppose so … it always seemed a bit sad to me to leave the ladies out."

"Thanks! Guys – and dolls too – let me introduce Goronwy Griffiths, one-time foreman of …" Jake checked himself. "Oh, I'd better not name the team but suffice to say, he's got loads of experience in teaching Morris."

The polite applause was spontaneous, and Gron allowed himself a smile.

Benji sauntered in, followed by a timid-looking thin girl and a fellow who shared the same kind of long straight blond hair and narrow features. I guessed they were twins.

"Sorry, man, got held up," Benji mumbled.

"Probably a good idea, now we're all here, to introduce ourselves, before we get dancing," said Jake. "I'm Jake Moses, and these are my housemates." He stretched his arm towards Dan, Benji and me.

"Robert Kiddecott." I acknowledged.

"Dan Chater."

"Benji."

"Linda Kesteven. But my friends all call me Kissy."

Sophie, Dicky, Rud and Huw all identified themselves. The late arrivals were next.

"Holly and Harry Dickens," they said together.

That left just two others, the aptly named Maurice Manley, a chunky mop-haired lad about my height, and Piers Walter, an athletic-looking six-footer.

"Over to you, then, Gron!" said Jake.

Gron cleared this throat. "Well now, gents – and ladies, too, of course – Jake here tells me you're all keen to learn a bit about the Morris dances from the Welsh borders."

We conscripts from Penybont grinned at each other. Perhaps the others were keen volunteers but I had my doubts.

"Now, I must admit that I know more about Cotswold Morris, but we used to do a couple of Border dances when we went out on Boxing Day."

"Is that what that bloke saw the men doing in the quarry?" Dan asked. I was impressed that he'd remembered anything of Jake's waffling.

"Pardon?" Gron looked confused, until the oblique reference clicked. "Oh you mean Sharp? No, Headington's quite different."

It was Dan's turn to look puzzled, but wisely said no more other than a sotto voce, "Of course."

"Right now, gents … and ladies, of course … if you form a circle around me we'll start with a bit of stepping. Quite easy, it's what we call single step, just right step, hop, left, hop, and so on." Gron demonstrated gracefully. "Now you have a go!"

We hopped around with somewhat less grace for the most part, with my limbs being reluctant to follow the brain's instructions precisely. Kissy, Sophie and the twins were looking more co-ordinated, however, while Rud had the right idea, albeit out of synch. with the rest of us.

"Good, good!" said Gron. "Now, I'd like you to grab a stick and form yourselves into groups of four, in a line." He caught sight of Jake making for the bell collection. "I don't think we'll be needing them just yet."

Gron soon had us hopping around in a sort of figure of eight weaving patterns and thrashing each other's sticks vigorously. I hoped there wasn't a witches' convention planned for Tencastle – they'd be seriously short of broomsticks. After half an hour we were all dripping buckets of sweat, with the exception of Gron.

"Okay, take a breather."

"Beer break!" gasped Dan. "Christ, I didn't realise it was so bloody energetic."

"Right," said Gron, when we'd all eventually reappeared from the bar. "We'll try it with music." He then thought for a moment. "Jake, did you find a musician?"

"No problem!. Huw here has volunteered."

"Excellent! What do you play? Can you read music?"

Huw, caught unexpectedly in the limelight, looked for somewhere to park his pint and stuttered, "Ye…yes, tha… that's right." He reached for his wooden casket and fumbled with the catches. As I had expected, he pulled out what looked like some giant long-legged spider.

"What on earth is that?" exclaimed Rud through a mouthful of crisps.

"Welsh bagpipes," replied Huw evenly. He adjusted one long tube over his left shoulder, put one end of another pipe into his mouth, and arranged his fingers along the length of the third. The creature gave a deep-throated groan, followed by a few high pitched squeaks, then sang sweetly in a rich melodic tone as Huw played a snatch of *Men of Harlech*.

"Bloody hell!" Even Benji was impressed. "That's so cool, man."

"Excellent, excellent!" Gron positively beamed. "You do read music?"

Huw nodded, still puffing at the pipe.

Gron retrieved his book, thumbed through it and handed it, page open, to Huw. "*Not for Joe*. Quite a simple little tune."

The instrument groaned and died. It squealed into life again as Huw tentatively played a few bars then picked up the feeling for the tune.

"Excellent! Right, back to work, folks."

You could see that Gron was really getting fired up. To be honest, so were we, and the next hour seemed to pass in seconds. As we became familiar with the pattern of the dance, so he introduced a couple of different movements which we took to like ducks to water. Rud still managed to hop about half a beat behind the rest of us. We were pretty knackered by the end of the session.

"Same time next week," said Jake, as the group made to filter out to the public bar. "And a big thanks to Goronwy for taking us on."

Gron looked a trifle embarrassed, though undoubtedly happy, as we gave him a round of applause.

"Where did you find him?" Dan asked, on the way home.

Jake did his best to swivel round in Jessica's rather cramped front passenger seat to answer.

"Gron? Purely by chance, as it happens. I was in the college library asking if they'd got any books on Morris dancing. He must have overheard me. 'I used to do that,' he'd said. Anyhow, we got talking, and he sort of volunteered."

"Really?"

"Well, I told him we'd got a group of students keen to have a go at dancing. Laid it on a bit thick, you know, and asked him whether he knew anyone who could teach us."

"Where did he learn to dance?" I asked.

"I'm not sure. I believe he was at Oxford before taking up a lecturing post at Tencastle."

"I've not seen him around college," mumbled Benji, and belched loudly.

"You wouldn't notice anyone unless they had a fistful of paint brushes," said Dan.

"S'not fair, man!" Benji protested feebly and promptly fell asleep, despite Jessica's rattles.

"He told me he also used to play the concertina, before his accident."

"What happened?" asked Dan.

"Motor bike crash, so he said. Afterwards, apparently, he tried strapping one side of the concertina to his leg, and just playing the right hand." Jake pondered a while. "I think he's quite chuffed to be involved with Morris dancing again."

Next Monday came round surprisingly quickly, and this time Jake didn't have to bribe us with beer. Even more remarkable was that nearly everyone else had turned up again, though Benji had offered cryptic apologies, something to do with four-dimensional expressionism, whatever that was. We were also missing the athlete, Piers Morgan, not that he'd said much at all last week, and he'd drank soda water all evening, which would have probably disqualified him anyway from the Morris fraternity.

Already in the back room when we filed through was a mousy slip of a girl with huge spectacles and a brimming pewter tankard that looked as if it would take all her strength to carry.

"Hi, I'm Min," she greeted us with a wide smile that revealed more metalwork than enamel. "Is this the fertility rites group?"

Jake and I looked at each other, gobsmacked. "Er, Morris dancing, actually," he said, lamely for him, I thought.

"That's what I mean ! It's all to do with fertility rites, isn't it?"

Jake was still rather nonplussed, "Er, um …"

Gron came to the rescue. "Well, young lady … er, Min …there may be something of fertility rites in the origin of Morris, long ago. We don't practice them today."

"Why not?" I heard Dan whisper.

"Oh!" Min looked crestfallen.

"But we do have a lot of fun," said Jake, recovering his usual composure. "And you are very welcome to join us."

"Can I? I'd love to!" Her face broke into a broad smile once more.

"Right," said Gron. "Down to the business. Dan, if you'd like to take Min in hand and join Holly and Harry. The three of you seemed to get on pretty well last week. I'll come in to make up numbers, so we'll have three sets of four again. We'll try to keep the sets the same for now, although you will probably have to get used to swapping round when you dance out."

Dancing out? I hadn't thought about that – and I was pretty sure that it hadn't hitherto entered into Jake's consciousness. Still for the present, Gron and I had other things to concentrate on in the only all-male set, like trying to get Rud to step in time with us and to avoid colliding with Maurice, who had a penchant for taking the most direct route between two points and expected everyone else to do the weaving. Sophie and Kissy seemed to be having fun with Dicky and Jake, frequently collapsing into bouts of laughter.

Min was a natural and more than made up for the missed week. In the bar afterwards Gron was so pleased with all our progress that he promised to introduce another dance or two next time. "I'm aiming for a modest repertoire of perhaps five or six dances in all," he said. "Which is all the border dances I know anyway!"

"And will they have some fertility rites for Min?" Dan asked innocently. He'd contrived to wedge himself next to her on the bench seat by the window.

"Only in your fertile imagination, I expect," Jake retorted.

Dan ignored him and turned to Min, for whom he'd just bought a third tankard of ale. "Tell me, is Min short for Minette?"

"No, I was christened Wilhemina, but it's a hell of a mouthful, so I've always been called Min, even at home. Or, as I've always been told, I was the smallest of all my brothers and sisters, so it may be short for 'diminutive'," she added with her now familiar great smile. "Not that any of them could have spelt it."

"Big family?" said Harry, opposite.

"Yeah, I suppose," she said, a little reticently.

"Blimey, and I thought our house was crowded with Holly and our younger sister."

"Moron!" said Holly, punching her brother playfully on the shoulder.

"Presumably you're in separate halls?" I asked. I didn't think Thomas or Abercrombie would bend their single sex rules even for siblings.

"No, we still live at home, just outside of Tencastle," said Harry. "Can't get away from her yet," he added, earning another thump from his sister.

Jake tapped on the table with a stick to gain our attention. "I've been thinking."

I rolled my eyes. Here we go.

"About what Gron here said earlier," he continued.

I knew it!

"It's now only the end of April," he said, "and we've got a couple of months to play with. How about we try to dance out, say, by the end of May? Long light evenings. What do you think? Possible, Gron?"

Gron stroked his beard. "Don't see why not."

Everyone tried to chip in at once.

"Where would we dance?" Dicky, I think.

"What would we wear?" This from Sophie.

"Yes, and who'd make the costumes!" Kissy sounded dubious.

"What about our exams?"

"What are we going to call the group?"

"How often …"

Jake raised his hands, "Okay, okay, one at time, I may have two ears but I've only got one brain!" He took his pint glass in both hands. "Right, exams – most of us are second years without any formal exams this summer. How about you, Maurice?

He gave his lopsided grin and raised his hand in acquiescence. "Third year, but I need some light relief."

"Holly and Harry?"

They looked at each other, and shrugged in uncertainty. "Not sure, really. Perhaps a couple of times. We're both first years and we'd really like to be sure we get through to next year."

"Min?"

"Definitely!"

"No exams?"

"Well, yes, but I want a life to!"

"Well, then, it looks like a green light. May I suggest that we all have a think about the other points like name and costume and so on and come back with suggestions next week."

Jake wasn't a natural gardener, so it was a surprise to hear him clattering about on Saturday morning in the old garden shed.

"Going to mow the lawn?" I asked hopefully. I'd done my best at least to keep the garden looking presentable since my father's efforts, but it seemed as if the grass grew inches overnight.

"No, can't find the combine harvester," came the disembodied voice. Jake emerged, brandishing the rusty saw. "Thought we had one of these somewhere."

I raised an eyebrow.

"Sticks!" he announced.

"Pardon?"

"Morris sticks. Those broom handles are full of splinters. We should be able to lop off a few bits from the trees out here."

"We?"

"I'll do the sawing. All you need to do is hold the ladder steady."

"We've got a ladder?"

"In here somewhere," said Jake and dived back into the shed.

Sure enough, he carried out an old wooden ladder which had definitely seen better days. I was glad Jake had volunteered to go aloft.

"Right," he said. "Which one's it to be?"

The cottage garden featured a couple of apple trees and a plum, none of which had yielded any edible fruit last autumn. Where the garden dropped away towards the river there were a few indeterminate saplings rising out of the bordering hedgerow.

Finding anything like eighteen inches of thin straight mature bough on the apple trees was nigh impossible, and the saplings were dubiously accessible and far too green. The plum tree had several boughs which were about the right diameter. Jake managed to scrape his way through a couple of suitable branches by reaching up from ground level, and then set his sights on two prime limbs higher up.

"Ladder!" he commanded.

We wedged it as firmly as possible in a fork in the trunk. Jake climbed up to the fourth rung while I held on to the sides. One branch yielded after a few minutes of Jake's grunting and cursing.

"One down, one to go." Jake took a couple of steps higher up the ladder and wriggled about, trying to get a decent angle to use the saw. "Can't see what I'm … Ouch! Oh bugger it!"

Jake dropped the saw and stuck a bleeding thumb into his mouth – and slid down the ladder as the rungs gave way in domino effect. Hitting the ground he toppled backwards into me, and we both ended up on our backsides, one behind the other sculler-like, with arms spread out to the side.

"Boat sank, did it?" asked Dan, who'd come out to see what all the kerfuffle was about.

"Piss off!" growled Jake. "Bloody plum tree's got bloody barbs in it." His left hand was dripping blood. He stumped off to the kitchen to clean up.

I examined our crop. Apart from a few vicious looking spikes which could easily be shaved off, the branches were fairly straight and smooth, and would probably yield several usable sticks.

Dan meanwhile was collecting the remains of the ladder. "Hey, Rob," he called, "I think these old rungs might come in useful."

When Jake eventually reappeared with plastered thumb, Dan and I presented him with two dozen Morris sticks – ten from the plum tree and fourteen from the ladder.

When we gathered for our next practice, Gron, true to his word, introduced a couple of different dances. Upton something or other I think.

"We'll use the short sticks, but ideally we need long ones for these dances," he said.

"I'm not going up that bloody plum tree again!" muttered Jake.

We'd not persuaded Benji to rejoin us, but fortunately no one else had dropped out, so, with a dozen dancers, including Gron, we were able to make up the three or six person groups that these new dances required. Things were getting a little more technical, with some new figures, new ways of beating each other to hell, and a not entirely successful attempt to get us to try a double-step, as Gron called it.

We hopped and pranced around for an hour or more with our usual exuberance, until, with everyone buzzing with ideas about going public, Jake suggested that we finish dancing a little earlier, collect a beer or two and bring it back to the function room for some detailed exchange of ideas.

"Okay, folks, let's get talking." The chatter fell away as Jake took control. "Now, there are three main points we need to consider, that is, where and when we dance, what we wear, and what we call ourselves."

"Isn't that four points?"

Jake ignored Dan and continued, "Now I take it that we all want to dance out in public this term, agreed?"

All hands shot up.

"Fine. Now can I suggest that we go for our inaugural performance over the Bank Holiday? That gives us three weeks to prepare."

"Will we need permission to dance?" Sophie asked.

"I doubt it, if we keep to pub yards."

"I was thinking about the Rag Day affair with the Mummers," she added.

"Ye…es. Not quite the same though. Gron?"

"Well strictly speaking I suppose you should have permission, but if you ask the Council they have to make a decision, and if they refuse, you're buggered." Gron quaffed a mouthful of bitter. "Sorry for the language, ladies. Best not ask in the first place."

"What about a couple of times during that week?" Dicky suggested. "Kids will be on holiday, there may be a few tourists around. Perhaps the market on Saturday, then again on the Monday?"

"Sounds fine. Agreed?" Jake looked round, as most hands went up, with the Dickens twins rather hesitantly. "Holly and Harry, are you both okay?"

"Yeah, guess so."

"What are we going to wear?" Min asked enthusiastically.

"That's the next thing to talk about," said Jake. "Any ideas?"

"Need to be kept pretty simple," Rud volunteered. "I'm no bloody good with needle and cotton."

A few other male heads nodded in agreement.

"And it wouldn't be fair to ask the girls to do it all, would it?" said Jake, hoping, I suspected, that they'd disagree.

"Too darn right it wouldn't!" Kissy said, leaving no room for doubt.

"If I might make a few comments," Gron came in quietly. "Traditionally the costume was simple – the ordinary working men didn't have much to spare for extravagance, a bit like students, I suppose. For Border Morris it was if anything even more basic, a few bells around the legs, a raggy jacket, and, of course, they often used to black their faces, as a kind of disguise."

"That's a brilliant idea!" Maurice said. "I'm up for that!"

I was not at all enthusiastic about the idea, and I expressed my point of view quoting my previous experience. But I was very much in the minority – the sole dissenter, in fact. Gron seemed rather embarrassed by the dissent his remarks had generated.

"Well, Rob, will you go along with the rest of us?" Jake asked, as conciliatorily as possible.

It was all right for him! I had an idea, "Okay, I suppose so – but on one condition."

"What's that?"

"That while we black up, you white up!"

I could see that Jake was quite taken aback. The room fell uncharacteristically silent.

Then Jake's serious expression gave way to a broad grin, "I could do that, I suppose. Be quite novel, wouldn't it?"

Harmony restored, everyone was keen to chip in with ideas about possible costume other than face paint. Rejecting some of the more bizarre suggestions such as black masks and highwayman's capes, we decided, with a few gentle nudges from Gron, on a pragmatic and unisex solution. Blue jeans, black trainers and a pale green rugby shirt – the college colours – to which we'd attach as many bits of coloured fabrics as we could get hold of. Holly and Harry were very concerned about the cost, but we reckoned we could scrounge a few old shirts from the rugby club.

"As long as they're washed," Holly said, wrinkling her nose.

"Nothing wrong in honest alpha male sweat!" offered Maurice, who looked as if he knew a thing or two about it.

"Ugh!"

Kissy and Sophie kindly offered to raid an imminent jumble sale on our behalf. Gron knew of a source of bells and thought that just a few attached on elastic around our legs would suffice. "You might even be able to get Union to cough up a few quid," he suggested.

"Good idea!" said Jake.

"What about headgear?" asked Rud. His mop of red hair would defy any disguise.

"Baseball caps, decorated?"

"Woolly knitted hats?"

"Why don't we leave it to individual choice?" Dan's glass was long overdue for a refill, and we were getting near to closing time.

"Good idea!" said Jake. "As long as it's decorated."

We all began to make movement to the bar.

"But we haven't decided on a name for the group yet!" called Min.

"Ideas on a piece of paper and we'll vote on it next week. Okay?"

Jake's suggestion satisfied her. At least she gave him the benefit of her radiant smile.

"Went well, I thought," I said, as I drove back to Penybont, having dropped Min off at 'Crombie Hall.

"Indeed!" said Jake. "Though you had me dead worried about the blacking-up issue. I seriously thought you'd bottle out."

"Well, I'm still not keen, but at least you'll have the same inconvenience."

"I'll look like a blooming Zombie!"

We didn't get to discuss a name for our fledgling group at the next practice. Even Min didn't bring it up, what with intense concentration on perfecting (in a manner of speaking) our dances and sorting through old rugby shirts in various states of decay. Sophie and Kissy had spent a lot of time slicing up a bundle of old brightly-coloured garments into inch-wide strips, and had thoughtfully stuffed a number of large envelopes with a similar assortment.

"How do we attach them?" asked Rud.

"Safety pins, if you're lazy, or just a simple stitching if you can be bothered," Kissy replied, dismissively.

We might not have even considered what we should call ourselves on the following week – our last practice – had not someone raised the question of posters to advertise our forthcoming inaugural performance.

"Good idea!" said Jake, as he examined the brass bells that Gron had dumped on the table in a large box.

"We could get Benji to do them," Dan suggested.

"I'm sure he'd love that!" I said. "If you don't mind abstract designs."

"But shouldn't we have a name?" asked Min.

"Does it matter?" said Maurice.

"You're all right – you've already got the proper name." This from Kissy.

Jake took charge. "It is something we've overlooked and I think it is important. Suggestions?"

Silence for a moment, then a few tentative ideas emerged.

"Tencastle Border?"

"Simple, Harry, but a bit unimaginative."

"College Caperers?"

"Black Sheep Morris?"

"Why?"

"Well, we'll be all blacked up, under the care of our good shepherd," Sophie indicated Gron.

"Not bad," I said, though I could see Jake wasn't keen. He'd been compared to a black sheep before.

"Sticks and bells?" said Holly tentatively.

"Hasn't quite got the ring to it," said Jake.

"Perhaps Gron could think of something in Welsh?" Rud suggested.

"What about 'Carpiog'," said Huw quietly.

"What's that?"

"It means ragged or tattered."

"I like it," said Jake. "Any other ideas, folks?"

There weren't.

"Shouldn't we have a dress rehearsal?" asked Holly.

"Not really time is there. Let's go for it, next Saturday morning at the market. Okay?"

A right ragged crew we certainly looked as we made our way from the Castle Inn to the Market Square, for, although there was a general compatibility in colour and costume, poetic license had run riot. Kissy and Sophie had gone to town with the rugby shirt almost completely disguised with carefully stitched rows of ribbons, and both sported straw hats bedecked with fresh flowers. Holly and Harry's outfits were nearly as impressive, with less floral adornment, but full blacking of their face, rather than just around the cheeks and chin. Min had somehow arranged her ribbons into a number of rosettes, including a couple on her kiss-me-quick seaside Stetson, which topped enormous psychedelic sunglasses. Rud had gone for the easy option of safety pin attachment of ribbons which would have been rather sparse had it not been for the bright red T-shirt showing through the threadbare rugby shirt. He'd also hung a couple of ribbons from his blue cricket cap.

The rest of us had done a reasonable job in bedecking the shirts with ribbons, but as for headgear we looked like refugees from the Mad Hatter's Tea Party. Maurice sported a very battered black topper, rescued, he declared, from a school production of Oliver. Dicky's bowler sprouted a single plastic daffodil from the crown, like some crazy antenna, while Huw had opted for a red and yellow hooped bobble hat. Dan, hatless until this morning, had found a Tommy Cooper fez in a second-hand shop in town. Beneath the ribbons falling down from the crown of an old deerstalker, Jake had dangled his plastic Christmas tree bells from the earflaps. He'd put a token daub of white greasepaint on his nose and cheeks. I felt quite under-dressed in my farmer's style flat cap to which I'd pinned best of breed rosettes from a Devon agricultural show.

Only Gron, in his black breeches, white socks, and proper bell pads looked anything like a conventional Morris dancer. He'd also spirited up some decent-length sticks from somewhere.

"Helluva lot of people here today," Jake observed, as we ambled into the Square.

"Good for collecting," said Dan, enthusiastically. He'd brought an old saucepan from the garden shed for this purpose.

"Perhaps Benji's posters worked," I said. "He did do some, I suppose?"

"Oh, yes, even volunteered to put them up," Jake replied.

Even though Tencastle's Saturday market usually attracted a lot of local support, there did seem to be an unusually large number of men milling around, not paying particular attention to the stalls of produce, garments and knick-knacks, more like farmers on the livestock day, and a few young sporty types in tweeds.

We dumped our gear at the northern end of the market square, where our appearance had attracted wary attention from the bystanders, and, in particular, from a stocky bald-headed official in a suit who came up to us, clearly agitated.

"I'm sorry, you can't perform here!"

"Why not?" Jake asked, reasonably. "There's plenty of space."

"Well, we're expecting … er … um … an … er … unexpected rally," he blustered.

"What kind of rally?" I asked, intrigued by his contradictory reply.

"Vintage cars, and … and … er … some livestock." He waved a sheet of paper at us.

"Can I have a look?"

The official, though surprised by Jake's request, seemed glad to be rid of the document.

Jake's puzzled expression soon changed to a broad grin, and, barely suppressing a guffaw, said, "I think I can explain."

"You can?" Baldy's eyebrows shot up.

"It's us."

"But …"

Jake showed us the poster. Benji, with artistic creativity worthy of Picasso, had intertwined garlanded geometric designs with a bell-bedecked pot-bellied porker around a headlined 'Morris Car Pig Show', whatever he thought that meant. He'd thoughtfully added the venue and date.

"It is meant to be us," Jake repeated. "A clerical error on the part of our graphic designer…"

"Clerical error?" said the official, puzzled but noticeably less worried.

"Some bloody error!" whispered Dan.

"We're Morris dancers. Carpiog is the name of our group – Ragged."

"I know what Carpiog means!" declared the official in exasperation. He breathed out a large sigh. "Well, your designer's caused me no end of worry, I'll have you know!" He waved his hand at the growing band of onlookers. "And all these people have been asking me about when the vehicles were coming and what was special about these ruddy pigs!"

"Sorry!"

"Well, it's a weight off my mind, at least." He thought for a moment, "You'd better get on with your display then!"

"Thanks ... and, again, sorry!"

He left with a dismissive wave of his hand.

"Didn't you ..." I began.

"Later, Rob!" Jake interrupted. "On with the show!" he announced to the bewildered but growing crowd.

There's something about a large virgin audience that gets the adrenalin flowing. With considerably more enthusiasm than expertise, we gave our first dance all our energy, amid calls of encouragement from the crowd to give even more welly to the sticking.

"Get the saucepan going!" Jake called breathlessly to Rud, as loud applause erupted after another frantic bout of bashing. Jake, every part a natural showman, wooed the audience shamelessly.

"Ladies and gentlemen, Carpiog present for you the best of your own Welsh Border Morris dancing ..."

According to Gron, the dances were collected from the English side of the border, but Jake wasn't bothered about the fine details.

"... resurrected from ancient rituals, you've never seen the like of for over a hundred years!"

Gron, puffing on his pipe, nodded his head with a wry grin.

It took virtually all of the next dance for Rud to make his way around the crowd rattling the old saucepan. He certainly had more aptitude for wheedling money out of the spectators than for the dancing – he still hadn't mastered the technique of hopping in time with the rest of us. During the third dance, a few people were beginning to drift away, until a roar of laughter greeted the demise of Dicky's daffodil, lopped off by a mis-timed swing from Min's stick.

"And now for our final dance," Jake announced. "We'd like to invite you to join us."

Consternation amongst our number. This wasn't in any pre-arranged plan!

"Jake," Dan called out. "We haven't got enough sticks!"

I was more concerned with insurance, given Dicky's close escape from decapitation.

But Jake pretended not to hear and about a dozen assorted volunteers, of both sexes and all ages, stepped forward to be hustled by Jake into a semblance of two lines. "Spread yourselves out amongst them!" he called to us.

We complied.

He paused, as Dan's observation dawned. "Ah! Hold on a moment!" He dashed to the nearby produce stall and scooped up a handful of early season rhubarb, to the astonishment of the stallholder.

A quick garbled instruction for a couple of basic figures and sticking then Jake yelled, "Gently now!"

Fat chance!

The tune came out in barely recognizable squeaks and grunts as Huw, blowing into his bagpipes, fought a losing battle to keep a straight face. Not that the music really mattered – our crew were more intent in parrying random rhubarb strikes than keeping in step or sequence.

"How much do we owe you?" Jake asked the stallholder, once we'd gathered up the shredded stalks.

"On me, boyo!" He wiped the tears of mirth rolling down his beetroot coloured cheeks.

"Went well, that!" declared Jake, wiping beer froth from his lips. We'd retired to the Castle for well-earned refreshment. "Brilliant job, Huw!" he added.

"I'll turn my back on you lot if you dance anywhere near a vegetable stall again!"

"Are we dancing again?" asked Kissy,

"What do you think, guys?" Jake looked round the group.

"Well, since we're all dressed up like lunatics, we might as well carry on," said Dicky.

"Sorry about your flower," said Min.

"Hey, what about doing it for Goliath?" Rud suggested enthusiastically. "You know, the fertility and suchlike?"

"I was thinking of leaving that for Monday. There'll be a lot of people around the park and down by the river ..."

"There's a good pub just across the bridge," Maurice interrupted. "I live near there."

"Yes, okay, that too, perhaps," Jake continued. "But for today, there will be more people in the town, so if we do a short show outside the pub here and another by the market before it closes. Okay?" He looked round and got nods of approval.

The lunchtime clientele at the Castle Inn showed mild interest in our capers at first before returning their attention to more serious business of drinking. The need to replenish their glasses or attend to the call of nature strangely coincided with Jake's announcement of a collection.

Back in the market square, our previous dancing spot was already taken. A buxom middle-aged woman in a smart grey tailored jacket and matching skirt was spouting on about the rural economy and suchlike to the modest gathering of afternoon shoppers who'd bothered to stop. The large red rosettes worn by her and her suited entourage reminded me that a parliamentary by-election was in the offing, following the untimely death of the popular incumbent in a road accident. A young cub reporter was scribbling furiously in his notebook.

"Ruddy political waffle!" muttered Jake. "Let's go round the other side."

A legful of bells and unconventional garb made discreet movement well nigh impossible, and the prospective candidate followed our progress around the crowd with her eyes, frowning, though barely pausing in her speech.

A few of the hustings crowd, expecting some light relief, peeled off and followed us to the southern end of the market, where we deposited our sticks and clutter on the wooden bench opposite the public conveniences. To a strident introductory wail from Huw's pipes six of us launched into the first dance, with newly found confidence and vigour.

Holly and Harry had wanted to browse through the market stalls, looking, they had said, for something for their mother. They'd almost joined up with us again when they were accosted, loudly, by the grey suited woman.

"You!" she bellowed. "You students should be ashamed of yourselves!"

Holly and Harry turned, open-mouthed in surprise at her angry tone. Other heads were turning, too.

"You … you! Blacking your faces like that!" she ranted. "Have you no respect for ethnic minorities? It's an insult to our black friends!"

The twins visibly cowered from the dragon's fiery onslaught. Not so Jake, who'd heard her last words. He strode purposefully up to her, and tapped her shoulder.

"Excuse me!" he said pleasantly, but firmly. I recognized well his battle tone.

The woman turned, and looked at him haughtily, with open disgust. "Young man …"

"May I ask how many black people have expressed their concern to you?" Jake cut her off.

"I beg your pardon!" she said huffily.

"Simple question. How many black people have you spoken to?"

She drew herself up, affronted. "I don't need your advice! As I said…"

"Strange," Jake mused, stroking his chin so that his negroid hand was clearly visible. "I am black. I am a voter. I live here." Jake pointed his finger at her, emphasizing each clearly enunciated statement. "You haven't asked my opinion. I am proud to be a member of this group. I AM insulted by people like yourself who profess to speak on my behalf about things you clearly know nothing about!" Jake turned to the reporter, "I hope you've got all that down!"

The reporter looked like a rabbit frozen in car headlights. He glanced at the woman whose face had turned beetroot then back at Jake, and swallowed, his Adam's apple bobbing up and down. The crowd had no doubts; they applauded Jake's stance.

Jake hadn't quite finished with the parliamentary candidate, now standing open-mouthed. "You do realise, I hope, that you have also been extremely rude to my young friends, whose father is an influential member of this town."

She turned on her heel and bustled off, trying to maintain some dignity, followed by her minions, all with glum faces.

"Silly bitch!" Jake muttered to us. Kissy and Sophie were consoling Holly who was fighting back tears.

"Are you? Is he?" I asked.

"What?"

"A voter? Holly's father?"

"Don't know, probably. I did fill in a form when we first moved into the cottage, and I am 21. Haven't a clue about the twins' parents, but I don't think she will be getting their vote!"

The reporter was still hovering round, recognizing that his piece was going to be substantially more than a dreary hustings report.

"Gentlemen …and ladies … ah … who are you?"

Even driving back to Penybont some time later we were still bubbling with enthusiasm over our inaugural public performance and Jake's taming of the dragon woman.

"That's Benji, isn't it?" said Dan. There was no mistaking the shock of black hair, even from a rear view.

"What's he got under his arm?" Jake said, leaning forward from the back seat.

"Looks like a bicycle frame," I said, as I passed by Benji and pulled Jessica to the side of the road several yards beyond.

He opened the passenger door. "Hey, man! That's real cool! I'm knackered!"

"Wheels drop off, did they?" asked Dan.

Benji ignored him.

"What are you going to do with that?" I asked

"Cyclic rejuvenation still life sculpture, man!"

If Jake had said it I'd have been certain he was taking the piss.

"I meant now. You're welcome to a lift but not your scrap metal."

Benji looked pained, "Aw, man! It's got to come with me. Someone might knick it, else."

"Ride off into the night with it, you mean?" said Dan unsympathetically.

"Hang on, Rob, couldn't we put it on the roof?" Jake suggested.

"I haven't got a roof rack, in case you hadn't noticed."

"We could tie it on."

"With?" I asked sceptically.

"No problem," said Jake. "Hop out of the car, Dan, and give me your belt."

"What!"

"Your belt." Jake was already following Dan out of the car and unstrapping his own belt. "Benji, lay the frame on top of this coat." He flung his raggy jacket over the car roof. "I hope you gave Jessica a wash," he said to me.

Right now I was more concerned about scratches to her body than her cleanliness.

"Right, Dan, now loop your belt round the frame and bring in the ends. I'll do the same on this side. Oh bugger!"

Traffic is quite light on the Penybont road, but the Saturday bus, full of shoppers returning from Tencastle, chugged up just as Jake's jeans slid down. With Jake hands stretching over the roof to the bike frame, Benji hurried round and attempted to rehoist Jake's breeches.

"Ouch, watch you're doing!"

"Sorry, man!"

On the passenger side, Dan was trying to hold his trousers up with one hand and loop his belt around the bike with the other.

"Will you lot hurry up before we get arrested for lewd behaviour," I yelled.

A few minutes and several curses later all four of us were squeezed in the car, with Dan and Jake hanging on tightly to their belts.

"Take it easy now, Rob," Jake advised, as I pulled away.

"I'm not at bloody Brands Hatch!" Gently was the only way I was going to do the couple of miles to the cottage.

"Hey, man, how did the old rituals go? Did my posters draw the crowds?"

"In a manner of speaking, Benji," I said. "Apart from a clerical error."

At the cottage Benji and I carefully removed the bike frame, and returned the belts to their owners.

"Why didn't you use Jessica's tow-rope, man?" said Benji innocently.

When we gathered by Goliath at 10.30 on Monday morning, the headgear had undergone a few changes. Still nothing like uniformity, but the fez and bowler had been replaced by bobble hats with the odd ribbon.

"Okay, guys," said Jake. "Shall we agree the day's itinerary? How about we do a display here for Goliath."

"Do you think he'll rise to the occasion?" Min whispered to me.

"… the Castle, for a quick jar, then back here, down by the river, and finish up at … what was your pub called, Maurice?"

"Fox and Shepherd."

"Right. Perhaps have a bite there."

Holly had been hanging on Jake's every word, like hero worship. She raised her hand tentatively. "We … er, that is, … er … my parents and us … I … um … we'd like to invite you all back for tea … And something to eat. If you'd like to …"

Harry nodded his head in confirmation of his sister's words.

"That's very kind of you … your parents," said Jake. "Are we up for it?"

Most hands shot up.

"Not you Gron?"

"Sorry, I've got another engagement later this afternoon."

"I'm afraid I'll have to opt out, too," said Dicky. "Love to otherwise."

"Where do you live?" Dan asked the twins.

"Between here and Pwllgoch – only a couple of miles."

Jake and Dan looked at Harry, then enquiringly at me.

"You're thinking Jessica's taxi service, I suppose," I said. "Okay, but it'll cost you a pint apiece."

"But you're driving!"

I made a rude sign at Jake.

"Our dad's going to pick us up at three o'clock," said Holly, "so we could take a couple more."

I reckoned I could just about manage with two trips.

Without phantom pig shows and politicians, our displays went surprisingly smoothly. The balmy May sunshine had brought a fair number of people to Tencastle – local families and their kids playing in the park, bank holiday day trippers, even the odd coach party stopping off for a comfort break. Any casual visitor could take in the sights of Tencastle quite easily within the space of half an hour or so – and those who asked about the castle were disappointed to be shown the few boulders and grassed mound at the north end of the park where the river had once cut out a low cliff.

Our audiences were appreciative, though fairly transient, with an attention span which barely stretched to the duration of our limited repertoire. Rud, de facto treasurer, worked wonders with the saucepan, timing his collection to perfection.

"Are you collecting for charity?" one matronly woman asked.

"Yes indeed," Rud responded, promptly moving on to his next target before having to explain that charity, for us, was very much likely to begin and stay at home.

Taking only one short beer break at the Castle, we danced almost continuously, with growing confidence (and also, as Gron commented, with some degree of proficiency) around the town, through to our finale, at the Fox and Shepherd. Elated, but, speaking for myself, bloody knackered, we spread ourselves and gear out over the benches in a corner of the riverside beer garden, to enjoy a well-earned pint of Hancocks.

"How much did we take?" asked Maurice.

"Give me a mo!" said Rud, who was busy arranging the heap of coins on the table into neat little stacks. He'd already tucked a few paper notes into his belt.

We gathered round to audit the bean counting.

A few minutes and nearly a pint later, Rud wiped the beer froth from his lips. "Well, added to the £12 or so we took on Saturday, I reckon we've got …" He did a quick calculation on the back of a beer mat. "Thirty three pounds seventy three pence and, er, foreign reserves of seventy centimes, twenty pfennigs, a ten pound monopoly banknote, one coat button and a few old pennies and ha'pennies."

A spontaneous cheer and applause caused a few turned heads from other tables.

"What are we actually going to do with the money?" asked Sophie.

"Drinks all round, for a start," said Dan. Which generated a few heads nodding in approval.

"Shouldn't we be giving it to charity?" Sophie persisted.

"Why?" Rud challenged.

"Because … you said so, didn't you?"

"Did I?"

"When you were passing the pan round."

"Oh that. I may have said something in passing. I didn't say which one!" Rud sighed, "Come on, Sophie, we've worked bloody hard for this, let's enjoy ourselves."

"Actually," Jake mused, "Sophie has got a point, of sorts. We've never talked about what we'd do with any money we collected. I don't think we really expected more than a few coppers at the most."

"What about expenses?" I said.

"What do you mean?"

"Well, Jake, like cost of bells, materials and so on. We've all probably spent out something."

"I have, certainly," said Kissy, "but that's not going to take thirty odd quid, or anything like."

"I've got an idea," said Huw. "I live near Haverfordwest. My father's got a field he sometimes lets scouts use for camping. We could stay there and use the money for transport and food. Have a holiday and perhaps do some dancing, and any money we collect then we'll make a point of giving it to a charity, if Sophie's got one in mind."

"Brilliant idea, Huw," Min bubbled enthusiastically.

"Be great to do some more dancing. I'm definitely up for it!" said Dan.

"Sophie?" Jake asked.

"I've no problem with that. Perhaps Holly and Harry could look into a local charity."

"One thought," said Kissy. "When were we thinking of doing this, and what about any of us who can't go."

"That's two thoughts!" Rud got a withering look from Kissy for being pedantic.

"Well, perhaps straight after end of term?"

"Would anybody not be able to make it then?" Jake asked.

"We're going away at the beginning of summer with our parents," Holly said. "So I'm afraid we'd have to decline."

"I've got a job for the whole of the vacation ... unfortunately!" Maurice said glumly.

"Me too, sorry." said Dicky.

"Camping's a young person's game, not for me, sorry," said Gron.

"Anyone else?" Jake asked.

No one else spoke up.

"Right, that leaves myself, Rob, Dan, Huw, Rud, Min, Kissy and Sophie. That's seven dancers plus music. Definitely do-able."

"One point," I said. "I don't mind ferrying you up to Holly and Harry's place, but I'm not doing a shuttle to ruddy Pembrokeshire!"

"That's not a problem, Rob. If some of you can make your way there by public transport, I'll be able to borrow my mother's car to ferry us around where needs be."

"Thanks, Huw. And for the idea," I said.

"I think that those not going should share in our profits," said Jake. "So how about we let Rud have our expenses, then divide the rest between us all. Those of us going camping can pool our share and those not going can get blind drunk, have a slap-up meal or give to charity as they wish."

No one dissented.

"Is everyone happy that we take some expenses for another pint all round to celebrate?

"Jake," said Holly, patting his arm tentatively. "Just a reminder, my parents are picking us up at three o'clock."

"Thanks, Holly. Can we all manage a pint in twenty minutes?

No one dissented.

Jessica was not exactly generously proportioned when it came to passenger comfort, but she seemed like a limousine compared to the little Fiat 500 which drew up by Goliath. A slightly-built woman in a pink summer dress but otherwise hidden beneath a huge straw sun-hat remained in the front passenger seat while a tall fortyish fellow uncoiled himself from behind the driving wheel. Slim but muscular, he was casually but smartly dressed in pale green slacks with beige open-necked shirt and a cravat. You could see where the twins got their facial genes from.

"Hi Pet, sorry we're late. Land Rover had a flat tyre." Educated neutral accent, definitely not Welsh. He held out his hand to Jake, "I'm Eric Dickens. You must be Jake. Holly's told me a lot about you."

"Dad!" Holly blushed.

"It's not all true," said Jake, in a touch of modesty.

"I'm afraid I can only take two of you," said Eric.

"Jake and I will come with you," Holly declared without hesitation. "Harry, perhaps you could show Rob the way?"

"Sure, Hol."

I squeezed Sophie, Kissy and Min onto Jessica's rear seat, with Harry in front. "Start walking along the Pwllgoch road," I said to the other lads, "I'll be back shortly."

A crow might have made the Dicken's place in two miles. Jessica certainly couldn't, and I was darn glad of Harry's directions, since the Fiat had sped off without waiting for us. We followed the main road along the river beyond Pant Gorau for at least two miles.

"Next left," said Harry.

There didn't seem to be any turning signposted.

"Here!" he yelled.

I hit the brakes sharply, the girls almost joining us in the front. I'd just passed the entrance to a narrow lane, which had appeared in a gap between tall hedges. Reversing, I noticed an old wooden signpost, green with lichen, which pointed to 'The Mount'.

More like a bloody mountain – the road, which as some consolation was metalled, led steeply upwards, winding through overhanging trees which let little daylight through. Jessica didn't like the gradient one little bit and made such sluggish progress that we could have been overtaken by a snail – if there had been room.

"Not far now," Harry said. "Turn off right where the main road bears left."

If this was the main road I dreaded to think what he considered a minor road.

Jessica just about coughed and spluttered into a stony track, which, a couple of hundred yards further on, led through a masonry arch into the gravelled courtyard of a large old house which commanded impressive views over the Tene Valley below.

"Thanks ever so, Rob. See you soon!" Min blew me a kiss, as I left my passengers and headed back.

Maurice, Dan, Rud and Huw had just about cleared the Tencastle boundary, and they waved furiously as I sped past, looking for a place to turn.

"Thought you'd got lost," Dan said ungraciously. I shoe-horned him into the back seat between Rud and Huw, with Huw's bagpipe box spread over his lap.

Even with previous knowledge I nearly missed the turning again. Jessica shuddered at the prospect of another hill climb with an even heavier load. I bungled the double declutch into bottom gear and the engine coughed and died.

"We're going to have to lose some ballast, guys. I'm afraid you're going to have to get out and walk."

Which was easier said than done in the straightjacket of the high-banked narrow lane, but they didn't fancy staying on board while I reversed the hundred yards or so snakewise back down to the junction.

Engaging bottom gear from the outset, I revved the engine, prayed, and let out the clutch. If Jessica had been a horse, I'd have probably given her a sugar lump. Slowly, surely she chugged upwards, past the lads who had to press themselves into a small gateway. We made the turn off, and waited for several minutes till the foot passengers puffed into view.

"Want a lift?" I said cheerily.

Their reply was unprintable.

Those who had arrived earlier were gathered on the lawn, glasses of wine or beer already well sampled. A smaller edition of Holly stood beside an elderly couple reclining in deck chairs. Several other folding chairs were interspersed with garden benches made from sawn logs.

"What kept you?" asked Jake. Holly clung to his arm.

"Jessica had a heart attack," Dan grunted.

"Grab yourself a drink," Jake waved his hand to the patio where Eric and his wife were attending to a smoky barbecue. "We're going to give our hosts a short display before we eat."

Huw retrieved his bagpipes from my car and played a couple of Welsh reels to attract everyone's attention.

Min parked her tankard, freshly brimming, on a bench, adjusted her Stetson to which she'd recently attached a forest of shrubbery that dangled over her glasses, and was first up on the lawn, stick in hand. The rest of us ambled on and milled around until some kind of regular formation became recognizable.

In a semi-inebriated manner of speaking, we gave a spirited performance of the three dances that were reasonably implanted in our memory – and received polite applause from the Dickens elders. I saw Rud making for the old saucepan and managed to catch his eye with a discreet waggle of my finger to abort a collection.

I would have stopped while we were winning, but Jake was all for a go at the stick dance supposedly from Upton-on-Severn, which, while quite showy, neither musician nor dancers had convincingly mastered. Without Gron's guidance and our ability to recall the order of the figures let alone distinguish between left and right, someone else always seemed to be occupying my patch of turf. Fortunately we emerged unscathed, though Grandpa Dickens had a close escape when the broken end of a stick landed at his feet.

"Bravo!" Eric cheered. "You've certainly earned your supper! Come and help yourselves."

Apart from a sandwich and a packet of crisps, our diet had been mainly liquid, and I for one was ravenous.

"This is really very kind of you, Mrs Dickens," I said, as she heaped burger, sausages and chicken legs onto my plate.

"Kathryn, please!" she said, smiling. "Not at all! We're so pleased that the twins have found such a lovely group of friends. They are normally so shy and you seem to have given them a lot of self-confidence. Do help yourself to salad!"

"Tell me," said Eric to Jake, when we were all sitting around the lawn munching, "I appreciate you rescuing Holly and Harry from that terrible woman, but how did you know I was, as you put it, an influential member of the town?"

"Er, I didn't, actually."

Eric's coleslaw-laden fork stopped between plate and mouth, and he guffawed with laughter. "You didn't ... you really didn't know that I'm the Editor of the Tene Messenger?"

It was Jake's turn to look amazed. "You are?"

"Indeed. My young reporter was falling over himself to tell me what had happened at the market on Saturday, and when I heard from Holly that she'd been directly involved, I wanted to see for myself what phenomenon had got Barbara Bowen-Martin's knickers in a twist, if you'll pardon my expression. It's not often, unfortunately, that she's rendered speechless."

"She really got up my nose!" said the phenomenon.

"She gets up everyone's nose. Can't stand the woman." Eric placed his plate on the grass, and leant forward in his seat, resting his chin on interlaced hands. "I'll be running the story of your encounter with her, with appropriate editorial comment, of course, and I'd also like to do a feature on your group here. If you'd like to fill me in on some background, about the Morris and its link to Wales in particular, I'd be very obliged."

Wow!

"What about the Messenger's owner? Won't you get some flak?" Jake asked.

"I own nearly half of the shares, Kathryn holds some, and a local Tory supporter has most of the rest. No problem!" Eric resumed his meal. "Perhaps you could give me an hour of your time this evening. I'll run you back to Tencastle afterwards if your friends don't want to hang around."

He looked around at us, relaxing, eating, drinking. "But you're all welcome to stay as long as you like. Have some more food and drink."

I felt that I'd better stick to Coke from now on, as I'd probably been over the safe limit to drive even before I'd got here. The others weren't showing much abstention, however, particularly Min, who, despite her small frame, was managing to down a fair volume. I was pretty sure she'd poured wine into her tankard at her most recent visit to the drinks' table.

The garden, facing westwards, was bathed in the early evening sunshine. Far below, the Tene shone like a silvery thread across the green patchwork meadows.

I'm not sure how long I'd been basking dreamlike in the blissful pastoral scene, not quite asleep, but definitely switched off, when I felt someone gently shake my shoulder.

"Sorry to disturb you, Rob, but is there any chance you could run us back into town? Kissy and I were meeting a couple of friends at the Union this evening."

"No problem, Sophie," I said, standing up and brushing the grass off my jeans and shirt. "What about the others?"

"The lads seem quite happy. Eric said he'd give them a lift later, and there's nothing to stop you coming back!"

"What about Min?" I glanced to where she was rolling on the grass, giggling, and trying to get Harry, Holly and the younger sister to do a stick dance horizontally.

"I think she might like a lift too. She must have hollow legs, the amount she's put away, but I guess she must be getting near to capacity."

Min took a couple of attempts to push herself to her feet and wobbled unsteadily towards her tankard. I headed her off.

"Going back now, Min," I said gently.

"Awright. Mus'avapee."

Sophie guided her up the steps and into the house. I hoped Eric and Kathryn didn't notice quite the state she was in. I wouldn't have wanted his article to associate Morris dancing with rolling drunkenness.

I picked up Min's Stetson and tankard. Kissy and I headed for the car after giving our farewells and thanks to Eric and Kathryn. When Sophie reappeared with Min, she volunteered to keep an eye on her in the back seat but I thought it might be prudent for Min to have quick access to the door in case she couldn't hold her drink.

As it happened Min sat quietly with a broad grin on her face all the way back and even seemed to be capable of coherent conversation again after I'd dropped the girls at the Union.

"Grea' party. What a place they've got!"

"Indeed. Quite a turn up for the book."

We drew up outside 'Crombie Hall.

"In f'ra coffee, Rob?"

"Okay." My need for caffeine probably wasn't as great as hers but I still felt a little concerned about whether she'd be able to find her way unaided.

We went arm in arm up the steps and a little more discreetly through the lobby for Percy the Porter's benefit.

"'Stairs," Min mumbled and dragged me away from the Common Room area.

I glanced at Percy in his cubby hole. He'd noted my presence but didn't seem unduly concerned that male curfew time in students' study bedrooms was less than an hour away.

Min's room was on the second floor, next to the communal toilets and showers. She fumbled with her key.

"Shall I do it?"

"Mmm, please." She took off her sunglasses and looked at me, with a rather whimsical expression. "You go on in. Need to get out these rags."

I entered, leaving the door ajar. The room was much like the one I'd had at Thomas Hall, though in delicate pastel pink décor. Min had a fluffy bunny on her pillow. No family photos, though.

I didn't hear the door close.

"Rob?"

I turned. Min was standing there stark naked, her clothes strewn on the floor. She had small but beautifully shaped breasts, with farthing-sized dark areolae and aroused nipples, satin smooth skin and a neat swatch of black pubic hair.

"Min! What…"

She fell on me, her tongue searching, pushing through my lips, as we tumbled back on the bed. She turned her attention to nibbling my ear, and murmured, "Show me your fertility rights, Rob."

One hand curled around my neck, the other began to explore my zip, already straining against a reflex action.

Next moment she was asleep, lightly snoring almost like the purring of a pussycat.

I extricated myself. She looked so delicate and innocent lying there, bosom heaving gently, and definitely pleasing to the eye. Apart from my younger sister before puberty and Sandra, briefly, I'd not had an unrestricted eyeful of fully naked female in the flesh before. Ever the gentleman, I resisted, with difficulty, the temptation to stroke her skin, caress her breasts.

Even so, I must have lingered for several more minutes before taking her in my arms to gently lift her from the bedcover so that I could pull back the sheets and tuck her safely in to bed. She murmured softly but to all intents and purposes she was out to the world. I kissed her softly on the forehead and took my leave.

"Goodnight, Mr Rose," said Percy.

Rose? Blimey, I didn't think he'd have remembered me from my previous fleeting visit to Abercrombie over a year ago!

Coming down to Earth from cloud nine was never going to be easy, and the next two days back at College were an anticlimax in trumps.

Min caught up with me on Wednesday morning in the main building coffee bar. Definitely not her usual bubbly self, in fact, she looked more than a tad worried.

"Rob, oh, I did need to see you! You haven't been deliberately avoiding me, have you?"

"Not at all. What's the problem?" Not that I needed to ask.

"Monday … I can't remember … I think I left the party with you, but … I woke up in bed with … with nothing on." She looked almost ready to burst into tears. "Did you … did we … er, you know … do anything?"

"Nothing happened, Min. I took you back to 'Crombie and saw you safely inside. You must have got undressed and crashed out." God's truth.

Her face lit up. "Oh, gosh," she heaved a sigh of relief, "I thought perhaps …"

"I think you'd had a fair bit to drink," I said diplomatically, "but your virtue is safe." I wasn't so sure about her reputation but it wasn't going to be me to gossip.

"I'm sorry, I suppose I got a bit carried away. I did enjoy the dancing, the party and everything so much. I hope we can do something like that again, don't you?"

"Um…"

"Thanks, Rob, for being so sweet." She threw her arms around my neck and gave me a full-bodied, passionate kiss.

"Careful you don't get carried away again," I said, as I came up for air.

"Have you seen the Messenger?" Dicky caught up with me on the way to the Union for a bite of lunch.

"Which one?" I said innocently.

"The paper, of course! We're in it!"

"Are we?"

"You don't sound surprised."

I wasn't, but of course Dicky had missed out on the jollies. "Can I have a look?"

Eric had really done us proud. Beneath the front page banner headline 'For Whom The Bells Toll' was a picture of Barbara Bowen-Martin ranting away on her soapbox juxtapositioned to us ragged lot posing for the reporter post-encounter in the market square. Two columns of text filled in the juicy detail, with a footnote that she had declined to comment. Inside, the editorial was given over to the various bandwagons that Madam B-M had ill-advisedly jumped on, while the features page gave an account of Welsh Border Morris and our part in its revival.

I caught sight of a small paragraph at the bottom of a page.

"Remember Joseph Carpenter, Dicky?"

"Holy Joe? What's he done, performed a miracle?"

"Not quite, though he tried. Fined and banned for drunk driving."

"You're joking! He was teetotal!"

"Well, he assisted at a number of services and it seems he was inclined to polish off the left-over communion wine. Prosecution rejected his claim of transubstantiation."

"Or was Christ's blood over the limit perhaps?" Dicky said irreverently.

"Have you seen the Messenger?" Jake asked, as soon as I got back to the cottage that same Thursday evening.

"Yes, indeed."

"Good, isn't it?"

I agreed.

"Eric rang me to check on a couple of details. Seems in fairness he also contacted Madam to get her comments and she went apeshit. Threatened him with all kinds of legal action until he called her bluff by pointing out that her deeds had been witnessed by a number of people."

"Stupid cow."

"I'm thinking of getting the gang together again next Monday."

Jake hadn't arranged another practice to follow our Bank Holiday capers, but it seemed a good idea – particularly if we intended to follow up Huw's camping offer.

"Can we get in touch with everybody in time?"

"Don't see why not," said Jake. "Pigeon-holes, personal contact and so on. I'll have a word with the Castle tomorrow."

"Kit?"

"I don't think so. Just business."

There was, of course, the matter of sharing the spoils.

Our gathering had something of a celebratory party atmosphere to it, with a buzz about how, in our short career, we'd made the headlines – even if was only in the local paper. Holly and Harry brought along glossy colour copies of the front page photo for each of us. Benji, wanting part of the action, brought along his sketch pad and, aided by the photo, began to churn out A4 size caricatures of every one of the team in full regalia – exaggerated head on diminutive body.

"Be priceless, man, when I'm famous, like."

"I thought artists only became famous a century after their death," said Dan, in a loud aside.

We refilled our glasses and got down to business. Min winked at me as she sat down opposite me, and raised her tankard. "Not getting carried away," she whispered.

Rud relished the role of banker, doling out the cash in accordance with the expenses chits he'd been given and an equal share of the remainder, which amounted to £3 a head.

"Right now," said Jake. "On to our next venture. Huw?"

"I've checked with my father, and he's happy for us to stay as long as we want."

"Brilliant! Now, are we still up for it? Any changes of mind?"

All the original hands went up. Dicky 's arm was at half mast.

"Dicky? Be good if you could come along."

"I'd like to, but I'm not sure. I'm trying to arrange a later start for my job. Let me have details and I'll join you if I can, even if for only part of the week."

"I'll give you my parent's home number," Huw offered.

"Thanks."

"Logistics," said Jake. "Transport. How to get there. Rob has some space in his car …"

"Not a lot," I interjected.

"…but for most of us it's probably the train. There is a train, I assume, Huw?"

"Haverfordwest is the nearest station. I could meet you."

"When would we go?" Kissy asked.

"Well, we've got this week and next at college, then we're free. How about a fortnight today?"

We thought about this for a while and no one raised any objections.

"That's it then," said Jake. "All sorted."

"Er, Jake," I said. "Tents. I assume we're not sleeping under hedges."

"Good point. Hadn't thought of that."

"We'll need space for seven people, eight if Dicky joins us," I added.

"Don't forget me," said Huw, "I'm camping too."

"Thought you'd be tucked up in your own soft bed."

"No way, the field's half a mile from our house. I'll rough it with the rest of you. I've got a ridge tent which will take three at a pinch."

"We bought a family frame tent last year," said Holly, "I'm sure Dad wouldn't mind lending it to you."

"But you're not coming with us, are you?" said Jake.

"No, but we're not using it on this holiday."

"Does it take the whole family?"

"It's supposed to. It's got two sleeping sections and the other half we use as a living area. Dad and Harry often usually sleep in the Land Rover though."

"Okay, so that would be best for Sophie, Kissy and Min. I presume you don't want to sleep with us lads."

Min looked disappointed.

Rud offered a small two-person hiking tent.

"That's eight, then. Great!" Jake rubbed his hands. "I'm sure we can roll over and make space for Dicky if he turns up."

CHAPTER FOURTEEN

Summer Days

The original intention had been for the three of us to stay on at the cottage and travel down together. Dan, however, decided that he needed to go back home to Brighton for his mother's birthday that weekend and also to collect a few bits and pieces. Which was just as well. With great difficulty we managed to squeeze the Dickens' enormous frame tent and all its accessories onto Jessica's back seat, though even with the front seats as far forward as possible Jake and I had our knees almost up to our chins for the return trip from The Mount.

"Can we get hold of a roof rack?" Jake asked as we approached the town centre.

I'd been thinking along the same lines and I pulled onto the forecourt of Owain's Auto Emporium.

Owain waddled out. "Looking to change your car, young man?"

"Not yet, thanks. She's still going strong. I was wondering, do you have a roof rack I could buy or borrow?"

He glanced in the back. "I'm thinking you'll need a trailer with that little lot, boyo!" He stroked his stubble. "Wait a minute, though, I may be able to help you." He disappeared behind the garage, and emerged a couple of minutes later with a tubular metal frame. "Here, took this off an old Ford I had in for breaking. Give it a bit of a clean, should be fine."

I looked dubiously at the obvious patches of rust. "How much?"

"Tenner to you, sir."

"Fiver, as seen and fitted," I said.

He adopted a pained expression, "Done!"

He demonstrated how the contraption should be secured, and I parted with the cash. The relocation of the frame tent could wait.

I doubt if Jessica had ever been such a beast of burden before. If she'd been a donkey, I would have been reported to the RSPCA for cruelty. However, she bore her load without protest, apart from a few more creaks and rattles than usual, and a laborious crawl up any gradient more than five degrees from the horizontal. The worst bit was getting her out of Penybont itself.

We weren't in any particular hurry – it would have made no difference even if we had been – with the plan to arrive at Huw's field in the afternoon and set up camp. Jessica had been excused shuttle duty, which left us plenty of time for a pint and a ploughman's just beyond Carmarthen.

"Time to test your skills at navigation," I said to Jake as we approached Haverfordwest.

"No problem," said Jake, scanning the used envelope on which Huw had scribbled directions. "According to this, we take a left turn on the other side of the town, then go on for another three or four miles towards Broad Haven and look for a farm track."

"Very helpful. Isn't he more specific?"

"There's a sketch, with several spikes coming out of the top of a circle marked HFW, and an arrow marked 'this one' and his phone number. That's all, apart from something so smudged I can't read it."

The local Ordnance Survey map would have been a sensible investment, but it's easy to be wise in hindsight.

"Which way?" I said, as we approached a junction at the top of a hill, having negotiated some narrow streets through the town.

"Left!" said Jake, and added, "I think", several hundred yards after I'd made the turn.

"Did you see the signpost?"

"I think I saw Broad Haven. On one of the signs."

"Recognise anything?" I asked, hopefully, ten minutes later. We'd already travelled more than four miles.

"Should I?"

"I take it you mean no?"

"Well, Huw's sketch is, well, sketchy."

We arrived at a small village with a multitude of junctions, a pub and little else.

"Where are we?" I asked.

"Tiers Cross."

"I thought you said Huw hadn't given any place names."

"He didn't. I saw the name as we came into the village."

"And where should we be?"

"Not here. We could always go back and try that other road."

I pulled Jessica to a halt near a telephone box. "Here, give me the paper, I'm going to ring that number."

Huw's mother, in a wonderfully lilting Welsh accent, confirmed that we shouldn't have been where we were, and gave me detailed instructions, with every minor landmark and place name. Fortunately we didn't have to retrace our tracks completely. Even so, we might still have missed the farm had it not been for Huw jumping up and down at the side of the road.

"Hi guys, glad you found us okay! I'll come with you and show you the way." Looking in the car, he could see the problem. "Or better, hang on a tick and you can follow me in the Land Rover."

Huw led us fifty yards or so up a stony track which sorely tested Jessica's ageing suspension, and into a small field just below the brow of a hill. From the evidence underfoot the rough grass had been recently cropped quite short by sheep.

"I'll see you later. Got to pick up the others from the station."

Jake stretched his legs and took in the view. "Hey, this is life! Sea, surf, fresh salt air! Don't get much of this in London!" Bordered on one side by a small wood, the aspect of our campsite to the west was fantastic, with distant white-crested waves rolling in towards the shoreline of a broad bay.

I fiddled with the ropes securing the frame tent to the roof rack. "Where do you think we should pitch the tent?"

Jake looked round. "Dunno, really. Near the trees? Close to the facilities?"

"What facilities?"

"Huw mentioned water and loos."

No modern toilet block was in evidence. A ramshackle corrugated iron shelter stood near the boundary with the wood. We went to investigate.

"Primitive," said Jake, wrinkling his nose at the earthy odour emanating from the pits over which two wooden toilet seats had been attached to a couple of lengths of four-by-two in each of the crude cubicles. A few drapes of hessian sacking held up by baler twine afforded the only modicum of privacy, while still giving an occupant a generous view of the trees.

"The girls will love this," I said, ruefully.

"Well they can at least sit down properly. Building site I worked on once you had to perch on rough sawn timber to shit. Had bloody splinters in my bum for weeks!"

A further search located a standpipe above a water trough, a few yards along from the gate.

"Bit small for a bath, isn't it?" said Jake. "Though Min might manage, sideways."

The best position for the tents, we agreed, was between the water tap and the bogs, not too close to the latter, of course. We laid all the poles, pegs, guy ropes and fabrics on the ground behind Jessica and stood contemplating a three-dimensional jigsaw.

"Any instructions?" asked Jake. "Should be, as it's almost brand new."

"Yes," I said. "But I'm not sure how useful they will be. The diagrams are minimalistic and the text a poor translation from some oriental language."

"Well it shouldn't be beyond the wit of two intelligent people to work out."

It wasn't, quite, but trial and error featured largely in our method since we'd tried at first to use all the poles for the main tent.

"What do you think these other bits are for?"

"It could be a toilet tent," I said.

"En suite?"

"I don't think so. Besides which we haven't got the portable loo to go with it."

"Not much use then." But we put it up anyway.

Alongside the green canvas ridge tent that Huw had left for us, the Dickens' dwelling appeared palatial, with an inner section with integral ground sheet divided into two sleeping compartments, and plenty of space to stand upright in the kitchen/diner area that boasted a large clear plastic window and a generous sheltered canopy.

A throaty roar heralded the return of Huw, and the Land Rover disgorged its human cargo with baggage of rucksacks and a couple of black bin-liners belonging to Min. She, along with Sophie, was dressed for the field in shorts and loose shirt. We shared hugs all round, like long lost friends, although it was only three days earlier that we'd still been together at Tencastle.

Jake and I presented the girls with their mansion-cum-community centre.

"Hey, this is brilliant, just brilliant!" Min enthused in her usual way.

"Sea looks wonderful," said Kissy. "Hope you've all brought your cossies."

While the girls were sorting out their gear and Dan helped Rud erect his small tent, Jake took Huw to one side.

"I started to make a list of various things we need. There wasn't room in Jessica for the kitchen sink."

"All sorted," said Huw. "I just need to go back to the farm. Ma's put together a whole load of things, probably including a sink, if I know her."

"That's great! And a watering can and an old metal bucket if possible."

"What on earth do you want those for?" I said.

"You'll find out," he said, secretively. "Could you add camping stools or folding chairs to your list, Huw?"

"I'll see what I can do. Anything else?"

"Where are the nearest shops? We'll need tea, coffee, milk, food for breakfast…"

"Loo rolls, beer," I added.

"… and there's probably a few more things we ought to buy."

"Broad Haven is the nearest place. That's in the bay you can see from here. It's only got a basic convenience store for essential goods plus buckets and spades."

"How far?"

"Couple of miles or so. Walkable, but it's uphill all the way back."

"We'll take the car," Jake decided, without asking for my approval.

"Look, why don't we rally the troops and all head down into Broad Haven? Do the shopping, have a swim, get some fish and chips, perhaps have a pint or two? I can pick up the things from home on the way back."

There's probably some exponential formula which relates the number of people in a group with the time taken to make a group decision, but a reminder from Huw that we had exactly half an hour before the shop closed, whether it was actually true or not, quickly focussed our minds. We took swimming gear and musical instruments, but didn't bother with Morris kit, on the basis that it would involve more time-consuming rummaging in kit bags. Besides, we needed to suss out the best dancing spots and the local hostelries, to see if the natives were friendly.

As it was still in school term time and any early season holidaymakers would have already started thinking about their evening meal, we had the beach almost to ourselves. While the rest of us frolicked about in the surf, Rud undertook – he might have even volunteered – to do the shopping, on the basis that he hadn't unpacked his swimming trunks. He also held the purse strings.

The ebbing tide had already left a wide expanse of golden sand exposed, with acres of space after our dip to play an impromptu game of tag rugby with an old plimsoll we'd found abandoned. Nobody bothered much about rules and nobody seemed to be sure whose team they were in, Jake's or Huw's. Exhausted, we eventually flopped out on the sand to soak up the early evening sunshine.

"Where's Rud got to?" Sophie asked.

"Shopping, but he should have been finished long ago," Huw said. "I gave him the spare key to put the stuff directly into the Land Rover, then join us. We're not exactly inconspicuous."

"Perhaps he's having a problem making himself understood by the locals," Dan suggested. "Or vice versa."

It was not until sometime later when we'd dried off and were getting dressed again that Rud appeared.

"What kept you?" Jake asked.

"A stupid old git and a copper."

"He hasn't rammed my Ma's car, has he?" Huw demanded, with great concern. "My Ma will kill me!"

"No, not that." He exhaled heavily.

We waited impatiently for him to elaborate.

"Well, I'd done all the shopping – four bloody great carrier bags, if you must know…"

"Get on with it," Huw said without sympathy.

"I was trying to unlock your car … at least I thought it was your car … when this old bloke rushed out of a cafe ranting and raving, and accused me of trying to break into his vehicle. I apologised and explained to him that I'd mistaken his car for yours. I pointed out that I would hardly be likely to burgle it to put more things inside. Silly bugger wouldn't have any of it, demanded I stayed put while he called the police."

"So what did you do?" I asked.

"Well, I wasn't going to be running far with four heavy …"

"Yes, yes, go on."

Rud glowered at Jake. "Anyway, I did eventually spot Huw's buggy parked further back in the car park, and I started to walk towards it…"

"Are you sure it was mine?" Huw interrupted.

"I recognised the mud on it," Rud said sarcastically. "The bloke went ballistic – grabbed hold of me, swearing about layabouts and vagabonds. I shook him off and started to tell him what I thought of short-sighted ignorant old fools…"

"It was your mistake. And his car," I pointed out.

"I suppose so," Rud conceded. "Things could have got nasty if a copper in a patrol car hadn't turned up. When he'd had an earful from the moron, I told him my side of the story, how we were staying at Huw's family's farm and so on. Fortunately he also recognised the vehicle, and when the key I had fitted, well, that was the end to the affair."

"What about the old bloke?"

"He wasn't happy. Claimed I'd assaulted him, but a young couple with a child who'd witnessed the whole incident spoke to the copper, who made it clear that no further action would be taken. Bloke stumped back into the cafe muttering about tearaways and taxpayers."

"I think we'll give that cafe a miss," said Jake. "Hope it wasn't the chippie!"

Which reminded us that we were getting hungry.

"Two options," said Huw. "We can find something here or go over to Little Haven. It's not far, and it's got three pubs."

We compromised. Instant attention to appetite where we were, then, because no-one felt like walking, a short drive over the hill to the next bay for liquid refreshment and an amicable banter over possible activities for the week ahead. One landlord seemed quite amenable to the idea of us dancing there during the week, and even offered to put some notices up. He would have been willing for us to have a music session in the back bar there and then, but Huw reminded us of some practicalities.

"It might be a good idea to return to camp while there's still some daylight. We've still got quite a bit of gear to sort out, which might be difficult in the dark, and I also need to pick up the stuff from home. Ma won't be happy if I roll in at midnight."

"Spoilsport!" said Dan.

"Hey, guys! Why don't we sing around the camp fire instead?"

"Great idea, Min. Should be plenty of dry kindling and old logs in the wood," said Huw.

While the girls busied themselves with sorting out all the pots and pans and whatnots that Huw had collected, and generally imposing some kind of order to the living area of their tent, we lads used the remaining daylight to gather fuel for the camp fire. Dan, who claimed some experience in this kind of field craft from his scouting days in Sussex, carefully built up kindling and small boughs then stood back to admire his handiwork.

"All ready to light," he declared. "Anyone got a match?"

None of us smoked.

"Why are you all looking at me?" said Rud.

"Didn't you buy matches?" asked Jake.

"Wasn't on the list."

"Looks as if you'll have to rub a couple of sticks together, Dan," Jake said.

"Or use the sun's rays and a magnifying glass," suggested Rud, unhelpfully. The sun had already dipped below the horizon.

"Hang on a mo," I said, and went to rummage in Jessica's interior. My father often squirreled away half-empty boxes of matches in any convenient nook or cranny once he'd tired of relighting his pipe. In the depths of the front passenger pocket I found a battered box with four vestas remaining – five, if you counted the broken one with only half an inch of stick below the head.

The first one snapped without igniting. The second burst into flame but blew out before the screwed up old copy of Llais y Castell caught alight.

"Save one for the morning, unless you want cold tea for breakfast," warned Jake.

Fortunately the third attempt was successful, and we soon had a good blaze going, though not before the girls had been half-kippered by eddying wood smoke. The gentle wind couldn't seem to settle on any one direction.

"You're a genius, Dan," said Min, planting a kiss full square on his lips. "Now, we could all dance around the fire, naked, like in a *Midsummer Night's Dream*."

My Shakespeare was a bit shaky, but I'm sure I would have remembered that scenario.

"Um, Min, can we stick to the singing?" said Huw. "I hate to disappoint you, but the people round here are, well, conservative, and I'm not sure my Dad would welcome reports of wild pagan orgies."

"But there's no-one watching!"

"Not yet, but we are near the road and the fire will attract attention. The local farm lads wouldn't be averse to a good oggle on their way home from the pub."

"Oh, right!" Min looked disappointed and Kissy relieved.

Sophie had missed this exchange. "Those loos are disgusting!"

"What do you mean?" said Kissy, concerned again.

"You'll find out! Be sure to take a torch, and don't have anything loose dangling out of your pockets or you'll lose it in the proverbial." She turned to Huw, "You might have warned us!"

"Sorry, I'm sure I said the facilities were basic."

We might have overlooked one or two items, like matches, but we did have the foresight to stock up on the essentials. The pile of empty beer cans grew larger as the night grew longer. Not that we were drunk, but the alcohol helped to lubricate the vocal chords, aid the recollection of half-remembered songs while dulling the senses to off key singing and dubious harmonies. Dan, who always claimed – with some justification – that he couldn't sing, amazed us with his repertoire of woggling ditties, while Jake and Huw produced some incredible duets on banjo and bagpipes, not the most likely pairing of instruments. Not to be outdone, the girls searched their mental archives for some contribution of their own, casting right back to Kissy's Sunday school days for inspiration. Silhouetted against the full moon, they stole the show with a rendition of *Little Donkey* a la Beverley Sisters, of whom Sophie's mother was a great fan.

With beer and fire both getting low, it seemed as good a time as any to crawl away to our sleeping bags.

The tent I shared would have been ideal for two people; with three of us, I felt a certain sympathy for sardines. If one of us really wanted to turn over, the other pair had little choice but to follow suit, while getting out for a leak, not to mention getting back in again, was logistically challenging. It would, I felt, have made more sense to have slept with our heads nearest the entrance. Nevertheless, once the excess beer had filtered through, I managed a couple of hours of unbroken sleep.

"'Morning, Rob!" called Sophie, as I stuck my head out into bright sunlight and sneezed. "Bless you!"

"Wassertime?" I grunted.

"About eight o'clock. Fancy some breakfast?"

I surveyed the scene. All three girls were dressed in shorts and T-shirts. Kissy was frying bacon over the double-burner camping stove that Huw had brought, while Min busied herself setting the large folding pasting table with plastic cereal bowls and plates.

"Are you going to shift your arse out of my face?" Jake had obviously risen. "I need a pee."

I crawled out. "Smells good!"

"Yeah, well we'll do the cooking, and you lot can toss for the washing up," said Sophie.

Returning from the loos, one would have thought Jake was the early riser.

"Come on, you dozy sods, reveille!" He rattled the guy ropes of Rud's tent, then tugged at the bottom of Dan's sleeping bag through the flap of our tent.

"Bugger off!" Dan's muffled voice became louder, as Jake hauled his cocoon out onto the grass. "You flaming pillock! What did you have to do that for?"

"Oh what a beautiful morning!" Jake burst into song and scooped a surprised Min off her feet into an impromptu waltz, and promptly caught his foot in a guy rope.

"Serve you bloody well right for disturbing my beauty sleep!" Dan complained as Jake picked himself and Min up off the grass.

Unconcerned, Jake went to inspect the remains of the camp fire, which he'd stoked up just before turning in. "Still glowing," he called to no-one in particular. "Soon have hot water going."

Among other acquisitions, Huw had produced an old galvanised bucket, an enormous black kettle and a garden hoe. Jake used the latter to lower the two water-filled vessels into the hot ashes. Meanwhile, we tucked into cornflakes, bread and jam and bacon sandwiches, leaving him to join Rud and Huw for the second sitting, assuming there was much left. Min had an enormous appetite for her size.

I'd more or less resigned myself to growing stubble for a few days and a quick splash under the cold tap for ablutions. Jake had other plans for us.

"Who's first for a shower?" he asked holding up a green plastic watering can with a sprinkler rose attached.

"You're joking!" I said.

"Not at all! I've heated the water over the camp fire."

"And the can? Are you going to stand and sprinkle naked bodies in the middle of the field?"

"The toilet tent. Stand on a stool and push the spout through the gap between the side and roof. Girls can wear their swimming costume if they're shy." Jake paused.

We looked at each other and burst out laughing.

"I'm game," said Min. She would be!

"With or without?" asked Jake, a twinkle in his eye.

"Without what?"

"Cossie."

"Definitely without!"

"Right, wrap yourself in a towel, then hand it out from the toilet tent to one of your handmaidens ..."

"Didn't the girls in those oriental palaces have eunuchs to attend them?" Min interrupted.

"Just close your eyes and imagine you're in a palace," said Jake. "If you keep your eyes closed you can pretend we're eunuchs as well, if you like."

Min dived into the inner sanctum of the tent and emerged a couple of minutes later with a huge towel wrapped around her and holding a bar of soap. She stepped into the toilet tent and thrust her hand out with the towel, which Sophie took from her.

"How would you like it?" Jake asked.

"What do you mean?" giggled the voice from within.

"Hot, cold or lukewarm water?"

"Warm would be nice."

Jake filled the watering can and tested the temperature with his finger. He climbed up onto the log he'd placed beside the cubicle and thrust the spout through a gap at the top.

"Ready?"

"Ready."

"Short burst to start, then more to rinse down, okay?"

"Wonderful!" cried Min as water started trickling from the bottom of the tent. "Oh shit!" she then exclaimed. "I've dropped it!" The bar of soap slithered out into a muddy puddle.

Jake handed it back.

"Thanks!" Min giggled.

Jake emptied the can. "That's it. If you want more it's another shilling in the meter!"

Min's hand came out for the towel. Wrapped up again, she stepped out in the sunlight, which caused the water droplets on her hair to sparkle like a tiara. Quite radiant, apart from muddy feet.

"And how was the palace, Princess?" said Jake, bowing from the waist.

"You're a genius! You should be knighted!" declared Min. With little regard for the security of the towel she flung her arms around him and gave him a kiss.

"I could get used to attending to fair young damsels," said Jake, grinning.

"You'd need the operation first," I said.

"Pardon?"

"Can't be a eunuch otherwise!"

I dodged the clod of earth.

"Who's next?" Jake offered.

Rud stepped up, dressed only in boxer shorts.

"Don't forget to give him a kiss, Rud," I said.

Huw and Dan having already declined, Kissy and Sophie were next in line to take advantage of Jake's improvisation. The patch of ground in and around the shower tent became increasingly waterlogged and slippery, however, and Sophie only just saved herself from embarrassing exposure by grabbing on to one of the supporting poles. I thought for a moment the whole caboodle would collapse.

While more water heated up, Jake used the hoe to hack a channel from the back of the cubicle, to divert water away from the main tent. We borrowed a few flattish rocks from the dry stone wall to line the shower floor.

I volunteered to act as shower power for Jake's ablutions, and he then reciprocated for me. By which time, however, whatever hot water remained was distinctly tepid, and, mixed with fresh water, bloody freezing. Once soaked, I didn't fancy hanging around for ten minutes or so for another bucket to heat up. I resolved that I'd be earlier in the queue if Jake operated the service during the rest of the week.

"Wow! That's some beach!" said Sophie in amazement, as a sweeping vista opened in front of us as Jessica began the descent on the minor road. "I don't get to the seaside much from Nottingham."

"Yeah, beats the pebbles of Brighton," said Dan. "Never could understand why it's so popular as a seaside resort. Apart from being only an hour from London."

I had to agree with Sophie. It could hold its own with the North Devon surfing beaches of Saunton and Woolacombe that I used to go to back home.

We'd discussed various plans for the day in the pub the previous evening, and the cloudless sky rendered most of them superfluous. Huw had suggested spending at least the morning on Newgale Sands, a few miles up the coast from our campsite, then working our way back to Little Haven, dancing en route at hostelries or wherever we might have an audience.

By lunchtime, it was too darn hot to contemplate doing anything other than keeping our bodies doused in the surf, and certainly no-one had much enthusiasm for dancing, other than cavorting around waving a few sparse fronds of seaweed at the water's edge. Besides which we'd hired some basic body boards and were determined to have our money's worth. Kissy and Dan were even beginning to look quite convincing while the rest of us wallowed around rarely judging the right moment to be driven ashore by the waves.

The afternoon was well advanced, therefore, when, salt-caked and sunburnt in equal measure, we eventually dressed up in our Carpiog kit. We didn't bother with any blacking up. There was a pub and shop behind the shingle bank at one end of the beach where we began our first performance. Though initially there were only a handful of people around to watch, the sound of our music gradually drew in a sizeable crowd who showed great appreciation for our show. Verbally that is. Rud, who could normally wheedle blood out of stone, was disappointed.

"All that bloody effort for less than four quid!" he moaned.

"People in swimming gear don't often carry cash," Kissy pointed out. "Except to buy an ice cream." She had a point.

We passed on dancing by the kiosks at the other end of the beach. On the way out we'd driven down by a couple of smaller coves, with a café or pub.

The first hamlet looked quite promising as the pub was already drawing clientele away from the beach for an early drink or late cream tea. Although we intended to dance in the road, we thought it politic to ask the landlord if he had any objection.

"Objection? Good Lord, no! If I had known you were coming I'd have put up a poster."

"Sorry, it was a, um, last minute change of plan;" Jake explained, off the cuff. If we'd known we were going there we might have sent him one of Benji's creations. "We're staying in the area for a few days."

"Well, if you can come back and dance again, I'll lay on some sandwiches for you."

Jake made a show of mentally checking his diary. "Thursday evening? We can play some music in the bar afterwards, if you like." As our arrangements were all pretty ad hoc, we could have easily returned on Wednesday and Friday as well, but we didn't want to impose too much on his hospitality.

"Thursday it is, young man!"

Marvellous what a bit of encouragement does for one's confidence, not to mention the liquid inspiration which I'm pretty sure we weren't charged for. We danced our socks off, with barely a foot wrong. Rud coaxed nearly twenty pounds out of the audience – our biggest bag ever for a single performance.

Huw and I, as drivers, were perforce obliged to maintain a modicum of sobriety, but, with further displays outside a hostelry in Broad Haven and a couple of short shows for holidaymakers enjoying the warm summer's evening in Little Haven, it was a merry band that finally settled into the back bar of the Castle Inn, almost like home from home. The singing party continued for those in the back of Huw's vehicle all the way back to the campsite.

Jake and Min were all for more camp fire songs. The rest of us were just happy to crawl into our sleeping bags.

"No stamina, you lot," grunted Jake as he cluttered into the tent some time later.

With just cold ashes where the campfire had been and no inclination to rekindle from Jake and Dan, both of whom were still snoring loudly when I stuck my head out next morning, I guessed a cold rinse down or at best a cold shower was all I'd get.

No sign of movement from the other tents either. I considered giving Jake the treatment he'd meted out to others the previous morning but thought better of it. His sense of humour could be a little one-sided.

I couldn't remember whether Rud, or anyone else, had bothered to replenish our larder. Wide-awake and with no desire to wriggle back into my sleeping bag just to contemplate the universe, I coaxed Jessica to life, probably waking everyone else in the process, and chugged off to Broad Haven in search of fresh bread and milk.

Surprised that such delicacies had made an impression on the local cuisine, I found croissants on offer and bought out their whole stock, no doubt disappointing any French tourists.

Hung-over humanity in various states of undress stumbled around the campsite like zombies.

"Wherroubeen?" mumbled Dan. "Left jeans in Jess'ca las'night."

"Hunting," I said.

"Whad'yer catch, apart from cold?"

"Breakfast treat." I pulled out the bag of goodies.

The bag made me the centre of attention for the rest of the group.

"Croissants!" exclaimed Min. "You're a star, Rob!" And in her usual show of appreciation, flung her arms round me, croissants and all, and kissed my stubbly face, which was as coarse as sandpaper. Min was wearing denim shorts and grey T-shirt. No bra.

The prospect of food brought a sense of order and purpose to the camp. It had been a long time since the bangers and mash we'd wolfed down the previous evening somewhere in between the dancing.

During the night the sky had become overcast, with a stiff breeze blowing in off the sea. Plan B, in the event of uninviting beach weather, was to take some towns by storm and collect some more money. One slight problem was that West Pembrokeshire didn't really go in for towns, and Huw had little regard for Milford Haven ('unless you're into oil') and Pembroke itself ('bit depressing'). Which really only left Haverfordwest and the pocket city of St David's within any reasonable travelling distance.

"Do we need permission to dance or collect?" asked Rud.

"Don't know," replied Huw. "But if anyone objects, we can plead ignorance and move on."

No one bothered us. We attracted indifferent interest in Haverfordwest, the kind where the townsfolk paused in their business, regarded us curiously from a safe distance, and continued on their way as soon as Rud got anywhere near with his collecting pot. Not much different to Tencastle, really. Anyway, we added a few quid to our coffers by dancing twice, at different locations by the river, then spent a leisurely hour or so mooching around the town and testing out a couple of alehouses.

St David's was altogether a different proposition, since tourists were attracted in appreciable numbers to the cathedral whose size was out of all proportion to meet the spiritual needs of the indigenous population. The happy snappers welcomed any kind of additional focus for their cameras, and we certainly provided a colourful spectacle. Jake's creative spiel about the traditions of the Welsh Border dances had the visitors, particularly from abroad, believing they were witnessing a genuine glimpse of local customs, and they were more than willing to donate generously to preserve the heritage.

We might have continued with another display or two, had not the grey skies begun to release precipitation, light drizzle at first, quickly threatening more serious and persistent rain. Too soon for opening time, we piled into the nearest café, to the consternation of a couple of elderly ladies daintily partaking of high tea. Well, I suppose with sweaty black faces and brandishing large sticks we probably looked a bit intimidating.

"My goodness, have they come to rob us?" one old dear twittered to her companion.

"Have no fear, madam," Jake oozed charm. "We're only poor Morris dancers."

She perched a pair of pince-nez on her nose and regarded him suspiciously. "Morris? Are you sure? I thought they were supposed to be clean and white and wave handkerchiefs."

I don't think any racial slur or criticism of our hygiene was intended. Jake didn't take offence. "Ah, that's because we're Welsh Border Morris. Much more primitive."

"They don't look Welsh, do they, Matilda?" said her companion. "And he certainly doesn't sound it."

She meant Jake. Huw responded on his behalf with a gabble of diphthongs and mutant consonants. The old biddies obviously didn't understand a single word, but it must have sounded authentic, for they seemed reassured that there was no threat to their well-being, and resumed their tea-time ritual.

We looked at the rain streaming down the café windows.

"No more dancing today, that's for sure," said Dan, stating the obvious.

"Any suggestions, Huw?" Sophie asked.

"We could stay in St David's and have something to eat. The rain might ease."

"What about nightlife?"

"There isn't any, Min. This place is dead after dark."

"Is Haverfordwest any better?"

"Not much. Greater choice of pubs though. Probably find one that's got something going on."

Huw's optimism with regard to the weather was unfounded. If anything, it got worse. Jessica's ancient wipers struggled desperately to clear the torrent of water and spray, and I held my face close to the windscreen to keep Huw's vehicle in sight. There was no way I intended to lose him once we got into Haverfordwest.

The pub wasn't brilliant. In fact it was downright dingy, and funereally quiet, apart from the clack of dominoes emanating from a fug of tobacco smoke over the corner table. Not the sort of place to welcome our kind of music, even if Jake had been prepared to risk his banjo strings rusting or Huw his bagpipes squirting out water. It was warm, however, and served a reasonable pint. Above all, we'd been able to park just fifty yards from the door, and, as our wet weather gear consisted of just one battered brolly, there was little inclination to seek out one of the pleasanter hostelries we'd discovered earlier in the day.

"How much did we take today?" Jake asked.

"Dunno," said Rud. "But the afternoon should have boosted the coffers a bit." He rummaged in his rucksack and pulled out a blue cloth bag. He removed a smaller plastic bag bound with a rubber band. "Yesterday's," he declared, then tipped out the remaining contents onto the table. A couple of pound notes and a fiver fluttered to the floor.

"Hey, that's good!" cried Dan.

We all helped sort the loose coin into manageable piles.

"Flippin' hell! There's over thirty pounds here!" Rud declared a few minutes later when it had all been counted.

"Do you think we'll make a hundred over this week?" asked Kissy.

"Don't see why not, if we have another good bag or two like this."

"We haven't made any decisions yet about a charity yet, have we?"

"No time like the present, Sophie!" said Jake. "Ideas?"

Ideas there certainly were, but no consensus, even by the second pint. If a vote had been taken there and then, eight causes would have had an equal share of the pot. Another pint and much discussion later, we'd whittled the possibilities down a little, though there was still no obvious favourite.

"Shall we come back to this later?" Jake eventually suggested. "We're not likely to agree on anything definite tonight, that's for sure. Something might come up, a natural disaster, you know, like Aberfan."

"That wasn't natural!" said Huw, heatedly.

"Sorry, it was more the scale of human tragedy I meant."

"I'd go along with that," said Dan. "We're not likely to give the money away until we get back to college in September, are we?"

"Probably not, if Rud can look after it."

We finally had a unanimous decision it seemed; not to do anything until a disaster, natural or otherwise happened, ideally a couple of months hence.

Though the rain had eased, I kept Huw's tail lights closely in view, back to our base. He swung into the field and I followed without a second thought. Only for a few yards. Jessica refused to go further as the wheels dug into the muddy ruts left by the Land Rover.

"There's someone in the tent!" Sophie cried in alarm from the passenger seat.

A dull glow from the girls' quarters was enough to outline a dark silhouette. Huw's group, climbing out of the vehicle, didn't yet seem aware of the intruder. I grabbed Jessica's starting handle and turned the headlights on again.

"Wait here!" I said, and clambered out with trepidation into the squelchy mud, Jake following.

A figure emerged from the tent.

"Christ, you lot took your time!"

"Dicky?"

"Who else were you expecting, you pillock! Didn't you get my message?"

"What message?" The rest of the gang had gathered round.

"I phoned yesterday, the number Huw gave me and spoke to a young girl. Said I'd be arriving about six o'clock today. She told me she'd let her brother know."

Huw said, "I haven't got a sister."

"Then who was I speaking to? I'm darn sure it wasn't your mother!"

"What number did you dial?"

"Yours." Dicky rummaged in his pocket.

I suggested we got out of the rain. Somehow, all nine of us managed to squeeze into the frame tent, where Dicky had got one of the camping gas lights working.

"Here!" Dicky showed a scrap of paper to Huw.

"That's not my number! You've got the 3 and 4 the wrong way round!"

"You're joking!" said Dicky, dumfounded.

"No matter, Dicky," Jake said. "Glad you could join us anyhow. How did you get here, as a matter of interest?"

"Hitched, didn't I? In the bloody rain, too."

"But how did you know where to find this place?" asked Huw.

"I didn't, but I remembered you'd said it was near Broad Haven, so I thought if I headed there I might find you in a pub, and if the worst came to the worst, I hoped to find a B and B for the night."

"And?"

"Well, this old gaffer gave me a lift, and we got chatting, and I mentioned your name. He said there were a few Parry-Evanses around. Anyway, I thought I saw a tent in a field, so I asked the chap if he'd hang on a tick while I took a recce. When I saw the stick bag I knew I'd got the right place."

We'd left the bag outside the tent and each of us had carried our own.

"So how long have you been here?" I asked.

"Couple of hours or so, I suppose. Still light when I arrived."

Moving as many bodies out of the way as possible, forcing us to overflow into the sleeping area, Min and Kissy got the kettle on the go for mugs of coffee. A plastic tooth mug was requisitioned for our new arrival.

"Have you eaten?" Kissy asked.

"Only a burger down by the station. Not since I've been here. I just, well, stretched out in there and had a kip." He indicated Min's room. "Guessed you'd be back sometime."

A logistical problem came to mind. "I don't suppose you brought a tent with you?" I said.

Dicky looked surprised. "No, you said there'd be space for me, didn't you?"

We looked around at each other. After what seemed like ages, Min spoke up, "If Sophie and Kissy don't mind, I could squeeze in with them. I'm only small." She giggled.

"Okay with us."

"It would make sense then if one of us joined Dicky in here," I suggested. "It's pretty cramped with three of us in the ridge tent."

"And we don't want Dicky getting up to mischief, do we?" Dan added.

We drew lots. Dan got lucky.

With Dan out of the way, Jake and I at least had a few more inches of space to manoeuvre and to exchange our damp clothing for a dry, warm sleeping bag.

I'd dropped off for an hour or so, until a vivid flash of lightning followed almost immediately by an enormous clap of thunder jolted me awake. The rain, accompanied by strong gusty winds, hammered down and shook the flimsy structure. I stretched out my arm, straight into a pool of cold water. By the next lightning bolt I could see that a broad rivulet was flowing from the front of the tent, over the non-integral groundsheet, to the foot of my sleeping bag, where it diverted around the right side of my body to pool close to my head, whence it trickled away under the canvas at the rear. Jake's side of the tent seemed perfectly dry.

I shoved at his bag, hoping he'd roll over and allow me to get away from the flood. He rolled towards me, amazingly oblivious to the storm. The inside of my bag was, thankfully, still dry, but, feeling the outside, it was obvious that it was only a matter of time before it became waterlogged.

I considered my options, all of them uninviting. If I stayed where I was, I'd become soaked. I wondered whether a water–filled sleeping bag had the same insulating effect as a wet suit. The living area of the frame tent had only a small plastic sheet over one part of the ground. Jessica was, I concluded, the only dry refuge. I rummaged for the keys in my discarded Carpiog jeans and grabbed my rucksack containing a spare jumper and clean clothes. I struggled out of the bag and prepared to make a dash next time the sky lit up.

"Closaruddydoor!" grunted Jake, from the depths of his bag, as a squally gust stretched the canvas like a balloon. I did my best to secure the flap and paddled over to Jessica, all the while getting drenched. It didn't help when I fumbled and dropped the keys by the car door, and, without another fortuitous flash of lightning, I'd have been very lucky to find them in the mire. I clambered into the back seat where, with many contortions, I managed to strip off the wet T-shirt and boxers and put on some dry jeans and a cardigan.

The unyielding nature of Jessica's upholstery, coupled with the light show of the electric storm denied any immediate possibility of sleep. I suppose I must have dozed off eventually, for the next thing I knew, someone was tapping on the car window. Jake grinned at me, all bright and cheerful, like the sun beaming through the windscreen. Apart from the copious mud, from which the water was already beginning to evaporate in wisps of vapour, there was little evidence of the storm.

All the rest of the crew were already up and about, draping various articles of clothing and bedding anywhere to benefit from the sun and light breeze. I'd probably suffered the worst discomfort, though Rud and Huw had spent most of the night clinging on to the inside of their little tent to prevent it from blowing away. Most of its pegs – glorified skewers, really – had lifted out of the soft ground.

Breakfast was a sorry affair, gastronomically. Soggy cornflakes with a sprinkling of evaporated milk for those who could stomach it, a lukewarm mishmash of tinned tomatoes, baked beans and the two remaining eggs and slice of bacon. The gas cylinder expired barely before the cooking had started, and Jake couldn't figure out a way to use the campfire without incinerating everything. Miraculously, he'd managed to get it going, thanks to some kindling and logs that he'd stashed in the loo block on the first evening, so coffee and hot showers were back on the menu.

"Gosh, I could fancy some more of those croissants," said Min, smearing a glob of marmite onto a crust. "Any chance you could pop into town again, Rob?"

"Sorry, I'm afraid Jessica's stuck." Not only gooed up to the axles, but blocking the gateway so that Huw couldn't get past in the Land Rover.

"So what have you planned for today?" asked Dicky.

"We haven't," said Jake "But I don't think we'll be going anywhere until we move that contraption."

"Do you mind," I said, "if it wasn't for Jessica you wouldn't be here."

"Sorry to hurt her feelings."

Nobody seemed in a great deal of hurry to rush off, anyway. Cleaning the mud off ourselves then restowing sun and smoke dried clothes and sleeping bags took some time, before we were ready to tackle Jessica's predicament. We piled a few stones and twigs by her wheels, and while I took my place in the driver's seat, the others prepared to push.

"I'm going to try to reverse out onto the track," I said. "When I begin to rev up, push hard."

A dozen hands rested on the front end in preparation. I blipped the accelerator, and the engine coughed and revved. I eased the gear lever into reverse and gave the thumbs up sign. "Push," I yelled.

Jessica resisted our combined efforts at first, the wheels spewing out great dollops of mud.

"Harder!"

All at once the rear wheels found purchase, and Jessica shot back, narrowly missing the gatepost. Caught out by the sudden movement, Rud and Kissy stumbled and fell flat into the quagmire that Jessica had just vacated.

Jake's whistling of the *Hippopotamus Song* was a little insensitive but one couldn't help laughing. Even Rud attempted a mud-caked grin, and grabbed Kissy for a Waltz, promptly toppling over backwards into the morass again. Give Jake his due, he offered to get the shower system going for them, and another bucket of hot water to rinse their clothes.

"Right," he said, when we were all more or less presentable again and ready to roll. "Priority one, provisions, priority two, a decent lunch. Any objections?"

"What then?"

"Well, Dicky, we've got the evening sorted at a pub just up the coast. Dancing and food. Why don't we just have a lazy afternoon on the beach?"

"Amen to that," I said. Although no great distances had been involved, it felt as if I'd spent quite a lot time driving during the week.

I thought we did laziness pretty well. Until the incoming tide made our position untenable, we established our own patch among the rocks at the north end of Broad Haven's beach where there was some natural shade to be found, for those who didn't want to get fried. In between frolicking in the waves whenever we need to cool off, we stretched out, snoozed, boozed and viewed the scenery. Kissy in her bikini would have made an enticing cover picture for the local holiday brochure. Jake plucked experimentally at his banjo, trying to find a tune for a song, he declared.

"What song?" I couldn't recognise any tune.

"I thought we could each write a verse for a song about Carpiog Morris?"

"Why?"

"Well, why not? We could do it as a sort of coming-on song whenever we perform. Gron once told me sword dancers do it."

"Really," I said unenthusiastically.

But being Jake, he wasn't going to let his idea drop so easily. "No, listen, each of us writes a verse about our attributes, to introduce ourselves to the audience."

I wondered what attributes he'd got in mind. "Wouldn't it be more fun for us to write verses about each other?" I had a sudden rush of inspiration.

"In comes I my name is Jake,
A fearsome sight to make you quake,
In banjo playing I am no sucker
I'm really quite a pleasant plucker."

"I don't think so, Rob." He didn't appreciate my doggerel. "I was after something more, er, …"

"Basic?"

"No, no no! More ephemeral, more cultural, you know."

I didn't know.

If anyone else in the group had been inspired by Jake's muses they kept their silence.

Dicky propped himself up on an elbow, "I've been thinking."

God, not another one. "Don't, it's dangerous!" I said.

"How far is it to the pub?"

"Back in the town, few hundred yards," Jake said. "Why, are you out of beer already?"

"No, not that. The pub we're going to this evening."

"Dunno. Huw?"

Huw remained prone on his towel. "Two or three miles, perhaps. As the crow flies."

"Why don't we walk there? Along the cliffs."

"Energy conservation," Huw murmured.

"What energy?"

"Mine. It's lazy day, remember?"

"Seriously, guys, who's up for it?" Huw and Rob could take our clobber in the cars and meet us there."

"It's all right for you, Dicky, you haven't been prancing your legs off for the last two days," Dan's level of enthusiasm matched that of the rest of us, even Min, who was usually a bundle of energy.

"Okay, you idle buggers. I'm going for another swim." Meanwhile we relocated to the top of the beach, kindly taking Dicky's clothes with us.

The landlord had certainly been busy. A large chalkboard outside the pub and another down by the beach proclaimed a display by the renowned Carpiog Border Morris. It didn't mention that until this week our fame had hitherto been limited to a square mile of Tencastle. Most of the tables outside were occupied by families, who cheered when we stumped up from the car park.

Inside, the main bar was heaving, but the landlord, when he caught sight of us, welcomed us like celebrities.

"Pleased to see you, my friends! I've reserved a space for you in the back bar for when you've finished dancing. But I expect you'd like a drink first?"

It would have been impolite to refuse.

Jake barely gave us a chance to sample the brew, "Bring them outside, our audience awaits us!"

We got another cheer when we emerged. A sizeable crowd had gathered.

"Christ, I hope they don't expect us to perform ruddy miracles," Dicky said.

Jake, of course, was not fazed by the spotlight, in fact being the centre of attention always racked him up a gear.

"Ladies and gentlemen of …" he paused, ever so briefly, the name of the hamlet having escaped his notice, "this fair land, I bring you the amazing Carpiog Morris, with their demonstration of ancient pagan rituals that have lain hidden in the annals of history since time immemorial. Not since the days of Owain Glyndwr have the people of Pembrokeshire witnessed the symbolism and splendour of these dances from the Welsh Border."

"Whose Owain whatsisname?" whispered Dan.

"God knows. He's really laying on the bullshit tonight," I replied quietly.

"And now, for our first dance!" Jake's elegant sweeping bow brought another round of applause.

If Jake's eloquent introduction raised the expectation of the audience, it also served to get our adrenalin flowing. We really laid into each other with the sticking! Just as well I'd brought the spares with me, as the second dance also sent the frayed end of a stick into the crowd, to huge roars of encouragement to thrash each other with even more fervour.

Acutely aware that our entire repertoire would not sustain a show longer than half an hour at the outside, Jake sought to milk the occasion for all it was worth, interspersing instrumental solos from Huw, "Who will delight you with mystic music drawn from the bards and played on this traditional instrument fashioned from the stomach of a sheep."

"Isn't he getting confused with a haggis?" Dan said.

"Probably. Hope there's no-one listening that's got a clue what it's really all about."

We rounded off our show with the Upton stick dance, for us the most technically difficult, but executed dynamically and with a modest degree of accuracy. No matter, the crowd loved it.

"And now, ladies and gentlemen, we give you the opportunity to partake in these age-old traditions, and perpetuate the magic of Morris in ensuring long health, wealth and fertility."

"I suspect Rud's removing them of their wealth," Dan observed, as the collecting pot was brandished once again to the throng of people preparing to claim their share of longevity or fecundity.

"He's probably charging them for the hire of the stick," I said.

There must have been at least two dozen men, women and children lined up and raring to go. Which presented some logistical problems as we'd only brought sixteen sticks with us in the first place. We encouraged improvisation amongst the latecomers, with beach cricket stumps and bats, a stick of rock, a walking stick and a plastic inflatable policeman's truncheon. Jake put Huw and his bagpipes in the middle of a triple circle of bodies, with us experienced dancers (!) strategically interspersed. Quite what dance we were supposed to be doing, I'm not sure, but incredibly Jake got everybody moving and stick clashing in some semblance of order. With Huw like the pied piper, he then led a whole crocodile up through the front door of the pub, out of the rear and back through the garden to the road, finishing once again in a huge circle with a rousing cry.

It was a standing ovation of sorts, since most of the audience had been dancing with us on the road, and those still on the pub benches rose to the occasion.

I was sweating buckets, the first pint long since evaporated.

"Well done, my friends," beamed the landlord as we filed tired and thirstily back into the pub. "If you would like to go through to the back, you'll find a little morsel or two." He dropped a folded note in Rud's pot.

The morsel was nothing less than a full scale buffet – chicken legs, pasties, sausages, sandwiches and salad, and two jugs of ale to wash it down.

"Bloody hell," said Dicky. "How did you stumble on this place?"

Rud fished out the note the landlord had given him. "My God, he's even put in a tenner!"

The word had also got around that a live jam session was on the cards, and, almost as soon as we struck up on banjo, pipes and guitar, the band was quickly augmented by a couple of fiddles, flute and a mandolin. One middle-aged bloke also had a one row melodeon, albeit in the unsociable key of C. I guess the flautist and one of the fiddlers were local, for they knew Huw, and rattled off a number of unfamiliar tunes together, which Huw told me were traditional Welsh dance airs.

No way were we going to leave that pub before closing time, and the landlord exercised a considerable degree of elasticity in relation to the licensing laws. Eventually, thanking the landlord profusely for his incredible generosity, which also warranted one of Min's famous kisses, we emerged from the fug of the bar into the warm night air. The road and car park were deserted. The moon, barely on the wane, reflected from the calm water of the cove.

"That looks gorgeous," said Min. "Anyone fancy a swim?"

"Our cossies will still be soaking wet!" Dan pointed out. "And cold."

"Skinny dipping?"

I was most surprised by several nodding heads that Min's suggestion was accepted, even by Sophie and Kissy. Well, who was I to be prudish?

In paradoxical modesty, we lads undressed a little way apart from the girls then sprinted down into the sea, so that any embarrassing arousals on our part to the sight of naked young females would be dampened by the cold water. Though I gave the pretence of not looking, even in the pale light of the moon, I could not help but be drawn to the sight of Kissy's most beautiful figure, so often camouflaged by baggy sweaters; generous rounded bosom with large areolae, hour-glass waist and neat swatch of pubic hair. Neat bum, too. Sophie's strangely thin and pointy breasts, swinging loosely as she ran towards the waves seemed by comparison out of proportion to the rest of her body. Min, of course, I'd feasted my eyes on before, but none the less attractive for all that.

We splashed around, splashed each other, played tag water polo with an old tennis ball someone had left lying around on the sand.

"Race you out!" Jake called eventually, when our bodies were beginning to feel the chill. He started to cavort to the water's edge, the water droplets glistening on his ebony skin. He stopped, and listened. "Someone's coming!"

We looked in some consternation towards the foreshore. Sure enough, two or maybe three men were rummaging in the back of an estate wagon. They pulled out long thin packs, fishing rods, I assumed, and turned towards the beach.

Jake responded swiftly. "Girls, stay in the water! Guys, quickly, follow me!"

We ran back to our clothes. "Grab your towel and form a line!"

We stood side by side with our towels stretched out to form a shield from knee-deep water to the shallows, moving as one towards where the girls had left their clothes, and thus keep their bare bodies from view from the fishermen whose attention we had certainly attracted. They were probably still too far away to see much, however. No mermaids in their nets tonight!

"That was inspired thinking," said Sophie, gratefully, when she'd rubbed herself down and got decent again.

"At your service, my lady!" Jake bowed. His towel came unhitched and slid to the sand.

Min giggled.

Reveille, on our last full day together, was naturally a very leisurely affair, since we'd not turned in to our beds until well into the small hours. We'd not even got back to the campsite until nearly one-thirty, then sat around drinking coffee and reflecting on the evening's success.

"Do we want to dance again today?" Jake asked over an elevenses breakfast.

"Do we need to?" said Sophie.

"I haven't counted up yet, but I reckon with last night's bag and the landlord's contribution, we might have reached our £100 target."

"Thanks, Rud. I suppose it's up to us then."

"We could have a free day and perhaps meet up this evening in the pub for a final session. Dance, too, if we want," Huw suggested. "In fact, we don't all have to stay together, if some of you want to do one thing and others want to go elsewhere, as long as we are split evenly between the cars."

"Good thinking. Ideas?"

"Sophie and I wouldn't mind a chance to look round the shops in Haverfordwest or even Milford Haven," said Kissy.

"I'm still keen to do some walking, perhaps another swim," Dicky offered.

"Can I join you?"

"Sure, Min. Anyone else?"

"I'm happy to walk. Not interested in shops!" said Dan.

"That goes for me, too!" I said.

"Right, that would be one car for walkers and one for the town, if you don't mind Huw."

"No problem."

Jake thought for a moment. "How many can you take, Rob? Assuming you use Jessica. You could always walk from here."

"Four ideally, five at a pinch, if it's Min."

"I can always sit on somebody's lap."

"I'll strap you to the roof rack if you don't behave, Min."

"Ooh, really!"

"Rud, what about you?"

"I'm not into walking, I'll go into town."

"Fair enough. Well then, Rob, if you can squeeze me in that will be four of us with you, and three with Huw," said Jake.

"Huw, where would it be good to go, that we haven't already visited, for walking and a swim?" I asked.

"Marloes or Musselwick would be ideal. Not so far from here, good cliff walking and fantastic beach at Marloes. You can only get to it on foot. You've got an OS map, I assume?"

"I have now."

While Huw showed me where to go, the camp bristled with life as everyone gathered up the appropriate gear for their chosen activity.

Jessica's suspension groaned in protest with the load of five adults, a tight squeeze in the back by any account, but Min didn't seem to mind, and neither Dan nor Dicky protested at each having to look after one of her legs. From Huw's description of the location, apparently in the middle of bugger all, we thought it prudent to stock up on some picnic fare before heading out into the wilderness.

That little corner of Pembrokeshire wasn't all that remote, but sparsely populated would have been a generous description of its human habitation. Two cars already occupied a large parking area on the outside of a sharp bend in the road. A track might have allowed us to get nearer to the beach, but I didn't want to risk Jessica encountering possible rough terrain. Anyway, we were supposed to be doing some walking.

We took the track, which led to a cliff-top path, still quite muddy from the storms on Wednesday night. It brought us down to a rocky high-tide mark beyond which a wide and a sandy beach dotted with several outcrops of rocks stretched out to the water's edge. I caught sight of a couple of people strolling with a dog at one end but otherwise we had the place to ourselves. I couldn't think of any comparable Devon location that was quite so stunning and deserted.

With so many rock pools and crannies to explore, not to mention the lure of the Atlantic rollers, it wasn't the sort of beach just to laze around on, and we rather forgot about alternative pursuits, until Dicky mentioned it.

"If we are going to do any serious walking, we ought to start thinking about it, otherwise we won't have time, particularly if we want to meet up with the others."

We thought about it, briefly. But Min wanted to dry off from her latest dip and add another shade to her glorious golden brown tan. Jake and Dan, meanwhile, were still keen to scramble up to the top of two neighbouring rocky pyramids exposed by the tide. Whence, each king of his own castle, they regaled us with bawdy sea shanties.

"If we head back up now, we should still have time to stroll to the bay on the other side of the village," Jake suggested when, voice or repertoire exhausted, he and Dan rejoined us.

We climbed a path which continued some distance along the cliff top.

"Hey, guys, hold on a tick!" Min called. "I forgot to take any photos!" She rummaged in her rucksack and brought out her old Kodak instamatic.

"Would you like me to take your photo?" offered Dicky. He dropped back from where we'd halted several yards further on.

"Would you?" Min handed over the camera and stepped back.

Whether she caught her heel against a rock or slipped on the mud, I don't know, but I saw her fall backwards, grasping desperately at the grass as she disappeared over the cliff. We ran back down, her screams followed by brooding silence.

Dicky was still holding the camera, in a state of shock. Jake prostrated himself and peered over the cliff edge, calling her name.

"Christ, she's not moving!" he yelled.

"Min!" I called, positioning myself beside Jake. I could see her motionless body where it lay on a grassy ledge perhaps forty feet below and perilously close to a vertical drop to jagged rocks on the foreshore. One leg stuck out at an unnatural angle.

"Rob, get back to the car, find a telephone and call the coastguards! Dan you go with him, and bring back that length of rope. I'm going to see if I can reach her either from here or below."

"Jake, take care, we don't want two de ..." I bit my lip, "two casualties." I tried not to think of the worst.

"Just go!"

We ran up the path and track as fast as we could, hearts pounding with foreboding and the exertion, even though the distance was probably less than half a mile.

Dan grabbed the rope – not that I thought it would be anywhere near long enough to serve any useful purpose – and I flung myself in the driver's seat, praying that Jessica would, for once, start on the first pull. There was the odd farm building dotted around, but I hurtled Jessica along the road to the village where I could be certain of calling for help. I screeched to a halt outside a post office, attracting the attention of a postman collecting mail from the nearby box.

"Girl over cliff!" I called at him, "Is there a phone box in the village?"

"Just along the road, sir, opposite the pub."

I hurtled a further hundred yards and dived into the kiosk. "Emergency!" I yelled, then responded to the calm questions of the operator. "Coastguard, ambulance, my friend has fallen over the cliff. She's badly hurt, she's ... she's not moving."

The operator clearly sensed my rising panic, and tried to reassure me that help would soon be on the way. "Where are you, sir?"

"I'm calling from Marloes village. She's at Marloes Sands. We were just coming back up from the beach." I described the location as best I could. I forgot about the map in the car from which I could have given a grid reference

"Just the two of you?"

"No, there's five of us, we're all students from Tencastle, on holiday."

She took my name. "We'll have help there within a few minutes," she said.

"I'm going back down there!" I said, and hung up.

The postman had pulled up outside in his van. "What happened?"

I explained quickly. "They'll be ages getting here!" I was having difficulty holding back tears, as I thought of Min lying there lifeless.

"Don't you worry, young man, there's a coastguard station a couple of miles away, and they'll probably scramble a helicopter from Brawdey – that's very close."

"Thanks," I said. "I must go back, and see if I can help." I bombed back along the road, taking Jessica part of the way down the track as well, to the edge of a field. I ran down the path to where Dan and Dicky were flat on the grass peering over the cliff edge.

"What's happening?" I called.

"Jake reckoned he might find a way to reach her from below. Definitely not safe to climb down from here, though he was all for trying," said Dan.

I joined them in their vigil, just as Jake's head appeared over a grassy clump near the ledge where Min lay. He pulled himself up and went over to her. He bent down beside her for a few moments, then looked up at us and raised his thumb.

"She's breathing!" he shouted.

"Thank God!" murmured Dicky, expressing what we all felt.

I heard the sound of a helicopter, which came into view over the nearby headland. We stood up and waved. It swooped over us, hovered above the fields beyond the path then disappeared, presumably landing. I caught sight of a four-by-four on the track above us. Soon, four men with ropes and harnesses ran down to us, and assessed the situation, calling down to Jake.

"She's unconscious but her breathing is steady. Her left leg is definitely broken and bleeding a little, but I can't say what other injuries she might have, apart from cuts and bruises," Jake answered.

"Thank you, sir. Stay where you are, we'll be with you shortly." The senior coastguard held a short discussion with his two colleagues, and with an RAF officer from the helicopter. The coastguard turned to us to tell us of their decision. "Right, we'll go down from here, and check her over. Depending on what we find, we'll either stretcher her up, or possibly down to the beach, if the tide's not come in too far. If her injuries appear to be more serious, then we may even have to winch her off the cliff. In any case, we'll need the chopper to get her to hospital pronto."

"Where will you take her?" I said.

"Haverfordwest, Withybush hospital. What is the girl's name?" the senior man asked.

"Min. Short for Wilhelmina."

"Surname?"

Dan, Dicky and I looked at each other. "Um, we don't know. We've only ever known her as Min," Dan said.

He raised an eyebrow. "Never mind, we can sort that out later. You'll be coming to the hospital, I assume?"

"Of course! We'll go back to our campsite first to pick up some of her things."

"Good idea. Find out if she's got any ID there."

He went over to his colleagues who were ready to descend the cliff. As they reached the ledge where Min lay, Jake began to make his traverse carefully back down to the beach. Dan picked up Min's rucksack from where she'd dumped it by the path, but, apart from a passport-sized photo of herself in a small clasp purse, there was nothing else to identify the owner. Several minutes later Jake rejoined us, out of breath and clutching Min's broken spectacles. The coastguards were already lowering a stretcher down.

"How is she?" Dicky still looked as white as a sheet.

"Her leg looks a mess but otherwise it's difficult to say."

"You don't happen to know her surname, I suppose?" I said.

"No, I've never asked. Why?"

The senior coastguard came over to us. "We're making your friend as comfortable as possible," he said kindly. "Apart from the leg we don't think there are any other bones broken, but she's probably concussed – banged her head, I expect, on her tumble. There's not a lot you can do here now, but it would be very helpful for the hospital if you could find out her full name, and her home address. Her parents will obviously need to be informed."

We made our way back up the path, Dicky mumbling about the accident all being his fault. We saw the flashing blue light at the top of the track just as we got to Jessica.

"Dicky, if that's the police, don't for Christ's sake say anything about you being to blame!" Jake warned. "You didn't push her or tell her to step back, did you?"

"Of course I didn't!" Dicky responded hotly.

"We know that! They don't!" Jake pointed to the policeman who was climbing out of his vehicle.

I wasn't quite sure whether we should stay where we were and let the police come down to us or drive up to them. Jake decided to walk up with Dicky and Dan, while I led the way in Jessica. The outstretched hand made it quite obvious that the top of the track was as far as I was going for the time being.

"Well, lads," he said, when we were all gathered. "You were with the injured girl?"

We nodded. We explained that we were all college friends on holiday.

"And who made the 999 call?"

I put up my hand.

"Right, can you give me your names, for a start."

We complied.

"And the girl?"

He wasn't at all happy when we could only give her Christian name. "You don't expect me to believe that you don't know your friend's surname, if, as you claim, you are friends from college. Do the four of you know each other's surnames?"

Of course we did.

"Now it seems a little odd, wouldn't you say, that there's you four fellows, who haven't the faintest idea of this girl's proper name…"

"It's Wilhemina," Dan said.

"Surname," he emphasised. "And one girl. Wouldn't she do what you wanted, then, didn't she like your advances?"

Jake was holding his temper with difficulty.

"It wasn't like that at all!" Dicky was also pretty annoyed that the copper was making ridiculous insinuations.

"So what was it like?"

Dicky explained.

"And the rest of you saw her fall?"

"Yes."

"I'm going to need your addresses. If the girl is able to verify your account then that's the end of the matter, but if she does not come round we will need to speak to you again."

We gave him our home details.

"And how long are you staying in this area?"

"This was our last full day," said Jake.

"And the four of you are staying … where?"

I gave him the name of Huw's family farm "There's nine of us. We four and Min. The others have gone to Haverfordwest or Milford for the day."

The policeman thought for a moment. "That's Parry-Evans place, isn't it? I had some incident the other day in Broad Haven with a student accused of breaking into a Land Rover, claimed he was camping up there. Friend of yours?"

"That would be Rud …Brian, rather," I said. "He's with Huw Parry-Evans and the other girls."

"I see." The copper seemed more ready to accept that we weren't rampant sex fiends.

"Will you be going directly back home tomorrow? Just in case we need to contact you again."

Dicky and Dan nodded.

"Jake and I have to go back to Tencastle first. We may stay here until Sunday, to see how Min is getting on," I said. I gave him our Tencastle phone number.

He had no further questions and headed off down the track to the cliff-top. I heard the helicopter clattering, and saw it hovering over the beach.

It didn't seem proper to rummage through Min's personal belongings back at the tent, but we couldn't see any alternative in trying to find out the information that the hospital would require. The search revealed only her student union card, with her surname.

"Smith!" said Dan. "I was expecting something much more exotic."

"Well, it's something, even if we still don't know where she comes from," Jake said.

"Must be hundreds of Wilhemina Smiths, though," Dicky added.

I had an idea. "Look, we know she's in Abercrombie, they're bound to have some record of her home address. We could ring up and ask."

"Good thinking, Rob! Let's do it!"

"Hang on a moment, Dan," said Jake, who'd been deep in thought. "We need to let Huw and co know what's happened…"

"Yes, but we don't know where they are!" Dan pointed out.

"Let me finish. We had planned to meet up in the pub sometime this evening but we don't know how long we'll be at the hospital. I suggest we leave a message here where they'll see it, and also at the pub, asking them to ring Huw's parents. If we go down to the farm and put them in the picture, then we should cover all possibilities. Perhaps they'll let us ring 'Crombie from the farm?"

Huw's father was not at home but when we told her the reason for our call, Mrs Parry-Evans fussed over us as if we ourselves had been injured, insisting that we should have a mug of strong sweet tea before anything else. "You'll be in shock, my dears!"

Apart from Dicky, who'd witnessed Min tumbling over the cliff, we hadn't really had time to be shocked, but sitting down in the comfort of the farmhouse, the horror of the incident struck home. Despite the warmth, I shivered as my mind uncontrollably imagined the most serious consequences. Judging by their silence, I suspected the others, too, were harbouring similar thoughts.

"May we use your telephone?" I asked, after the tea had done its work.

"Of course. Do you know the number?"

"Well, the hospital, but first we need to find out some details from Tencastle."

I had to get that number from Directory Enquiries. The phone rang several times before a gruff male voice answered.

"My name's Robert Kiddecott, and I'm calling about a student at Abercrombie…"

"They've all gone home for the Summer."

"I know. She's on holiday with us and …"

"Then why are you ringing if you know she's not here?"

"She's had a serious accident and we need to know her home address."

"We don't give out personal information to any Tom, Dick or Harry over the phone."

I was losing patience with his unhelpful attitude. "Look, we need to let her parents know what has happened."

"Why don't you ask her directly?"

"Oh, for Christ's sake! If we could we would! She's unconscious, in hospital!"

"There's no need to get stroppy with me, young man."

Officious sod. I wondered, "Is it Percy I'm talking to?"

That took him by surprise. "Yes, it is," he said cautiously. "And who did you say you were?"

"I'm a friend of Min … Wilhemina Smith, the injured girl, from room 207. You may remember me as Matt Rose."

Jake looked at me, puzzled. "Explain later," I whispered, with my hand over the mouthpiece.

"Yes, I do recall that name. But you gave a different name just now, didn't you?"

Bugger! "Yes but …"

"I'm sorry, Mr Rose, or whatever your name is, it's more than my job's worth to give out confidential information to anyone over the phone. I'd need proper authorisation from her parents."

"That's the whole point, I am trying to contact her parents!"

"Sorry, I can't help you." Percy hung up on me.

"Bloody moron!" I exploded.

"Let me try, dear," Mrs Parry-Evans offered when I'd calmed down and explained the impasse. She rang, and firmly insisted on speaking to the Warden. Giving the brief response, "Smith," to whatever Percy, presumably, had asked, was enough for her to be put on hold until the Warden, or someone else in authority came to the phone. Brooking no interruption, Mrs Parry-Evans gave a concise account of the emergency, and the urgent need to contact Min's family.

"Thank you for your help," she said a couple of minutes later, after scribbling down an address on a notepad. "Min lives in Leeds. Would you like me to ring? The news might be better coming from a woman."

We agreed to her offer. When the phone was answered, she asked if she was speaking to Mrs Smith, then held the phone away from her in surprise at the response. She barely managed to give the reason for the call before she was silenced, the expression on her face registering disbelief and anger in equal measure. She was left looking at a silent handset.

"What's wrong?" Jake asked.

"I've never heard anything like it!" she said, and slumped into a chair. "That, I understand, was her aunt. Seems the poor girl lost her parents when she was very young, and has been pushed around from pillar to post amongst various aunts and uncles. God help her if they're all as foul-mouthed and uncaring as that one! Blamed Min for being a good-for-nothing troublemaker and washed her hands of the whole affair."

"Min? But she's a great girl, always full of fun," I said.

"Well, she's not going to get much fun with her aunt," said Mrs Parry-Evans.

"What are we going to tell the hospital?" asked Dan.

"Say that we have been unable to contact her parents, I suppose," said Jake. "But we'd better find out what's happening there."

Jake did the honours this time, ringing the A&E unit and listening intently to the answers they gave to his questions. He took a deep breath. "She's had x-rays. She hasn't regained consciousness, but they don't think her condition is critical. It's likely to be another hour or so before they've finished all the tests, so there's no point in us going down there until later."

"Then why don't you stay and have some supper with us? My Dai will be back shortly."

"That's very kind of you, Mrs Parry-Evans, but we don't want to impose on you," said Jake.

"Nonsense! It's no trouble. And anyway, Huw may return in the meantime."

I wasn't really hungry, but I was quite happy to accept her offer and stay there for a while. Moping around the campsite or sitting in a pub nursing a beer for a couple of hours didn't have much appeal at that time.

The huge steaming cauldron of beef stew which she set before us on the table would have kept just her and her husband well-fed for a fortnight, so generous were the portions she ladled out. Served with boiled new potatoes dripping with butter, I rediscovered my appetite and was even able to do justice to a second helping of rhubarb tart.

Whether by design or not, throughout supper and coffee, Huw's parents kept us chatting about ourselves, our course – anything to stop us from worrying conjecture about Min's prognosis. Eventually I could see Jake was getting restless, glancing at the grandfather clock and biting his knuckle.

"Do you think we…" Jake didn't finish.

"Ma! What's happened!" Huw burst in. "I got the note! "He saw us. "What …why are you here?" He paused, confused, "Isn't Min with you?"

"She's had an accident, Huw," said Jake. "We were just getting ready to go to the hospital."

"Accident? How did it …? Is she … is she alright?"

"She isn't in danger, we've been told, but she had a pretty nasty fall." Jake filled in the details as Huw sat with his head in his hands.

"Where's Rud and the girls?" Dan asked.

"I left them at the campsite. I came straight here when I found your note."

"Okay, let's pick them up and we'll all go into town," said Jake. "Huw, you'll know where the hospital is, we'll follow you."

"Just a moment, Huw," said his mother. "Have you eaten? There's stew if you'd like it. Enough for your friends too."

"Thanks, Ma, we had a Chinese takeaway earlier."

We reshuffled ourselves around the two vehicles so that we could make everyone who'd been with Huw fully aware of the facts. Kissy and Sophie had been distraught when they had first heard the news, initially fearing the worst, like I had, and had only slightly been consoled when we told them that Min was not believed to be critically injured. Kissy had gathered together some of Min's belongings that she thought she might require.

"Has Min ever mentioned anything about her home life to you?" I asked.

"Not as such," Kissy pondered. "I think she comes from up North somewhere, but she's never volunteered any personal information about her background. Almost seems to shy away from attention when family life is being discussed. Why do you ask?"

I related what Mrs Parry-Evans had discovered.

"Oh the poor girl!" cried Kissy. "How on earth does she manage to be so bright and bubbly with a background like that?"

I didn't know the answer.

"What is she going to do when she comes out of hospital? Even if she's only broken her leg, she's not going to be able to look after herself for a while, and it sounds as if her aunt would be worse than useless."

I didn't know the answer to that either.

Ahead of Jessica, Huw signalled to turn into the hospital car park.

We all piled into the foyer and made for the reception desk.

"Might be better if just one of us made the enquiry," Jake said.

I volunteered. "Good evening," I began. "Our friend, Wilhemina Smith, was brought into casualty this afternoon, after an accident at Marloes. Could you please find out for us how she is getting on? We did ring earlier and were told she was still unconscious."

"Just a moment, sir." The receptionist lifted up a phone and spoke quietly. She nodded several times in response to what she heard then glanced at me and the rest of the gang. "If you'd like to take a seat someone will be down to see you shortly."

"Is she going to be okay?" I asked desperately.

She nodded again.

Taking a seat was easier said than done. The foyer hadn't been designed as a waiting room. We squatted round the edge of a large concrete planter until, several minutes later, a short dark-haired man, thirty-ish, with rimless spectacles, white coat and the obligatory stethoscope, came through the inner double doors and headed straight for us.

"You are the young lady's friends? I'm Doctor Wallis."

"Is she going to be okay?" I asked again.

"She's been very fortunate in the circumstances. Her leg is badly broken, and we've had to pin it, but apart from minor cuts and bruises, there's no sign of any other major problem. Crucially, no head injury."

"Can we see her, then?" said Dicky.

"I'm afraid not, she has not regained consciousness yet."

"How long is she going to be like that?" I asked.

"Difficult to say. She's concussed but the brain scans show no cause for concern. Sometimes unconsciousness is nature's own healing mechanism."

"I see."

"Can you provide us with any more details about her? Our information is very sketchy, only her name."

"Not really. We understand she has lost both of her parents. We think she may have some relatives in Leeds but we don't know how close they are."

"We'd like to be able to get some medical background for her, family doctor, for example."

"I'm afraid we can't help you there."

"Wait a minute, Rob," said Sophie. "She should be registered with the doctor in Tencastle. We all had to, remember?"

"That would indeed be useful," said Dr Wallis. "Now, unless there is anything else I can do for you?"

"Doctor," said Kissy, "when … when Min wakes up, would it be helpful if she had a friend with her?"

"Possibly," he said thoughtfully. "You might have a long wait."

"I'm willing to sit with her all night, just in case. If it's allowed."

"I think that could be arranged."

"I'm happy to keep you company," said Sophie.

"Thanks, Soph, but there's no point in two of us having a sleepless night. I'll be okay here. Perhaps you can take over from me in the morning if necessary. I'll ring your home tomorrow morning, Huw."

"What about your train home?" said Huw.

"Let's worry about that tomorrow!"

There was little else we could do at the hospital. Although I'm sure Min would have wanted us to carry on and enjoy ourselves, we didn't feel much in the party mood and just went for a quiet pint. There were decampment and transport matters to reconsider.

I doubt if I got much more sleep than Kissy. I suppose I must have nodded off intermittently but each time I looked at my watch, the minutes seemed like hours. Jake's snoring didn't help.

I rose early with the intention of going into Broad Haven to get something for our breakfast. Rud stuck his head out of his tent as I tried to coax Jessica into life. "You didn't buy anything yesterday, I suppose?" I asked, after the second abortive swing of the starting handle.

"Um, no. Didn't even think about it."

On the third attempt, as was her habit, Jessica spluttered and roared, with a loud bang from the exhaust that shattered the tranquillity of the early morning, and likewise the dreams of anyone sleeping within a hundred yards. Except, possibly, Jake.

It was nearly nine o'clock when I returned. As I slowed down to turn into the track I saw Huw walking back up the road from the farm. I waited for him to catch up. He was smiling.

"Good news," he said. "Kissy's just phoned. Min regained consciousness about six this morning, and she's sitting up chatting! Ravenous, too, I gather."

"Sounds like Min! Christ, I'm so glad she's okay!"

The huge relief I felt was quickly shared by the others. If we'd had a bottle of bubbly we would have broken it open. We toasted her recovery with orange juice.

"I assume we can all go and see her?" said Rud.

"Try stopping us!" said Jake.

"We must get her a card. And some flowers," Sophie suggested.

"Knowing Min, she'd probably prefer something edible," said Dicky.

"Grapes?" Dan said unimaginatively.

"Why don't we dress up in our Carpiog gear and surprise her?"

"Probably surprise a few other people, Dicky!" said Jake.

"Seriously, we might not dance in the ward, but perhaps we could dance in the hospital foyer, in the town too. Collect some more money?"

"Which we could donate to the hospital. I'm pretty sure they've got a 'Friends of the Hospital' charity."

"Brilliant idea, Huw!" said Jake. "Add to the rest of our bag? How much have we taken so far, Rud?"

"Not sure, hang on." He rummaged in the back pocket of his shorts and pulled out an old envelope. "I'd say one hundred and three pounds, and, er … no, make that hundred and four, round figure."

"That's incredible!" I said. It was truly far more than I'd ever expected, particularly as fund-raising hadn't been the prime aim of our week.

"All agreed then?" asked Jake.

No dissent.

"Now I know some of you have a train to catch this afternoon," he continued, "but Rob and I are quite prepared to stay on another day at least. Kissy, too, I think. So you can leave all the clearing up, just get your gear together and we'll head off in to town. Any questions?"

"Just one concern. What's Min going to do when she comes out of hospital? She can't go home, can she?"

"No problem, Sophie," Huw replied. "She'll be welcome to stay here on the farm. My Ma's quite insistent that she shouldn't have to go back to that bitch of an aunt. And I'll be here all summer to keep an eye on her."

Our appearance in costume at the hospital did raise a few eyebrows, and some consternation at the reception desk, even though we'd thought it prudent not to black up. When I explained who we were and why we were there, the receptionist's frosty glare melted, and the mention of a donation to the hospital charity smoothed any obstacles she personally was likely to make to our presence or performance. She made a couple of phone calls.

"All right, you can go on up. Strictly speaking she should not have more than two visitors at a time, but we'll turn a blind eye provided you keep the visit short and don't annoy the other patients."

We promised to be on our best behaviour and asked for directions to the ward.

Kissy saw us first. "Min, you've got visitors," she whispered.

The way her eyes lit up was a joy to see. "Hey, guys! You're not going to dance here are you?"

"We've got permission to dance and collect in the cafeteria and in the foyer," I said. "We're so pleased to have you back in the land of the living!"

"Amen to that," said Jake. "We were so worried about you."

"Sorry for all the bother. I don't really remember much about what happened. One moment I was with you on the beach, the next thing I find myself in bed with my leg in a sling and Kissy fussing over me like a broody hen." She giggled in her unique way. "Thanks, though, Kissy."

"We're going to give all the money we collect to the Friends of the Hospital, if that's okay with you, Min?" said Rud.

"Only if I can have my photo taken presenting the cheque."

"Of course!"

Her forehead creased slightly, "I suppose you are all off home today?"

"Some of us," said Dicky. "But we'll keep in touch with Huw."

"Jake and I will be in to see you again this afternoon, and tomorrow before we head back to Tencastle."

"I'll be around too," said Kissy. "Have you been told how long you'll have to stay in hospital?"

"Not really, but not before they get this contraption off me, anyhow. And I don't think I'll be dancing for a while!"

"I'm home for the summer, so I'll be checking up on you each day," said Huw, "to make sure you're not terrorising the doctors."

"Would I?" Min said wickedly. No broken spirit that's for sure.

"Is there anyone you would like us to contact? Your family?" Jake broached the subject gently.

Min grimaced briefly, "I haven't really got any family. I was going to spend the summer with a friend. We'd got a job lined up working at a holiday camp in Skegness."

"We can let her know."

"It's a him, actually. Yes, please, Jake, if you would. Er, where exactly am I at the moment?"

"Haverfordwest, Withybush Hospital."

I glimpsed a nurse hovering nearby. "I think our time's up," I said, "but we'll be back later." I gave Min a kiss on the cheek, the others following suit.

"Hey, I could get to like this!" said Min.

"We've brought your Morris kit, if you'd like to join us, Kissy."

"Thanks, Sophie, I'll do my best but I'm pretty knackered."

The receptionist had obviously been busy spreading the word around, and, much to our surprise, a goodly number of walking and wheelchair patients had been ushered into the cafeteria to join the visitors having their elevenses. Jake quickly switched to showman mode, announcing the purpose of our appearance, but cutting out a lot of his usual bull. The response was fantastic and the collection reasonable, considering that many of the people there were in their dressing gowns.

In the foyer, the situation reversed, with an ever-changing, moving audience, nevertheless happy to dip into their pockets. When a reporter from the local paper turned up, Jake was more than ready to fill him in on the story and extracted from him a promise to fulfill Min's request when our cheque was ready to be handed over.

"Have we got time to dance up in the town?" Dan asked, as we headed back to the vehicles.

"Pushing it," said Jake. "Depends whether you want to dance and drink or eat and drink!"

"Drink and dance!" said Rud. We accepted his priorities.

The campsite seemed so strangely calm and peaceful that night. Kissy had struggled to keep her eyes open from the moment we'd left Min again late that afternoon, and crashed out on her sleeping bag as soon as we got back from the hospital. Jake and I relocated to the spare compartment next to her since Huw had taken down his tent earlier and retired to his proper bed at the farm.

Jake and I sat outside the main tent drinking coffee and gazing at the waning moon over the sea.

"What are your plans for the rest of the summer?" I said.

"Oh, I don't know. Get a job stacking supermarket shelves or something. You?"

"Driving my dad's tractors I guess."

Jake was silent for a while.

"Been a good week, hasn't it? Generally, I mean."

"Highs and lows, but, yes, it's worked well."

It could have turned out so differently.

CHAPTER FIFTEEN

School of Wales

With the Dickens away for most of the summer, Jake and I had brought their tent back to Tencastle and left it stretched out in our lounge. I'd thought it prudent, however, to return to Ty Melin a couple of days before the start of term, in case Benji felt the urge to convert the tent into an Indian tepee or Mongolian yurt. It had also given me time to lay the tent out on our lawn (once I'd mown it), brush off all the mud and fold it carefully so that it fitted properly back into its bag.

I dropped off the tent before picking up Jake from the station. Holly and Harry naturally quizzed me intently about Carpiog's activity in Pembrokeshire, and I tried to minimize the horror of Min's accident, reassuring them that she was making good progress, even though I'd not had any recent news as such.

Jake was already waiting, with two enormous suitcases and a rucksack that would have challenged the toughest soldier.

"Christ, Jake, spare a thought for Jessica!" I exclaimed. "I've still got to get a load of stuff from the supermarket." I was determined that we should not repeat the previous year's foodless arrival at the cottage.

"I'm sure the old girl will cope," he declared cheerfully. "I can always walk, if it's a problem."

"I'm probably going to need you to push! What on earth have you got in there anyhow?"

"Oh, this and that, you know." He didn't elaborate.

I turned my attention to manoeuvring the rucksack through the passenger door and onto the rear seat. I reckoned Jake's superior height qualified him to hoist his cases on to the roof rack. Fortunately I'd reversed into the parking bay, because I could no longer see a darn thing out of my inside mirror, and the outside mirror never had been aligned to serve any useful purpose.

Jake must have used his charm on Jessica, for she chugged along as sweet as a bird, slowly of course, but surely.

"You're dead lucky in getting a placement in Tencastle," I commented en route. Jake, falling on his feet, as usual, had somehow secured one of only four places at the local comprehensive for his final teaching practice in Physical Education.

"Just the old black magic at work," he replied deprecatingly. "You know that Huw is in my previous school?"

"Pwllgoch? No I didn't!" I thought for a moment. "Have you spoken to him already then? Did he say how Min is getting on?"

"No, just saw his name on the list. And Dan is only up the road at Tenbridge."

"That's great! We'll all be at the cottage again this term."

For the first term of the third year, it was by no means a foregone conclusion that students would be in their Tencastle pad. If first teaching practice placements were achieved through a certain amount of imaginative planning, the main, and final, placements were Machiavellian in the complexity of the arrangements, not to mention disruptive to the normal pattern of student life. The problem, of course, was the location of Tencastle in the middle of bugger all, in terms of population other than sheep. Within reasonable commuting distance there were just not the number of Secondary level schools available, though final year Primary level students did fare a little better. It was quite common – in fact, it was positively encouraged – for students to secure a placement in a suitable school within reach of their own home or rather, their parental home. This minimised the need to pay both a retainer for their Tencastle accommodation as well as bed and breakfast near their placement school. In some schools just beyond commuting possibility of Tencastle, the college had developed a working arrangement with teaching staff who had a spare room and were willing to take in students temporarily. The wide geographical spread of the placements also meant that the furthest flung students only received the barest minimum of visits from their tutors.

"What about Benji?" I asked, as he was the only one unaccounted for. I'd been fortunate, I thought, to be foisted onto a traditional grammar school in the distinctly up-market town of Carrick Major, about 30 miles from Tencastle, and feasible, Jessica willing, for daily commuting.

"Dunno. I don't think he'd sorted himself out last time we saw him."

That would have been a couple of weeks before the end of the Summer Term, before we had our camping jaunt. Most placements were resolved before the end of the June, since we had only barely two weeks back at college in the Autumn before they began. Just enough time to be reminded what a one-horse town Tencastle was and to make a preliminary visit to the chosen school.

From the moped leaning against the porch we deduced that Dan had already returned. From the boxes and bags cluttering up the lounge we concluded that he'd also had some help with transport.

"Hi guys! Welcome back! Fancy a coffee?"

"That would be great!" we both replied. "Any sign of Benji?"

Dan looked surprised. "I thought he was coming back with you, Rob."

"First I've heard of it," I said, puzzled how Dan could ever have got that idea.

We weren't particularly worried by Benji's non-show, however. He tended to live on a different astral plane altogether.

"There's a fair bit of junk mail mounted up over the summer," said Dan, pushing a pile of the envelopes from the coffee table onto the floor to make space for the steaming mugs. "Haven't had time to go through it yet."

"No time like the present." Jake scooped up a handful and thrust them at me, taking another bundle for himself.

"Bills … junk … more junk …" he muttered. "Ah, what's this?" Jake waved a psychedelically decorated envelope. He extracted a single sheet of plain paper on which was drawn two squiggly lines, one like the upper half of a low amplitude sound wave, the other descending deeply downwards and back, not quite a smooth or symmetric curve. Between the two stood a cartoon figure not unlike a Robinson's jam golliwog, emblazoned with a large B. Beneath the sketch was a legend:

C U B4 L

"What the devil is that supposed to mean?"

"Search me, Dan!" replied Jake. "Anyone sign up for spook school over the summer?"

We all studied the paper for several minutes, looking for clues.

I had an idea. "What's the postmark on the envelope?"

Jake rummaged amongst the debris on the carpet. "Not terribly clear. Looks like '…elte…ha.'"

"Cheltenham?" suggested Dan.

"Could be," said Jake. "So what?"

"That's near Gloucester. Doesn't Benji come from that way?" I asked.

"I think so," Jake conceded. "And I suppose that could be Benji's self caricature, with the shock of hair and big B."

"But what's the message? Why can't he write a letter in plain English like any normal person?"

"He's not a normal person, Dan, you know that! And he doesn't do writing!" Jake added.

"Why has he crossed out the 'L'?"

"Doesn't want it?" I offered.

"No 'L'," mused Jake. "No L. NOEL!" He exclaimed. "Christmas!"

"So, no B4, either!" I said sceptically.

"What if it means 'not B4'? Not before!"

"Well done, Dan!" Jake exclaimed. "You should be with MI5. It's clear, Benji's saying, see you not before Christmas!"

"We don't know it's Benji," I objected.

"Well, who else do we know who's such a prat?" Jake declared.

We couldn't think of anyone else.

"Okay, so we know – or, we think, he's not coming back to Tencastle this term? So where is he?"

Jake and Dan considered my question for a moment before Dan proposed, "Perhaps the sketch is a map."

"B marks the spot where Benji's buried his paint brushes?"

"Don't be flippant, Rob! Look, does the sketch look like any country you know, you're supposed to be the geography expert?"

"Geography, not Picasso impressionism." I looked again. "Could be the Indian sub-continent, perhaps, with the blob at the bottom being Sri Lanka – that's Ceylon to you – and the Himalayas the squiggles at the top. Or South America," I added helpfully.

"India I'd go along with," Dan agreed. "He's probably gone to find the meaning of life."

"Bloody long way for teaching practice!" I responded.

"So, gentlemen," Jake summed up. "We have Benji somewhere in curryland until Christmas at least, and, presumably, a spare room here."

We could have managed quite happily without Benji squirting paint everywhere, but the implications for our finances with one less tenant were another matter entirely, and reduced us to deep thought once again.

"Could we manage with just three of us?" I asked. I wouldn't have minded having a room to myself.

"Stretching it, I think."

"Isn't Benji required to give notice?" Dan queried.

"Yes, I suppose so," Jake conceded. "But how do you suggest we get in touch with him? I don't think 'Benji, India' will impress the postman one little bit!"

"Do you have his parent's address," I asked. "After all, my parents had to act as guarantors when we signed up for this place last year."

273

"Good idea, Rob!" Jake brightened, then knitted his brow again."Only problem, I'm not sure whether I've still got it. It's not the sort of thing you keep to hand, you know."

"You could look!"

With that we left the matter, and went about our own business of stowing our gear and getting some semblance of order back into the place. We left Benji's room untouched until we'd resolved the issue of his absence. One good piece of news, however, was that our landlord had written to say that the rent would stay the same for the coming year.

The Union coffee bar had a buzz to it, mostly from freshers in their first flush of freedom from home. Third year students were thin on the ground. Several students didn't return to college at all until after TP if they were using family or friends elsewhere as a base during this period.

"Jesus," Jake observed. "They're getting bloody younger every day! Look at that girl over there, she hardly looks out of gymslip and knickers!"

The object of his attention was a very waif-like young thing with gorgeous long blonde hair, blue eyes and a lightly blushed innocent angelic expression to match. And those were only the assets above her neck!

"Wouldn't mind seeing her out of knickers myself," leered Dan.

"Shall we offer to show her the sites of Tencastle?" I suggested.

"Too late, I think," said Jake. "Looks as if she's got a babysitter." A great swarthy beefcake, six-foot-six in his socks, came up beside her and handed her a mug of coffee. Barbie meets Superman.

Jake drained his coffee and pushed his chair back. "Must be off. Going to pop into the school."

"Keen all of a sudden aren't we?" I commented. Most of us weren't planning our preliminary visit until Thursday.

"First impressions, you know!"

"I'm off too," said Dan. "Thought I'd see how long it takes to get to Tenbridge on the moped. I'm in two minds whether to use the train."

"It's a long walk from the station," I advised. "Uphill all the way."

I'd got no particular plans for the day, since any necessary meetings with our tutors were officially scheduled for Wednesday. That left Friday for a follow up meeting to sort out any problems or queries that arose from the school visit and a few days for essential preparations. I needed to borrow a couple of items from the science departmental library, then intended to take in a pie and a pint perhaps then spend the afternoon pottering around at the cottage. In the autumn sun, I even considered giving the garden a bit of a facelift and hopefully harvest some of the vegetables that the birds and bugs had left us.

Beyond the brouhaha of the freshers' registration circus, which was in full swing, the corridor upstairs was almost deserted. Freshers were more concerned with goody bags than academic study for this week at least. I quickly recognised the lone girl who was scanning the teaching practice lists on the notice board with some degree of concern, since she seemed to be holding her hand to her face and biting her nails.

"Hi Sunny," I said. "Problems?"

She took another anxious glance at the lists before turning to me, brushing her hair back from her brow. "Oh, hello, Rob!" And turned back to the notice board again.

"What's the problem?" I tried again.

"Oh, Rob, I really don't know what to do!"

I don't think I'd ever seen Sunny without a smile on her face, let alone sound distressed.

"Why's that?" I enquired gently.

"My placement! I thought they were going to send me just up the valley to Tenbridge, but they've sent me miles and miles away! I've been trying to see Dr Williams about it, but he's not in until tomorrow, and I don't know whether he can do anything about it now anyway. I'm going to have to get bed and breakfast I suppose, I can't travel every day, and my landlady will have kittens if I tell her I'm not going to be there for eight weeks or so!"

After her outpouring Sunny seemed close to tears. "Not that I'd mind getting away from her, she's a spiteful old bitch, and I'd be there on my own. Suzy and Kissy have both got schools near their home, so won't be back for ages."

She held her head in her hands. I put my arm around her to comfort her, and she wept buckets on my shoulder, deep sobs welling up, shaking her body.

After a couple of minutes, though it seemed much longer, she calmed down and looked up at me. I offered her a tissue, fortunately fresh that morning.

"I'm sorry, Rob, I shouldn't be burdening you with my woes."

"That's okay," I said. "Look, shall we have a coffee, and we'll see if we can find some way through the problem?" Though in truth I didn't feel I'd be able to offer much practical help. "And I'll come with you tomorrow to see Dr Williams, if that would help. You know, moral support."

"That's very kind of you."

Sunny allowed me to steer her towards the stairs and to the small snack bar situated off the rear of the atrium. The freshers hadn't discovered it yet, so it was nearly empty.

"Black is how you like it, if I remember," I said, handing her a steaming cup.

"Thank you!"

We sat silently for a while, Sunny staring into the cup cradled in her hands. I wasn't quite sure whether to raise the placement issue or try for small talk. Oh well!

"Where is it they want to send you?"

"Some place called Carrick Major. It's miles away!"

"Thirty, to be precise," I said.

"Do you know it then?" she asked, surprised.

"I'm doing my teaching practice there, at the Sir Wilfred Roberts Grammar School. But you're Primary, aren't you?"

"Yes."

"Which school?"

She thought for a moment, "I'm not sure, I think it just said Carrick Major." Another pause. "Are you lodging in Carrick?"

"No, I'm going to do the round trip each day with Jessica. That's my car." I made the next step without even thinking. "Look, Sunny, I'd be very happy to give you a lift each day, if that would help."

"Would you really?" her eyes lit up for the first time since we'd met. "I'd share petrol, of course!"

"Thanks. Makes sense, with two of us going to the same town." Some practicalities then dawned on me. "By the way where do you live?"

"Outskirts of Tencastle, beyond Pant Gorau."

"Um…" That was not so practical. From Penybont, I could join a B road to Carrick Major without heading into Tencastle. To Pant Gorau would add a full ten miles and at least half an hour onto my journey.

Sunny could sense my hesitation. "It's not going to work, is it?" she said despondently.

"Well, it would be quite a detour. However …" I tried to sound positive.

Sunny's head hung low again.

"Wait a minute!" A brilliant idea struck me – well, perhaps not brilliant, but possible. "You said you're not happy with your digs. Well, we've got a spare room until Christmas." I only hoped we'd interpreted Benji's message correctly. "You could use that, then there would be no problem at all with transport. And save you finding somewhere in Carrick!"

The suggestion took Sunny by surprise, but she was obviously thinking about it.

"You already know Jake and Dan, my housemates," I continued, enthusiastically, then saw a problem that Sunny might have. She hadn't yet given a reply. "Ah, Sunny, just wondering ... with your religion ... you are Moslem, aren't you? Would it be difficult for you to share a house with three blokes?"

"Yes I am nominally, but no, it wouldn't be a problem. My father's always been very broad minded and he trusts my judgement." Sunny paused for a moment before continuing. "Rob, it's really ever so kind of you. If Jake and Dan are agreeable, I'd like to take up your offer. It would be good to have some sensible company."

I wasn't sure about the sensible bit. She hadn't lived in close proximity to Jake!

"Right! I'll speak to them tonight and meet you tomorrow, say, elevenses here?"

"That's fine. And, Rob, thanks so much!" Sunny planted a kiss firmly on my cheek.

"I've been thinking," said Jake, almost as soon as he had crossed the threshold. "If Benji's not coming back yet, you may as well have his room."

"I've got another proposal ..."

But Jake was still in full swing, "And if we can get his parents to cough up the rent, we won't ... "

"Jake, listen!" I demanded.

"What?"

"I've found someone who would be interested in taking Benji's room on a temporary basis."

"Who's that?"

"Sunny, you know, Suhindra ... the Turkish Delight?"

Recognition was slow in coming until the image of the Mummers Play dawned.

"Sunny? She's a girl!"

I clapped slowly, "Your powers of observation are incredible!"

"But ... how would she feel being with three fellas?"

"She's prepared to chance her virtue. Best that you find somewhere else other than the Rayburn to dry your jockstraps though."

"What about rent?"

I must admit I hadn't even thought about it. "We'll sort something out. I suggest that you still try to contact Benji's folks in the meantime. I don't see why he should leave us in the lurch."

Sunny was looking chirpy, much more like her usual demeanour, when we met next morning.

"Hi Rob! I've just seen Dr Williams. It seems I'd got my wires crossed somewhere along the line, and Carrick was always my intended school. Have you spoken to Jake and Dan?"

"Yes, no problem at all." Actually I hadn't spoken to Dan, he'd been very late back and hadn't surfaced before I'd left. Anyway, he was unlikely to make a fuss.

"What about rent? We didn't even mention it yesterday."

"Well, it's a little bit complicated." Jake had managed to get through to Benji's parents, who confirmed that he was expected to be in India until Christmas. They'd no idea that he'd left us pretty much in the dark and were horrified he'd not made any arrangements about rent. They were quite prepared to cough up his rent until Christmas, but we did mention that we might have someone to take his place. "What have you agreed with your landlady?"

"I've given her a month's notice. The stupid old cow was making such a song and dance, and making all sorts of ridiculous accusations and threats that I told her what she could do with her flat. She wanted to charge me a term's rent, until I pointed out that our contract required just a month's notice on either side. I shall probably have to chase her for my deposit, but I'll deal with that later." She smiled wryly, "I'm afraid I've rather burnt my boats!"

"Well, at least you're okay now until Christmas."

"Mmm, yes. Thanks again for your help."

"What I suggest is that we get Benj's folks to pay for the first four weeks, then you pay your share from then on. They'll be happy, we'll be happy, and you won't be out of pocket."

"That's absolutely brilliant!"

"When do you have to move out?"

"I told her I'd probably be out by the weekend."

"Right. Can you bring a few overnight things with you today, then we'll make an early start for Carrick tomorrow, and I'll help you with the rest of your stuff on Saturday. You can also see whether you like the cottage."

"I don't think I've got the option not to like it now!"

In truth, Sunny fell in love with the cottage the moment she saw it.

"It's gorgeous! Fantastic! How did you ever come across a place like this?"

"To cut a very long story short, some relative of Jake."

A touch of concern. "But it must cost a fortune…"

"No, usual level of rent. We're, er, sort of house sitting for a couple of years while the owner is abroad."

"Really!"

I showed Sunny to Benji's room and told her to ignore discarded tubes of paint, psychedelic murals and any other artistic debris. From the distinctive whistling and odd tuneless vocal from the bathroom Dan was obviously back in the land of the living.

I suppose I should have remembered the usual sequence of events once the bath time recital ceased. Dan strode out, still wiping his face on the towel, but otherwise naked. Sunny chose that moment to come out of her room. Her barely suppressed giggle alerted Dan to the fact that something wasn't quite in order.

"Wha...?" He gaped and blushed bright pink. Trying hard to cover himself one handed with the towel he sidled past Sunny, mumbling, "'Scuse me" and dived into his room. Not before he'd shot an accusing glance in my direction.

After I'd given Sunny a short guided tour of the cottage and garden, which was showing the result of recent attention – as in one hour of my frenzied activity – we flopped out in armchairs to talk about other practical issues in our household.

Dan, more respectively clad, joined us. "Sorry, Sunny, if I embarrassed you. I'd no idea you were here." He turned to admonish me. "That was a rotten trick to spring on me, Rob. You might have given me some warning that you were bringing your girlfriend back."

"Not a..."

"Not my..."

Sunny and I both tried to speak at once. We burst out laughing.

"What's so funny?"

"Sorry, Dan. Meet your new housemate!"

"Not his girlfriend!" added Sunny.

"Housemate? What ... what about Benji? And does Jake know?" He turned to Sunny, "You wouldn't want to catch Jake like you did me!"

"Why's that?" Sunny asked mischievously.

Dan managed pink again, "Well ... you know..."

I thought I'd better rescue him before Sunny teased him further. "Benji's definitely away till Christmas, and Jake's happy with the arrangement. I'm sorry we didn't manage to catch you last night, but we hoped you wouldn't object. You don't, do you?"

He couldn't really veto the plan, with Sunny right there, but to seal the matter, I added, "She'll share the rent."

"No problem. Welcome to Ty Melin, Sunny," he said magnanimously.

Thursday was one of those fresh autumn mornings that promised a bright sunny day when the early mist cleared from the valleys. Jessica gave a short cough in surprise, no doubt, at the unaccustomed right turn downhill and over the stone bridge. The road then climbed up though the wooded hillside until we levelled out on moorland, just before the junction with the high-level route to Carrick Major.

Although we'd known each other for some time – since our first day of registration two years ago – we'd never been in the situation of sharing each other's company uninterrupted for a period of forty five minutes or so. So, inevitably, by the time we descended the escarpment to Carrick which lay at its foot, Sunny had been given a potted history of my life, and I had learned that she was the London-born eldest daughter of an Indian mother and exiled Iranian father, with further international ancestry thrown in for good measure. Whether she was fluent in her parents' native languages and what nationality she was officially remained to be discovered on future commuting journeys.

I dropped Sunny off at her school, a modern single-storey construction adjacent to extensive playing fields on the edge of Carrick Major, or Carreg Mawr, as the bilingual town sign informed us. My academy, however, was an imposing grey sandstone edifice that dominated one of the three narrow streets that led into the central market square. Although pedestrian access was obvious, I wasted at least fifteen minutes trying to find a way to get Jessica in before settling, begrudgingly, for the pay-and-display car park that occupied the square on all but market days.

A large ornate wooden plaque on the high stone wall declared the Principal of Sir Wilfred Roberts Grammar School be one Dr M.O. Bedford-Dickson. An arched gateway opened into a claustrophobic twelve foot or so strip of tarmac – hardly big enough to be classed as a playground, unless skittles were in vogue. In the old building which towered high in front of me I faced a choice of three entrances, above which, nearest to me, on the right, I could just make out the word 'Boys' in weathered stone lettering. Reasoning that the left hand entrance probably had a similar legend for girls I opted for the central door, and entered a parquet-floored vestibule from which an empty corridor stretched ahead way into the distance. A prim, grey-haired woman bearing a handful of folders appeared from a transverse corridor.

"Can I help you?" she asked, rather brusquely, adjusting the rimless spectacles on the end of her nose.

"Thank you. I'm Robert Kiddecott, from Tencastle. I'm starting final teaching practice here next week."

Her look suggested that she thought I'd be more suited to starting A levels. "Wait here."

She strode purposefully through an open doorway on my right. The small wooden sign above modestly stated 'Reception'.

A few minutes later she re-emerged and addressed me formally, but somewhat less frostily. "Mr Kiddecott, I see you are to be attached to the Science Department. I've let Mr Ramsbottom know that you're here. He's teaching at the moment, but he'll be with you shortly, at morning break."

She turned to go back into the reception office.

"Do you want me to wait here?"

Any alternative obviously hadn't occurred to her. "I suppose you had better go to the staff room. First door on the left, round the corner." And she was gone.

The large solid oak door also had a small high level sign beside it, 'Private – authorised staff only'. How the youngest pupils were ever expected to read such notices I had no idea. I hoped I qualified as authorised.

I entered another short corridor with further identical doors, thankfully clearly marked 'Ladies', 'Gents', 'Resources', and a stone staircase with an arrow directing 'Staff' upwards. At the top I briefly considered whether I should knock, but took my shortly-to-be temporary trainee staff appointment seriously and entered unannounced. The spacious room appeared to be unoccupied. An assortment of armchairs lined the wall beneath the tall windows, and one end was fitted with a bank of lockers and a nest of pigeon-holes. The central area was taken up by several wooden tables and chairs, mostly laden with an assortment of exercise books, brochures, folders and the odd newspaper and cup.

"Hello there," came a voice from the far end of the room. "You look as if you're lost!"

The voice belonged to a six-foot mountain of muscle in a tracksuit who emerged from a steam-filled alcove with an enormous coffee mug.

"Care for a coffee?"

"Yes, er, thanks. I was told to wait in the staffroom for Mr Ramsbottom," I ventured.

"Ah, you must be one of Arsenic's young protégés."

"Sorry?"

"Student on TP with Nick Ramsbottom?"

I nodded.

"Thought so. Kids all call him Arsenic, on account of his poisonous tongue. Don't tell him I told you, though will you? I'm John, by the way, John Rhys-Price, head of games."

The lock of fair hair tumbling over a crooked, flattened nose in a well-tanned face gave him a rather lopsided, conspiratorial grin.

"Rob Kiddecott," I offered my hand. "And you're right, it's my final teaching practice from Tencastle."

"You'll do fine with Nick, he's very supportive of his students, as longs as you treat his sarcastic humour with a pinch of salt. Is Chemistry your only subject? Not a rugby player by any chance?"

"No chance! I once made the reserves at school when most of the squad were on county trials and got stretchered off after ten minutes with concussion."

"Shame!"

I wasn't sure whether his remark was in sympathy for my accident or disappointment for whatever he'd had in mind.

"I'm hoping to do a bit of Geography as well."

"Then you'll probably be with my flat-mate, Mark Matthews. You must come round for a drink some time and we'll show you the flesh pots of Carrick!"

"Thanks, I might do that!" Not that my travelling arrangements were likely to accommodate such dubious delights. Still, a friendly gesture, after Miss Iceberg downstairs.

A shrill bell shook the room, almost causing me to drop my cup in surprise. Less than thirty seconds later, the staffroom began to fill up rapidly, with some teachers showing obvious signs of stress or thirst or both. I couldn't help but notice that the early arrivals were predominantly male but before I could comment on this, John called out.

"Hey, Luke, come and meet the latest lamb for the slaughter!" To me, presumably the lamb, he added, "Luke's my other housemate."

A slightly-built young man with a neatly-trimmed brown beard and an expression of utmost calm politely threaded his way across the room.

"Hello," he said pleasantly, offering his hand, "I'm Terry Osborne. Pleased to meet you."

"Rob Kiddecott. Er, excuse me, but didn't John just call you Luke?"

"Yes, his little joke."

"I don't understand."

"Well, John and I, and Mark Matthews all started here at the same time, and, since I'm an R.E. teacher, John thought that it only right that all four gospels should be represented. Unfortunately he's rather indiscreet in his comments and I'm afraid the alias has rather caught on with the children."

John was unmoved by this mild admonition, "Well, you do have a saintly air about you!"

The rejoinder was given and received in good humour, but I wouldn't have put discretion high up the Rhys-Morgan agenda. I felt I needed to be a little cautious in what I said to him lest he should saddle me with a nickname before I even got into the classroom.

Beyond John and Luke's effective shield I noticed a short middle-aged man in a lab coat. His hair follicles had retreated from the crown of his head and relocated in his ears and nostrils. He seemed to be purposefully surveying the assembly for an unfamiliar face.

"Excuse me," I said, and made my way towards him, as he caught sight of me.

"Robert Kiddecott?"

I nodded, and offered my hand.

"Nick Ramsbottom. Sorry I couldn't meet you before. Miss Ellis told me you'd be here. She's the Headmaster's secretary, a bit of a dragon, but very efficient."

I didn't need to comment, for he rattled on, in an accent indisputably northern English. Yorkshire, I'd guess.

"Now, I see you've already got a coffee. Let me grab a cup, and we'll head up to the labs. I'm free now until lunch, so we should have plenty of time to sort out what you can do for us. And us for you, of course."

Caffeine fix soon in hand, he breezed out with me following, down the stairs and along the now busy main corridor that had stretched away from me when I first entered the building. He barely paused to admonish a youngster who had allowed a crisp packet to fall to the floor. Out we went then into a large quadrangle beyond which at least three modern two-storey blocks were sited, and I caught a glimpse of green turf behind them.

"How did you get to Carrick?" Nick asked, now that I was able to walk alongside him. "Will you be staying in the town for the duration?"

"No, I'm driving in each day. It's not too far, and a student at the primary school is sharing the cost."

"Good idea! Carrick's a bit dull in the evening."

Except John's supposed fleshpots, I thought.

"By the way, is there any on-site parking? I left my car in the square."

"Eh, now, lad, you won't get in from the town centre."

"So I discovered!"

"You have to come in the back way, take the first left after the primary school and just follow your nose. You come in on the other side of these annexes. There's plenty of space to park, but don't take any of the numbered bays or the Head will go berserk."

"What's he like, the Head?"

"Bedford-Dickson? He's okay, rather aloof and pompous, but a good administrator, and he's got a knack of screwing the bean counters at County Hall for every last penny, not to mention any other funding available for the latest Government wheeze of the day. Result is, we've probably got the best funded and resourced school anywhere in Wales, even if we do have to shift our goal posts every season. He'll probably want to meet you once you've settled in."

We entered the furthest annex, all glass and dark slate.

"Our newest addition," said Nick, quite proudly. "Built to accommodate the extra kids when the school leaving age was raised to sixteen. Not that it really affected us, as all but a handful stayed on to O levels and beyond anyway. Too good an opportunity for the Head to miss, though, and I'm pleased to have modern purpose-built laboratories instead of the glorified garden sheds we'd been squeezed into previously."

"How many labs have you got?"

"Two biology on the ground floor, together with a couple of seminar rooms, office and main prep room, then two each of physics and chemistry upstairs and another equipment store and prep room. Come upstairs, and I'll show you round. C1's free where you'll be doing most of your teaching."

From the top of the central staircase a door marked 'Staff only' faced us, while a short transverse corridor led to a wide balcony either side each accessing two laboratories. C1 was first on the right, and quite impressive compared to the dingy, smelly laboratory I'd been obliged to occupy for my schooldays. It sported a well-equipped demonstration bench in front of a rolling blackboard, facing two longitudinal island benches with facilities for four pairs of students on each side. It meant of course that they had to sit sideways on to face the teacher, but it made it easier for supervision – no hiding behind the old-style high transverse benches. Further workstations were available beneath the windows along two sides of the room.

We soon got down to business. Nick certainly had a brisk no-nonsense approach and though seeming to involve me in the decision making, cleverly steered me towards the programme he'd almost certainly predetermined. After three days of observation, I'd work effectively nearly a half-timetable, mostly with the 11-14 age group, but with active participation in an O Level group and observation with some sixth-formers. Two classes would be with the other full-time chemist, Jenny Pagitter.

"Well, I guess that's about it!" declared Nick, after half an hour of intense concentration on my part. "If we go next door, I'll give …"

A loud three-note tone interrupted his gift intentions. "This is the Headmaster," boomed a rich baritone Welsh accented voice, from a speaker high up in the far corner. "All third years please report to the hall at the end of morning school!"

"Head's new toy," said Nick. "Bloody tannoy. Overrides the radio network system we acquired to allow every room to receive BBC education broadcasts. The kids have got their own pet name for it."

"What's that?" I asked.

"Not for me to say. You'll find out soon enough!" he replied enigmatically. "Now, to those textbooks and worksheets you'll need!"

I followed him through a door beyond the demonstration bench into a prep room. A girl was half-hidden by a large cardboard box she was carrying.

"Rosetta, this is Robert Kiddecott. He'll be joining us next week on teaching practice."

A freckled round face framed in dark bubbly hair peeped from behind the box. Her eyes opened wide, as if she'd been surprised by an alien, her mouth forming a perfect O. As she stepped forward, she stumbled and the box tipped its contents of polystyrene packaging generously over the floor.

Nick rolled his eyes. "Meet Rosetta Cledwyn, our lab technician."

Rosetta was on her knees, trying to scoop up the white chips with her hands. "Sorry, Mr Ramsbottom," she said, then to me, "Hi!" with a toothy smile and a wave which scattered a few chips further afield. "Oops, sorry!" she apologised again.

I noticed a dust pan and brush on the table. "Here, let me help," I offered, slipping instinctively into my white knight for damsel in distress mode. Nick looked on impassively. Between us we soon managed to return most of the escaped plastic tadpoles to their box.

"Oh thank you ever so, Ro … er … Mr?" From her confused expression she was either unsure whether to use my Christian name or had forgotten my surname. Or both.

"Kiddecott. Robert Kiddecott."

If I'd said, 'Bond, James Bond,' I couldn't have elicited a more dewy-eyed look of awe from Rosetta. She didn't match up, however, to any of double-o-seven's bimbos, being oddly proportioned, small -breasted in relation to her chunky body mounted on long legs that were surprisingly shapely from what I could see below the knee. She did have a smooth sexy voice, though, with a gentle soft Welsh accent.

Nick meanwhile had gathered an assortment of folders and textbooks for me in a Co-op carrier bag. "Mustn't keep Mr Kiddecott any longer, Rosetta, he's still got a lot to sort out today."

Had I? Nick was already half out of the prep room door, still holding my bag of goodies.

"Bye," I said. "See you again next Wednesday!"

"Rosetta's very well-meaning," said Nick when we got out into the corridor, "if somewhat accident-prone. Anything you need for your lesson, just fill in a requisition slip the day before, and Rosetta will have it ready for you. Just don't get too close to her when she's carrying concentrated sulphuric acid!"

"Does she make up all of the reagents?" I asked, wondering how far I could rely on their accuracy.

"No, that's usually done by Aubrey Turner, our chief technician. He can be an awkward sod and quite intimidating to any young person. That's anyone below forty in his eyes, so it's probably best if you just go through Rosetta."

The clarion bells sounded again.

"End of morning," said Nick, "I've got to rush off now, to take fencing club, but I think we're just about done, don't you? Any questions?"

He obviously wasn't wanting any. We'd already reached the quad, and pupils were spilling out of classrooms.

"I don't think so, thanks."

But after he shook my hand and began to turn away I remembered something. "Oh, just one thing, I was hoping to do a bit of Geography as well."

"Ah, yes, I'd forgotten," replied Nick over his shoulder. "Mark Matthews is out with some sixth formers today, but I'll speak with him tomorrow. Take care now!" And with that, he was off to another of the new buildings.

I'd arranged to pick Sunny up at three-thirty since neither of us knew how long we'd take at our respective schools. Which left me with three hours to kill. I spent a few minutes getting a feel for the geography of the school campus until I was sure that I could find my way from the car park to the labs and the main building. The road which gave access to the car park was blocked to four-wheel traffic just beyond the gates, but on foot I soon found myself in the market square. Although two inns were in prime position on adjacent sides of the square I decided my hunger and thirst could wait a while until I'd done a perambulation to see what else was on offer. Apart from a Boots and three banks, other national chains were refreshingly absent. Even so there was a good selection of shops selling all the essentials, with little obvious pandering to the tourist trade.

I was tempted by the butchers selling hot fresh steak pies and by the amazing selection of calorie-laden cakes in the window of the bakery, which also had a small cafe attached. I opted for the Bull and Dragon's special of the day, a generous shepherd's pie and veg, washed down with a pint of Brain's Best Bitter, a beer I'd not come across before. Apparently Cardiff students were weaned on it.

Suitably fed and watered, I still had a fair bit of the afternoon free to explore Carrick. One street led away from the square down past a livestock market and abattoir – the only possible fleshpot location as far as I could see, and not what John Rhys-Price had in mind. At the bottom of the hill a roundabout gave access to a main road from the south which then branched left over a bridge towards Carmarthen. Another avenue, lined with trees ran beside the riverbank, I assumed, towards Tencastle. In the warm Autumn afternoon a few late season tourists were strolling along the well-maintained grassy bank of the river, which was shallow enough to see the rocky bed but quite fast flowing despite a fortnight without rain. Broad, too, about the width of a dual carriageway.

I cut back up a steep narrow lane which sported a couple of interesting looking pubs and led, so I hoped, more or less back to the square, in time to indulge in a cream cake at the bakery cafe.

Sunny had arrived there first and had already made substantial inroads into an enormous slice of cream-topped apple pie. She was one of those fortunate people, she had told me, who could eat like a horse without any effect on her figure, whilst I, though not fat by any means, nevertheless had to be on my guard – sometimes – against temptation by stray calories.

"Hi there. Surprise!"

"Hi, Rob. Yes, I finished early so thought I'd wander into town. Quaint place, isn't it?"

"Er … yes, I suppose it is. Everything go okay?"

"No problems! The deputy head is half-Indian, like me, so the children shouldn't be put off by my oriental appearance."

I wondered how Jake would make out this time. Still, Tencastle, though almost exclusively Anglo-Saxon and Celtic, was used to seeing the odd student from various ethnic backgrounds around the town.

"Have you been down by the river?" I asked, when my carrot cake arrived.

"Not yet. It took me fifteen minutes to walk in."

"How about we drive back that way? The road probably leads back to Tencastle."

"Sounds fine."

We finished our respective gateaux and coffees at leisure and rejoined Jessica basking in the sun. I followed my earlier pedestrian route to the roundabout and turned along the leafy avenue. Apart from a couple of other lanes similar to the one I had taken, the road meandered uninterrupted along by the river beyond the limit of Carrick's habitation, becoming narrower.

After about three miles, the road turned left at right angles to cross the river over a stone humpback bridge. Then it began to wander through a deeply wooded side valley, making it very difficult to tell from the sun in which direction we were heading. We passed a couple of unmarked side roads, the odd farm and isolated cottage, but little else that told of civilisation. I was hoping that we'd strike a major crossroads before too long, to verify our whereabouts.

Fifteen minutes more driving through similar landscape brought partial fulfilment of my wish.

"Llanfihangel left, Cwmgruffyth ahead and lord knows what to the right," I said, peering through the windscreen at the signpost half obscured by hedgerow. "Can you find them on the map, it's on the back seat?"

The tattered road atlas had come free with Jessica, and must have been years out of date. Still, the roads had been there for much longer.

Sunny studied the map intently for a couple of minutes. "I've found Carrick," she said helpfully, "and Tencastle. What place did you ask me to look for?"

"Let me have a look," I said. After all, I was supposed to know about maps and things.

Sunny pointed out the position of Carrick and Tencastle, both represented by a single small black dot. From the former I could see a spidery red line following an even fainter blue squiggle. After a couple of inches – as the crow flies- it was bisected by another spider thread, if anything further away from our destination. Llanfihangel was another inch or two off course and Cwmgruffyd was nowhere to be found. The unmarked road at least started in the right direction but naturally fell off the dog-eared edge of the page. It did appear, however, to continue overleaf and link up with our B road home.

"Right or back to Carrick?" I asked.

"You're the driver!" Sunny shrugged, unhelpfully.

"Right!" And I took the unmarked road. If my reading of the map was correct, we would travel about four miles to the next crossroads where a right turn should bring us back to our desired route.

Two miles along we came to an unmarked T-junction. I turned right again, only to meet with a similar dilemma a couple of minutes later. Another right brought us to an unsigned five-way junction. I rested my chin on my hands.

"We're lost, aren't we?"

"No, not lost," I said, trying to sound more optimistic than I felt. "I'm just re-assessing our coordinates."

"We are lost!" Sunny said decisively.

"Well ... yes," I conceded.

"What do we do now?"

"Safest thing would be to go back the way we came, I suppose. Though to be honest, I'm not even sure I can remember all the turnings."

We sat silently, pondering our predicament. The peace was broken by a rising cacophony of bleating as a flock of sheep appeared from the road diagonally right. I hoped they didn't want to come our way as Jessica was taking up most of the width of the road.

"There should be someone with the sheep," suggested Sunny. "We could ask."

Sure enough, as the flock passed in front of us, a bent old man wearing a long brown coat over corduroys tied up with string came into view. He tapped the stragglers gently on their back.

I scrambled out of the car, trying not to scare the sheep.

"Excuse me, we are trying to find our way to Tencastle."

"Well now, boyo, most folks don't go to Tencastle from here."

"I don't think we've got much choice!"

He leant on his stick and thought. "Most of us go to Carreg Mawr, if we have to go at all." He adjusted his shabby flat cap. He caught my look of frustration – or desperation. "Mind you, you could go up this road," he said pointing along the lane sharp right, "and take the next turning right. It's a bit narrow, look you."

His sheep obviously knew their whereabouts better than us and were already fifty yards or so ahead. The old man touched his cap and hurried after them.

We looked at each other and shrugged.

"Carry on?" I said. I was also concerned that Jessica's fuel gauge, dodgy at the best of times, was hovering around the quarter mark.

A couple of hundred yards along the road a potholed track with a central green reservation led steeply downhill.

"Is this it?" Sunny asked, dubiously.

"Don't know!" I replied, but turned anyway. The brambles brushed Jessica's sides, squashing a few juicy berries against her paintwork. I took the track very carefully in bottom gear. Jessica's crude suspension transmitted and amplified every bump.

Down and round a sharp bend we went, and came upon a rare sign. 'Ford' it declared, and next to it stood a weathered white pole showing depths of up to six feet, while beyond gurgled a ten feet width of babbling brook.

"I hope Jessica can swim!" I said, and edged forward. Turning round was not possible anyway, and I didn't fancy reversing up half a mile of steep winding road. She took it like a duck to water – too readily, in fact, for as the front wheels touched the tarmac on the far side, Jessica decided to cool off a little longer in the water and stalled.

"Bugger!" I exclaimed. then remembered Sunny. "Sorry!"

She seemed quite amused, which I suppose suppressed a few Anglo-Saxon expletives that I'd have normally expressed in other circumstances. I pulled on the starter knob, and was not surprised by an apologetic splutter from Jessica.

"You or me?"

"Pardon?"

"You or me for a paddle? I presume one of us has got to get out and push?" Sunny had assessed the situation perfectly.

"I'll go. You're lighter. Can you steer?" I was pretty sure Sunny didn't drive. I took off my shoes and socks, rolled up my trouser legs and eased myself out of the door. The water was bloody freezing!

When Sunny manoeuvred herself over the gear lever into the driver's seat I started to push. Jessica wouldn't budge.

"Have you got the handbrake off?" I yelled.

"I don't know. Which one is it?"

"The short stick with the button at the top. Press the button and push it forward!"

"Okay."

Jessica now moved slowly forward. Fortunately the road on the far side was level for twenty yards or so. One last heave ....

I felt Jessica pushing back.

"Pull the brake on again, for Christ's sake!"

Sunny poked her head out of the door. "Are you all right?"

"I'm okay now, thanks. But I'm going to need you to help a little more." If I knew Jessica, she'd probably fire up after a few swings on the handle, but the trick was to keep her going with a blip on the accelerator.

Time for Sunny's next driving lesson! "When I swing the handle, and you hear Jessica cough, just push down on the pedal nearest the door, but take your foot off if she doesn't start."

The first four swings barely raised any reaction. I was concerned about flooding the carburettor, and, abandoning the starting handle, I leant in through the driver's window to ease back the choke knob. My next attempt with the handle triggered a brief ignition and an explosive exhaust emission.

"This time," I called hopefully. "Get ready!"

The engine caught and I just got my hand away in time before Sunny floored the accelerator, sending the starting handle spinning furiously and the engine racing.

"Steady, steady," I shouted above the din. "Now just ease your foot slowly off the pedal," I said, with careful encouragement to Sunny who was looking very startled and nervous.

Slowly the revs dropped and Jessica sat purring gently. I retrieved the starting handle which had rattled free. We reclaimed our proper seats and, barefooted, I eased the car forward in first gear until we were firmly on dry land.

"Well, done, Sunny! That was perfect!" Not quite, perhaps, but what the hell! Without her help we would have still been marooned.

Jessica seemed none the worse for the experience and chugged happily up the long hill on the other side. We caught sight of traffic moving along the top of the escarpment, and breathed a sigh of relief when we eventually came to the main road. 'Carrick Major 5 miles', the signpost advertised.

Fortunately, I'd noticed two garages along this road on the morning's journey, so a further detour into Tencastle was unnecessary.

Jake and Dan were already home, and a saucepan was bubbling on the stove with some indeterminate gruel which smelled quite appetising.

"Hi, wondered where you two had got to."

"We went for a ride in the country," said Sunny, innocently.

"Very pleasant!" commented Dan, suggestively.

Apart from helping Sunny to transfer the rest of her belongings – three round trips with Jessica – the following few days were unnaturally quiet as the members of the household took their forthcoming teaching practice seriously, with heads down in earnest preparation of lesson plans. Though I was only a few years along from first-hand experience of schoolboy chemistry, several things seemed to have moved on. The new textbooks focussed much more on observation and deduction, with hypothesising, testing and analysing results all the rage. Quite different from the rote learning of chemical facts and formulae.

When Sunny and I set out for Carrick Major on Wednesday morning I suppose we were as prepared as we were ever likely to be, though we didn't discuss the prospects much on our journey. There was no problem finding the rear entrance to the school as Nick had directed, and I even managed to find my way to the staffroom without getting lost. Already there was a hive of activity and a pall of tobacco smoke. There was no sign of Nick, but I recognised John Rhys-Jones in tracksuit chatting with Terry Osborne and a clean-shaven fresh-faced colleague of medium build and curly blond hair. He looked to be in his early thirties, and, dressed in brown tweed jacket and cords, could have been taken as a young country squire.

"Hey, Rob, come and meet Mark!" John called across the room as he caught sight of me.

"Hello there," said Mark, offering his hand, "I'm Mark Matthews. Sorry I wasn't around when you were here earlier. I understand you'd like to escape from old Nick's lab from time to time."

"Rob Kiddecott. Yes, if it's okay with you I'd like to teach a bit of Geography."

"I'm sure we can sort something out for you. Now, you've ..."

"This is your Headmaster speaking," the tannoy blasted into our conversation. "Lower School assembly only this morning. Seniors are to stay with their form teacher. I repeat, Upp..."

He didn't get the chance. John reached across to the volume control on the nearby wall.

"We heard you first time, Moby!" he muttered. "Bloody Radio Whales! More bloody announcements than Cardiff Central."

"At least you don't hear him out on the rugby pitch," Mark observed, tartly. "We can't turn him off in the classroom."

"Missed his blooming vocation, look you," John grumbled on, with what was evidently a well-worn subject.

The bell silenced any further comment.

"As I was saying," said Mark, "you've been assigned to me as a form tutor. Delightful bunch of second year scallywags. Care to meet them?"

We made our way to the door. "John seemed a bit put out there," I ventured.

"Oh, he's always bolshie. He'll get himself in trouble one of these days with his indiscreet use of the kids' nicknames for the staff. You've probably gathered that our noble Headmaster is known as Moby Dick behind his back."

Mark's classroom was in the main building two corridor lengths and one right angle from the staffroom steps. The hubbub of chatter ceased the moment he entered, and the children – two dozen or so shining smart, well-scrubbed individuals – mostly – stood in silence, their eyes turning en masse to the stranger in their midst.

"Please sit down," said Mark, in a friendly tone. "I'd like to introduce you to Mr Kiddecott who will be helping me to keep you lot in order this term."

A gentle chuckle from the youngsters. It was pretty obvious to me that Mark didn't need any assistance in keeping his charges under control. He had that natural air of authority and easy manner that commanded immediate respect from the pupils without any need for him to raise his voice or threaten harsh penalties, though I suspect that he would soon put any miscreant firmly in his – or her – place. I hoped I'd be able to develop similar attributes in my teaching career.

I survived the first couple of weeks pretty well, I thought, all things considered. While my time at Abergwnwyn had given me a taste of life from the teacher's side of the desk, I'd not really had to seriously concentrate on subject matter in the context of working to a set curriculum, and ultimately delivering part of the preparation for examinations. Though Nick, Jenny and Rosetta all gave me tremendous support, anticipating in those early days some things that I didn't even realise myself that I was going to need, I often felt as if I was going round blindfolded since the whereabouts of even basic and essential items of equipment were part of a very steep personal learning curve.

The kids were no trouble at all, but possibly I was just enjoying a honeymoon period while they assessed my ability to keep control. Of course, their regular teachers were usually still hovering around as well.

"Got a few minutes before you go?" Nick asked me at the end of the second full week. "Just need to check some things with you."

"No problem." I'd made a standing arrangement with Sunny that, unless we agreed otherwise beforehand, she'd get on with some work in her school until I turned up.

Jenny joined us in Nick's office. She was a tall, slim woman in her early thirties, at the most, I would have guessed, with short cropped hair and wire framed spectacles perching on a short, slightly beaky nose, which gave her a rather wise owl appearance. She seemed very quiet and reserved, not given to public expressions of hilarity other than a slight wry smile. Nevertheless I found her easy to get on with and very professional in dealing with any queries that I had.

"Well, young Robert, you seem to have made a good start," Nick began. "No real problems that I can see, though you should take care not to get sidetracked. There's one or two of our scallywags who could get an O level in diversionary tactics, and they were testing your awareness yesterday. I don't expect you even realised."

"No, I didn't. Sorry."

"Anything you'd like to add, Jenny?"

"Not really. I think, Rob, you perhaps need to slow your delivery down a little, and perhaps break down procedural instructions into smaller, single steps, particularly for our less gifted pupils."

"Okay, thanks for that. I'll try."

"Well then, Rob," Nick concluded, "next week you can go solo. We'll be on hand if you need us."

The weekend passed in minutes, it seemed. Whatever apprehension I had about going solo, as Nick had put it, disappeared as soon as I stood in front of my first class without the safety net: a fresh faced bunch of eleven year olds. As the week progressed, I began to feel like a real teacher. Nick hadn't mentioned any particular class or names with regard to the sidetrackers, but I think I nipped one of them in the bud when he asked, innocently to all intents and purposes, an obscure question about car batteries. He wasn't so keen to stay behind for the detailed answer I offered to give him at the end of the lesson.

Mark's tutor group were a delight, and I found it easy to enter into the good natured repartee in which he interacted with them. They seemed to know just how far to go, and anyone who strayed over the mark was gently but firmly reminded where the line was. Taking them for Geography, too, I got to know all of their names very quickly.

Travelling back to Penybont we both felt in quite buoyant spirits, pleased with our week's work.

The next Monday was a different kettle of fish. It hadn't started well. In fact Jessica had been reluctant to start at all, and after much vigorous swinging of the starting handle and some equally vigorous cursing, I'd only just managed to get the old girl to splutter into action on a rolling start downhill to the bridge. And then, setting off some fifteen minutes late, we got caught up in a ruddy tractor convention – it seemed as if all the farm machinery in mid-Wales that morning was on the move, very slowly. The B road to Carrick was scenic though anything but straight, and no sooner had we squeezed round one tractor, another hove in view.

Consequently, I was not in a good mood when I arrived with barely five minutes to spare before my first lesson, having missed both registration and assembly. My weekly encounter with 3D, the lowest set of 14 year olds was not my favourite lesson. It wasn't that they were badly behaved, they were just, well, bloody thick, with the attention span of seconds and seemingly incapable of remembering even the simplest instruction for much longer. To give them a series of procedures in one go would be sure to end with the final action being attempted first. One small, simple step at a time was the only way any meaningful practical chemistry could be chanced. The lesson was, for some quirk of timetabling, in one of the downstairs Biology labs, next to the main prep room.

Simple electrolysis even so was a bit ambitious with this group, but having suggested to them previously that they could transmute copper coins into silver they were anticipating the chance to get rich quick. I spent nearly half the lesson getting all the wires, crocodile clips and electrodes issued, and then I checked each group before I even considered pouring out a small measure of the electrolyte. Which should have been in the bottle so labelled. The half-litre bottle contained just about a centimetre depth of cloudy liquid. I knew, however, that the prep room usually had Winchesters of all the common reagents, so, telling the class to copy the diagram from the blackboard, I headed for the side door, followed inevitably by one Peter Allen, a tall gangling lad who had an unlimited store of inane and usually inconsequential questions to which he sought immediate answers.

"What are you doing in here?"

The brusque challenge caught me by surprise. "I beg your pardon?"

"You're not allowed in here. Get out!" The command was barked by a tall, ramrod-upright, bald man with a brown toothbrush moustache and dressed in a pristine white lab coat.

"Mr. Turner, I presume?" I said, more politely that I felt. "I've got a class out there and I want …"

He didn't let me finish. "You're a student. I don't take orders from students. Now get out of my prep room!"

I'm not one to easily lose my cool, but I wasn't giving in to this martinet, particularly with Peter Allen looking on in the doorway.

"As far as you are concerned, I am a member of staff, and I will not be spoken to like that in front of the pupils!" I said with as much authority as I could muster.

"What! Let me tell you, young …"

I'd had enough. "No, let me tell you! I need this bottle filled. As on my requisition. Now! Please!" I was bloody furious, but tried to keep my voice, albeit louder, still just respectful.

Aubrey Turner's face looked like a boiled beetroot. I doubt if anyone had spoken to him like that in years. The other door from the corridor opened, and Rosetta caught us in cameo. Her mouth formed its classic

O of surprise. Nick eased past her and took in the expressions on the face of Aubrey and myself.

"Problem?"

"Not now," I replied, and headed for the shelf of stock reagent bottles.

Aubrey gave me a death ray stare and stumped off. Peter Allen had obviously broadcast our exchange to the rest of 3D, who sat in awed silence when I returned to the lab with a fresh bottle of electrolyte.

Nick caught up with me at morning break. "Seems you've crossed swords with Aubrey. He's claiming you stormed in, demanded chemicals which he'd already put out, and swore at him when he pointed that out."

"I felt like swearing at him. He was so darn rude when I went in there to get some chemicals that hadn't been put out."

"He's demanding that you apologise."

"I'm sorry, Nick, but no way am I apologising to him! His version is a complete fabrication of what actually happened – and I'm pretty sure that Allen in 3D will bear me out." I could have stopped there, but I was still pretty pissed off. "If anything, Aubrey should be apologising to me for unprofessional behaviour. He's arrogant and overbearing, and a liar to boot."

Nick stroked his chin thoughtfully, "Aye, lad, I'm inclined to believe you, but don't press for an apology from Aubrey. You did well to stand your ground," he added.

The rest of the day was a piece of cake.

Though Rosetta had regarded me from our first encounter rather like a knight in shining armour, I think I became even more godlike in her eyes after the confrontation with Aubrey. She seemed to follow me round the lab with almost dewy-eyed devotion whenever I was there preparing lessons, ever eager to help, and falling over herself – literally, sometimes – to fetch and carry whatever I needed during a lesson. I can't say that I actually encouraged her, but neither did I discourage the attention that subconsciously boosted my ego and made my practical lessons the best equipped of any.

I was rather surprised nevertheless when she turned up on Mark Matthews' field study trip.

At his suggestion I'd 'volunteered' to accompany his GCE group at the beginning of half term on a coach trip to visit some caves and waterfalls. I didn't recognise Rosetta at first amongst the two dozen or so teenagers milling around the school car park, all similarly clad in jeans, anoraks and assorted headgear. Mark had also insisted on stout walking boots and all had complied. All apart from the one pair of legs that descended into calf-length furry footwear with an inch of heel. They began to move in my direction.

"Hello, Rob … er … oh … er … Mr Kiddecott." Rosetta wasn't sure whether out of school activity in the presence of pupils required formality.

No problem for me. "Hi Rosetta, I didn't know you were coming," I said pleasantly.

She giggled.

Mark called the party to order. "Gather round, folks, just need to give you a final briefing before we set off."

The group fell silent as Mark stood in front of the coach, fellow geographer Patricia Prior by his side. A good few years older than Mark, and slightly taller, she looked as fit as a fiddle, slim, upright, an unwrinkled squarish face with a thin upturned nose and greying hair beneath a neat black beret. She tolerated no nonsense but had a reputation for showing a gentle, caring approach in counselling any girl with a genuine problem.

"We're going first of all to the show caves at Dan-yr-Ogof and then on to …"

Standing at the back of the group, I missed the next destination as a heavy lorry revved up.

"… walk to meet the coach. We will keep together as a group – no solo adventures please! And if you have any problems like blisters, calls of nature or whatever, then please have a word with me, Mrs Prior, – or Mr Kiddecott or Miss Cledwyn," he added, waving a hand in our direction.

Rosetta beamed at the recognition of her role.

"Now, please make sure you all have a notebook and something to write with, a drink and your packed lunch. And if you must stuff yourself all day with Mars Bars and crisps, no litter or crumbs on the coach, otherwise I'll hand you over to Mr Powell to scrub it clean with a toothbrush!"

The kids chuckled but knew Mark Matthews didn't make idle threats. He'd once got a trespasser to cut the grass on an out-of-bounds verge with a pair of nail scissors.

Powell's Pleasure Tours of Tencastle had obviously acquired new livery which I hadn't recognised and a far better vehicle than the old boneshaker that had taken the eisteddfod party to Aberystwyth. Apparently they had taken over a small family firm in Carrick itself.

The kids piled on, the lucky first few making a bee-line for the back seats.

"Can I sit next to you?"

I couldn't really say no to Rosetta. Mark and Patricia sat up front, and we were in the row behind, across the aisle. One row of empty seats separated us from the nearest pupils.

"Isn't it exciting! This is the first field trip I've ever been on." She babbled on like a junior schoolgirl.

"I think you'll have problems on the walk," I said pragmatically.

"Oh!" she said, surprised. "Why do you say that?"

"Your boots aren't really designed for rough terrain."

"They're my very best pair!"

"Perhaps, for a night out in town, but they won't be much good across muddy fields and stony paths."

"Do you think so?" She sounded dejected. I'd pricked her bubble of enthusiasm. A few brief moments of concentration with furrowed brow, and her eyes lit up again. "But you will help me over the rough bits, won't you … Rob?"

Oh God!

As it happened neither Rosetta nor I ended up doing much walking at all. And it wasn't her fault. We'd shuffled round the show caves at Dan-yr-Ogof, marvelling at the fantastic limestone formations, whose origins Mark described in great detail. We were making our way back to the coach, as tail-end-Charlies, shooing the stragglers along, when one large and overweight girl, calling back to a friend, snagged a lead connecting a West Highland terrier to its tweedy female owner.

The mutt yelped and narrowly avoided being flattened by the falling girl, who, grabbing at anything which would save her from the effects of gravity, pulled Tweedie down on top of her.

I rushed forward to help. The woman, suffering little damage other than to her pride, was quickly on her feet, scooped up her Scottie and began to berate the girl still lying on the ground for her clumsiness, among other things.

"Go and get Mr Matthews!" I urged Rosetta, who stood pretty well frozen to the spot. Snapped out of her trance she scuttled off to the coach where Mark had already started a head count.

Ignoring the ranting woman, I knelt beside the girl who was sobbing and holding her left ankle.

"It hurts! It really hurts!"

"There, there!" hardly seemed an adequate response but I wasn't a first aider.

I don't know what Patricia Prior said to the woman with the dog, but she laid off her tirade and stomped off towards a swanky looking limousine. Supported between us, Patricia and I managed to get the girl upright and half-carry her over to the steps of the coach. Mark had got the rest of the party aboard and came to examine the girl's ankle.

"I'm pretty sure it's not broken, Shelley," he said. "But you've twisted it quite badly, I fear. No more walking for you today, young lady!"

Shelley seemed to take it quite well, her face still grimacing with pain but also showing disappointment at missing out on the rest of the action.

Mark carefully removed her boots and socks and strapped up her ankle firmly, also applying some pain-killing spray. We managed to lift her onto the bus and to the middle of the back seat where she could rest her injured foot on a rucksack.

Mark called Patricia, Rosetta and myself together for a discussion.

"It looks as if we're going to have to call off the rest of the day," he began. "No way can Shelley walk. I can't leave Patricia with her and do the walk without a female member of staff. I can't leave you, Rob, with the girl – not that I don't trust you!" he added.

I thought for a moment. "Can I make a suggestion, Mark?"

"Go ahead!"

"How about if you leave the girl with Rosetta and me on the coach? You've got a teacher, even if I'm still training, an adult female chaperon, and there's the coach driver too."

Mark considered this proposition. "What do you think, Pat? Can we do it that way?"

"I don't see why not," she mused. "If there's any comeback, I'll take the responsibility. Are you sure you don't mind, Robert?"

"It seems a pity for the rest of the group to miss out."

"Okay then, Rob, now here's what we'll do," he said, pulling out an Ordnance Survey map. "The coach will drop us off here at Ystradfellte. We'll cut out some of the study of the cave system there, and just do the walk. We'll meet you here." He pointed at some fiddling hamlet a couple of inches away on the map. "Should be a couple of hours maximum."

"Where in the village do you want us to wait?"

"By the pub, I think. Young lady might need the loo. We'll see you there. And, thanks again! Remind me to buy you a pint sometime."

The party were somewhat subdued as the coach made its convoluted way to the drop-off point, where Mark showed the driver, Wally, the rendezvous on the map. And then there was just the four of us. Rosetta and I, well, mainly I, tried to make small talk with Shelley, who, bless her, was taking it well and didn't want to be any trouble.

"I'll be alright, really, Mr Kiddecott. It's not so painful now. Really."

I think she was trying to show a brave face. "Okay, well let me know if you need anything."

It wasn't far to our chosen hamlet which rejoiced in a name even more unpronounceable than most, with a string of 'l's, 'w's and 'y's and hardly a recognisable vowel in sight.

"Where to, then, boyo?" called Wally. We had pulled up outside a few cottages that constituted the community, situated on a fairly main road, probably B rather than A. There were no other buildings that I could see and definitely no pub.

"Um, we need the village pub," I said helpfully, hoping that a hostelry would appear before my eyes.

"Looks like a church up there," Rosetta offered.

There was indeed a small bell tower just visible half a mile or so away up the hill to our right. "Well, I suppose there might be a pub there as well."

"We could ask someone."

'Someone' was about as apparent as the pub. A few moments later, however, a builder's van pulled up in front of the bus, and a wiry little man in overalls hopped out.

"Ask him," urged Rosetta.

I clambered out and caught the fellow just as he was about to disappear down an alleyway between the houses.

"Excuse me, is there a pub in this village?"

He looked at me quizzically. "Yes there is. But it's not open till 7 o'clock."

"Where is it?"

He pointed with a spirit level in his hand up to the church. "Up there. Miner's Arms."

"Can we get the coach up there?"

"There's a lane just beyond the next house over there. The rugby club go up there."

"Many thanks!"

"You're welcome. You've got a long wait, mind you!"

I told the driver where we needed to go, and he edged forward. He looked at the track and obviously wasn't happy.

"Looks a bit narrow."

"The builder chap said the rugby club go up there."

"If he says it's okay, we'll give it a go."

The road was narrow and twisted between three-foot-high dry stone walls on either side. Fortunately there were no sharp bends but even so Wally needed all his skill to squeeze the coach up the hill.

"Only hope I can turn this bugger round. I don't fancy reversing back down!"

I could see his point.

He needn't have worried – then. The shared pub and church car park – hard packed earth after a fortnight of dry weather – had room for half dozen coaches parked side by side, and then some. I wouldn't have fancied venturing on the car park after prolonged rain, however. The pub was decidedly closed, but had a primitive outside loo from which a black-faced sheep emerged. Forgot to pull the chain though.

Shelley had drifted off into a nap, so Rosetta and I parked ourselves on a rickety wooden bench in front of the pub and tucked in to our packed lunch. Very pleasant, too, in the late October sunshine. We chatted or, rather, Rosetta chattered away, requiring relatively little response or input from me. She was an only child, in her late teens, with a domineering father who worked in a quarry and an over-protective mother who gave her very little freedom at home and little social contact with others of her own age. They lived in a two-up, two-down terrace in the old part of Carrick, and her job, which she'd been in for three years since she left school, seemed to be the only time she was allowed to mix with other people.

"So, are you working during half term or confined to home?"

"No, we're going to visit my auntie in Tenby for a few days."

"Where's that?"

"Oh, it's a little seaside town in Pembrokeshire. Quiet this time of year, but very busy in the summer with holidaymakers. My aunt runs a small bed and breakfast."

"Bring me a stick of rock!" I said, jokingly.

The next time I checked my watch I realised we'd already been there for an hour and a half. Mark and co. would soon be putting in an appearance. Another forty minutes went by, and I was beginning to get a little concerned.

I reassured Shelley, who'd woken up, and was feeling uncomfortable again. "Soon be on our way!"

Ten minutes later, I saw Mark approaching, up the lane, followed by the kids.

"What are you doing up here, Rob? We've been looking everywhere for you!"

"By the pub, as you said."

"Not this one!"

"But there isn't another one!" I protested.

"Down on the … Oh Christ, I forgot they closed it a year back. Sorry!" He thought for a moment. "How did you get the coach up here?"

"With difficulty, but a local said the rugby club come up here to the pub."

"So they do. I've been here myself. But we always leave coaches at the bottom. You can't get anything bigger than a minibus up here."

"But…"

We looked at the coach.

"Right," said Mark. "Everyone on board! And say your prayers," he whispered to me.

It must have been God's day off, for though we made it about half way down, with much manoeuvring inch by inch, we came to a point where a deceptively gentle S bend trapped the coach firmly between the stone walls. Powell's livery had already acquired a few scratches and gouges, and we seemed to have found an exception to Newton's Law in that what goes up doesn't always come down!

Mark, Wally and I got off to assess the situation. We could just about squeeze out of the door. The problem was obvious; about half way along the right hand side of the coach and about a foot from the top of the wall, a large stone protruded just a couple of inches out of line from its neighbours. It had scored a deep silvery gouge into the bodywork and had come up against a rivet or bolt. The solution, too, was obvious; the wall would have to be taken down, stone by stone, until we could remove the offending boulder. Easier said than done, however, for there was no room for a person to stand roadside.

As I'd got us into this predicament, albeit inadvertently, I felt some sort of responsibility for resolving the situation, and so volunteered to attempt the demolition. I found a gate to clamber over into the field and, half leaning, half lying on the top of the wall, slowly began to pull off the stones. I soon had an audience; five heifers on my side and two dozen or so kids in the coach, all excitedly brandishing their cameras. The keystone was a bugger; its girth was larger than apparent from the road, and it extended under its neighbours on either side, thus requiring even more dismantlement. Eventually, with help from Rosetta, who looked quite cute leaning over the wall with furry boots in the air, the slab yielded, and a great cheer went up from those in the coach.

Wally acknowledged our efforts at freeing his coach, but I could tell he was not relishing what his boss would say about the damage. And, of course, he still had to negotiate the rest of the lane. Fortunately there were no further obstructions, and though tight, with just inches clearance, we made it back to the main road without further incident. Just as well we didn't have the larger 53 seater coach. I suppose we should have tried to rebuild the wall, but it had already taken over an hour to travel the half mile from the pub, and we were definitely behind schedule. I hoped the cows weren't feeling adventurous.

There was something of a party atmosphere on the coach, with the kids chatting animatedly about the unplanned entertainment. No doubt the highlight of the field trip would be all round the school complete with photographs after the half term break.

By the time I got back to Penybont with Jessica, the sun had long since set, and I was starving.

"Want some? "asked Sunny, who was dishing out a pile of stir-fry onto plates.

"Love some!" I replied. "If there's enough to spare."

"Have a good day, did you?" inquired Dan, through a mouthful of noodles.

"Interesting. Spent most of it at a pub."

"Bet you got stoned!" Jake commented.

"In a manner of speaking. But the pub was closed."

I tucked into the stir fry while they considered the conundrum.

True to form, my fame as the hero of the field trip was already established in the staff room when I turned up on the Monday morning after the holiday. No doubt John Rhys-Price had a hand in its propagation, for he greeted me with a slap on the back and a town crier style broadcast. "Ah, the famous Robert Stonewall Kiddecott! The man who moves mountains with his bare hands!"

Well, not quite. But I had no doubt what my nickname was going to be for the rest of my time at Carrick.

My first class, a lower set of second years, held me in awe as I stood in front of them, with no need for the usual exhortations for silence. With the assessment visits from my college tutors fast approaching, I anticipated that the field trip would yield unexpected dividends.

Bright and bubbly as pink champagne, Rosetta caught me in the prep room at the end of morning school.

"Hello, Robert. Er, can I call you Robert? You don't mind, do you?" A brief wrinkling of her brow in case she'd been too bold.

"Not at all, if I'm not with the kids."

"I've brought you something." She rummaged in a brown carrier bag. "Here, I couldn't find any rock, but I hope you like this."

She held out a hand-sized gift-wrapped package for me.

I was taken aback, and, to be honest, more than a little embarrassed.

"I was only joking about the rock," I said lamely. "I didn't expect …"

Her face fell. "Don't you want it? Oh, I'm sorry …"

"No, no, no," I recovered graciously. "It's … well, unexpected, and thank you very much, Rosetta."

I took the package from her.

"You can open it now if you like."

"Yes, of course!"

Carefully removing the wrapper, the white cardboard box inside yielded a china coffee mug marked 'Tenby', with a picture of a beach and cliffs.

"That's very sweet of you, Rosetta. Thank you very much."

Her cheeks blushed with pleasure at my words.

I didn't see much of her over the next couple of days to speak to. Last thing Thursday afternoon, however, Rosetta came up to me as I was writing up some lesson plans in the empty lab.

"Robert," she started, coyly, "I was wondering…"

"Uh huh," I said, still writing.

"I was wondering whether you've ever been to a twmpath?"

"I dunno, what is it?" I looked up, intrigued.

"It's like, well, like a Welsh barn dance."

"Oh, right. No, I haven't come across one before. Why?"

"Well, I've got two tickets for the PTA dance tomorrow night, and my friend's ill and can't come."

I thought for a moment. I hadn't been to a barn dance of any kind since I'd been at Tencastle. Logistically it would be possible, as Sunny had gone back home for a funeral, so there'd be no problem staying on in Carrick.

"I don't want to go on my own," Rosetta said.

"What about your parents?" I asked, remembering what she'd told me about their strictness in letting her go out.

"They'll let me go, as it's at the school. As long as I'm back by eleven o'clock. My friend, Jill, lives near me."

"Well, I …"

"I'd really like to go."

I couldn't think of any reason at the time why I shouldn't go. And by all accounts Rosetta didn't get much chance to let her hair down.

"Okay, then, I'll come. But I'll pay for the ticket. There's no reason for your friend to lose out on the fun and the cash."

"That's kind of you, but I'm sure she won't mind."

"I insist."

"Thank you … Rob." Her eyes lit up and she blushed. "Seven-thirty at the school hall, it is."

"I'll see you there!"

I mentioned to Jake next morning as I was leaving that I'd probably not be back until late, and not to bolt the bloody door again.

"Got a date then?"

"Not at all. PTA function."

"Shame."

I'm not sure why Jake was so concerned for my love life. I did tell Sunny more about the PTA event as I ran her into Tencastle to catch an early train, before I drove on to Carrick Major.

Rosetta said nothing more to me about the dance during the day, but gave me the benefit of a beaming toothy smile whenever she saw me. She hadn't mentioned whether any food would be provided during the evening, so I stuffed myself with school stodge at lunchtime, and promised myself an early evening pint and pasty in the Bull and Dragon. There was no problem filling the couple of hours between end of school and opening time with lesson plans and marking exercise books.

I got to the school hall in good time, since Rosetta still had both tickets. On the stage, which predictably had been lined with straw bales, the band were still setting up. A couple of middle-aged fellows with bass guitar and accordion and a dishy redhead with a fiddle tried out snatches of tunes, while a bearded bloke with a bright check shirt straining over a substantial beer gut made hand signals to adjust the sound level and balance. Eventually satisfied, the band launched into a set of bouncy tunes with Beer Gut first testing his mike then thumping away on a tambourine. Actually they didn't sound half bad, and the decibel level was comfortable enough to allow conversation and avoid a splitting headache.

People started arriving, mostly casually dressed in jeans and open-necked shirt. I spied the odd cowboy hat and toy six-shooters from Wales' Wild West. I'd swapped my jacket for a sweater but still felt rather formally attired in conventional dark grey trousers. Rosetta, when she arrived, stood out like a sore thumb. Actually, that's unkind, she'd made a real effort, with a thigh-length pleated skirt that showed off almost the full extent of her shapely legs and matching pale green short-sleeved blouse with little lacy frills around the neck. Perfect for a disco club and eye-catching certainly amongst the barn dancers. She'd applied powder and paint to her face.

I was taken completely unawares by her kiss on my cheeks as she greeted me – and it must have showed.

"Ooh, sorry, Rob, that was a little bold of me!"

"It's okay," I said, with some embarrassment. I only hoped she hadn't been too liberal with the lipstick.

I don't think anyone had noticed, and I didn't see anyone else I recognised, apart from a couple of members of staff with whom I'd had just a nodding acquaintance. Beer Gut, or Tom, of Tom's Twmpers, as he introduced himself, was already exhorting everybody to come on to the floor with their partners and make a big circle.

"Shall we dance?" Rosetta grabbed my hand and dragged me up.

I had no choice, but then I didn't keep her company very long. One good thing about this kind of knees-up is that you often change partners during the dance, and this first dance was just like that – Rosetta was whisked off in one direction, and I was swung and do-si-doed and whatever by a succession of females, some of whom were young and very attractive. I couldn't tell whether they were sixth formers or parents. By the conclusion of the second dance, which followed without a break from the first, the caller somehow managed to get us, or at least most of us, back to our original partner.

"That was fun, wasn't it?" declared Rosetta, flopping onto one of the wooden chairs around the side of the hall.

"Yes, it was, actually," I agreed, taking the seat next to her.

"Have you done any of this before?"

"Once or twice. My father used to let the church social committee run the odd hop in one of his barns."

"Do you live on a farm, then?"

"Yes, my father's got a small dairy herd in Devon."

"Ooh, how lovely!"

I'm not sure that's the epithet I would have used. Cold, wet, muddy and dark it was, milking in the depths of winter.

"Not sure for how much longer, though. He's not getting any younger and he's beginning to suffer with back problems."

"Won't you take over the farm?"

"Not me. I like the countryside, but I've no interest in farming. He'll probably retire and move to the coast. My brother's doing most of the heavy work anyway."

"No other brothers?"

"No, just a sister."

Twmper Tom was calling people up for the next dance. I took the initiative this time. Welsh, or whatever, the formations and figures seemed much the same as the barn dances back home. This one had us all in a line, with much to-ing and fro-ing, but we kept our partners. Rosetta, belying her clumsiness in the classroom, was a surprisingly good dancer, and nimble on her feet.

"You've certainly danced before!" I said, as we finished a long bout of stripping the willow.

"Used to do it at school, and I came to last year's PTA dance."

"With Jill?"

"Who? Oh, no, with my parents."

I couldn't quite see her parents hopping around on the dance floor, from what she'd told me about them, but you never knew.

I was hoping that Rosetta might attract the attention of some other young fellow for the odd dance and give me the chance to try my charm on a couple of young maidens who didn't seem to be with anyone else. No spare young beaux appeared however, and Rosetta was nothing but keen for us to whirl through every kind of caper. Thirsty work, too, and the two or three white wines she had and the shandies for me barely replaced the liquid we lost through perspiration. Despite the pasty earlier I had no problem making short work of my ploughman's supper, as well as half of Rosetta's.

After the supper break, the dances got even more frenetic and complicated, requiring almost as much time in instruction from the caller as the actual dance took to do, and frequently Tom called on the band to play the dance a second time. Once on the floor, you couldn't really escape, and we'd being repeating a rather silly square – the grasshopper dance I think they called it – when Rosetta panicked.

"Oh my God! Look at the time!" She grabbed my arm. "My father will kill me! We must go!"

"Hang on, we can't just walk out of the set! Another minute's not going to make a difference if you're already late."

Rosetta stayed, but in obvious agitation and even as the band played the finishing chord, she dashed off to grab her coat from the chair. I glanced at the clock, which showed just 11.05, and caught up with her.

"I'll run you home, if I can find my pumpkin."

"Please." I think she missed the Cinderella allusion.

Out in the clear cold night air she regained her composure. Jessica, good as gold, started on the first pull, and Rosetta directed me out to an unfamiliar part of town.

The car having all the warmth of a refrigerator, Rosetta nestled up to me, as far as the bucket seat and gear lever would allow.

"I did enjoy this evening," she murmured.

"Me too."

"Honestly?"

"Honestly!" Truly.

We turned into a dimly-lit narrow street lined with plain terraced houses. We passed a couple of similar streets leading off at right angles.

"Drop me here, Rob," she called suddenly, and I pulled into the kerb just before another junction.

"Rob," she said, looking up at me, with dewy eyes. "Can I kiss you properly?"

"Well … er." Oh what the hell, I wouldn't have had a good evening without her.

She embraced me and locked her lips to mine, passionately, tongue probing into my mouth. It would have taken a better man than me to resist, and I responded in kind. I could hear her breath panting, and her arm began to stray lower down my back. Without thinking, I started to move my hand towards her breast, and involuntarily felt myself harden. And promptly deflate as someone hammered furiously on the passenger window. Rosetta broke off quickly as the hammering continued and an angry face pressed to the misted window.

"Ma!" Rosetta yelped.

Ma wrenched the door open, "Come out of there, you brazen hussy!" she shrieked, "What do you mean by this? You told me you were just going out with Jill! Do you know what time it is? Jill didn't know what you were doing, but my God, I can see for myself!" All this in one breath, her fat jowls quivering with rage. Her piggy eyes fixed on me, "Tomcatting with this … his …"

"Mrs Cledwyn, let me explai …"

"You shut up! My Dai'll deal with you!" She dragged Rosetta out of the car, "Come here, you little whore, I'll show you not to lie to me!"

Rosetta was clearly agitated but didn't resist. "Best go, Rob! Don't let my father catch you!"

I suppose I should have stood my ground and defended my honour – and hers – but in my rear mirror I caught a glimpse of some bloody great mountain of a man striding purposefully up the hill. I doubted that he'd an exchange of pleasantries in mind.

Rosetta had seen him too. "Go, Rob, go, for Christ's sake, go!"

Lights were going on in upstairs windows and I needed no further bidding. I revved like hell, let the clutch out sharply, and Jessica lurched forward. I hadn't a bloody clue where I was, and I hoped that I wasn't in a cul-de-sac. When I thought I'd put a reasonable distance between myself and the unfolding domestic scene, I pulled up and took a deep breath. Below me I could see the lights on the town centre. I reckoned that I should be able to take a parallel road back into town.

I had plenty of time for reflection on the drive home on deserted roads. Had Rosetta told her mother where she was going? Probably not. Had she told me the truth about her friend Jill? I had my doubts. Had she engineered the whole story to get me to go out with her? Quite possibly. I could not help but feel sorry for Rosetta with parents like that, but I was going to have to keep her a bit more at arm's length over the next couple of weeks.

The first phone call started soon after breakfast. I'd not long surfaced and I was still in my pyjamas.

"Phone for you, Rob," Jake called, holding his hand over the mouthpiece.

"Who is it? "I said sleepily. I wasn't expecting anybody.

"Dunno, but he doesn't sound a happy bunny." He spoke briefly down the phone, and turned to me again quizzically. "Says his name's Clegwyn or something. He's ranting on about his daughter."

I woke up sharply. "Tell him I'm not here! I'm … I'm away for the weekend!"

"I've already implied you're not around. Didn't like his attitude."

I made for the stairs. "I'm going out! I'll be out all day – and tomorrow probably! Hang up if he calls again!"

Jake nodded, "What did you do, put a bun in her oven?"

"No, no, nothing like that. Just a … misunderstanding."

I could see Jake wasn't convinced.

I had no idea where I was going to go. I certainly had no intention of hanging around the house. Whatever Rosetta's dad intended, I didn't want to find out face to face. If he'd got our phone number out of his daughter he might well have got our address as well – not that I actually recall giving either to her. Tencastle still seemed a bit obvious so I headed out on the road to Tenbridge, by which time the coffee was playing havoc with my bladder.

Other than passing through during my first teaching practice, the only time I'd visited Tenbridge as such was with my parents the previous Easter. It was a quaint, unspoilt little town, its fortunes – and its brief spell in the media spotlight – were all down to quarrying. All the shops up the steep winding main street were built of the grey local stone, as were most of the houses. I sat nursing a coffee in a little cafe next to The Picturedrome, the town's only apparent concession to twentieth century entertainment, and contemplated how to spend the day.

Thinking back to my earlier journeys in this direction, I found a local Ordnance Survey map in the newsagents and discovered a whole network of forest trails and footpaths around Lake Dynad, which I remembered passing everyday on the way to Abergwnwyn. I bought a cheese roll, a Mars Bar and a tin of Coke and headed back to Jessica.

Whilst a walk in the wilderness hadn't featured in my original plans for the weekend, not that I'd had any plans as such anyway, the day was perfect for such activity, crystal clear and, for November, still relatively warm. There were no other vehicles in the car park, just off the main road at the eastern end of the lake, and not a soul anywhere. In the unspoilt tranquility of the location, I soon forgot the reason why I was there, as I sauntered along the full length of a lakeside track, taking in stunning views and clear upland air. Following the natural contours of the hillsides, it must have been some five miles to the far end, and to the settlement of Pentredynad itself, little more than a smattering of small stone built cottages, and, most welcoming, a pub. The sign outside was badly faded but appeared to show some four-legged black beast that could have been a dog, a pig or a bull. Inside, Y Mochyn Ddu, as the name above the low wooden door stated, was no bigger than someone's front parlour, with half a dozen chairs, an old wooden bench and a plain scrubbed wooden table. Get a football team in there and it would be bursting at the seams, though I doubt if Pentredynad's whole population amounted to more than that anyway. The roaring log fire gave a warm welcome, as did the landlady, once she'd got over the obvious surprise at seeing a lunchtime customer at this time of year.

"Would you like a bowl of cawl, young sir," she asked as she handed me a foaming pint of dark ale.

"What's that?"

"It's a stew with vegetables, ham and lamb."

"That would be marvellous!" I'd not really expected to find a pub, let alone hot food.

Delicious it was, too, with a huge great chunk of home-baked brown bread and a wedge of cheddar to go with it. The landlady, once she'd ascertained that I was on a walking break from work – which was sort of true – chatted away with minimal interjections from me on the history of the village, what it had been like in her younger days before the reservoir had displaced half of the then population from their homes and livelihood, and how only a few hardy families had remained to scratch a living, mostly from forestry.

"Do you get many tourists here in the summer?"

"It's certainly busier, particularly at weekends. There are a few holiday lets in the area, and a couple of farms do B and B, mostly for people, like your good self, who like to get off the beaten track."

"How on earth do you keep going through the winter?"

"We manage. My husband works in Tenbridge. We've already lost half the village and the shop, the school is always under the threat of closure.

We feel it's vital to keep the pub going. There's no other place where people can get together and chat. Without it the village would die."

She clearly felt quite passionately about the small community. I wished that there were a few more people like her back in Devon, where uneconomic village pubs were being bought up by developers and converted into swish eateries full of plastic beams and ersatz horse brasses, or otherwise turned into luxury second homes for London stockbrokers.

If I could have whistled for Jessica, I'd have been quite happy to nestle in the warmth of the hostelry all afternoon, but, after a second pint and an enormous helping of bread and butter pudding which the landlady insisted I try, I needed to work off my lunch. The track continued round the lake, parallel to but well below the level of the main road. The light was just beginning to fade when I got back to the car park. Jessica was still alone.

Though feeling considerably more at ease than at the start of the day, I was still reluctant to head back to Penybont until later, so escaped into fantasy with James Bond at Tenbridge's Picturedrome.

"What's going on Rob?" Dan greeted me as soon as I stepped inside the cottage. "Bloody phone's been going mad. Left it off the hook all afternoon."

"Girlie trouble," said Jake.

I shot him a withering look. "Not what you think at all," I retorted.

"And what are we supposed to think, Casanova?"

I suppose I had to end the speculation. "Ruddy father can't accept that his daughter's grown up into a young adult with desires of her own."

"Which you were willing to satisfy?"

"Not as much as she would have liked, I'm sure! I took her back home in the car after the PTA dance and just gave her a goodnight kiss – at her insistence, I might add."

"Yeah, we believe you." Which clearly they didn't. "And?"

"And nothing! Bloody mother went ballistic!"

"Was she in the car as well?" asked Dan innocently.

"Probably wanted a bit of the action," Jake said. "You should have kissed her too."

I'd rather have kissed a rhinoceros. "I don't think she'd been entirely honest with her parents." Or, probably with me, for that matter. "Anyhow, I skedaddled pronto."

"Gallant of you," Jake commented.

"I was bloody scared. I reckoned her Pa was a raving psychopath!"

"Yeah, he sounded like a nutter on the phone. Swore you'd seduced and molested his little girl."

"Did you?" asked Dan.

"No, I bloody well didn't!"

Next morning it was pissing down with rain. Not the weather for another nature ramble, so I headed into Tencastle and spent all day moping around the Union and the library, which I was surprised to find open. The place was fairly busy but I didn't see anyone I knew. When I got back, I learned, to some relief, that the phone had been silent all day. Either Pa Cledwyn had got the message that I wasn't around or he'd been pacified. I sincerely hoped for the latter.

I was not looking forward to coming face-to-face with Rosetta on Monday morning. As it happened, I need not have worried. She had taken the day off, called in sick, according to Nick, and there was no sign of a burly Welsh giant waiting at the school gate to hammer me to kingdom come. Consequently, I was a little less apprehensive the next day and felt further reassured by Sunny's pragmatic assessment of the episode, as we drove in on Tuesday morning.

"Probably all a storm in a teacup, Rob. They'll all have come to their senses by now."

"I hope so."

Sunny, of course, had missed all the drama, having only returned from the family funeral the previous evening.

Still no Rosetta.

Even on Wednesday, though I caught sight of her once or twice, I managed to avoid contact with her, as my timetable put me with Mark Matthews' geography classes, and I'd volunteered to accompany him on a 'town trail' study of Carrick during my free time.

Eventual direct contact was, of course, unavoidable, given our respective roles in the school. Although Rosetta was ill at ease in my presence, I tried to maintain a pleasant, but strictly professional tone in our exchanges during Thursday's school day. After the kids had all dispersed, I slipped out of the science block with my briefcase and a pile of books, and headed for the car park.

"Rob!" Rosetta came scurrying after me, and caught my arm. "Rob, I must talk to you!"

"Uh huh."

"You've been avoiding me all day!" she said, a touch of accusation in her voice.

"Not really, I've had a full teaching day." We'd almost reached Jessica. "Just let me put these things in the car."

She fidgeted while I dumped my clutter on the back seat. "I'm sorry about Friday and my parents. I hadn't told them I was going with you."

"Why not?"

"They wouldn't have let me go!"

"And what about your friend Jill?"

Rosetta hung her head and looked ready to cry, "She didn't know anything about it."

"But you told me …"

"I so wanted to go to the dance with you, but I thought you'd turn me down if I asked you directly." She began to sob, "I couldn't bear that."

"Rosetta, I …" I turned to face her and put my hands on her arms.

"Would you?"

"Have turned you down?" I thought it quite likely but I replied gently, "I don't know." And added, "But I'm not happy that you misled me and lied to your parents."

"Oh, Rob, I wanted … I want …" Her shoulders heaved with deep sobs. She pulled a linen handkerchief from her pocket, and blew her nose.

"What happened with your parents? Have you sorted it out?"

"They wouldn't stop shouting at me! They … they threatened all sorts of things, they demanded to know your name and made me give them your telephone number."

"I didn't know you had it!"

"I got it from Nick … Mr Ramsbottom." She didn't say how. She leant against me, crying softly now, "I got up to my room and locked the door. I wouldn't come out. Not till they promised not to shout at me anymore."

"I told them about you," she murmured.

I waited.

"They've never let me have a boyfriend. I'm nearly nineteen, Rob." She looked up at me, cheeks streaked with tears. "I've told them I want to … to … to move out. Do you think I should, Rob?"

I didn't know quite what to think. "It's a big step," I said neutrally, and should have left it there. "But if you want your own life…"

She perked up, "You'll help me then?"

"Just hold back there a minute, Rosetta." The last thing I wanted was to be the cause of further family strife.

I don't think she heard me for she buried her face in my arms again, and whispered, "Rob, would you run me home?"

"I don't think that's a good idea!" I was pretty sure that getting Rosetta out of the car might prove more difficult, and I certainly didn't fancy another run in with Ma and Pa Cledwyn. She caught my terse tone.

"What? Why?" The cause of my concern, or one of them, dawned on her. "You're worried about my Mum and Dad? They're not back till this evening. We could, er, you know, we could ..."

"Rosetta," I said firmly, but I hoped not unkindly. "I hope you're not getting the wrong idea."

"What do you mean?" Tears were welling up again.

"I like you as a person, as a colleague but I'm not your boyfriend."

She pushed away from me and bit her lip. I opened the driver's door and slid in.

"Rob, you know ... I'd do anything ... anything for you." She pressed herself to the window, which I'd left partly open.

"Rosetta, let's not go there."

Her tears gave way to incredulity and quickly to anger. She curled her lip.

"What! I suppose I'm not good enough for you! No more than a little scrubber from the back streets! When you've got all those fancy college tarts!"

"It's not that ..."

"Good enough for you on Friday wasn't I! Like you weren't enjoying snogging me!"

"Your suggestion, if I remember."

"You bastard!"

"Rosetta, please forgive me." I did feel sorry for her, but things were getting out of hand, "I'm sorry if can't give you what you want. Now I've arranged to meet my friend after school, and I'm already late. She ..."

Rosetta's outburst had subsided, and she had pulled back, looking utterly crestfallen. But she caught the last word, and screamed, aghast, "You've got a girlfriend?"

"No, we just live togeth..." I wish I'd chosen my words more carefully.

"Bastard! Bastard! You damned bastard!" Rosetta was screaming like a banshee and hammering with her fists on Jessica's bonnet. Even if Jessica had miraculously fired on the starter button, there's no way I could have driven away.

Her yelling attracted the attention of Nick Ramsbottom and Moira Bunn, the Senior Mistress, who were just leaving the science block. They hurried over to see what all the commotion was about.

"Now then, young lady, tha's no way to treat a gentleman's car!" said Nick.

"Bastard!" Rosetta gave a couple more thumps and scurried off, wailing and holding her head in her hands. Moira headed off after her.

"What's that all about, lad?"

I told him, in brief.

"Aye, lad, I could see yon lass had got a bit of an eye for you."

I slumped at the wheel. "I don't know what to do, Nick. God knows, I didn't encourage her!"

"I believe you. Impressionable young girl." He stroked his chin. "Look, Robert, why not take the day off tomorrow, let things cool down a bit. I'll fill Moira in on the situation and ask her to speak to Rosetta."

"Thanks, Nick. Look, I don't want her to get into trouble on my account."

"She won't. Moira will give her some TLC and help her sort herself out."

"Thanks."

I breathed a few good sighs of relief to gather my composure and set out with Jessica to meet Sunny, who, I guessed, might have been getting anxious at my non-appearance.

"Staff meeting?" she enquired.

"Not quite." I told her. "Rosetta got jealous of you."

"Me? Why?"

"She thought you were my girlfriend."

"How come?"

"I let slip that we were living together."

Sunny giggled, "You idiot!"

I suppose it was talking about living together but on the journey back Sunny fell uncharacteristically quiet for several minutes.

"Penny for your thoughts?"

"I've been wondering. Are we going to be able to continue living together?"

"What do you mean?"

"Well, I took Benji's place on a temporary arrangement. Isn't he supposed to be coming back after Christmas?"

I must admit I'd given the matter no thought. "We don't know," I said truthfully, "but in theory, yes."

"I'll have to try and find somewhere else, I suppose. I'll be sad to leave."

"I'd be sad to see you leave, too." Sunny seemed naturally so much part of our domestic set-up now.

I didn't really want to entertain the idea of her being replaced. "Look, don't do anything yet. We'll see if we can find out what Benji is up to." I also offered to ferry her up to a bus stop on the main road to Carrick next morning, and pick her up again in the evening. I was fully intending to keep well away from the school that day.

My worries about possible repercussions from our playground contretemps increased when I was asked to see Moby Dick himself on the following Monday morning. Miss Dragon Ellis ushered me into his office, which was carpeted and spacious, with a bay window overlooking the front playground. Dr. Bedford-Dickson rose from his leather upholstered chair behind a large mahogany desk, and came to greet me. As was his custom, he was wearing a dark suit, stiff wing collar, bow tie and full academic gown. I noticed a mortar board on the filing cabinet.

"Good morning, Mr Kiddecott," he boomed, in a rich, plummy voice, and offered his hand. "I regret that I have not had a chance to meet you before."

He returned to his chair. "Please be seated," he said, authoritatively, though not unkindly.

"Now, tell me how you are getting on here. Any problems? You're in good hands with Mr Ramsbottom."

"No, Sir." If he didn't know about Rosetta, I wasn't going to burden him. "Everyone has been very kind and helpful. And the pupils have been good, too."

"Well, we pride ourselves in running a tight ship. Good discipline is essential."

Images of a whaler flashed involuntarily through my mind.

"We welcome students here at Wilfred Roberts. Always keen to hear the latest trends from the colleges. Keeps us all on our toes, wouldn't you say?"

I smiled in acknowledgement. I don't think he was expecting any reply.

"What is the latest initiative in the teaching of science, Mr Kiddecott?"

God knows, I thought. I wasn't certain, but I got the impression that his background was more in the arts.

"Well, the Nuffield Science project is still going strong, though it's been around now for a few years," I began. "It is moving the emphasis from rote learning of facts and formulae towards scientific process, hypothesis, experimentation, evaluation, deduction. Trying to make young people think scientifically."

"Good, good. I'm pleased to hear it!" Obviously my waffle sounded more convincing to him than it did to me.

"Now, I mustn't keep you any longer from your lessons. I hope you'll welcome me into one of your lessons, if my diary permits."

Like he'd need an invitation even if he did feel inclined to sit in on one my classes, which I strongly doubted. He stood again, and showed me out. That was it!

Mark Matthews had just sent his form off to assembly. "Hello, Rob, what kept you? Did I hear you'd had a bit of a bust-up in the playground last week?"

"Rumour is grossly exaggerated, no substance whatever," I replied. Whatever he'd already heard – and I'm pretty certain it wouldn't have been from Nick – I certainly wasn't going to enlighten him further. If he passed any juicy titbit on to John Rhys-Price, I might just as well emblazon the school with six-foot banners.

"Okay."

I'd anticipated Nick would have something to say, however. I was relieved that there was no sign of Rosetta.

"Well, Robert, do you make a habit of breaking young girls' hearts?"

I mumbled, "Sorry!"

"No need to apologise, I don't think it was your fault."

"What's happened to Rosetta?"

"She poured out all her woes to Moira – about her parents, you. She adored you, saw you as her Sir Galahad, to carry her away into the sunset on your white charger to live happily ever after. Or something along those lines."

Bloody hell! Jessica would be flattered.

"Next day they talked things through again, and Rosetta had more or less made up her mind what she wanted to do. Moira went round to see her parents, and they had a long chat. Upshot is, she's handed in her notice, with immediate effect, and she's going to stay with a cousin up in Caernarvon."

I sighed with relief, "I'm glad she's being positive. It would have been a very difficult two or three weeks for both of us."

"I agree," said Nick, and added, smiling, "and at least our equipment is safer!"

The remaining couple of weeks at Wilfred Roberts passed without any further hitches. I had two visits from my tutors, John Tudor Evans, and Stephanie Ellison, the Geography lecturer. Both professed themselves satisfied with what they observed. Moby Dick, unsurprisingly, didn't put in an appearance at the lab. The loss of Rosetta in the prep room caused a little inconvenience at first, with Aubrey taking on the extra burden with his usual bad grace, but Nick filled the gap with help from willing sixth-formers until a new assistant was appointed to take up duties at the start of the Spring term.

Strictly speaking, our teaching practice ended on the Friday, but both Sunny and I had accepted the invitation from our respective schools to join them for their end of term jollies on the following Wednesday.

Sunny was feeling much more relaxed now the worry of accommodation had been resolved. In the end it wasn't another cryptic letter from Benji, but a phone call from his mother to say he would not now be returning until March at the earliest. Jake had made it clear to her that we wouldn't expect him to return to Ty Melin.

"Care to join us down the pub at lunchtime?" Mark asked as we elbowed our way across the staff room to the mince pies, traditionally provided, I was told, by the PTA.

"I'm not sure – I've got to drive back, and …"

"Of course he'll bloody well join us!" John Rhys-Morgan interjected, reaching past us to grab two pies. "Merry Christmas and all that!"

"Well …"

"It's on me, Rob. I haven't really said thanks for helping out with the field trip."

I doubt that that Mr Powell of Powell's Pleasure Tours would have been so magnanimous.

"We always have a jar or two on the last day," added John, spilling crumbs down his tracksuit. "Helps us sleep through Moby Dick's waffle".

"Well, okay, then … just a quick one."

Nick had evidently overheard the conversation. "You'll be lucky to get away with a quick one with that bunch of boozers," he commented as we walked back to the lab. "They don't take prisoners – no shandies or soft drinks in their company."

"Surely they don't come back drunk, in front of the kids?"

"Not drunk, but definitely well-oiled. And there's no lessons, just the carol service and the Head's Christmas message." He pondered a moment. "Take care you don't lose your license if you've got to drive."

I was tempted to opt out of the Christmas drink, but it did seem unsociable to refuse. Looking at some clutter in the prep room that Aubrey hadn't bothered to put away – beneath his dignity, I suppose – I had an idea. I borrowed a couple of large squeezy wash-bottles, a length of clear flexible tubing and a plastic filter funnel.

Any chance I'd entertained of bunking off was scuppered as soon as I left the science block.

John caught sight of me straight away. "Ready then, Rob, to paint the town?" He put his muscular arm on my shoulder and guided me towards the back gate. "Rear exit, don't want to catch Moby's eye."

Not that I think it would have bothered John unduly.

The Bull and Dragon was already heaving, hot and smoky, and I was perspiring within seconds. It was necessary, however, for me to keep my parka on.

John called out to Luke and Mark who were at the front of the melée at the bar. "Make that two more!" Turning to me he asked almost as an afterthought, "Bitter?"

"I'd prefer the dark."

The message obviously didn't get through and a glass of Brain's Best was soon thrust into my hand.

"Cheers!"

We raised our pints in seasonal greeting and the liquid level in the Apostles' glasses rapidly fell to barely a quarter full, to my few sips.

"Same again?" John gathered their now empty glasses. "Rob?"

"Give me a moment," I said. Time to test my apparatus. Turning away from them, I raised my glass and, with my other hand, I carefully manoeuvred the filter funnel hidden beneath my coat so that I could pour the beer apparently into my mouth. Brief consternation as the funnel nearly overflowed, then a glugging bubble as an airlock released and the liquid trickled down the tube into the plastic bottle. Impressively I shifted nearly half a pint at one gulp. I shared the rest between the funnel and my throat.

"Dark for you, wasn't it?" John handed me a handled mug. Their glasses were already going down, but thankfully not quite at the same rate as for the first round. There were no spare seats, but we managed to push our way to one of the old wooden pillars that had a shelf around it. Soon they were in loud and animated discussion about the fortunes of Llanelli's rugby club, to which I could add nothing. It slowed their drinking a little, and allowed me to enjoy half of my pint at my own pace.

The final whistle suddenly blew on the verbal rugby scrum, glasses were drained, and John saw my generous measure still unimbibed. "Drink up, Rob, Foresters' Arms next."

I wasn't at all sure how much more the wash-bottle could take but Mark's hearty slap on my back dislodged the tube and I felt a spreading dampness.

"Sorry, fellas, gotta take a leak! Catch you up!"

I pinched the end of the tube as best I could through my coat and dashed to the loos. Not before time I aimed the end of the tube down the toilet bowl and carefully extracted the brimming wash-bottle from my belt. Although most of my left torso felt soggy, not too much beer had escaped. It took me several minutes and half a roll of bog paper to make myself comfortable and reasonably presentable again. The Apostles, of course, hadn't wanted to waste drinking time, and there was no sign of them in the pub or the street. I'd no idea of the whereabouts of the

Foresters' and frankly didn't feel too inclined to look for it. I settled for a pasty and headed back to the school staffroom.

For the final carol service the whole school crammed into the main hall, where the pupils had to remain standing throughout; no space for chairs and the opportunity for chaos was too great to allow the kids to squat cross-legged on the floor. Eric 'Eleanor' Rigby, the Deputy Head, was well-practised in shoe-horning the classes into more or less orderly lines. The staff, which included me, sat comfortably on the stage behind the seats reserved for the Headmaster, Eric and senior staff.

I perched on the end of the back row. The Apostles just made it in time, John whispering loudly as he squeezed past me, "Whatappendchou?"

We stood as Dr. Melville O. Bedford-Dickson made his grand entrance. In full academic gown now complete with kingfisher-blue hood, over his usual dark pinstripe suit and wing collar, he mounted the steps, head aloof, like a peer of the realm. Following discreetly, Moira Bunn, the senior mistress, looked more like a private secretary to his lordship in her usual attire of pale blue trouser suit. The Head nodded to Tim Pintwhistle, the music teacher and Bob Dylan lookalike, to lead in to the first carol on the piano. The service was conventionally predictable; carol, reading, carol and so on, with a procession of pupils from different year groups carefully chosen no doubt for their lack of nerves on the big occasion and clarity of delivery.

As we sat down after the eighth carol, John took its message to 'Rest Ye Merry Gentlemen' to heart. "Time for a kip," he said softly, "Headmaster's sermon on the mount."

Sure enough, the Headmaster approached the lectern, puffed out his chest and drew himself up to his full height.

"I am proud," he began, "to be the Head of one of the most distinguished schools of Wales…"

John spluttered and barely managed to disguise a loud guffaw in a fit of coughing. Mark blew his nose loudly and Luke was finding it difficult to keep a straight face. Even Nick couldn't hold back a smile. There was a low murmuring and fidgeting from the body of the hall and only 'Eleanor' Rigby's piercing stare dared any youngster to laugh outright.

What else Dr M. O. Bedford-Dickson said about his school of Wales no-one remembered or cared, and it was fortunate that only one carol followed. As the pupils filed out it was like releasing the steam from a pressure cooker.

"Good on yer, Moby!" chortled John, wiping tears of mirth from his eyes as we entered the staffroom. "Best end to a term yet. God, I nearly peed myself in there!"

Nick came over to say goodbye. "Take care, young man," he said, offering his hand. "Good luck for the future. I trust you'll remember your time with us."

"No doubt about that!" I said, in all honesty. "And thanks for your help!"

"By the way, I had a postcard from Rosetta."

"Oh yes?" I said warily.

"She's got a job at Wylfa."

"Where's that"

"Nuclear power station on Anglesey."

"Should we all start building fall-out shelters?"

"Come, now, Rob, don't be unkind to the lass! Loves it, she says. And she sends you her love. Says to thank you for giving her life more meaning."

Well, well! Every cloud and all that!

Sunny's last day had been far more predictable and orderly. Pass the parcel and other rationed fun activities, carefully choreographed carols round the Christmas tree, and a neatly wrapped present of crayons or notepad for every child.

"Gosh, you smell of booze!" she declared, as she climbed into Jessica's passenger seat. "Are you sure you're fit to drive?"

"Believe it or not, I only had one pint. Someone spilt beer down my jacket."

"Bet you really had a whale of a time," she said, unconvinced.

CHAPTER SIXTEEN

Annie

Apart from occasional forays into town at weekends, work commitments for our respective school placements had kept us out of regular contact with our friends for much of the autumn term. Even two weeks into the new term we were only just getting back to the routine of normal college life, after the formal debriefing sessions with our tutors. Far more interesting, however, were the exchanges between fellow practitioners during coffee and lunch breaks. My experiences at Carrick, prudently edited in the telling, paled in comparison with some of the salacious stories I heard. Rud, for example, had narrowly escaped termination of his teaching practice for trying to seduce the headmaster's teenage daughter, while in Dilly's school, the police had been called to arrest a drunken paedophile.

Though we had been rather on the sidelines for three months with regard to Union matters, no student could have been unaware of the way in which one person had dominated the headlines.

"Rusty's put his foot in it again," said Jake, flinging the latest issue of the college newsletter to the refectory floor. "God, I can't believe he's so bloody insensitive!"

"What's our esteemed Union President done now?" I asked.

"Only said that Tencastle would be a cultural and economic backwater living in the dark ages if it weren't for the students."

"He said that?"

"Not in those words but the message was unambiguous. Also criticised the college elders for having their heads stuck up the arses of the local councillors."

Rusty MacDowell had run a good campaign a year earlier, with eloquent passionate speeches promising action on a number of fronts to improve the lot of impoverished, exploited students. Actually our lot wasn't really that bad, but his rhetoric had struck a chord amongst the student body. I'd even voted for him, mainly because I hadn't a clue who the other candidate was. His predecessor had been much more low profile, working diligently enough behind the scenes while remaining pretty anonymous.

In office, however, Rusty had been a disaster. Full of hot air and fancy ideas, he'd achieved bugger all in his first six months of office apart from alienating townsfolk, the academic council, the rest of the student executive, and anyone else who had the misfortune to be caught in his radar. At a National Union of Students conference he'd been dubbed the clown prince by claiming, among other daft things, that Tencastle stood on a par with Cambridge in the academic world. Most of the delegates hadn't a clue we even existed. He'd had a flaming row with the Editor of Llais y Castell, who'd dared to publish a report of his contribution to the conference. He'd threatened to sack her, which constitutionally he was not empowered to do, but it didn't stop him trying.

"That's going to give fresh ammunition to T.H.E.M.," I said.

It was unfortunate timing that the failed candidate in last summer's parliamentary by-election, battleaxe Barbara bloody Bowen hyphen Martin had seen fit to set up the new Tencastle Householders, Employers and Merchants organisation, with herself as self-styled president and her meek husband as secretary. Whatever its declared objectives may have been, it seemed to function as a pressure group against anything to which its president objected, the Union of Students being high on her target list.

While there had been the odd contretemps between town and gown, such as Goliath's erection, relationships over the years had been good, both sides co-existing largely to mutual benefit. In recent months, however, the on-going arguments between THEM and US had raised unnecessary tensions. Some students were finding difficulty in getting customary part-time work to supplement their grant, and others were withdrawing from voluntary community service work with the aged and handicapped. All because the two main protagonists both had a bloody great gob and nothing else between their ears.

"I've a darn good mind to stand for Union President myself," said Jake.

"You're not serious? You've already crossed swords with Blooming Big-Mouth!"

"Yes, but she might be wary of personal attacks, if she's really as sensitive to the feelings of the black community as she would have us believe."

"It didn't stop her making disparaging remarks about the Scots."

"Our present haggis-hunting incumbent, you mean? That's different, he's a total pillock, acting like he's got a thistle up his backside. Probably something to do with wearing kilts." Jake paused for breath. "Besides, I'm more diplomatic."

"You are?"

I dismissed Jake's sudden interest in student politics as a flash-in-the-pan expression of frustration with our inept president, and I gave it no further thought.

Evidently Jake hadn't shared his thoughts with Dan and Sunny, so when, a week later, he breezed into the kitchen where the three of us were in the midst of a late Sunday breakfast to declare he'd got all the necessary forms, our response was at best mild curiosity.

Jake was somewhat taken aback by our general disinterest. "You've only got to sign them," he exhorted. "And you can be my agents."

"Sign what?" asked Sunny.

"Official secrets act?" I said.

"He fancies himself as the next double-o-seven, I expect," said Dan, scraping carbonised bread into the sink.

"I hoped I'd be able to count on your support!" Jake sounded somewhat miffed.

"In what way?" I said.

"At very least nominate me."

"What for? Prat of the year?" Dan was used to Jake's schemes.

"Union president, of course?"

Dan stopped scraping the toast and looked at Jake. "You are joking ... of course?"

"He did mention something to me in passing, Dan." I came to Jake's rescue. "I didn't think you meant it."

"Why not?"

I couldn't answer that.

"It's the first we've heard of your intentions," Sunny said, more co-operatively.

"I thought I'd told you."

"Not until a couple of minutes ago. What is it you want us to do?"

"Thank you, Sunny. Nice to know someone takes me seriously."

Dan and I exchanged wry grins.

"First of all, I need to be nominated – that's what these forms are for." Jake waved some pieces of paper. "Then I need a campaign manager. I thought you could do that, Rob. And agents to handle the publicity, drum up support ..."

"Whoa, Jake. I've no experience of anything like that," I protested.

"... arrange interviews, hustings ... you know." Jake was on a roll.

324

"Jake! Just shut up a minute!" said Dan. "Let's take things slowly."

Jake straddled a chair, chin and hands resting on its back.

"Right! Now, are you really going to run for president?" Dan asked. "You know that means a sabbatical – another year here – if you're successful?"

"Yes, to both."

"Okay. And you'd like our support?"

"I was hoping I could count on you."

"Well, that's fine by me. Rob? Sunny?"

"I'm willing to help," said Sunny.

"Me too. Though I don't know whether Tencastle students really deserve him."

"Pillock!" Jake said to me. "But thank you all."

"When's the election?" Sunny asked.

"Three weeks Thursday, so we need to get organised."

"I thought it was usually later," I said.

"Normally, yes, but you have Heath and Scargill to thank for that. Students will want to be out on that campaign trail no doubt."

"Do you know yet who you might be up against?" asked Dan.

"Not certain, yet, but there's a rumour that Tom Merchant will stand."

Tom was Chairman of the Drama Society, and a good speaker. A pleasant enough chap, I hadn't marked him out as a student union activist, but then I hadn't cast Jake in that role either.

"And one Rhiannon Legge-Upton has already handed in her nomination forms, I believe."

"Never heard of her. Who is she?" said Dan.

"Some pushy second-year, so I'm told."

Though there were no rules to the contrary, it was always assumed that the in-coming president of the Students' Union would be selected from the final year students. The post brought with it a modest stipend, funded out of our compulsory union subscription, and it provided a comfortable transition between student life and the real world of work.

Whatever vague plans we'd had for the day went by the board as we spent several hours chewing over various ideas and generally planning Jake's campaign. Personally, I wasn't sure that Tencastle would be prepared to replace a fiery red-headed Scot with the college's only black student, but nevertheless we resolved to give Jake's campaign our best effort. At least we wouldn't have the problem of recognition of our candidate. Jake was adamant, however, that we should make no attempt to play the racial card and Dan's suggested slogan, 'Things can't get blacker – or can they?' promptly ended up in the waste bin.

Jake had certainly dumped us at the bottom of a very steep learning curve. We spent three intense days reading up on the Union constitution, finding out the mechanics of the election along the lines of what we could and could not do in the way of campaigning, the support that was available for printing and distributing publicity leaflets and such like – and that was before deciding what we were actually going to put down on paper.

In the Union refectory my third cup of black coffee was already lukewarm, ignored in my so far futile attempt to devise a catchy headline to accompany Jake's photograph on a poster.

"May I join you?"

I looked up to behold a copper-haired girl with the most perfect complexion I'd ever seen. Her straight shoulder-length hair framed a heart-shaped face with blue eyes and a short straight nose with the hint of a few freckles. I almost pinched myself to make sure I wasn't dreaming.

"Er, yes! Please do." I barely registered that most of the other tables in the refectory were empty.

"You look worried. Are you working on an assignment?" She pulled up a chair opposite me, and smiled.

Wow.

"Sort of. It's for the Union elections."

"Is that the candidate?" she said, picking up Jake's photo. "He's very handsome."

Did I feel a twinge of jealousy? I rather lost my concentration on the poster. She was definitely more pleasing to the eye than Jake's ugly mug.

"Sorry, I'm not very good company at the moment. Bit of a headache, trying to get everything together for the campaign."

"You should take an aspirin." Her smile was like a magnet for my attention.

"Giving my brain a rest might work better," I said. I reached for my cup, and realised it was cold. "Can I get you a coffee or something?"

"That would be nice."

It barely flitted through my mind that she hadn't brought a drink with her when she sat down. I returned with two cups of hot brew. The girl was looking through the bumf I'd pushed to one side.

"It's the first time I've thought of a Union President as a real person. They always seem remote, well, like up on a pedestal."

An image flashed through my mind of Jake replacing Goliath on his plinth. "Oh he's real enough. We share a house."

"What's he like, you know, as a person?"

"I've known him ever since I came to Tencastle. He's, um ..." I'd never really given much thought to how he would come across to someone who didn't know him. I suppose as his campaign manager it was something I should address. "He's dynamic and focussed when he gets an idea into his head." Which was quite often, I could have added. "Bit like a whirlwind. He sweeps all of his friends along with him."

"Even if you don't agree with him?"

"He's very persuasive, and if we're sceptical at first, he has a knack of bringing us on board for his pet projects."

"Like this one?"

"Well, this is certainly a major undertaking, bigger and far more reaching than anything we've done before. But we're all firmly behind him."

"He sounds like a paragon of virtue."

"Well, I wouldn't have quite described him in that way."

"He's human, then? He's got his faults, like the rest of us mere mortals?

"Definitely human. I suppose he has got weak points, but I can't say that I know of any, or unsavoury vices."

"You reckon he stands a good chance in the election?"

"Jake? To be honest I don't know. Students can be a fickle lot at times. Depends on the strength of the opposition I suppose, and what's on at the cinema."

"Really?" Her delicately prepared pencil eyebrows shot up.

"Only joking. We'll have to see. Anyhow, let's forget Jake for a moment, tell me about yourself."

It might have been my imagination but I thought I caught a brief flash of concern on her face.

"What do you mean?"

"Well, it's not every day a pretty girl sits down at my table. And I don't even know your name."

The blush was genuine. "I'm Annie."

"Rob." Impulsively, I took her hand and kissed it.

"You are quite a gentleman!" she chuckled quietly.

"How come I haven't seen you around college before?"

"Perhaps you haven't been looking." A coy smile.

"I'm sure I would have noticed you. Are you first year?" Being at Carrick for most of last term did limit the amount of time I'd spent on the college or union premises.

"No, I'm second year. I assure you I've been around."

"Well, I must have had my head in the clouds for the last eighteen months."

She laughed, an infectious gentle sound which quivered her breasts, generous but shapely under her tightly fitting roll neck sweater.

"Listen," I said. "Would you like to come with me to the cinema this evening? If you're not doing anything else?"

"Were you going on your own, then?"

"I was thinking about it." I lied. To be honest, I hadn't a clue what was on at the local flea-pit.

"I'd like that very much." She took my hand and looked innocently into my eyes.

"I need to finish these things of and just pop back to my digs, but shall we meet here, say, six-thirty?"

"Let's make it in the park."

"Goliath?"

"Goliath. See you later, Rob." She stood up and drifted over to the door, then looked back and waved.

I did pinch myself. I looked at Jake's photo and the poster template. Something she had said gave me an idea. Aspirins.

Jake didn't get it. "'Nothing's written in tablets of stone.' What's that supposed to mean?"

"Tablets, Moses, you know, the ten commandments and all that."

"Um …"

"They'll like the play on words. And it implies strength of character, but willingness to listen and not be bound by preconceived ideas."

"You think so, Rob? Seems a bit dubious to me," said Jake.

"I think it's a brilliant idea!"

"Thanks for your support, Dan."

"Should I also offer to lead them to the Promised Land?"

"No, but we could say something like, Moses – keeps his promises."

"But I might not be able to."

"Well don't make any – or at least don't make any that you can't be certain of fulfilling."

Jake at least appeared to be giving the matter serious consideration. "How did you come up with this slogan?" he asked.

"Well, I met this girl, and she gave me this idea."

"What, tablets and all?" said Dan, incredulously.

"No, not as such. Just something she said inspired me. I'm meeting her again this evening."

"For more inspiration?"

"Maybe. You never know." I touched the side of my nose. "And also, we need to think about your personal image, like how you come across to the voters."

"And we should make a big point about your role in the Dome project," said Dan. "It should attract the Thomas Hall vote."

Before meeting Annie, I took the chance to call by the Olympus to check on the programme and the times. Not that there was really any choice, since the impressively named cinema was only one in Tencastle, and the last outpost on the distribution network before films began their cycle of repeats on television. It also catered for the popular taste; nothing too obscure or intellectually demanding, and definitely nothing erotic. Unless, of course, Sean Connery's rompings with his leading ladies turned you on, for its current promotion seemed to be a re-run of old Bond movies. Roger Moore's re-incarnation of double-O-seven was yet to reach Tencastle's silver screen and I'd already seen *Diamonds Are Forever* in Exeter, but then it wasn't the action drama I was looking forward to that evening.

My first impressions of Annie had, if anything, been understated. Even wrapped against the winter chill in a fleece-lined leather coat, she had a grace and beauty that would turn many a male head.

"Hi, Annie, I haven't kept you waiting, I hope."

"Not at all, I'm a bit early."

We crossed the road and started walking towards Castle Street. Wondering whether it would be premature to take her arm, she took the initiative.

"It's James Bond all this week, I'm afraid. Is that okay with you?"

"That's fine. I'm sure I've missed one. His wife was shot in the last one I saw."

"That's right. It didn't seem right to have someone else playing Bond, though. I'm glad Connery's back."

By unspoken consent we took to the back row of the stalls. It was too much to expect us to be like courting couples snogging throughout the film. I was just happy to have her nestle up contentedly in my arms, her delicate fragrance gently keeping the usual cinema smell of stale cigarette smoke at bay. I wouldn't have minded if the movie had been on a continuous loop, with Blofeld surviving to launch another scheme for world domination. Perhaps he did, for even before the credits were rolling, I'd practically drifted off into my own fantasy world.

"It's over, Rob."

It's pleasant to be woken with a kiss. "Sorry, I wasn't really asleep."

"You had your eyes closed, and the most contented smile I've ever seen."

"I am contented. Must be the company."

She punched me lightly on the shoulder, "Come on, you daydreamer!"

We were among the last to leave the auditorium and venture back out into the chilly street.

"Fancy a drink?"

"Nothing alcoholic. A coffee perhaps?"

A coffee at her pad sounded good to me. "Where do you live?"

"'Crombie, I'm afraid."

"Oh …" Not all my dreams were going to come true tonight, it seemed. "How about The Rivers Hotel?" I didn't fancy the goldfish bowl of the Union refectory and the mega-decibels of the re-branded Bard Café in Castle Street definitely didn't suit my mood.

"Isn't that expensive?"

"Not really. I've been there before. It's quiet."

Our breath steamed in the cold night air as we sauntered arm in arm across the park towards the Rivers. I chanced an embrace and found Annie responsive, her lips soft and her tongue probing.

Annie gently resisted an encore. "I need to be back before eleven. I didn't get a late pass. Let's have the coffee."

As I expected we had most of the hotel lounge to ourselves, and a choice of deep real leather to bury ourselves in, discreetly of course. Although I tried to get Annie to talk a little more about herself, she seemed a little reluctant to do so, turning the focus back to myself and Jake and our house at Penybont.

"Why don't you come over this Sunday for lunch?" I suggested. "Meet the gang. I could pick you up."

"That's very kind of you, but this weekend is not possible. I've really got a hell of a lot to do."

"When can I see you again? I'd really like to."

"You'll see a lot of me, I'm sure," she said, enigmatically.

"Monday?"

She thought for a moment, "Okay, if you like."

"Lunchtime in the refectory?"

"Mmm. Look, I must be going."

I called the waiter to settle the bill, and helped Annie on with her coat. "I'll walk you back."

"It is only across the road, Rob."

"Yes, but, you know, I've enjoyed the evening with you and …"

"You are a romantic aren't you?" she teased.

"Well … yes."

Longer this time, we embraced outside Abercrombie, passionately, though restricted in our mutual fumbling by duffle coat and fleece. We came up for air as the town clock began to strike the eleventh hour.

"Must go, Rob." She broke away from my arms. "Thank you for a lovely evening." She planted one more brief kiss on my lips.

"Till Monday!" I called as she ran up the steps and disappeared inside.

Monday seemed light years away. I looked out for Annie around college and the Union on Friday without success – when I wasn't in lectures or seminars or chasing around getting Jake's campaign leaflets to the printers. We now had just over two weeks before the election day, and the first priority was to get his mug shot in the face of every student whenever and wherever they set foot on college premises. Then there would be personal appearances at as many of the union activities as possible and in the final run up to the formal hustings Jake would undertake a whistle stop tour of all first and second year lectures – or as many as were physically possible to fit in – at which he'd introduce himself and give a quick sound bite either at the start or end of a session. We didn't think this method of making contact with the students had been tried before, and we were pleasantly surprised when the lecturers were for the most part supportive of our innovation. Dr. Cruikshanks, naturally, rejected the request out of hand.

Over the weekend, back at the house, Sunny, Dan and I took it in turns to groom Jake for his public exposure, testing him on his views on all the various issues we expected to be raised, acting as devil's advocates to his responses. By Sunday evening he was mentally drained.

"Christ, give it a rest, you lot! My brain hurts!"

"We're only doing it to give you the best chance," said Sunny.

"Yes, I know, and I appreciate your efforts, but I don't want to spend the next couple of weeks like a walking zombie."

"Talking of zombies, do you want to see *Live and Let Die*? Coming soon at a cinema near you. It'll give you a break," I suggested.

"I'll pass on that, thanks. You weren't suggesting I address the audience there I hope?"

"No, they'd probably think you were Baron Samedi in person."

"By the way, Rob," said Dan. "Can't help noticing you've had quite a spring in your step the last couple of days. Anything to do with some female inspiration?

"May be."

"Come on, you can tell us"

"Not much to tell. Pretty girl, cinema, coffee, you know. I'll be seeing her again tomorrow."

"Don't let yourself get too distracted from my campaign," warned Jake.

"Inadvertently she gave me some good ideas. And she seemed quite interested in you as a person. Can't think why, though."

I dodged the cushion.

Monday morning dragged on. God knows what John Tudor Evans was waffling on about, catalytic conversions or something, but I was glad to get out of the laboratory and down to the refectory. I needn't have rushed. Annie wasn't there. I grabbed a Coke and sandwich anyway and took a seat where I could see any new arrival.

Distracted briefly by a slice of tomato that had sprayed pips out over my T-shirt, I glanced back up and caught sight of Annie bidding farewell to someone in the doorway. Rather too fondly, possibly, or had I imagined the kiss?

Whatever, she had saved one for me, along with a gorgeous smile. "Hi, Rob, sorry I'm late."

"Old friend?" I said, as innocently as I could manage, nodding towards the entrance.

"Oh. Yes, old friend." She wasn't more forthcoming and changed the subject. "Been busy this weekend?"

"Pretty well, getting Jake up to speed. We've got some of the posters up already."

"Really?" She sounded surprised. "That's very quick!"

"What about you? You've been working too." She had a thick envelope folder under her arm.

"I had a lot of catching up to do."

"Annie, are you doing anything this evening? If you'd like to come back to my place, perhaps?"

"I've still got a lot of unfinished work."

My disappointment was obvious. "Tomorrow, then?"

"Rob, I do like you. Really. But I've also got this project which is going to keep me out of mischief for a week or so. Afterwards, perhaps." She actually made the perhaps sound definitely positive.

"Anything I can help you with?"

"Not on this occasion, but thanks for the offer. Now, I'm sorry, but I've got an appointment in fifteen minutes, so I'll have to love you and leave you."

"I'd prefer the first."

"You're sweet, Rob." I got a farewell kiss. "Bye."

"Au revoir!" I said, as she weaved through the tables, and I was obliged to put my passions on ice. For the time being.

I suppose I must have sat huddled over my Coke for several minutes, various thoughts, mostly concerning Annie, turning over in my mind.

Someone tapped my shoulder. "Hey, great thinker, aren't you going to say hello?"

I turned. "Min! Good to see you! Come and sit down!" She was probably the next best person to restore my spirits at that moment. "How are you? How's the leg coming on?" I noticed she still walked with a bit of a limp.

"Pretty well, considering. The plaster's been off for ages now but it still aches at times. You saw the photo I suppose?"

"Yes, they gave us a good splash." The Haverfordwest rag had published a photo of Huw and Min, still half mummified, presenting an outsize cheque for £130 to the hospital. Together with a half-page background account, there was also a picture of the rest of us dancing in the foyer.

"Huw arranged all the publicity," she said, proudly.

"Are you able to dance again?" After Min's horrific accident no-one had been particularly enthusiastic for Carpiog Morris to meet during the Autumn, and we'd more or less agreed to put things on hold at least until the days drew longer again. Besides which, the prolonged final teaching practice prevented many of us from making a regular commitment.

"I'm hoping to be okay. Actually, that's what I'd like to talk to you about. We're thinking of starting up again."

"Not for Rag?"

"No, I don't think that would be a good idea with Lady Muck throwing her weight around."

"I agree."

"We're thinking of Ivdif."

"What's that? Sounds like a medical procedure."

"I.V.F.D.F, it's a festival of folk dance between different universities. It takes place every year, at different venues."

"And you're thinking Carpiog could take part?"

"Yes!" Min beamed her signature smile; she'd lost none of her enthusiasm. "Huw's keen." I caught a flash of light as she waved her left hand. "We're engaged, you know?"

"I didn't. Congratulations to you both." I really meant it.

"He was absolutely wonderful to me, all the time I was in hospital. He came and visited every day, literally helped me back on my feet again."

"I'm so pleased for you. What about the wedding bells? You'll want us to dance, I hope?"

"Absolutely. But it won't be for a while yet, not until we've both finished our degree. We are sharing a house though. Do come and see us!"

"I'd like that."

"Anyhow, are you interested in going to London? Jake and Dan, too, of course."

"Possibly. Where and when?"

"First weekend in March. You'll come?"

"Min, I'd like to, but I'm not sure we'll have the time to practice. You know Jake's running for President. Dan and I are supporting him."

"Yes, so I've seen. Surprised you're consorting with the opposition as well."

"What do you mean?"

"I was standing in the lunch queue. Saw Leg-Up giving you the lovey-dovey."

"What are you saying, Min? I don't understand." Even the hint of cattiness seemed out of character for her.

"Rhiannon Legge-Upton. You two seemed quite friendly."

"Annie, you mean?" I had several conflicting thoughts running through my brain.

"Yes," Min sighed. "She does call herself Annie when it suits her. Probably did the same with the other fellow in Tom Merchant's camp."

"The other …?"

"Just before she met you."

"Oh my God!" I held my head in my hands. What had I told her about Jake?

"She's in my tutor group. She's very ambitious and well prepared to use all her assets to get what she wants. Quite ruthless but she can charm the leg off a donkey. That's how she got her nickname."

"Bloody hell!" Donkey or ass, she'd taken me for a ride.

Min put her hand on my arm. "Don't take it too personally. I don't like her very much, but I'd have to agree she's very attractive."

"Thanks." My air-balloon had rapidly deflated. "You won't mention this to Jake if you see him?"

"No way! But I'll vote for him. And please, have a think about the trip to London."

Though we'd been first to get our posters up, it didn't take long before every inch of display space, permitted or otherwise, was covered with mug shots of all the candidates, not only for the presidency but for the rest of the union executive positions. I took some solace that Rhiannon's photograph, surprisingly, did not really do her justice – she was far more attractive in the flesh. Being directly involved it would have been easy to assume that everyone was as enthusiastic as we were, but we also knew, not least from our own personal experience in previous years, that student apathy was the biggest hurdle to overcome. In truth we had little feedback on which to judge how Jake was faring in the popularity stakes compared to the other candidates. Any straw polls would have been time-consuming and pretty pointless.

It wasn't as if students could ignore the fact that elections were imminent. In addition to the leaflets liberally distributed, and regularly replenished, to refectories, coffee bars and halls of residence, the Union newspaper, Llais y Castell, gave two double pages to the aspiring presidential candidates. Reason and reconciliation were the cornerstones of our platform, but whether it would strike the necessary chords was anybody's guess.

The final hustings, however, were usually well attended and regarded by many as akin to a gladiatorial contest, candidates battling for dominance over their rivals with the cut and thrust of barbed rhetoric. In practice a candidate was more than likely to make an utter fool of him – or her – self, and suffer the ignominy of being laughed off the stage.

The lesser bouts out of the way, Jake, Tom and Rhiannon took their seats in the spotlight in the drama studio borrowed for the occasion, while myself and the other campaign managers were allocated the front row in which to bite our nails. Neil Tredinnick, Tom's agent, I already knew, of course, but it was the first time I'd come across Rhiannon's second. She seemed familiar, however, and though I couldn't quite place her, I thought I caught a flash of recognition from her.

I was pleasantly surprised to find the event chaired not by Rusty MacDowell but by his vice-president, Helen Alexander. The rules were quite clear: a maximum of five minutes address by each candidate in turn, followed by an open question and answer session. As campaign manager I was not permitted to put a question directly but supporters were always primed to raise points of order or targeted queries should the proceedings become too mundane.

Helen spoke briefly to the candidates before addressing the gathering, her voice calm but authoritative.

"Ladies and gentlemen, fellow students, thank you for giving up your valuable time to hear the presidential candidates speak for themselves. You will, of course, have the opportunity to ask questions. The candidates have agreed to go in alphabetical order, which also absolves me of the accusation of putting ladies first."

The audience laughed politely, easing the tension.

Rhiannon Legge-Upton exuded sensuous charm, guaranteed to give male students wet dreams for a week, regardless of what she said, while her cleverly constructed address, in its bare bones, focussed largely on women's rights, to get students of her own gender on board. Tom Merchant, as I expected, was eloquent, with all the right dramatic hand and facial gestures, but far too erudite. Like spouting Shakespeare to five year olds, I doubt if most of the assembled body understood what the hell he was on about.

Jake rose from his seat. I gave him a thumbs up in encouragement.

"Madam Chairman, fellow students, I appreciate that I have a slight advantage in being the last to speak. The other candidates have already said much with which I would agree. The role of females in our society is indeed often undervalued, but I question whether the Union presidency is the appropriate vehicle for Miss Legge-Upton's campaign about which she feels so passionately. Mr Merchant was also passionate and eloquent, as befits the chairman of the Drama Society, but was it all an act? I am not sure I understand quite what he is proposing. What do I stand for?"

Jake paused briefly, and took a sip of water from the tumbler.

"You can see that my ancestry is neither Celtic nor Anglo-Saxon …" A few titters from the audience. "But I do not want you to vote for me for the novelty of being possibly the first student body to elect a black president. I want you to vote for me, the person, on what I believe I can contribute to benefit your life in this community. We may not be, as some would have us think, on par with the likes of Oxford and Cambridge, but I am very proud to be a Tencastle student, and I believe we can make a valuable contribution to the national student scene in highlighting issues which are particularly relevant to a small and fiercely independent establishment. Perhaps the most important among these is our partnership with the town. It will not have escaped your notice that in recent months our relationship with the wider community has deteriorated with detrimental effect on part-time employment prospects for students, difficulties in finding accommodation etcetera. I intend to start building bridges, to re-establish trust and good communications, instead of the counter-productive inflammatory rhetoric that has been the norm of late. I hope you will support me. Thank you."

Jake's speech, short and to the point, went down well. Except for one prominent individual who shot to his feet and barely waited for the applause to subside before launching into a tirade.

"Hae dare ye use yon pla'form tae attack me, ye black bastard!"

The room fell silent, the assembled body scarcely believing their ears. All eyes were on Jake, who turned to the chairman, and said calmly, "May I reply to that question?"

Helen looked grim. She nodded. Jake stood and looked at the audience for a few moments, and then towards his antagonist.

"Our honourable President is correct. I am black, as you can all see, and, I am a bastard – my mother hardly knew my father. However I have purposely refrained hitherto from referring by name to any individual in the present administration, but if Mr MacDowell wishes to indulge in personal comments then I am happy to respond. You, sir, have made Tencastle the laughing stock of the NUS. You have soured relationships with the college authorities and caused discord and suspicion among the town folk in your petty, ill-tempered feud with Mrs Bowen-Martin. You have brought the office of President into disrepute. You should resign, forthwith."

As Jake sat down, the auditorium erupted. Almost to a man, the students stood and cheered and clapped. Even so, above the din, those of us at the front heard Rusty yell, "Aw, bollocks!" as he stormed out.

Helen Alexander did her best to bring the meeting to order. She looked round in vain for an object to use as a gavel, then resorted to standing, her hands held up like a priest about to give a blessing.

"Ladies! Gentlemen! Please! Please be seated!"

Slowly at first, the students took their seats again, and a hush descended on the room.

Tom leant across Jake and then spoke quietly to the Chair. He stood to address the meeting.

"Ladies and Gentlemen. I have known Jacob Moses almost from the first day I came to this college. He is an honourable and honest man, and I am deeply ashamed at the abuse he has been subjected to this evening. He has responded with dignity. He has also had the guts to state in clear, unambiguous language what should have been said long ago, and which none of us, myself included, have had the courage to voice in public. I cannot now in all honesty stand in opposition to him in this election, and therefore I am withdrawing as a candidate for the presidency."

He sat down, his last words coming out with difficulty. He looked emotionally drained.

For a second time the assembly was taken aback, before bedlam broke out, everyone talking, hands shooting up to attract the attention of the Chair, some heated arguments as well. I felt sorry for Helen, having to preside over a completely unanticipated set of circumstances. She spent the best part of a minute in animated discussion with Rhiannon, Jake and Tom, after which she again called the meeting to order. Even when the hubbub died down, many students still had their hands waving, intent on having their say.

"Ladies, gentlemen, if I may have your attention. I am aware that many of you wish to speak. However, we find ourselves in a situation without precedent, and I am therefore adjourning this meeting for half an hour in order to discuss the matter in detail with the candidates, and take appropriate advice as to procedure. You may remain, quietly, in the auditorium if you wish, but you may prefer to take the opportunity to grab a coffee and talk things over yourselves."

She paused to let her message sink in. Most students began to make their way to the exits. "I should be grateful if the respective campaign managers would join us on the stage. Tom's manager, too, please."

We hurried to join our protégés. Rhiannon's agent touched my arm as we mounted the steps to the stage.

"Don't you remember me, Rob?"

Recognition hit me in the gut. After all, it had been eighteen months ago in dim light, and some twelve months since our correspondence had dried up.

"Mary?" I stuttered.

Helen gave us very little opportunity for private discussion. "We have very little time at our disposal, so I suggest we get down to finding a way out of this constitutional mess. Tom, I am still prepared to let your name go forward, if you wish to reconsider your withdrawal?"

"Thanks, Helen, but I don't think that's an option."

"Tom, I am grateful for your comments, but really, you don't need to do this," said Jake. "I'd rather take my chance than have you ditch your ambition."

"I've already done that, I think. I'd have no credibility if I went back on what I said just now." Tom and Neil stood up to leave.

I looked at Rhiannon. She hadn't said anything since Rusty's outburst had sent the proceedings pear-shaped. It was impossible to read anything into her serene expression.

"Very well," said Helen, "I understand your position, but nevertheless I regret that you have pulled out." She then addressed those of us remaining. "Now, as you are well aware, the election is tomorrow, and the ballot papers have already been printed, of course. Where there are more than two candidates, voters can indicate an order of preference. If no single candidate achieves an absolute majority over all of the others, then the candidate with the lowest support is eliminated. Second choice votes from those who voted for that candidate are then counted, and so on, until one person has an absolute majority. In the present situation we now have only two candidates but three names on the ballot paper. As I see it, there are three ways to proceed. Firstly, we cancel the whole process, and re-run the election, with the possibility, of course, of new nominations. Secondly, we postpone the election for a week in order to print fresh ballot papers. Thirdly, we go ahead with the ballot tomorrow, and count the second choice votes on any papers that list Tom as first choice. Your comments, please?"

"I'm not keen to go through the whole rigmarole again," said Jake.

"I don't like the first option either," Annie said softly.

"Is the third option legal? I mean, constitutionally?" I asked.

"There's nothing as far as I can see in the constitution that would preclude this solution, providing both of you are in agreement, and, as a safeguard, the agreement is witnessed by your campaign manager. I don't want any writs flying onto my desk from whoever loses the election, declaring that anyone was pressurised into making a decision they were not happy with! Do you want a few minutes to talk it over?"

Jake looked at me, shrugged, and made up his mind, "I'd rather get it over with. I'm happy to go ahead tomorrow."

"Rhiannon?"

For her the decision wasn't going to be so clear cut. She and Mary were obviously not in full agreement with each other, though, keeping their voices low, I wasn't sure which of them had the serious misgivings.

"We'll agree to the election going ahead tomorrow, on one condition," said Annie eventually.

"What's that?"

"We run the whole hustings again when the audience reassembles. Five minutes each, as before, with question and answer session. And I'd like to speak last this time." She looked at Jake, "It wasn't your fault, but you rather grabbed the limelight earlier."

"Is that acceptable to you, Jake?"

"I've no problem with her request."

Helen breathed a sigh of relief, which I'm sure we all felt. "Now, if you'd be so good as to get that agreement in writing and witnessed." She looked at her watch. "Ten minutes. I'm just going to ask the stewards to chivvy the great unwashed back into our presence. Don't quote me on that, will you!"

Her attempt at light-heartedness broke the tension. I blessed the fact that she had the tact, common sense and presence of mind so demonstrably lacking in the President.

I was anxious in a way, though also with some apprehension, to speak to Mary but she and Annie were in deep discussion.

When the students had re-assembled, Helen apologised for the interruption in the proceedings and summarised the position on which we had agreed. She explained that notices would be displayed at each polling station to publicise Tom's withdrawal as a candidate, and what would happen to any votes still cast for him.

Jake rose to speak again. "This has been an unusual and dramatic evening in more ways than one. I should like to thank you, Madame Chairman, for your steady hand and guidance through this, and to welcome the consent of Miss Legge-Upton in allowing the election process to continue. I would like to pay tribute, also, to Tom Merchant for his most unselfish action. It is not what I would have wanted, but I respect his decision. However, I would not automatically expect his supporters to transfer their allegiance to me, though I would of course be happy for them to do so. I would urge you all to vote, and to vote for whichever of us you believe will bring respect for the presidency again, and to best serve the interests of all of you. You have already heard me present my intentions in that respect and I do not intend to bore you by repeating them in detail. I will work for your best interests, I will seek to re-establish co-operative relationships with the townsfolk and with the college administration. I will represent Tencastle responsibly in the National Union of Students. Thank you."

The applause was generous even though I felt Jake's address was much lower key than earlier in the evening.

Not so Annie. I gave her all due credit for delivering, off-the-cuff, a completely revamped, punchy speech, nothing short of brilliant. While not abandoning her support for women's rights, they were presented in context as one of many issues facing all students. Without appearing to steal Jake's ideas, reconciliation featured prominently as a recurring theme, and she gave the impression of having thanked Jake, Tom and Helen even though I don't recall her actually doing so. There was certainly more substance to her than met the eye – and that would in itself have been enough for most males!

I'm sure the clapometer recorded a higher level than for Jake.

After the earlier shenanigans the questions seemed pretty mild, even trivial, and were fielded competently by both sides. The meeting, thankfully, wound down, rather as an anticlimax. I rejoined Jake on stage where we all cordially shook hands.

"Christ, I could do with a beer!" said Jake.

"Sounds a good idea," I agreed.

"Helen?"

"Thanks, but no. I've still got a few hours work ahead of me back at the office sorting things out on your behalf!"

Jake turned to Rhiannon. "Would you care to join us? After all, it's all over bar the counting now."

Annie was as surprised as I at his unexpected magnanimity, and, for a moment, lost for words.

"Er, yes, why not? Would you mind the Rivers? I'd prefer a coffee."

I wondered if she was being provocative. "It does a good pint as well," I said to Jake who looked uncertain about the venue. "And it's definitely more comfortable than the Castle."

"You've been in there?"

"A few times. On special occasions."

"You're on."

Jake found himself strolling over to the Hotel with Mary. We still hadn't had a chance to talk. Which left me with Annie, and not sure how to play it.

"You made a good pitch in there tonight."

"Thank you, Rob."

"Listen, Annie," I said. "Earlier, you know, the other week. Were you, I mean, were you just leading me on? To get me to open up about Jake."

She didn't answer immediately.

"Well?" I pressed.

"That was the plan, initially, yes. But you didn't tell me anything other than what a good fellow he was."

"Initially?"

Unexpectedly, Annie took my hand. "Yes. But you seem to be a very natural person, guileless and completely up front. I genuinely enjoyed being with you that evening."

"We could have met again."

"It didn't seem a good idea."

"Did you try it on with Neil Tredinnick as well?"

"Guilty, as charged. Same result, nothing on Tom. And Neil was a cold fish."

"We can meet again," I said, but without much optimism.

"Let the dust settle on this election first."

I wondered whether she was aware of my distant relationship with her agent.

Electioneering wasn't permitted on the day the votes were cast but we all did what we could to persuade students to rise above their apathy and participate in the democratic process. Shortly after the poll closed at seven o'clock, Jake and I arrived at the Union offices to witness the count. Rhiannon and Mary were already there.

"There's an Executive Committee meeting still going on, apparently."

I took the opportunity afforded by the delay.

"Mary," I said. "Can I have a quick word with you, please?"

A brief flash of concern knitted her brow. She looked round at Annie, who was surprised by my request. Jake, too, looked at me quizzically.

"Be back shortly," Mary said to Annie.

We walked in silence to the end of the corridor and down the stairs. She turned to look at me, jaw set straight. I couldn't really fathom her expression.

"Mary, I'm really sorry I didn't recognise you yesterday. You've changed your … your … um … you look so different." Even to me it sounded pretty feeble. "I didn't even know you were back in Tencastle. Why didn't you write?"

"I did write, Rob, but you didn't reply."

"When?"

"Last February."

"I've heard nothing from you since your card the Christmas before last. I assumed you had found someone else back in Cheshire."

"I did, briefly. That's why I called off the invite to my place. It didn't last," she said wistfully.

"I really can't understand why I didn't get that letter." I was, indeed, puzzled, since she'd used the correct Ty Melin address previously.

"I don't know either." She shrugged. "I guessed you had got another girlfriend by then, anyway. And then when I saw you with Rhiannon …"

"I hadn't, really. And Annie, that's very recent. I didn't know her until a couple of weeks ago." I thought it unnecessary to elaborate on the circumstances.

Mary suddenly put her arms round me, and rested her head on my shoulder. "What a bloody mess, Rob," she sighed. "What on earth did you think of me?"

"Probably much the same as your opinion of me." In all honesty I didn't really know what to think. The missing letter, if it had ever existed, was a conundrum.

"I think we'd best be getting back," I said.

"Uh huh." She looked up at me with her deep brown eyes. "You're very sweet, Rob," she said. And kissed me.

When we rejoined Jake and Annie, we waited for another quarter of an hour until the door opened and Helen ushered us in. "Sorry to keep you all waiting. Jake, you should be the first to know that Rusty

MacDowell has been suspended with immediate effect as President by the Vice-Chancellor pending an investigation into his racist comments last night. He is banned from all college and union premises until further notice. We have endorsed that decision, and have in addition called for his resignation. We can't actually sack him, but in practice the investigation will probably drag out for several weeks. He's unlikely ever to show his face round here again."

"I can't say I'm sorry," Jake commented. "He's an uncouth, foul-mouthed ba … I'd better not use that word … foul-mouthed moron."

"I'm Acting President in the meantime. So, let's get on with the count. Take a seat, if you like."

"What's the usual turn out in these elections?" I asked Helen.

"Anything over forty percent is doing well. It can drop to around thirty percent in a lacklustre campaign. I don't think that's going to be the case, this time."

The ballot boxes were brought in from a locked storeroom next door, and, one by one, their contents tipped out onto the cleared tables, one hell of a lot of paper, I thought. The members of the union executive acted as tellers and the ballot papers began to accumulate in two roughly equal stacks, and a third much smaller pile. Jake seemed unaccustomedly nervous, drumming his fingers on the table. The result was far from a foregone conclusion.

Helen was going round the tables, making regular checks. She glanced at the stack of empty boxes and frowned.

"I think we're missing one box."

Everyone stopped and looked at her. She grabbed a sheet from her desk and checked each box against her list. "Arts Coffee Bar. Where is it?" She demanded of no-one in particular.

Coffee bar hardly described the location in question. It was no more than a vending machine in an alcove on the second floor wing of the main building.

"Christian Guild secretary was responsible for that one," offered the Union Treasurer.

"Well, what the Christ has he done with it?"

"Helen, I may be able to help," Annie said. "While we were waiting – before Jake and Rob came along – a short, dumpy chap with glasses brought a box up, and took it away again."

"That's him! Okay, the couple of you that have finished your count, go and find out where the hell he's got to. With any luck the box will be on the premises somewhere."

Two people scurried out. They returned a few minutes later with the missing box. "Silly sod was sitting in the corner of the Llais office clutching the bloody thing like it was his favourite teddy bear."

"Why was he in there?"

"God knows."

Apart from this last box, all the other votes had been counted. The provisional result was certainly close so far, with 357 votes for Jake against 338 for Rhiannon, including about thirty second-choice votes, honours roughly even from those who had still voted for Tom, despite the bloody great signs stating he was no longer standing.

"I don't believe it, the stupid pillock!" exclaimed the teller who had started sorting the contents of the final box, which certainly had the potential to change the outcome.

"What's up now?" called Helen, whose exasperation was beginning show.

"It looks as if he's crossed out Tom's name on all of the ballot papers. Technically, that means they are spoiled papers, I suppose."

"Oh hellfire! That's all we damn well need!" Helen put a palm to her forehead. "Look, I'm sorry, I'm going to have to ask you to leave until we've got an answer to this latest cock-up, if you'll excuse the expression."

"Will we still have a result tonight?" I asked.

"I don't know … I just don't know. Hang around for a while anyway."

Jake kicked a chair in the corridor in frustration. "God, I thought all students were supposed to have an IQ at least in double figures."

"If the papers in that last box are void … does that mean they will have to run the whole election again?" Mary voiced a thought that had also occurred to me.

"If that were the case, I'd be sorely tempted to stuff the whole bloody show." Jake was rarely despondent but I saw his point. "You'd do a fine job, Rhiannon."

"I'm not sure I'd want the job under those circumstances."

Nobody spoke. There didn't seem much to say beyond meaningless speculation. The door opened, and the Union Secretary came out.

"Any news?" Jake asked.

"Not yet, but I think we're getting there. Something I need to check on first." He disappeared down the corridor. He returned several minutes later, and gave a thumbs up sign as he went back inside.

"I'm going to get pissed, whatever the result, after this evening," said Jake.

"But it might spoil your squeaky-clean image!" Difficult to tell whether Annie was being serious or taking the piss.

We lapsed into brooding silence again.

"Would you please come back in?" Helen held the door wide.

"This has been a very difficult time for all of us, as I'm sure you will agree. We had to consider the outcome of the election if all the votes in the last box were declared void against the result if they were all valid. A change in outcome would certainly have required us to declare the whole election void, and organise a re-run."

Jake perked up.

"As it is, we have counted all of the votes again, and given particular attention to the rogue box. The maximum number of votes for Rhiannon Legge-Upton, including the dodgy ones, is 356. The number of votes cast for Jacob Moses, without the last box, is 357, or 363 with."

I saw Annie wince. So close.

"That's nearly sixty percent turnout. Well done, both of you. You know that either of you have the right to request a recount."

Annie shook her head. "That won't be necessary."

"I therefore declare Jacob Moses to be the president-elect of Tencastle Student Union."

Under any other circumstances I might have punched the air.

"Thank you," said Jake, closing his eyes momentarily. He turned to Rhiannon who was being consoled by Mary. "I'm sorry."

"One of us had to win," said Annie, close to tears. "But congratulations." She kissed him on his cheek, and turned to me. She put her arms round me, burying her face in my shoulder. I could feel her chest heave as she tried vainly to control her sobs. Jake, I could see, was talking quietly to Mary.

"Could you spare a few minutes, Jake?" Helen said. "There are a couple of things I'd like to discuss with you as soon as possible."

"Sure," said Jake. "Just give me a moment." He turned to say a few more words to Mary.

I caught his eye and mouthed 'Castle Inn' silently over Annie's shoulder, and made a gesture of raising a pint glass with my spare hand behind her back. Jake nodded.

Annie showed no inclination to leave my arms, but I steered her gently to the door. "Take you home?" I whispered.

Mary began to follow us, then stopped and looked back at Jake, undecided as to what she should do and confused, among other matters, that I had taken her role in consoling Annie rather than celebrating with Jake.

Outside, it was drizzling and chilly. Annie still kept her head down in my arms, and it wasn't until we were close to Abercrombie that she looked up into my face.

"I'm sorry I've made a fool of myself, Rob," she murmured.

"You've nothing to be sorry for. I can imagine how disappointed I'd be in your position."

"Not only that. I feel so ashamed…"

"There's no need, the turnout must have been the highest ever."

"For trying to use you. And I still lost, didn't I."

"You've already made up for that, last night. I wondered why you didn't ask for a recount, though. One vote."

"Which would have meant a re-run. I didn't want that." She put her head on my shoulder again. "You'd better go and help Jake celebrate with that pint."

"You would be welcome to join us." I had a suspicion Mary might be there with Jake.

"I don't think so," she sighed. "I think I'd like to be on my own for a while. But thanks for the offer." She kissed me on the lips, and eased away from my arms.

"I'll be in touch," I promised.

She nodded and turned towards the steps of Abercrombie.

When I'd eventually pushed my way into the snug of the Castle, word of Jake's triumph had already got round, and two pints of best bitter were already lined up in front of him by way of congratulation. I'm sure that they weren't the only ones he would put away, though I was confident he would avoid getting legless. Mary had tagged along, a bit like a fish out of water, I thought. I contemplated asking if I could see her home, to start again, as it were, with our strangely broken relationship, but I heard Jake take the initiative. I would have been prepared to wait discreetly and give him a lift back to the cottage, until I discovered that Mary wasn't still in Abercrombie as I had assumed, but up near Thomas Hall. No chance was I going to wait for him to trail all that way even supposing he was actually capable of finding his way back again unaided. Neither did I feel entirely comfortable about playing gooseberry to him and Mary in the back of Jessica. I quietly suggested that he should order a taxi.

"Hail, O mighty one!" Dan prostrated himself at the foot of the stairs as Jake descended for breakfast. "Thy word is my command."

"Well, you can get up and stop pratting about, for a start!" the Almighty replied. "And find me an aspirin."

"Jake! You did it!" Sunny breezed into the kitchen and hugged him.

"Careful, he's rather fragile this morning," I said.

"No, it's all right, I'm okay, really. If someone can lend me their head."

It took three cups of strong black coffee to restore him to normality, as far as anything about Jake could be regarded as the norm.

"What's the plan now, O master?"

"Oh, piss off, Dan, I'm nobody's master!" Jake took the leg pulling in good stead. "Various meetings in due course with Helen. She's got a cool head in a crisis, I must say, but for the present, I need to wind down. I've been running on adrenalin these last weeks."

"How about a weekend away?" I said.

"What do you mean?"

"I've been intending to tell you, but, well, course of events and so on…"

"Yes, go on."

"I met Min the other week. She's trying to get Carpiog together for a trip to London."

"Really? What for?"

I told him.

"And when is this supposed to happen?"

"Next weekend."

"Bloody hell, that doesn't leave much time for us to practice, does it?"

"Are you interested then?" I was surprised he'd be so enthusiastic, given his recently elevated status. Carpiog had, of course, been his inspiration in the first place.

"Certainly! It will be great for us all to get together again." He detected some reticence on my part. "You will both come too?"

"I'm up for it," said Dan.

It was probably totally illogical, but I'd always regarded London with suspicion, and, given a choice, always avoided it like it still had the plague. Prancing around hot dusty streets, choked by traffic fumes and hemmed in by brick and concrete wasn't my idea of fun, and I said so.

"It's not all like that, Rob, there's lots of green spaces as well," said Jake.

"Bet he's got a date with his new girlfriend," said Dan.

Despite more of their cajoling and enticements, I stuck to my prejudices. I was not going to dance in the capital. Besides which, Dan's comment suggested a far more attractive alternative worth pursuing.

Strangely, it didn't occur to me to ask how Jake had made out with Mary.

CHAPTER SEVENTEEN

Field Studies

In retrospect, I wished I had gone to London since my desires to get in close contact with Annie proved totally unfulfilled. I suspected, possibly uncharitably, that I'd served my purpose with her, and she would be seeking to use her physical assets to further her career in other ways. And Mary seemed to be keeping me at arm's length, with pleasant conversation but no encouragement whatsoever to rekindle passions. Furthermore, Jake and Dan both returned full of renewed enthusiasm for Carpiog, with all of the original members, apart from myself and Maurice Manley, who had graduated last year, having made the journey. The Dickens twins assured Jake that their father would give his electoral triumph a front page column in the Tene Messenger.

Jake, naturally, had returned with even more ideas for extending our experience into the other dance traditions he had encountered. Personally, I took some comfort in the fact that our remaining time at Tencastle would curtail the possibility of being shanghaied into any further bizarre activities.

I felt the need to escape from the almost carnival atmosphere in the house. For nearly an hour I vented my personal frustrations and disappointment on the garden weeds. With minimal effort on our part since the previous summer, we had enjoyed the results of my father's initiative, with a supply of fresh sprouts, savoy cabbage and parsnips. We still had a string of onions hanging up in the shed. The dandelions and daisies, not to mention a host of other unwanted tenacious green intruders, were now intent on claiming the patch for themselves. My attack with the hoe seemed to be making little impression, and I didn't see why I should be the lone crusader when my housemates had also enjoyed the garden's bounty. With the proximity of the Easter vacation, I felt that urgent joint action should be taken, lest the plot revert to the near wild state my father had seen fit to tackle the previous year.

Dan was unenthusiastic. "What's the sense of planting more

vegetables when we're unlikely to be here to reap the benefit."

"He has a point, Rob," said Jake. "And with our finals coming up, can we really afford the time for agriculture?"

"It would be nice to leave the garden in a tidy state for the owners when they return."

I was pleased of this support from Sunny, who was usually happier to process the vegetables than be hands-on in their cultivation.

"Look, at least give me a hand this weekend to clear it. We don't need to do anything else until next term, or even until we've got a better idea what we'll be doing after the summer. Only Jake's got his future settled at the moment."

Fortunately, Sunday was one of those days which challenged anybody to stay cooped up indoors when spring was at its best. I volunteered to set an example by doing the first stint of digging, while the others tried to look busy doing as little as possible.

No sooner had I handed the fork over to Jake than he cocked his head to one side.

"Isn't that the phone ringing?"

I suspected a ploy to divert my attention.

"I'll go," said Sunny. She emerged a few moments later. "For you, Rob."

"Who is it?"

"Not sure, think he said his name was Mark."

The name didn't immediately ring any bells. I couldn't think of who'd want to cold call me on a Sunday.

"Rob Kiddecott here. Who's calling?"

"Rob, hi! Mark here, Mark Matthews." He added, "you remember me from Carrick?"

"Yes, indeed." He was the last person I expected to hear from.

He read my mind. "I expect you're wondering why I'm calling. I'm really going to ask you a big favour, and I shall fully understand if you tell me to get lost."

"What is it?" I was intrigued.

"Well, I've broken my leg playing rugby ... no, no need for sympathy," he added, as I begun to express my condolences. "Thing is, I'm due to lead a field trip to Devon for the lower sixth this Easter, and no way can I do that in my present state."

"What about your colleagues?"

"I've been trying for the last few days to get someone to step in, but seems they've all made other plans. Patricia Prior – she suggested you. She's going, but she doesn't know Devon at all. I've done all the recce and planning. You are familiar with the school, you come from Devon, and you are a geographer."

"Well, I ...er ... I don't know." Genuinely, I had some strong doubts, though I was quite flattered to even be considered as a last resort.

"We may have to cancel the whole trip if I can't find someone suitable by tomorrow. And you're the best hope I've got – no, scrub that, the only hope, to be honest."

Moral blackmail and flattery.

"We could probably manage to pay you something, even if I have to raid my own piggy bank, and there would be free board and lodging ..."

The carrot dangling.

"Where and when?" I asked "Not that I'm saying yes." Though I knew I probably was.

"The group leave Monday week. Four nights at Millworthy Centre, it's near Bideford. You know it?"

"Not from personal experience, but I know the area."

"Excellent!"

"How big is the group? It wouldn't just be myself and Pat as staff, would it?"

"No, there are about two dozen students, mixed. Tim Pintwhistle's got a PSV license, so he'll be driving, and Moira Bunn is in charge of all the domestic arrangements."

It was feasible I suppose. Probably look good on my CV too.

"Are you still there? "

"Uh huh."

"Will you do it?"

What could I say? "Okay, if you think it will be all right."

The relief was evident. "Thanks, Rob, you're a star!"

"But I'll need to know a bit more about your programme, at the very least."

"Yes, that's the next point. Can you come over to Carrick?"

"To school?" That would be difficult, as the programme for college was pretty tight in this final week before the vacation.

"I'm at home. All the time for the next week or so I guess."

"Of course. When do you suggest? I've got very little free time this week during the day."

"Any chance you could make it today? This afternoon?"

I expected Jake and co. might have something to say about leaving them to tend the garden while I went gallivanting off in the car. But as I took down the directions to Mark's house, I had a brainwave.

"Nice of you to join us," said Dan sarcastically.

I couldn't detect any noticeable change in the state of the garden. I ignored his comment.

"That was Mark Matthews, head of geography at Carrick." I explained the situation. "Fancy a trip over there? Have a pub lunch, you three have a potter round – I'm sure Sunny will show you the sights – while I meet Mark. Head back this evening."

"Beats buggering around with Mother Earth," said Jake. "I'm up for it!"

So were Dan and Sunny.

I doubt if Dan and Jake had ever explored the road uphill beyond Evan's cottage, far less ventured in the direction of Carrick. With windows wound down to enjoy the warm spring sunshine, it was also something of a first for all four of us in the house to be taking a trip purely, or rather, largely, for pleasure.

"Where did you have in mind for lunch, Rob?" asked Jake. "I thought the pubs round here were closed on Sundays?"

"Carrick's in a different county," I replied. "And the Bull and Dragon is open for food every day."

"What about a country pub instead?" said Dan.

"Rob has a habit of getting lost in the country lanes," said Sunny.

"That's not fair! It only happened once," I protested. "And we didn't even come across a pub anywhere on that occasion."

All the way to Carrick we didn't pass another pub that was open, but the Bull and Dragon did us proud with a massive Sunday roast and all the trimmings. I left the others to enjoy a second pint and arranged to meet them at five o'clock, or thereabouts.

The directions Mark had given me led to a small modern estate of semis and link-houses just off the Carmarthen road on the other side of the river.

"Come in, door's open!" Mark called when I rang the bell on the middle of three houses.

The door opened directly into a small sitting room, cosy and compact in agent's language. Mark was stretched out in an armchair, his plaster-encased leg resting on a footstool. A pair of crutches lay propped up within easy reach.

"You'll excuse me for not getting up," he said. "Bloody nuisance! Fortunately we've got a downstairs loo. Fancy a beer?"

"Thanks, but I've just been in the Bull and Dragon with my housemates."

"Would you get one for me from the fridge?" One empty lager can already sat on the coffee table.

The kitchen had a woman's feel to it. Difficult to describe, but we experienced the same subtle change when Sunny replaced Benji, even though she was far from being our galley-slave.

"I thought you shared a flat with John?"

"We did, until we had a disagreement." Mark took a swig of lager. "Actually, more like a blazing row. Couldn't keep his hands away from my girlfriend when he'd had a jar or two. In the end it was him or Karen. No contest really. I moved in with her, six weeks ago, now."

"I hope I'm not inconveniencing her."

"Not at all, she's out playing hockey this afternoon, so we can get down to business. I'm really glad that you can help me out."

I pulled up a chair, and he spread out a number of sheets from a folder on the coffee table.

"Right, now as I said, we're staying at The Millworthy Centre, about three miles from Bideford. It's independently owned, a bit like a Youth Hostel, though we don't have to do our own catering. How far is it from where you live in Devon?"

"About forty minutes drive, I guess."

"And you are intending to go home for the holidays?"

"Yes, I usually do."

"Now, we're leaving Carrick on the Monday morning, and we'll spend some time in Bristol, so we won't be at the Centre until the evening. There's no need for you to arrive until next morning if you prefer. You might prefer to travel up each day, but if you could stay overnight, it would be very helpful."

"No problem."

"You'll have to share a room with Tim Pintwhistle."

"Okay."

"Tuesday the intention is to study transport links past and present, road, rail and sea, in relation to the industry of the area over the years. Wednesday is more geologically biased, looking at coastal features in the Hartland area. Thursday is a bit more fluid, depending on the weather, we can either go to North Dartmoor, or undertake a detailed study of Great Torrington."

Off the top of my head I couldn't imagine how Torrington could warrant a whole day's attention. I'd be hard pushed to justify a couple of hours and said so.

"You'd be surprised," said Mark. "Once you throw a bit of history in for good measure, and there's always the option of letting them have a swim. You'd need to confirm that in advance though. Now, Patricia will obviously have full details of everything I've planned, and I've prepared a copy for you too. I spent a week in the area last summer doing all the preparation on the ground, but I'm relying on you to provide that bit of local knowledge which will make a big difference, I know, to the success of the week, and, even more importantly, stop Pat worrying her head off."

Mark had certainly been thorough. The thick A4 folder would take me a fair time to plough through.

"Any questions?"

"Will I need a sleeping bag?"

"No, all bedding provided."

"What about Friday?"

"Ah yes! We leave the Centre after breakfast. If we haven't done Torrington, then that's the morning taken care of, otherwise we do a river profile on Exmoor. In any case the intention is to travel back over Exmoor to the North Somerset coast. You'll need to use your car that day, but if you want to take your leave after lunch that's no problem. I wouldn't expect you to travel half the way back to Wales!"

We spent some time going through the material in the folder, which, I was glad to discover, was very comprehensive, down to large-scale maps, with marked routes, parking places for the coach and even location of public loos, telephone boxes and shops in the remoter areas.

"If you think of anything else, please give me a ring. You've also got Pat's home number and that of the Centre. And, I will make sure that you are appropriately reimbursed for your time and expenses."

We shook hands.

"Don't get up, Mark, I'll see myself out."

I met a dishy young blonde in a tracksuit coming up the path.

"Hi, you must be Rob. How's grumpy?"

"Okay," I said. I assumed she meant Mark.

"Probably done him good to talk shop. He's been feeling so sorry for himself ever since the accident. I'll be glad when he can get round a bit more."

"Rugby injury, I gather."

"Well that's what he'd like everyone to think. Actually fell awkwardly in the car park after the game, pissed as a newt. Don't tell him I told you." She gave me a conspiratorial wink.

I couldn't imagine being grumpy with her to keep me company. Still, a leg in plaster must cramp one's style a bit.

Jake, while not exactly grumpy, was far more subdued than usual when I met up with my housemates in a riverside café.

"What's up? Lost a pound and found a penny?"

"He's embarrassed?" Sunny giggled.

"That I don't believe!"

"It's true." Dan too was enjoying himself at Jake's expense.

Jake munched on a Bath bun. Whatever he'd done he knew his warning glare wouldn't stop the deed being described to maximum effect.

"Well?"

"We found a boating lake," Sunny said.

"Like, a lagoon or tributary, you know," Dan continued. "Only twenty pence an hour, which we were persuaded by you-know-who was unbelievable value."

"They took it in turns to row me," Sunny added.

I visualised several possible scenarios, mostly on the theme of being upstream without a paddle, but I wasn't even close.

"Anyway," said Dan, "we'd been out nearly half an hour when Jake's third pint started working its way through."

"Busting for a pee, I was," Jake grunted.

"Well, what could we do? Nowhere to get ashore, he couldn't stand up for fear of capsizing, and with Sunny on board …"

"So what did you do, Jake?"

He wouldn't say, just rested his chin on his hands.

"I lent him the Sunday supplement," said Sunny.

"Which he rolled up to cover his whatnot, and aimed over the side of the boat."

"What, standing?"

"No, no, sort of kneeling on the seat while we leant to the other side to balance."

"That doesn't sound embarrassing."

"No, but just as Captain Codpiece started bailing out his bladder the boat drifted past a clearing full of a group of birdwatchers with their binoculars and cameras. Christ, I nearly wet myself!" Dan chortled.

If he'd had a fair skin, Jake's face would have been bright red. Again.

"Well, it could have been worse, Jake," I offered.

"How?"

"You saved Sunny from embarrassment."

She giggled again.

"Wonder if they'll publish photos in their magazine," Dan said. "Cock Robin?"

"Greater Spotted Dick?" I suggested.

"Can we go home now, if you comedians have finished?"

I toyed with the idea of doing a recce myself for the Hartland day since it was seven years or so since I'd last visited that stretch of coast, and at that time the attraction of ice cream at Hartland Quay had made more impression on me than the geology. As it happened, my free Sunday back at my parents' farm was seriously wet, and I opted for the cosier option of studying Mark's notes and the large-scale maps.

Setting out early on Monday morning, I found the village of Millworthy quite easily, even though I'd not been there before. It was only a couple of miles off the main road which ran alongside the River Torridge from Torrington to Bideford. Millworthy Centre was in fact the old school in the middle of the village, across the square from the pub and post office. Single storey, for the most part, with an upper storey over the main entrance, it reminded me of Abergwnwyn, though undoubtedly larger and built of local stone. A small coach which would not have looked out of place in a transport museum stood in the car park, formerly the playground. I added Jessica to the vintage display.

The main door led into a short corridor with a store room and office on one side and a stairway opposite. Beyond, another door opened into the main hall, with dining area at one end and a lounge area with armchairs and television at the other. Having arrived a good half hour earlier than the time I'd agreed with Mark, breakfast was still in the toast and marmalade phase. I got a few puzzled glances from the students before Patricia Prior caught sight of me from a table near the serving hatch.

"Good morning, Robert," she called. "Do come and join us!"

"Toast? Coffee?" she offered, once I'd weaved around the other tables.

"Thanks very much." I shook hands with her and Moira Bunn.

"Moira of course you know, but did you meet Tim when you were at Carrick?"

"Not really," I said. I'd seen him a few times behind the piano during assemblies, but never to speak to. I was surprised how short he was when he stood up to greet me, barely five foot two, and thin as a rake. The straggly beard and leather jacket I did remember.

"Pleased to meet you." Tim held out a bony hand with long thin musicians' fingers.

Patricia rapped on the tabletop with a dessert spoon, and waited briefly while the chatter died. Having gained the students' attention she rattled off a whole string of instructions, from preparing packed lunches, clearing the tables and generally getting ready for the day's excursion.

She then added, "I'd like to introduce you to Mr Robert Kiddecott, who will be helping us this week. Some of you may recognise him from when he was with us at Wilfred Roberts last autumn."

I doubted it. I'd had hardly any dealings with sixth formers then. A thought struck me.

"Pat, what's the protocol on these field trips?"

"In what way?"

"Are the students still expected to address staff as 'sir' and 'miss' or is it more informal?"

"Well, to be honest, it's a bit of a grey area. Mark was very much in favour of the informal Christian name approach on these residential visits. The students appreciated it and never took advantage of the privilege. I'm not quite so comfortable with the arrangement, but I go along with it, but it would be a brave or foolhardy youngster who'd ever dare to address our senior mistress by anything more familiar than Mrs Bunn. Isn't that right, Moira?"

"Very true!"

"So really, I suppose it's up to you. Play it by ear. If they all keep to Mr Kiddecott, no problem, but if they ask permission, you can agree without any loss of respect. I wouldn't let them just assume that they can call you Rob, however. It's possible one or two wags might test the water. Use their Christian names if you get to know them."

"What about you, Tim."

"I'd be happy for them to call me Tim," he said, in a resigned manner.

Patricia chivvied the students to get themselves moving ready for a prompt departure at nine thirty. I attempted to make myself useful, though everybody else seemed to know what they were doing. We were rattling out of the village before the scheduled time.

By mutual agreement I sat next to Pat in the front seat, with Moira across the gangway behind Tim.

"Where on earth did you acquire this old bone shaker from?" I asked Pat, as the coach transmitted and magnified every minor deformity in the road surface. Even the grottiest vehicle from Powell's Pleasure Tours would have been a luxury by comparison.

"Quiet, don't let Tim hear you," Penny cautioned. Not that there was much chance over the labouring of the engine.

"Why not?"

"The coach belongs to Tim, a remnant of his hippie days, I think. He's happy to help out on trips like these, if the school contributes towards the licence fee. It works out considerably cheaper. It may be noisy and shake up your breakfast, but it's never let us down."

Yet.

"What would you like me to do when we get to Barnstaple?" I asked.

"We'll split into four groups, with specific areas of study and meet up again at lunchtime. Any preferences?"

"I'll take the railway, if that's okay."

As I didn't know any of the students, it didn't really make much difference to me, but I anticipated that the topic would have less appeal to the fairer sex. I was a little surprised therefore when we disembarked to find my group consisted of three nubile females and a couple of timid looking lads.

For some reason Tim seemed very disappointed to be landed with a bunch of alpha males. He sidled up to me and said quietly, "Care to swap groups. Rob?"

I didn't get a chance to reply before Patricia had shepherded all but my party towards the road leading to the town centre.

"You may as well start this side of the river," she called to me. "We'll see you by the Civic Centre at midday."

Tim looked as if he'd swallowed a lemon. He gave me a grimace and hurried to catch up with the main body.

"Right, gather round," I addressed my group, hoping I sounded more confident than I felt. "We'll go first to Barnstaple's only station that is still open, then later to the old town station. You all know what to do?" The question was intended to be rhetorical and thankfully nobody asked for clarification.

We'd hardly set out over the car park to walk the short distance to the station when two of the girls took position either side of me.

"May we call you Rob, Mr Kiddecott?" This from a brunette with a wonderfully clear smooth complexion and an hour-glass figure which the light anorak she was wearing did little to disguise.

"If you wish. I may take a little while to get to know your names."

"I'm Annabel. My friend's Yo."

"Yo? That's an unusual name."

Her companion giggled and blushed. She was also quite attractive, taller and slimmer than Annabel, long red hair and freckled around the nose and upper cheeks.

"Short for Yolande," said Annabel. "Were you really teaching at Carrick last term? I'm sure we would have remembered you, wouldn't we, Yo?"

Yo giggled again and nodded her head vigorously.

"I was there on my final teaching practice, Chemistry mostly."

Annabel screwed up her nose. "Ugh, with old Arsen ... sorry, Mr Ramsbottom?"

I ignored her minor indiscretion. "Correct. I also took some of Mr

Matthews' geography lessons. Not with the sixth form though."

"So you're not really a proper teacher?"

"I haven't received my degree yet, if that's what you mean, but as far as you are concerned, yes, I am. I'm covering Mr Matthews' commitments whilst he's off sick."

Annabel stayed quiet for a few moments, weighing up, no doubt, how forward she could afford to be.

"Are you married?"

We'd now arrived at the station so I didn't reply, but set them about their tasks. I resolved to keep Annabel strictly at arm's length during the week. The last thing I wanted was another Rosetta incident.

As it happened, I received no untoward direct attention from her or from her friend for the rest of the morning, though on a couple of occasions I noticed the pair of them chatting and glancing in my direction with a cheeky smile. The programme for the afternoon, however, gave little opportunity for further interaction since, when we split at all, in Bideford, it was only into two groups. At Fremington Quay, Appledore and Westward Ho we stayed en masse.

Tim and I had been allocated the only staff bedroom in use on the first floor over the entrance area. The advantage in being furthest from any night time noise the students might make was countered by the fact that we had to go downstairs for toilet facilities.

Not surprisingly, Moira and Patricia were located in the second staff room, adjacent to the girls' dormitory. It did, I believe, have en-suite facilities.

It wasn't until after supper though, that I had a chance to retrieve my kitbag from Jessica's boot and haul it upstairs. Even so, unpacking had to wait until we'd finished the evening seminar, reviewing the day's activity, in which I was obliged to waffle in length about the axe of Dr Beeching in North Devon, aided by reference to large-scale Ordnance Survey maps where the former extent of the rail network could clearly be seen.

I'd got as far as laying out my change of underwear on the bed when someone knocked gently on the door.

"Come in!" I called in reflex reaction and looked up.

Annabel stood in the doorway, looking even more surprised than I was.

"Oh, I'm sorry … I was looking for Tim, er … Mr Pintwhistle."

"He popped out for a few minutes, to see to the bus, I think. Can I help?"

"Er, no … not really." She stood there undecided. "I … er … had a bit of a headache and I wondered if … if he could give me something for it."

"If you need an aspirin I think you'd be better asking Mrs Bunn."

"Yes … yes, you're right." She backed out of the door. "Sorry!"

I'd pretty well got the rest of my stuff sorted when Tim returned.

"Young girl called Annabel came looking for you."

"Oh … oh really?" He didn't seem too surprised despite an attempt to sound casual.

"Got a headache, she said, so I sent her to find Moira."

"Oh, right."

"Fancy a quick jar at the pub? I don't think we'll be missed for a while."

"Well, I … um…"

"No rules about staff abstinence after the day's work is over, is there?" I couldn't really imagine Mark on the wagon for a week.

Tim thought for a moment. "Not that I know of. Okay, why not?"

The Wagon and Horses was one of those idyllic rural hostelries, with ivy-covered stone walls under a thatched roof. The board outside advertised good wholesome food, beer from the wood and accommodation.

As we reached the wicker gate which opened into the small beer garden in front of the pub, three youths came out of the door and lurched unsteadily along the path. Seeing us, their leader, a strapping big lad with a pug nose and close cut hair, held the gate ajar, belched and exaggerated a bow.

"Half-pint for you, sir?" His cronies laughed at his mocking tone.

Tim muttered something and, head down, stepped briskly towards the pub door. I started to follow, then changed my mind.

"Wait a minute!"

They stopped and turned back at the unexpected challenge.

"Have you been drinking?"

"What's it to you …Rob?" Pug Nose sneered.

"Mr Kiddecott, to you! Now, please answer my question!"

The other pair seemed uncertain how to respond, but not so Pug Nose, confidence fuelled no doubt by alcohol.

"Yes, Mister Kiddecott, we have been drinking. Lemonade, if you must know." He belched again and turned to his friends, "Isn't that right?" They grinned inanely.

"Laced with vodka? Your breath smells like a brewery! Didn't the landlord ask your age?"

"Not really."

"Explain yourself!"

"He asked if my friends were as old as me. I told him they were." He smirked. "Didn't lie, you see!"

I'd had enough of his attitude. "Okay, smartass, get yourself back to the hostel right now, and don't think about coming to this pub again. I'll make sure that the landlord and his staff know you're under age!"

"You can go and …"

"I suggest you shut your big mouth now! Unless, of course you want me to report this incident to Mrs Bunn. You know darn well she'll send you straight back to Carrick!"

I didn't know whether she would but it was enough for the youths to believe it.

"C'mon, Gary, leave it be!"

Gary Pugnose started to argue, but thought better of it and slamming the gate, stalked off across the village square.

Tim had already got a couple of pints in and was sitting hunched up in an alcove by the window.

"You didn't need to make an issue of it," he said.

"Sorry, Tim, but I'm not prepared to ignore loutish behaviour. Besides which, they were drinking illegally."

"Nasty piece of works, that Gary. Believe me, he'll try to get his own back."

"You're not scared of him are you?" Looking at Tim's face I knew the answer before he replied.

"Bane of my life, ever since I came to the school. I'm sure he's the one who coined my Half-Pint nickname."

In other circumstances I might have found the alias amusing.

"How long have you been at Wilfred Roberts?"

"This is my fourth year"

"Your first appointment?"

"Good Lord, no. I was in Manchester for three years before that. Not a happy experience."

I could imagine, if he was having problems in a quiet backwater like Carrick. Tim was obviously a few years older than I'd thought.

"Another pint?"

"Thanks, Rob, but I think we'd better get back before Mother Hen starts clucking."

Heavy overnight rain had given way to clear sunny skies, with a freshness in the air ideally suited to the coastal studies to be undertaken.

Mark's notes had recommended leaving the coach on the main road and walking down to the hamlet of Buck's Mill, our first stop. I was surprised, therefore, when Tim pulled to the centre of the road to turn right, waiting for the oncoming traffic to clear.

"Tim, we need to park up here. It's not suitable for a coach in the village."

"There's no restriction sign, is there?"

"But…"

Tim took advantage of a gap in the traffic and swung the vehicle over. "See, no problem," he said, as the coach trundled down the narrow, winding road, which did, however, just leave enough room to avoid brushing both hedgerows.

A little further on Tim said, "Car park, too," then, as we got nearer, he saw the problem.

There was no way the coach would make the sharp right-angled turn into the car park, even if the horizontal bar had not imposed a six-foot height restriction. Other than reversing half a mile or so, Tim had no option but to carry on. Though the road widened, the village centre, such as it was, offered no obvious turning place for such a large vehicle, and a few parked cars further restricted the opportunity to manoeuvre.

Elbows on the steering wheel, Tim rested his chin in his hands and considered his limited options.

"Look, Pat, why don't you and Moira take the group down to the beach and I'll help Tim get the bus turned round. I'm sure we can get someone to move a car."

"That makes good sense, Rob."

"You might have to walk back to the main road," Tim warned. "Even if I can turn it round, I don't think I can leave the coach here."

"Well, at least we didn't have to walk down as well," said Moira.

After the party had set off down the track past the village shop Tim climbed out of the driver's seat to assess the situation.

"I'll ask in the shop. They may know who the cars belong to," I said.

"Okay, but I think I can make it if I can squeeze back into that driveway."

Our arrival had already attracted the attention of the shopkeeper, but at first he seemed unable or, more likely, unwilling to identify the car owners. Until it became obvious that Tim wasn't going to make it; the coach was sideways on across the road, the back inches from a newish Datsun estate, and the front blocked by a Land Rover.

"The estate belongs to Miss Childs but she's not at home. The Colonel owns the … Oh dear, that's him now!"

A man, probably in his early sixties, came storming out of the house opposite.

"Thanks," I said to the shopkeeper, and hurried out to give Tim support. The colonel was already waving his stick at Tim, demanding that he get out. He caught sight of me and redirected his attention with renewed vigour, his white moustache quivering.

"What the blazes do you think you are doing?"

"Trying to turn the coach round, as you can see. Would you be kind enough to move your Land Rover for a minute?" I said, politely.

"Yes I bloody well would mind! You've no right to bring that thing down here!"

"There's no sign at the top prohibiting access by coaches."

"Any fool knows you can't bring a coach down here!"

"Local people perhaps. We're not."

"I'll have you know I'm the Chairman of the Parish Council. I'm telling you that you can't bring a coach down here!"

"Perhaps you should be telling the Highways Authority instead and ask them to put up a sign to that effect."

"Damn your impudence young man! I've a good mind to call the police."

"I'd be delighted for you to do so, sir. We are here quite legally, as far as I can see. I'll ask them to remove your vehicle for causing an obstruction, since you are parked on a public highway and are refusing to agree to a reasonable request. Unless, of course, you'd prefer we leave the coach here straddling the road."

If I'd been serving in the ranks I would probably have been shot for insubordination. The Colonel went red in the face, opened his mouth to speak but seemed lost for words. He stumped round to the rear of the coach and scribbled something down on the back of an old envelope he'd fished out of his jacket. He glared at me, then tapped on Tim's side window with his cane.

"I'll be reporting you to your superiors!" he barked, then muttering loudly about bloody hippies and beatniks, he climbed into his Land Rover and pulled away up the road.

Tim revved, releasing a huge malodorous black cloud of diesel smoke, and edged forward to complete the turn. I trotted after the coach and gave the Colonel a friendly wave as I climbed on board.

"Thanks for that, Rob."

"No problem."

"And apologies. Mark was right, we should have parked at the top."

"He will report you, you know."

"To the school?" Tim sounded worried. "You didn't tell him the name of our school?"

"No way! He jotted down something from the back of the bus. Not the registration number."

"He did?" Puzzled for a moment, Tim suddenly started chuckling. "The old phone number! He won't get far with that! The coach company went out of business long before I bought this bus."

We chugged up to the main road, squeezing into the hedge on one occasion to allow a carpet company delivery lorry to edge by. I wondered what kind of greeting he'd get.

I'd guessed that Pat and Moira would spend half an hour or so around the old lime kilns at the edge of the beach, and it was certainly getting on for midday before the first students appeared.

"Hi there!" I said. "What have you done with Mrs Prior and Mrs Bunn?"

"Oh, they're probably still pacifying some pompous old git who was ranting on about undesirables invading the village."

Tim adhered precisely to the directions Mark had given me to our next destination, an isolated car park near to Hartland Point. Despite its remote location, there were several vehicles already there, and an elderly couple enjoying a picnic. They didn't look too happy when the coach disgorged our party of youths, but we soon left them in peace again as we headed off, not towards the lighthouse which was the usual focus for walkers, but over to the next cove.

On the seaward side of a grassy meadow where a few sheep were grazing, the path descended steeply. Still muddy from the recent rain, great care was needed in picking our way down, single file. I was startled therefore when someone tried to barge past me and I instinctively barged back, managing to steady myself with a hand to the ground above me. My assailant was less fortunate; staggering onto the field, he slipped onto his backside, and, with gathering momentum, slid out of control over the wet grass. We all momentarily froze, open mouthed, for despite his yells, there was nothing we could do to arrest his free-style tobogganing, as he disappeared from view over the convex slope.

Pat and I hurried down as quickly as we could, and when we could see the bottom of the field, there was no sign of him, fuelling our worst fears that he could have plunged over a cliff. Except that the lower boundary of the field was marked by a stone wall and an extensive brown morass stretching almost to the stile in one corner.

A filthy, chocolate-coloured apparition rose from the mire, spitting mud and foul language in equal measure. He didn't appreciate being the object of mirth for his peers.

"You f... well pushed me!" he pointed a grimy hand at me.

"That's enough of the swearing," Pat remonstrated, showing little sympathy.

"But Miss, he pushed me over!"

Moira was even less charitable, "Nonsense, Gary! Don't be a big cry-baby. I saw exactly what happened. You tried to push past Mr Kiddecott. No one else to blame for your own stupidity!"

I don't usually put the boot in when a man's down, but with Gary I couldn't resist, "Making a habit of getting plastered aren't you?" I said quietly, as he dripped sullenly past me.

Moira hadn't finished with him. "Now get yourself cleaned up as best you can while we get on with our work. There's no way you're getting back on the coach looking like the beast from the swamp."

"But Miss, I haven't got a towel and my clothes are soaking …"

"You'll just have to drip dry, won't you? Rinse your jeans and jacket in the sea."

Moira thought for a moment. "Has anyone got any spare clothes they could lend him?"

There was no rush of volunteers. After a long pause, a tall raven haired girl spoke up, "I've got a spare jumper you can borrow, Gary."

"Thanks, Ellie."

"Only thing, it's bright pink."

Which would have matched the hue of Gary's face beneath the mud.

By the time we'd finished exploring the rock formations and were ready to return, Gary was clean and fairly dry, even if his top clothes were still damp. His cronies did their best to form a body shield in the now busier car park. Only the hairy legs below the thigh-length jumper exposed the cross-dressing.

"I'm not getting out of the coach like this, Miss!" Gary protested when, some twenty minutes or so later, we arrived at Hartland Quay, our last stop for the day.

"Well you'll have to put your jeans back on, won't you." Moira gave him no leeway. "You're not staying in the coach."

Gary muttered and grumbled but complied. I even felt a little sorry for him. Only a little. I suppose I was thankful we hadn't had to scrape him off the rocks.

With the tide almost at low ebb, the contortions in the rock strata around the bay were truly spectacular, and gave me the opportunity to prattle on at length about folding, faulting and tectonics in general. We'd brought a few hard hats, but not enough to go round, so close contact at the cliff face with hammers, clinometers and such like was restricted to small groups at a time, while the others made sketches. The bay formed a natural sun-trap, enhancing the warmth of the spring afternoon, and we'd all shed a layer well before we climbed back up to the Hotel on the

Quay, where ice-creams all round seemed an appropriate way to conclude the day's field work. I noticed Gary handing over a soggy banknote in exchange for cornets for Ellie and his bodyguards.

I was looking forward to a day out on Dartmoor, but the weather forecast on Wednesday evening cast doubts on the practicalities. After supper and the usual seminar to review the day's activities, Pat and I spent some time going over alternative programmes, deferring a final decision until the following morning.

From the moment I drew back the curtains, I knew Dartmoor was a non-starter. Even at this lower altitude the visibility in the heavy drizzle blanketed out the view across the Torridge valley, and I didn't fancy us being the focus for a Dartmoor search and rescue. I knew from experience how easy it was to get disorientated in the swirling moorland mists, and no-one would get lost in Torrington.

I'd been surprised that Mark's research on Torrington had produced a range of study topics that would certainly keep us busy. Even though the town was only a short drive from my parent's home, almost on my doorstep, so to speak, I'd not been aware that there had once been a large leper colony nearby at Taddiport, nor of the town's significance as a Royalist stronghold during the civil war. Not much remained of the castle, but one could certainly imagine it in an imposing position, high above the river Torridge.

Rather than moving round all together like a flock of sheep, we divided the students into three groups. Tim dropped most of us off on the main road opposite the church then drove the small railway party that I'd escorted on Monday back to the outskirts of the town to explore a section of the abandoned line than stretched from Barnstaple via Bideford and Torrington deep into the Devon countryside. As Moira and I headed off in the rain with the others down the steep footpath to the river I envied those who were staying in the town with Pat, where they would be able to undertake work under cover if they had a bit of common sense.

Both Pat and I arrived with our groups at the rendezvous in the main car park near the town centre before the agreed time of 2 p.m., and quickly decided that, rather than stand around in the now persistent rain, we could take shelter under the canopy of the town hall, leaving one volunteer on the corner of the square to look out for Tim's coach. There was no way he could get to the car park unobserved.

We waited. We relieved the observer, and waited longer.

"Where the devil has he got to?" said Pat, in frustration. "I've booked us all into a tour of Dartington Glass Factory at three o'clock."

Twenty minutes to spare.

"He can't have got lost, could he, Rob?" asked Moira.

"I wouldn't have thought it possible. He was only going less than a mile away."

"Could he be waiting elsewhere?" Pat suggested.

"Well, he was given pretty clear instructions."

"But are there any other public car parks? He may have made a mistake."

I considered the possibility. "Oh hell, he could have pulled into one off the main road, near where he set us down. Or even, I suppose, up on the common." I thought for a moment. "Look, you go on ahead to the Glassworks, you know where it is. I'll try to track him down. Probably best if you leave a reliable runner here for a few minutes just in case he's still trying to find a way in."

Bloody Tim! No sign of him at the first possible location, which meant jogging on half a mile to the common at the western edge of the town.

I heard it before I saw it. Tim still had the engine running, parked opposite the public toilets.

"Hi Rob," he greeted me nonchalantly. "Thought you'd all be here long ago. We've only just arrived. 'Fraid our walk took longer than expected."

"We've been waiting for nearly three-quarters of an hour! In the town centre car park where we agreed."

"Not here, you mean?"

"Definitely not here!" I cast my hand around. "Does it look like the blessed town centre?"

"Oh! Sorry!"

"Look, we're due at the Glass Factory in five minutes, so can you get this old crate moving!" I was wet and cold and annoyed at Tim's apparent lack of awareness. That's artistic types for you!

Tim looked a little put out at my description of his beloved vehicle, but shoved it into gear and pulled out.

We made it with a minute or two to spare.

I felt considerably more charitable, however, not to mention warm and dry by the end of the factory tour. Pat had certainly made a wise choice for the final venue for the day.

"Mark would usually organise some kind of entertainment on the last night," said Pat, rather wistfully, as the two of us sat with a mug of coffee after conducting the evening seminar.

"What sort of thing?" He hadn't mentioned anything to me.

"Oh, you know, talent contest, d-i-y disco or such like. That young Annabel, for example, she's got a beautiful voice. Always stars in the school musical each spring."

"Pity I didn't know, I could have brought my guitar."

"What do you play?"

"Not much really. I strum along to a few folk songs." Which made me think of our Bob Dylan lookalike. "What about getting Tim to lead a singaround on the piano?" I nodded towards the old upright instrument opposite the television.

"It's a thought. He's quite shy, though."

"I'll give him some support." I thought I could rattle up the spoons again, perhaps warble the odd song. I wasn't going to see this lot again so I could probably afford to make a fool of myself. "I'll go and put it to him."

Few people remained in the dining room. Many students had gone to their rooms to do some packing ready for the early start next morning.

Tim, however, wasn't in our room. I gathered up a bag of my clutter to take out to Jessica. Outside it was still damp, the odd street light across the square glimmering in a hazy halo of mist. Not the sort of weather that Jessica enjoyed, and I hoped she'd start tomorrow morning without having to dry out the leads. As I stowed my bag in the boot, I felt sure the coach next to me rocked. I stood quietly. I could just catch the sound of murmuring voices from inside the vehicle, and the suspension was clearly being tested.

I was considering whether it was any of my business to investigate when a sharp cry from a girl's voice made up my mind for me. I assumed that a couple of the students had found the coach unlocked and were up to a bit of hanky-panky that might be getting out of hand. I hurried back to the dining room.

"Pat, would you mind coming outside for a moment? I think we may have a problem."

"What's up, Rob?"

I led her across the tarmac to the coach. "Listen!"

The old coach was rocking. The odd grunts and short squeals were definitely human, not mechanical.

Pat looked at me and grimaced, "Fetch Moira, will you?" Pat hammered on the door of the coach. The rocking and voices stopped. Pat thumped again, "Come out of there at once, both of you!"

As Moira strode over, myself following, the coach door opened, and a girl peered out. Annabel's clothing was in disarray, the blouse only partly buttoned up, and she was desperately trying to smooth down her skirt.

"Oh, bloody hell!" She brought her spare hand to her face.

"Annabel Lewis! Come here!" Moira commanded. "And your boyfriend too," she called through the open door.

A few moments passed. Tim appeared, dishevelled and head down in his beard.

Moira and Pat looked at each other in disbelief.

"We love each other, Miss," Annabel was the first to regain her composure, "We're going…"

"Be quiet!" Moira snapped. "I'll deal with you later!"

"We've done nothing wrong!" said Annabel truculently. "I'm sixteen and I can do…"

"Young lady, that is not the point!" Moira pointed to the hostel. "Now, go back to your room. Immediately!"

Annabel tossed her head and flounced off, muttering about her rights.

Tim still hadn't spoken. He stood leaning against the coach.

"Well, Tim, this is a difficult situation you've got into," Moira said, more calmly. "What on earth were you thinking of?"

"What are you going to do?" Tim said nervously.

"I really don't know at the moment. I can't believe this is happening."

"How long has this been going on, Tim?" Pat asked.

"About two months – ever since the musical. But this is the first time we've ever … ever …"

Moira came to a decision. "Tim, would you please go with Rob, and it would be best if you stay in your room for a while. Don't try to speak to Annabel before I've seen her again. Pat and I need to think this through carefully."

I waited while Tim locked up the coach. I didn't know quite what to say to him and he stayed silent as we walked back to the hostel. When we got to our room, he slumped on the bed, head in hands and broke down.

"Oh Rob … what am I going to do? …Oh shit! … what will happen to Annabel? … I'll lose my job, won't I? … My wife … when she finds out …"

"You're married?" I was really surprised.

"Yeah. Sort of."

"What do you mean?"

"She walked out on me just after Christmas. Went to her bloody mother's and never came back."

"Kids?"

"No, thank God! But she'll go ballistic if she finds I've been seeing another student."

"So Annabel's not the first?" I felt like a priest taking confession.

"Rob! You won't say anything to Moira will you? Or to Annabel?"

"Not to Annabel. I'm not sure whether I ought to keep it from Moira."

"It wasn't at Carrick. Just a harmless fling at my previous school. Nothing serious you know."

"And this one is?"

"I thought so. Silly, really. We'd even started talking about setting up home together when she left school. She's very attractive."

"I had noticed. Quite a flirt, I imagine. I even thought she was trying it on with me the other day in Barnstaple."

"You don't mean that?" Tim looked up sharply.

I shrugged. "I don't know."

Tim polished his glasses with his shirt cuff. "What do you think Moira will do?"

"I don't know that either. You probably know her better than I do."

"Uh huh." He put his head in his hands again.

"One thing, Tim. I do wonder whether you should look at some job other than teaching. You already admit that some of the kids make life difficult for you, and if you're inclined to get romantically involved with the girls ..."

"Yeah, I suppose you're right." He lapsed into a contemplative silence.

Sometime later – probably half an hour or more – there came a knock on the door, and Pat called softly, "Tim?"

"Come in," I called.

"Tim, Moira would like you to join us downstairs. You too, Rob."

"Are you sure you want me there as well?" I asked.

"We think so."

Moira had sequestered a table for us at one end of the dining room, well out of earshot of the few students that were watching television at the other end. She began her judgement, bluntly.

"Tim, I find it incredible you have been so stupid and unprofessional. I have talked at some length with Annabel. Quite a feisty young madam, that one. She obviously has some strong feelings for you, and was fully prepared to accept all the blame for leading you on."

"But..."

"Hear me out, Tim. I don't believe for one moment that all the encouragement came from her. Now, technically, I suppose, you haven't committed any offence that would need to involve the police, since she has turned sixteen."

Tim blanched at the mention of the law.

"But you realise," Moira continued, "that your position at Wilfred

Roberts is untenable. If you hand in your resignation to the Headmaster as soon as we return to Carrick then I shall not inform him of this evening's events. I don't think Annabel wants the affair brought under the spotlight, and I have her assurance that she will keep her silence."

Tim couldn't believe that Moira was effectively going to brush the whole affair under the carpet. "You mean you're not going to tell the Head about this?"

"Not if we can avoid the inevitable scandal and media spotlight. It might be better as well if you can make up some plausible excuse for immediate leave of absence. The longer you and Annabel are working in the same establishment the greater the likelihood that something of this episode will get into the public domain. That's certainly not going to help you, and it could put me in an awkward situation too."

"I don't really have any choice, do I, Moira?"

"In my view, no. Whatever you and Annabel may decide to do about your relationship is up to you to sort out, but I would suggest that you both keep a very discreet, low profile over the next few months if you continue to live in Carrick. Do not, under any circumstances, make contact with her at school, do you understand?"

"Yeah, I suppose so," Tim sighed. "I'm sorry."

Moira turned to me. "I've asked you to be here so that you are fully aware of the situation. I hope we can rely on your discretion, particularly if you should have any further dealings with Wilfred Roberts School. We have really appreciated your contribution this week."

"Thank you. And thank you for your trust. I can assure you that this evening's affair will remain confidential." I wasn't expecting my involvement with the school to last longer than a few more hours.

I didn't think anyone was going to be in the mood for a sing-song around the piano.

Pat and Moira assured me that unless I really wanted to follow the coach half way across Exmoor they would manage to cope with the various activities planned for the return journey. I was glad to accept the opt-out in the circumstances.

A little colour had returned to Tim's face when we returned to our room. He'd been close to tears earlier, but now all he wanted to do was to pour out his life story. I listened patiently to his catalogue of woes and misunderstandings. Until I fell asleep.

CHAPTER EIGHTEEN

Maddy

When I had first arrived at Tencastle for the start of my degree course, three years had seemed a hell of a long time. With less than three months to go before graduation, I wondered how the time had gone so quickly. More to the point, I realised that my days of relative independence were numbered, and the prospect of a life beholden to an employer loomed ever closer. I suppose it was when I found a cheque for forty quid from Mark Matthews on my return to the cottage that I realised my freshly acquired teaching skills were a marketable asset. I'd not hitherto given the matter of job searching much serious consideration. Thus, that first weekend back at the cottage found myself, and Dan too, scouring the Times Educational Supplement far more earnestly than the casual glance we'd previously given it. Jake, of course, was settled for the next year, following his elevation to president-in-waiting.

"Here's one for you," said Dan, who'd got to the paper first. "Enthusiastic young science teacher for progressive department in popular school."

"Translated into plain language that probably means the faculty head is full of half-baked ideas and the school is the only one for miles around," I replied. "Where is it, anyway?"

"Plymouth."

"I'll pass on that." I didn't like Plymouth – all brick and concrete.

"Or, here. Newly qualified teacher, science and environmental studies. Whatever that is."

"Possible. Devon?" In my mind I'd harboured the assumption that I'd just drop into a plum job within commuting distance of my parents' farm.

"No, Central London."

"Not bloody likely!" I had visions of a Friday afternoon trying to instil an appreciation of the wonders of science into inner-city no-hopers forced to stay an extra year at school. Not an environment I wanted to study first hand.

"I must say, you're being very fussy."

"I'm not that desperate, yet!" I said. "Since you've obviously found no joy for yourself in the Maths section, why don't you just pass the whole lot over so I can have a proper look."

"Okay, no need to get shirty! I did find a couple, actually, one in Worthing and another in East Sussex."

"What about you?" I said to Sunny who'd just joined us at the breakfast table. "Have you been through the jobs yet?"

"No I haven't. Not sure I'm going to."

"What do you mean?"

"I'm thinking of applying for another course."

"In Tencastle?"

"Probably not. I'm still trying to make up my mind whether to stick with teaching or go for something else."

That was a surprise. I'd thought she was quite committed to the classroom.

A scrutiny of both science and geography posts yielded bugger all. Perhaps I was being too picky. The problem of course with Devon was that, being such a pleasant place to live, people once in post tended to stay put. I resolved to wait one more week before casting my net wider.

The following week the Times Educational Supplement had grown substantially fatter as the hiring season gathered pace. Before I had a chance to study it, however, it disintegrated into a soggy mess. Jake apologised for taking the nearest thing to hand to mop up a saucepan of soup he'd tipped all over the kitchen floor. The science section had, of course, been in the front line of action. It was a fortnight, therefore, before I found anything remotely interesting.

In the meantime, Dan's applications had secured two interviews, and Sunny had opted for a post-graduate diploma in something nebulous like educational psychology. While pleased for them it did nothing to improve my growing sense of concern.

"Where's Steyning?" I asked Dan, reviewing one possible destination for my talents from the paper spread in front of me.

"It's a small market town in West Sussex, only a few miles from the coast. And it's pronounced 'Stenning' not 'Staining'."

"Whatever. Know anything about the school?"

"Not really. If I get the Worthing job, we could share a house."

"Hang on, I haven't even applied yet, let alone got the job."

"Are you going to apply?"

"Probably." Along with about half a dozen other posts scattered across the southern half of the country from Worcester to The Wash. I'd sketched out my curriculum vitae, trying to flesh it out so that it appeared less like a skeleton on hunger strike. My extra work at Carrick had certainly helped, and both Mark Matthews and Nick Ramsbottom had readily agreed to act as referees if required. I made as much play as I dared about keenness to undertake extra-curricular activities, field trips and the like, and, for what is was worth, my interest of sorts in traditional customs.

One thing Dan and I had quickly discovered was that there was no such thing as a standard application. Every local education authority seemed to operate a different system, let alone the individual schools who added their own measure of autonomy. Some were quite content with a handwrittten letter and CV, while others sent a sheaf of forms that required one to itemise everything from religious background to the colour of one's underpants. In the space of a week I reckoned I jumped through more hoops than a troupe of performing dogs at the circus. All this in addition to maintaining some momentum in preparation for the final examinations.

The mail never reached outposts like Penybont until well past the time we normally set out for college. That particular Thursday, Dan had arrived back first. Grinning like a cat that got the canary and the cream, his face told me the news.

"They've offered me the job!"

"Congratulations," I said, automatically. "Which one?" He'd been back to Sussex for the days either side of the previous weekend.

"Worthing. The Boys' High School."

"Is that the one you wanted?"

"It's the better school, though further from my parents' home than the other one. It's a newish building though, very handy for the train from Brighton. You've got some official-looking letters, too."

Like the proverbial buses, three replies together, after waiting ages for something to turn up from the eight posts for which I'd applied.

"Well?" asked Dan, hovering over me as I slit open the envelopes.

"Three interviews!" I studied the invitations in detail. "Oh, bugger! Would you believe it? Two on the same ruddy day!"

"Where?"

"Exmouth and Steyning."

"It's 'Stenning'," Dan reminded me, pedantically.

"It's a flaming nuisance!"

"One of them might be prepared to change the day, if you explain," said Dan, helpfully.

"Probably scupper my chances if a school thought I was making it my second choice."

"You don't need to tell them that you got both invites on the same day."

"I suppose not. Which one do you think I should make my priority?"

"Hell, I don't know! Depends what you're looking for."

"A job, obviously," I said sarcastically.

"Okay, don't jump down my throat. Nice area, round Steyning. Close to the night life of Worthing and Brighton, too, if you're more adventurous, and handy for the sea."

"Exmouth's actually on the coast," I pointed out.

"Well, you know it better than I. What kind of school is it?"

"Large – one of the biggest comprehensives in the country."

"Um …" Dan wasn't taken by the concept. To be truthful, I'm not sure I was either, even though it was virtually home territory.

"What about the third one?" Dan asked.

I looked again. "That's for a girls' school in Worcestershire."

Dan raised an eyebrow, "You'll not be turning that down, I bet!"

Jake arrived, sweating from the exertions of the bicycle. He tipped a whole bundle of folders out of his rucksack onto the table. "Never thought there'd be so much bumf to get my head round in being president." He saw the letters. "Good news?"

We told him. "Hey, that's great! Calls for a celebration!" He dived into the kitchen. "Where's that bottle of champagne?"

"Toasted you with it last term, remember?"

"Oh yeah. Well, drinks on me in the Union tonight!"

"I've only got interviews, not a job," I said. "It's Dan who's got his foot in the door."

"Only a matter of time! Celebrate in anticipation."

I anticipated who'd be doing the celebrating. I'd be driving. Still, it wasn't often Jake let the moths out of his wallet.

The Worcestershire job interview came first and I'd felt really confident, particularly after a pleasant early morning drive through green rolling countryside. That was, however, the only good thing about the day, apart from an unexpected glimpse of a couple of well-endowed sixth formers sunbathing topless in the school's inner quadrangle. The building was depressing, all pitted red sandstone on the outside, dark and dingy within, with laboratories that probably predated Sir Isaac Newton. I didn't take to the Head of Science who struck me as bossy and overbearing. Ugly to boot.

The interview itself had been a total farce. The Headmistress, Ms (insistently Ms!) Amelia Lovebody, was a large, buxom woman with a round, florid countenance, which competed in colour with the giant yellow and mauve floral pattern on her voluminous kafkan-style dress. She had dominated the proceedings by relating, in a rich Roedean-cultured voice and at a high decibel level, all the contents of my CV, plus a few irrelevant anecdotes, to her two companions, the Head of Science and an old bewhiskered gentleman whom I assumed was the Chairman of Governors. Both had looked totally bored but impotent to stop the verbal flow in which she had referred to me throughout in the third person as if I wasn't there. The only question, when it came, had caught me unawares, my attention having begun to wander. I'd cobbled up an unconvincing response as to what I could contribute to the school.

"Good, good!" she'd boomed. She'd turned first to the old boy. "Any more questions, Mr Hampton? Miss Rudge?" And before either had had a chance to say anything, she'd dismissed me with the promise of letting me know her decision once she had talked to the other three candidates, all female, whom I'd briefly met over lunch.

Jake and Dan were, of course, keen to know how I had fared.

"Not quite my scene," I said.

"You didn't turn it down?" Dan exclaimed.

"Didn't actually get the chance to."

"Oh, right, some other bloke got it?"

"Woman, I think."

"Figures," said Jake.

"Still you've got two more chances," said Dan.

"Yes, indeed. In fact I need to talk to you about that. I've got Steyning this Friday, and Exmouth on Monday."

"I thought they were both the same day."

"They were, but I spoke to Exmouth and it seems a second candidate also had a clash of dates, and the two others both pulled out. So they've agreed to reschedule."

"So, what's the problem?" asked Dan.

"Well, I was wondering the best way to get there, train or Jessica. I need to be in Steyning for ten o'clock. Also I don't really want to come all the way back here and then to Devon. I was thinking of going to my parents' for the weekend direct from Sussex."

"Train from here is not easy and you would certainly have to stay Thursday night. No way you'd get there for ten." Dan thought for a moment. "You be best by car, if the old girl is up to it. Tell you what, my Ma wouldn't mind putting you up Thursday, and it's only a half an hour or so from there to Steyning."

"Would she really?"

"No problem. You could stay Friday too if you didn't want to tootle on down to the West Country straight after the interview. I'll ring her now if you like."

"Thanks, Dan, I'd really appreciate that."

Mrs Chater fussed over me like a mother hen – when I eventually found her house. Even with Dan's detailed directions, I got lost in the backwaters of Brighton since someone had obviously shuffled the roads around in the week or so since he'd last been home. Six hours on the road, not counting the stop for a ploughman's in rural Wiltshire, was far longer than I'd previously been in close company with Jessica, and her springs weren't kind to my undercarriage.

"You'll be hungry, Robert, I'm sure. Would you like a cup of tea – oh, no, you'll be wanting to see your room and freshen up won't you."

"I'm fine, Mrs Chater, really, though a coffee would be welcome, if it's no trouble."

"Dorothy, please. No trouble, dear, not at all! Make yourself comfortable!" She pottered off into the kitchen leaving me flopped out in a chintzy sofa.

You could see where Dan got his brown eyes and short snub nose from. In fact, his face and build generally suggested a dominance of his mother's genes. He'd never talked about his father, who I assumed was the ramrod stiff young man in uniform with a young woman, undeniably Dan's mother, in their wedding photograph on the mantelpiece.

"Daniel's told me so much about you, well, all of his friends, you know." Mrs Chater handed me a cup of coffee. "I'm so pleased to meet you – you've been very good for him, bringing him out of his shell, you know."

I couldn't imagine Dan as ever being in a shell, but perhaps he was different at home. "Thank you, Mrs Cha ..., er, Dorothy." I took a bite of the flapjack she proffered. "Wow, these really are delicious!"

"Daniel's also told me what a beautiful place Tencastle is. I'm really looking forward to seeing for myself."

I wasn't sure I'd have described Tencastle as beautiful. Interesting and quaint, perhaps. "You'll be coming up for the graduation, I presume?"

"Yes, indeed. Daniel has invited me to stay at the house."

"Right." I could anticipate a slight logistics problem. I'd already hinted to my parents that it might be possible to stay at Ty Melin, and if Sunny and Jake had had similar ideas ...

"Of course, I shall be seeing a lot more of him when he starts work. He says he'd like to live here, at least until he finds somewhere of his own nearer the school. Another flapjack?"

I declined, though tempted.

"Perhaps you might be thinking of sharing a house again if you get a job this way as well."

"Perhaps. I've got to be offered the job first."

"Of course you have. Now, remind me where you're going tomorrow."

"Steyning. I gather it's not too far."

"Not far. You could go the back way over the Downs but you might be safer to stick to the main A27 and the main road up the Adur valley."

"Main road, definitely. I need to be sure of getting there before ten o'clock." If Sussex back roads were anything like those of Devon, tractors, cows and sheep could play havoc with one's timings.

Dorothy Chater showed me the accommodation, an under-the-eaves boxroom at the front of her thirties-style semi on a quiet residential road. "Is dinner for six alright?"

I assumed she meant time rather than diners. "Fine, whatever is best for you."

Over the excellent generous helping of shepherd's pie, Dorothy chatted almost constantly, requiring very little input from me. I got the impression she was glad to have someone to talk to.

"Have you any plans for this evening, Robert?"

"No, not really. I could go into the town I suppose."

"I'm not forcing you out, you know, you can stay in, watch television, if you like. Daniel said that you were a folksinger, is that right?"

"That's a little exaggeration, but, yes, I am interested in folk music." I wasn't sure why she had brought up the topic.

"I believe they have a folk club or something at the pub just down the road on a Friday. Daniel's been there a couple of times."

"That's interesting! Shame it's not tonight though."

"You're welcome to stay another night."

"Thanks very much, Dorothy, but I was planning to head back home straight after the interview." I paused. "I might wander down there for a quick drink anyway. What's the pub called?"

"The Springfield. You can't miss it, it's the only one on that road."

With a slight hangover even though I'd only had two pints, I borrowed a couple of aspirins from Dorothy, to rinse down with black coffee. I passed on the fry-up she was eager to cook for me, and settled for toast and marmalade and more coffee.

Jessica seemed a bit hung-over too, and wasn't keen at all to be aroused. I gave up after several unproductive swings of the starting handle and an increasing whiff of petrol, which probably meant a flooded carburettor. The Chater house was near the top of a long hill, so I reckoned a bump-start would soon bring Jessica to life.

She didn't appreciate the rude awakening, but, with coughs and splutters, settled down into her usual routine, ticking over with her familiar rattle by the time we reached the main road at the bottom of the hill. The steady stream of rush-hour traffic into the town left me no option but to nose out into the procession, unless I was prepared for a long wait.

Jessica didn't approve. She backfired, jerked forward into the busy flow, stuttered along into the roundabout a couple of hundred yards distant and stopped dead. Good, faithful Jessica, who had never let me down – well, never seriously – came to a halt next to the central island, engine lifeless, the starter raising a mere flutter of sound, in contrast to the cacophony of hooting and shouting that quickly developed in my wake. With little real hope of success I climbed out with the starter handle and tried to ignore comments which would have embarrassed the old girl. Jessica would not respond. I shrugged helplessly at the motorists snagged up behind.

One middle-aged fellow, two cars back, had the sense to realise that no amount of cursing and horn blowing would move the obstruction. Enlisting the help of another stationary motorist to hold back the traffic, which wasn't going anywhere fast, he helped me push Jessica to a forecourt on one side of the roundabout. The vehicles began to move again.

I'd left, so I thought, plenty of time to get to Steyning, but without Jessica's co-operation I was, well, stranded. As I stood contemplating her, a police car drew up alongside.

"You can't stop here, sir," the officer said, firmly.

"I don't want to stop here!" I said, a trifle sharply. "My car's broken down."

"You're blocking the fire station," he continued, unhelpfully. "You'll have to move."

"How?" I asked. "The car won't go."

He seemed at last to get the message. He stroked his chin and looked up and down the busy roads, still backed up with commuters. "There's a garage just up there. Wait here!"

As if I had a choice.

He trotted off up the road and returned a few minutes later with a mechanic in a greasy green overall.

"What's the problem?" he asked. Unnecessarily, I thought.

"My car's died."

"Right." He looked around. He spoke to the copper. "If you could just hold the traffic for a while, we'll push this young man's car along to the workshop and have a look at it. No point in bringing out the breakdown truck for the sake of a hundred yards."

Fortunately this part of the town was on the level.

The mechanic stuck his head under the bonnet and fiddled around. "I think there's a problem with the distributor," he said when he emerged.

"Can you fix it?"

"Yes, but not immediately. We'll need to do a more thorough check and get spare parts."

My face dropped.

"Where were you going?" he asked.

"I'm supposed to be in Steyning for an interview at ten o'clock."

"Well, you'll not make it in this car. It will mid-afternoon before it will be ready, assuming we find no other problems."

"What do you suggest? You haven't got a spare car I could borrow by any chance?"

"'Fraid not. Your best bet is to get a train to Shoreham and change." He looked at his watch. "You'll be hard put to make it by ten, but with luck, perhaps half past."

I wished I'd come by train anyway. "Where's the station?"

"About ten minutes walk or you can get a bus here. Won't take a jiffy."

His jiffy lasted at least fifteen minutes. I'd have probably been quicker walking, even up the steep hill. I dashed from the bus into the station, searching for the ticket office.

"Return to Steyning, please."

The clerk muttered something. 'Shorum ' was all I caught.

"When is the next train?" I asked.

"Seven minutes, platform three," he replied, without looking up.

I glanced at my watch. It was already gone nine-thirty. I pulled out the invitation to interview letter from my jacket, hoping it would have a phone number so that I could tell the school I was on my way but I'd been delayed.

Reassured by the school secretary who told me she would pass on the message, I flopped down gratefully in the compartment, its sole occupant, and tried to recover my composure for the interview.

I hadn't even thought to ask the ticket clerk how long the journey would take, how long I'd have to wait for a connection at Shoreham or even how far that place was along the line. The train, economical with its speed at best, gave me more than enough time to register the name of each fiddling little station it stopped at – there must have been four or five at least – before pulling in to the one I required.

The timetable showed many destinations, but no mention of Steyning, which, I assumed, must have been a minor halt on the way to somewhere important. With the time ticking away, I was beginning to get more than a little frustrated and desperate.

"Can I help you, sir?" This from a porter who had noticed my bewilderment.

"I'm trying to find the time of the next train to Steyning."

He gave me a strange look. "I'm afraid you've missed it, sir."

"What!"

"Last train ran years ago. The line was axed by Beeching."

"But … I was told to change at Shoreham!"

"Well, yes, this is as near as you'll get by train. You have to get a bus from here. Or a taxi."

My jaw dropped – as did my hopes of ever getting to the bloody place this side of Christmas.

"How far is it?"

"Oh, only about five miles. There is a bus goes by the station or more frequently from the High Street – that's just down past the shops and church until you come to the footbridge."

"Thanks," I said grimly. I made my way quickly out of the station to see a bus disappearing over the level crossing." I ignored the taxi waiting for custom at the rank, uncertain whether the school would meet the extra travel expense. If the bus service was actually frequent, I reckoned I still might make it to my destination by eleven o'clock.

The porter's directions were, thankfully, easy to follow, and the High Street was only about three minutes' brisk walk. No buses were in sight, but at least none were accelerating away from me.

"Excuse me, could you tell me what time the next bus to Steyning is due?" I asked of a couple of elderly ladies waiting at the bus stop.

One of them peered along the road, and the other replied "Very soon, young man, it should be here any minute."

Her last words were almost drowned out by the siren of a police car which sped past with blue lights flashing. Vehicles in the busy street pulled over to let it by. As I turned back from watching it disappear, a green double decker pulled in.

"Return to Steyning, please."

"High Street?"

"Um, I'm not sure. The nearest stop to the school."

"The grammar school?"

"Yes, that's right."

"Upper or lower?"

The other passengers waiting to board weren't happy with the game of twenty questions. It hadn't dawned on me that it might be a split site.

"Are they far apart?" I fished in my pocket again for the invitation letter.

"More than you'd want to walk if it was raining."

The weather was fine, but I was in a hurry. "Shooting Fields is the address I've got."

"That's on the far side of town. Return, you said?"

"Yes please."

Inquisition over, I settled down in a vacant seat for what I hoped would be a reasonably short journey. Leaving the high street, which I noticed featured several interesting looking pubs – to explore on another occasion, perhaps, if I got the job – the bus headed out of the shopping area, along by a river. And stopped.

The traffic queued up in front for as far as I could see – or as far as the flashing blue lights visible in the distance. Nothing came in the other direction, apart from two or three cars which had pulled out of line and executed a three point turn. The driver of one of them stopped and spoke to the bus driver, who then just rested his head on his hands in resignation.

I wondered what I'd done to so upset the Almighty, beyond my usual apathy to religious matters. The imprecations I now muttered under my breath to God and Jesus Christ weren't likely to be in the book of Common Prayer. Steyning could have been on the other side of the moon for all the chance I had of getting there before the end of term.

Trying to think positive, I went up and asked the driver how long we might be delayed.

"Multiple collision on the junction ahead at Old Shoreham. Debris everywhere, I'm told, and probable fatalities. Nothing can get in or out of Shoreham this way. The road could be blocked for hours." He let out a long breath. "Sorry"

"Not your fault. Is there any other way I can get to Steyning? I'm already late for an interview."

"Not easily. You'd have to go to Worthing and get a bus from there."

There didn't seem much point in staying on the bus going nowhere. I started walking the few hundred yards back to the High Street. Several other passengers followed my lead.

I hadn't a clue how long a detour via Worthing would take, but I doubted I'd now arrive before lunch. I popped into a newsagents to get some change for the phone.

"Just a moment," the school receptionist interrupted, after I had introduced myself and had started to explain my predicament. "I'm putting you through to the Headmaster."

"Mr. Kiddecott," the deep voice began pleasantly enough, "I understand you are not able to join us."

"Yes sir, I …"

"I am not really interested in hearing your excuses. I attach great importance to punctuality, and I was not at all impressed to hear of your earlier call. We have several excellent candidates who have met their obligations to arrive on time, and I do not believe we need to look further."

"I am truly sorry but …"

"If you were really interested in this job you should have made arrangements to stay locally than be beholden to the vagaries of public transport."

Pompous fart. Brighton was hardly Timbuctoo. "I really think …"

"Good day, Mr Kiddecott!" He didn't give me chance to air my thoughts. Probably just as well, since I would have very likely told him where he could stick his precious school.

Angry and frustrated, I just stood there, breathing heavily and staring at the handset, now burring away gently in my grip. Until a constant tapping on the kiosk glass cut into my trance. Some old boy waved his walking stick at me.

"About time, too, young fellow!" he growled.

"Sorry – I had a little problem."

"Trouble with your generation. Always causing problems." He made a show of taking a huge great watch out of his waistcoat and grumbled on, "No consideration for your elders! I always make a call at eleven o'clock precisely – and it's now six minutes past!"

"Be my guest, grandpa!" You'd have thought the silly old goat owned the bloody phone box.

Indecision and worry soon replaced the anger, though not the frustration. I was stuck in a strange town, with uncertainty over Jessica's reliability, a repair bill and a ruined job prospect, not that I really cared a rat's arse about the latter, the way I'd been summarily cast aside.

I needed a drink. And I was hungry.

The plump middle-aged woman behind the bar of the curiously named Marlipins was one of those naturally cheerful chatty types, and though I wasn't in the mood for socialising it would have been rude to ignore her, particularly as I was the only customer in the pub, so soon after opening time. She bustled around wiping the tables which already looked well polished, and gave me barely five minutes uninterrupted with my beer.

"Up here on business, love?"

In my best suit I could have passed for a salesman or executive I suppose. "No, I came for an interview."

"I hope you were successful."

"I'm afraid it didn't work out. Mutual unsuitability."

"I'm sorry to hear that. Have you got anything else in the pipeline?"

"Another interview in Devon on Monday?"

"Devon, really? What a coincidence!"

"It is?"

"'Scuse me a moment, love. Your food's ready." She disappeared into the kitchen behind the bar. I caught a glimpse of a pretty young girl with auburn hair.

"There you are, love." She returned with a plate of ham sandwiches and a bowl of soup.

"Thank you. You were saying about Devon."

"Indeed. My daughter was supposed to be going to Exeter tomorrow. She's been offered a provisional place at the University and wanted to have a look round. See if she liked the place before committing, you know."

"So isn't she going after all?"

"Oh I don't know. Seems there's some problem with the trains, and she's not sure whether she'll get there – or get back again."

I knew the feeling. God, I hoped Jessica had recovered. I'd had enough of travel disruption in the last few hours.

On an impulse I said, "I might be able to help." The idea of six hours in pleasant female company certainly had appeal. "I had a little problem with my car today but, assuming it's been sorted, I shall be driving down through Exeter tomorrow. Your daughter would be welcome to a lift."

The landlady blinked, and thought about it, a brief furrowed brow as she probably tried to weigh up whether I was a sex fiend or upright citizen.

She decided I was respectable. "Yes, well … that would be helpful, of course. And very kind of you to offer. What time would you be leaving?"

"I'm staying in Brighton." At least I supposed I was. I'd have to get it touch with Mrs Chater again. "I need to check that my car will be ready." Another phone call. "But all being well I'd like to set out after breakfast, about nine o'clock."

"So about nine-thirty here?"

"I guess so. I'll have to ring to let you know that I have transport."

"You can ring the garage from here, if you like."

"Thanks very much." I rummaged and found the card the mechanic had given me and made the call. I was enormously relieved by the response.

"Everything's fine," I said. "The car will be ready for me to collect later this afternoon."

"I'm sure my daughter will be delighted. Just knock on the pub door."

"What's her name?" I was surprised she didn't ask her there and then to come out and give her approval to her chauffeur.

"Madelaine. Would you like another beer? Have one on me and I'm not going to charge for the food." She thought a moment. "I'm going to have to trust you to turn up, aren't I?"

I accepted, just to be sociable, of course.

I took the landlady's advice on how to kill a couple of hours in Shoreham before I could collect Jessica. After phoning Dan's mother to check I was okay for a second night, I strolled over the footbridge and down to the beach, where, at high tide, the onshore breeze drove waves crashing down on the shingle. I wandered along to a busy road, beyond which light aircraft were landing at a small aerodrome, then returned over a girder-like bridge into the High Street, and back to the station. Quite a busy town, but, apart from Woolworth's, most shops seemed to be small independent businesses.

I suppose I should have learnt from my experience the previous night at The Springfield but I'm afraid I'd yielded to temptation. The pints of ale had slipped down very easily, partly to drown my sorrows but mostly due to the friendly reception from the local folkies, who had welcomed me like a long lost brother, even though I didn't know any of them from Adam. I'd been persuaded to do a couple of songs during the advertised 'Come All Ye' session at which any singer from the floor – and there were quite a few, all far more accomplished than I – could put their name down to perform. I hadn't needed to worry about driving home, either, since the pub was only a couple of minutes walk from the Chater home.

Before I set out on Saturday morning, having further depleted Dorothy's reserves of aspirin, I'd had a look at the map, primarily to check my route to Devon, but also to see whether there was an alternative route to Shoreham, wary of chancing fate a second time at the roundabout. There were only two viable options, both through urban Brighton, other than a long detour on a minor road through quaintly named Fulking – with 'Shorum' and 'Stenning' I did wonder about its local pronunciation.

I took the coast road, through the gentile suburb of Hove and past the commercial port of Shoreham. Jessica positively purred along, like a mischievous mog making amends to its owner. As it happened the bill had been nowhere near as much as I had feared, and the mechanic had also done an oil change and checked the brakes.

Yesterday's debacle behind me, I was feeling quite bright and breezy when I pulled up opposite the Marlipins.

I waited a couple of minutes for someone to respond to my knocking, surveying the early morning bustle of the High Street. I turned as the door opened to face not the gorgeous brunette but a tall gangly blonde girl with buck teeth and glasses. She took in briefly the fellow standing there in jeans and T-shirt then glanced over my shoulder at the cars parked nearby. She probably didn't spot the disappointment in my face.

"Madelaine?" I asked, tentatively. "I'm …" I paused. I wasn't sure I'd even given my name. "I'm Robert … Robert Kiddecott."

She looked at me. "Yes, I'm Maddy. Er, where's your car?"

"Over there. The old Ford."

"Oh!" Her turn to be disappointed. "But Ma said you were an executive, or something!"

Presumably she was expecting a ride in a Jag or a Porsche. "It's the something. I was in the area for an interview yesterday. I'm a student teacher."

"Where at, Exeter?"

"'Fraid not. I come from Devon, but I'm at college in Wales. Tencastle, if you've heard of it."

She shook her head. Her brow was still knitted.

"Um, do you want a lift to Exeter or not?" I didn't want to waste time hanging around on her doorstep like a cold-calling salesman. "Jessica – that's my car – is quite reliable. All patched up now and raring to go." Not the best choice of words to convince a doubter, perhaps.

"Oh well," she sighed. "It's you or nothing, I suppose."

Hardly a vote of confidence, but she grabbed a rucksack and followed me.

"You want to get on to the A27," she said.

I knew that, but acknowledged, "Thanks."

I took the route my bus should have followed. Skid marks, a pile of broken glass still by the roadside and a badly bent bollard marked the site of yesterday's accident.

Maddy didn't say much at all for the next hour or so, beyond monosyllabic responses to my attempt at polite conversation. I guess she was still moping over being downgraded from her expectation of first class executive travel. She underwent a remarkable transformation, however, after a coffee and loo stop the other side of Southampton. Almost exuberant and chatting almost non-stop she quizzed me about what Exeter was like as a city, my background and my family. To the latter I kept the answers fairly general, a little uneasy about what was driving her, but it gave me the opportunity to squeeze in a question of my own.

"Do you have any brothers or sisters?"

"Only a kid brother. He's a total wimp." So much for sibling love.

"Right. I wondered whether the girl I caught sight of in the pub yesterday was your sister."

"Oh her! She only works in the kitchen Fridays and weekends."

"Do you help out at other times?"

"Me? Not bloody likely!"

The minor digression into her own family life quickly stifled, Maddy focussed her questions on my student life. Probing, for that's what it seemed like to me, far beyond polite conversation, her questions and comments became more overtly charged with sexual innuendo, leading eventually to her direct question.

"How many girls have you slept with?"

I didn't reply immediately. I distinctly got the impression that a flippant response wouldn't satisfy her and the honest truth only encourage her. I muttered something non-committal about having several female friends but no regular girlfriend.

She thought about this for a minute or two. Her hand then started to brush over my left knee, creeping up my thigh. Steering with one hand, I guided her wrist back to her own lap, which she took as the signal to grab my hand and thrust it down to her crotch.

Only the blaring of a horn and an instinctive one-handed swerve on my part avoided a head-on collision.

"Don't bloody well do that again!" I yelled, as I restored both hands to the wheel.

She seemed totally unfazed and unbelievably responded in a soft voice, "I could make you come at the wheel." Her hand once again began to stray.

"No, Maddy! You may have a death wish, I don't! Now keep your hands to yourself when I'm driving!" I was finding it difficult to concentrate on the road ahead, for fear of what she'd get up to next.

A brief silence. Then, "If you want to have sex with me, we could pull off the road …go into a field…"

"No, Maddy, I do not want to have sex with you."

"Don't you find me attractive?" Her voice was becoming rougher, accusing. When I didn't reply, she sneered, "I get it, you don't want sex with me because you're a queer!"

I kept my cool with difficulty. "No, I'm not homosexual, it's just I have no intention of having casual sex with a girl I didn't know before this morning."

"Bet you'd have gone for that tart in the kitchen."

She seemed to go into a sulk, for she made no further lewd comments for the next few minutes. Her next sly remark, when it came, shook me with her twisted, malicious turn of mind. "I'll go to the police, tell them you've molested me, tried to rape me ... if you won't ..."

I turned off sharply.

"Where are you going!"

I'd had enough. We'd entered Dorchester and during her last outburst, I'd noticed a fortuitous sign.

"Here we are. The police station. You can make your report right now. I'll come with you. And then I'm going to phone your mother and tell her why her scheming sex-crazy little daughter is going to have to make her own way from Dorchester."

"What! You can't do that! You can't just dump me here!"

"Try me." I hoped she wouldn't call my bluff. I wasn't sure I'd still got the piece of paper with her mother's number. Nor was I sure that the police would take my word against hers.

"My mother will kill me!" She broke into huge great sobs of tears. I didn't offer her a shoulder to weep on.

"Well, are we going in?" I waved towards the door of the police station. "They might be interested in what else you took with your fix of caffeine."

"No!" She sobbed some more. "Oh God!"

I made no further move, just gave her a little while to calm down. "Well?" I said.

"Oh Robert, please! Please don't leave me here!" She gulped. "I'm ... I'm so sorry ... I don't know what came over me."

I could guess, but I didn't say anything.

"I didn't mean any of ... of that ... of reporting you ... I promise I'll not be ... difficult. Please, please, take me on to Exeter!"

Despite all the trouble, I didn't really like the idea of abandoning her. "Okay," I offered. "But you travel in the back and any suggestion of a repeat performance, I promise you I will do what I said just now."

Thankfully she was as quiet as a mouse for the rest of the journey. Normally I would have stopped for a pub lunch but we made do with a burger at a roadside kiosk, and I kept a close eye on her manner after she'd used the loo in a lay-by.

"Do you want me to drop you at the bus station or the university?" I broke the silence as we approached Exeter city centre, a good five hours or so after we had left her home.

"Bus station will do."

I parked opposite to let her out.

"Thank you, Robert … I'm sorry I was so stupid earlier."

She might have kissed me if she'd been in the front seat.

"Good luck," I said by way of farewell. And breathed a sigh of relief as I started on the last leg of my journey to my parents' farm.

Although I valued my independence and I would no longer consider living with my parents on an extended basis, it was always comforting to return to the home of my youth, an oasis of peace and tranquillity in rural Devon. Looking out over the rolling hills to the backdrop of Dartmoor, even the environs of Tencastle would be hard pressed to compete with its idyllic location. Not that life on a working farm was a bed of roses, as my father sometimes reminded me. I think he'd have appreciated my commitment to his way of life, even so.

My parents, bless them, were as usual eager to catch up on the news of my exploits, and I quickly gave them an expurgated version of my job seeking to date. As for general life at Tencastle, the odd things that I found memorable or inspirational seemed quite mundane in the retelling. Dad, of course, wanted a root and branch account of all the activity in the vegetable garden he'd helped to establish. Since our belated attempts to tackle the encroaching weeds back in the Spring, we'd rather let the plot, well, go to seed. I made a mental note to give it a blitz before they came up for the graduation ceremony.

His enquiry also reminded me that I needed to ring the cottage to see whether any further invitations to interview had arrived in the post. There were still one or two schools in southern England that hadn't yet been tempted by my talents, and it didn't make much sense to return to Tencastle only to set out on another jaunt possibly the following day.

"Hi there, Rob! How did you get on?" It was Dan who picked up my call. I told him, complete with the saga of my most recent journey.

"Reminds me of that old joke, she was only a publican's daughter but she preferred men to …"

"Yes, yes, I've heard it before. Do please thank your mother again for letting me stay, particularly the extra night. Tell me, are there any more official looking letters for me?"

"What? No, sorry. You did have a phone call, though."

"Really? Who from?"

"Hang on a mo. Jake, who was it that phoned Rob?"

I heard a distant anguished cry. "What's he up to, strangling a cat?"

"Jake's taken to walking around the house in bare feet." Dan elaborated. "I think he's just found the ice cube I dropped."

"Why?"

"I'm practising making cocktails."

"No, I mean, why's Jake … oh, never mind! What's the sudden interest in cocktails?"

"For the cocktail party. Didn't I tell you?"

"No, but it can keep. Now, about the phone call …"

"Oh yeah. Be right back."

I waited a minute or so.

"Well?" I asked when Dan returned to the phone.

"Nick somebody or the other. Wanted you to get in touch with him as soon as possible. Something about a pregnancy." He paused. "You haven't put some girl in the club again have you?"

"What do you mean again? No! Have you got the number?"

Another wait.

"Here we are." Dan reeled off the digits which I instantly recognised as Wilfred Roberts in Carrick. "There's also a home number. Sounded urgent. You sure you've not been up to mischief, like with that lab technician who had the hots for you?"

"She's moved on. And I wasn't. See you late Monday, probably."

I hoped Nick Ramsbottom – I didn't know of any other Nick from Carrick – wouldn't mind me ringing on a Sunday morning. He didn't seem the church-going type to me.

A woman answered. "Just a minute, I'll get him. Who is calling?"

No doubt about the accent on the phone. "Rob, I'm glad you've called. I've got something that might be of interest to you."

"Go on."

"You remember Jenny Pagitter, the other chemist? I think you took some of her lower school classes last autumn. She's expecting her first baby soon, and …" He paused. "I suppose I should ask first whether you've already got a job lined up."

Interesting. "Not yet, but actively looking."

"That's good. I mean, good that you might be available. Rather than go through all the rigmarole of advertising and interviews, I … we wondered whether you would consider covering her maternity leave. It's only a temporary post for six months, but, knowing Jenny, I wouldn't be surprised if she opted to become a full time mum, or at least work only part time. So, although I obviously can't promise, there is a possibility of a permanent post. I thought you did a very good job on your spell here, and I heard complimentary remarks about how you handled situations on the field trip with Mark and Moira."

"Thanks very much, Nick. I appreciate your confidence in me."

"Are you interested, then?"

"How soon do you need to know?"

"Well, pretty quickly. If you are not available, we'll need to get on with other arrangements."

"I am certainly interested, but I've got an interview here in Devon tomorrow. I'm at my parents' place now. Can I let you know tomorrow evening, or Tuesday latest?"

"That would be fine. I'm not sure whether in self-interest I should wish you good luck, but I'll understand if you want to accept something more secure closer to your roots."

"I'll be in touch. Cheers … and thanks again."

"Good news?" Mum asked.

"Yes, I suppose it is. I've got a job, even if temporary, from September, if Exmouth doesn't turn up trumps."

I was far more relaxed for my appointment at Exmouth, which was due in part to a lazy day lounging around my parents' garden but even more down to the fact that I knew my immediate future on the job front no longer depended upon idiosyncratic interviews or temperamental transport.

Jessica behaved impeccably and the interview process was very business-like and efficient, though conducted with a degree of informality that allowed myself and the other candidate, from Bristol, to feel at ease. Talking with him over lunch, however, his feelings about the post pretty much mirrored my thoughts. For location and sense of co-operation and purpose within the science department, it had much going for it. The drawback, we both agreed, was the strong likelihood of a timetable heavily weighted towards the lower age groups and the lower ability CSE students, with little prospect of sixth form work until we had proved our worth. Nick had given strong hints that I'd have some access to the higher echelons.

Before our final interview, Exmouth's Head of Science asked whether we would consider accepting the post, if offered. My fellow applicant shook his head and politely declined.

"Mr Kiddecott?"

The job was clearly mine for the asking. I mentally tossed a coin.

"I regret that, though in many ways I am tempted, I would also like to withdraw at this stage. I have this morning received another offer which, on balance, will offer greater scope for my personal development."

I hoped it didn't sound like the load of old cobblers I knew it to be. The poor guy gave a slight shrug of disappointment, and, spreading his hands, said, "Well, gentlemen, if that is your decision, so it must be. Thank you for your time."

Nick on the other hand would be very happy.

CHAPTER NINETEEN

Cupid's Dart

"Seems a bit of an anticlimax," I said. I'd only been back at the cottage for a couple of days after my travels, and the euphoria at having a job for the autumn had already worn off.

"What do you mean, Rob?" said Dan.

"Well, our future's all settled, so to speak, no real challenges left at college." Foreseeable future, I should have said, which for me was just the next six months.

"There's still the final examinations. You've got to pass, I suppose?"

"I suppose." Nick hadn't made it clear whether my temporary appointment was conditional on graduating. "Still, most of it is based on continuous assessment and our teaching practice performance. I've no worries there."

"And there's the Graduation Ball, don't forget!" Jake said. "And the graduation ceremony itself to look forward to."

Neither prospect turned me on. The ball was always on the evening before the results were posted – the graduation day itself as far as the students were concerned. "Getting dressed up to prat around dancing? Over-bloody expensive, if you ask me! And we've got to fork out to hire fancy dress to shake hands with the Vice-Chancellor and receive a piece of paper!"

The Ceremony was, well, just that, a glorified photo opportunity for proud parents to acquire the standard sideboard portrait of their son or daughter in full regalia. And of course, a lucrative business opportunity for guest houses, restaurants, gown hire and the services of Dafydd ap Thomas who ran the only specialist photography business in Tencastle.

"My, we are grumpy today!" said Dan, "Hangover?"

"Piss off!"

"I think we should set up a blind date for him at the ball," Jake said in a theatrical aside to Dan.

"You bloody dare!"

"You should think yourself lucky that we don't have to hire gowns for the exams as well," said Dan.

"True," I conceded.

It had made a big splash in Llais y Castell in my first year. The college authorities, in an absurd attempt to add gravitas to the proceedings, had insisted that all students in their final examinations should wear academic dress. Pointless, because the examination hall, a.k.a. the sports hall, sweaty and airless at the best of times, was unbearably hot on a sunny summer's day, and the practically-minded invigilators had allowed students to stow the heavy robes by their desk. Provided one was seen to be carrying a gown, the rules were unofficially relaxed so that a student hadn't actually needed to wear it to the examination. Some residents at Thomas Hall had exploited the situation, offering to hire, for a nominal fee, the black liners from their bedroom curtains. The proprietor of the sole outlet for academic attire in Tencastle must have complained about lost business, or else the cleaners at Thomas had spilled the beans, for on one memorable occasion, the Vice-Chancellor himself had appeared at the examination hall, and insisted that all candidates be suitably dressed. The furore which followed when he had then sought to exclude all those – the vast majority, in fact – with fake drapes had caused a stand-off with students refusing to leave the hall, and the Vice-Chancellor bawling them out and refusing to back down. Common sense had eventually prevailed, but only when the Union President and senior lecturers had intervened, drawing attention to the likely damage to the Vice-Chancellor's precious image of the college. The question of academic dress had been quietly forgotten when the following year's examinations came round.

While the cottage should have presented, in theory, the perfect location for quiet study, Jake and Dan always preferred to work with the radio blaring out the latest hits. Sunny and I often set out after breakfast to seek the peace of the College Library, where, with finals fast approaching, only early arrivals could be guaranteed a decent seat. I'd long discovered that the padded chairs on the first floor gallery of the huge church-like building offered far more comfort for prolonged study than their wooden counterparts in the main ground floor area. Besides which, the study bays on the balcony were out of view of the librarian's desk below, and rules of silence, if not broken, could at least be discreetly bent. It was also possible to observe one's fellow students working at the long mahogany tables below.

I'd brought Sunny in that morning as usual, dropping her at the station to catch an early train to visit a friend for a long weekend, and I'd already spent three hours on intense, if not particularly organised, revision. In the pleasant warmth of a June afternoon and the aftermath of a liquid lunch, I was currently in 'thinking' mode. Others might call it daydreaming. My attention drifted towards a particular table below, where, for the past three days Kissy had taken up residence adjacent to the social science section. I'd known Kissy, of course, from day one at Tencastle, and ever since she had always been part of a special group willing to get involved with Jake's schemes, like the Mummers play and Carpiog Morris. As she leaned back and yawned, her full rounded breasts stretched against the cotton of her light summer blouse, I wondered why I'd never really made any romantic advances towards her. I didn't count flirting banter between friends. Oblivious of my interest she leant forward again over her books, and I wished I had a pair of binoculars to get a better view of her cleavage, exposed by the unfastened top buttons of her blouse.

Over the past month or so she'd taken up with a burly rugby forward, who, according to Llais y Castell, had been hospitalised with a crushed testicle after an ill-tempered needle match with arch rivals Lampeter. On an impulse, with the opposition partly neutralised, so to speak, I scribbled a message on a sheet of foolscap, folded it into a paper dart and launched the missile, and my hopes, towards Kissy's heart.

To avoid obvious eye encounter, I ducked behind the wooden panelling of the balcony whilst my cupid's arrow sped downwards, so I didn't actually follow the dart's progress. Raising my head carefully a few moments later, I smiled in anticipation as I saw Kissy glance upwards, and a short time afterwards gather her books together and depart.

I was a bit secretive with Jake when I returned to the cottage briefly to smarten myself up.

"Got a date then, Rob?" he asked.

"Sort of."

"Who's the poor girl?"

"Ahah," I replied, and tapped the side of my nose.

"Do you want me to move into Sunny's room for the night?" Jake inquired helpfully.

I'm not sure whether Sunny would have been happy with Jake intruding on her personal patch. I couldn't really see that I was going to strike that lucky, anyway. Indeed, I wasn't even sure that I was going to have a date at all. So I just said, "Don't think that will be necessary, thanks. But don't bolt the door like you did last Saturday night!" Returning at two o'clock in the morning it had taken ten minutes of loud banging on the door and handfuls of gravel at his window to rouse any signs of life.

Jessica may have been a touch jealous since it took several swings of the handle before she spluttered into life with a burst of blue exhaust smoke. She made more hard work than usual crawling up the long hill from Penybont. However, I was still in good time for my chosen rendezvous – by Goliath, of course. Seven thirty came and went, and, although there were a fair number of townies and students about, none were in the fair form of Kissy Kesteven. I looked at my watch again and decided to call it a day.

"Hello, Rob."

I recognised the 'Ooh Aarrh' accent. "Oh, hi there, Liz. I was just …"

Liz Burke had been a surprising hit as Mother Wayles in Jake's rag production, since when she had politely declined his invitation to her to join Carpiog Morris, and had once more tended to keep her own counsel. She brushed away her long, mousy hair from her moon-like face with a pudgy hand.

"I'm sorry I'm late …"

"Sorry?"

"You must have been getting tired of waiting."

"I … er,"

"I wasn't sure what to wear. The invitation didn't say." She gave an embarrassed little giggle and blushed.

"The invitation …?" But I already knew before she produced a familiar sheet of multi-folded foolscap from her handbag. With an unflattering surname and a solid figure unlikely to ever grace a Pirelli calendar, she would not have ignored Cupid's arrow.

"This is from you, isn't it?" A look of concern clouded her face.

My few cryptic words 'Tonight. Goliath, 7.30. If you're free. R.' I could not deny it.

"Ye…es, but …"

"Oh, it is so kind of you to ask me, Rob." She gushed on, unaware that I'd suddenly gone slack-jawed. "What a bolt from the blue it was, you're quite a surprising person, you know."

My thoughts exactly.

"Have you planned anything for this evening, Rob?"

"Well, er, not really. I hadn't … actually …" Such plans as I had envisaged were already history. "I didn't know if anyone would turn up." I hoped there was a sufficient suggestion that I hadn't got Liz Burke specifically in mind.

But Liz was oblivious to hints.

"I'm not terribly keen on the cinema, it hurts my eyes." Liz continued. "But I'm happy to go for a meal if you like. Chinese is my favourite."

My appetite had rather deserted me, but I couldn't see any half-decent way out. Grin and bear it.

"Okay, fine by me, if that's what you'd like." I tried to put a pinch of enthusiasm in my voice, however reluctant.

Her saucer eyes fairly lit up behind her wire-frame spectacles.

"Kowloon, then?" I suggested. "Unless you'd prefer the Ganges?"

When it came to ethnic cuisine in Tencastle, choice was not high on the menu. The Ganges Indian Curry House down by the station by all accounts had a reasonably good reputation, whilst the Kowloon, on Castle Street was basically a take-away with a few tables crammed into a small upstairs room. Intimacy with one's neighbours was unavoidable if the restaurant was more than half full. One of the hotels on the posh edge of town also advertised speciality Thai dishes for the discerning diner with a deep pocket. That didn't include students.

"Oh, definitely Chinese. I've always wanted to try chopsticks!"

"Right." We might be in for a long evening.

I'd left Jessica parked near the College, so there didn't seem much point in moving her when Castle Street was only a short walk away. I hoped not to meet anyone I knew.

Being still quite early, the Kowloon was almost deserted. Business at the take-away on a Friday evening would become very brisk once the pubs turned out on, but for now the young Chinese girl at the counter was watching some soap on the TV suspended from the ceiling.

"Have you got a table for two?" I asked. I wouldn't have minded if she'd said no.

She turned away from the screen briefly, and waved with her hand in the direction of the stairs. I took that to mean yes.

Indeed, in the small room over the shop front, only one of the seven tables was already occupied, by a young couple with two pre-pubescent children, a boy and a girl. The decor was pretty basic – the odd Chinese lantern and ornate dragon illustrations on the whitewashed walls – but it was clean, with fresh linen and posy bowl on each table.

"Window seat?" I suggested.

"That's great, yes!"

It was in fact the only table by the window. Outside, the evening sun caught the upper parapets of Gwilym Williams' electrical store opposite. A waiter brought us menus. Liz looked as excited as a kid on her first visit to the seaside.

"What do you recommend, Rob?"

"Well, er," I hadn't a clue, but scanning the menu rapidly, I replied, "the set meals for two give a good variety of dishes." They were also the most inexpensive, all things considered, since, a la carte, the separate items would have cost an arm and a leg. "Unless you've got a particular yen for something."

"No, good idea, Rob!" Liz beamed at me.

"Would you like a drink?" asked the waiter.

"White wine for me!" Liz responded quickly.

"Make that two!" I said.

Although still not fully reconciled to the twist of fate, I was beginning to relax. There were no uncomfortable silences as Liz kept up a flow of conversation greater than I would have ever expected from her, and I began to participate with more than just the minimal responses that politeness required. Some people will tell you their whole life story at the drop of a hat, but Liz wasn't like that at all – much more of a two-way exchange of two people with a nodding acquaintance getting to know each other better. The last time we'd been quite so intimately confined was on the minibus rat-run in the first teaching practice and then not with just each other for company. By the time the steaming salvers of oriental fare arrived, I'd already discovered that she was the youngest of eight children from an old Quantocks family, and the first one to ever go on to higher education.

"How come you don't have a strong Devon accent, Rob?" she asked, after I'd commented – kindly, of course – on her rustic burr. She heaped a pile of noodles onto her plate to join the generous helping of sweet and sour pork and egg fried rice.

"That's because I'm not a native Devonian. I was born in Guildford and moved to Devon when I was six. My father came from Devon originally but he worked on a farm in Surrey for a few years, and my mother came from Hampshire. So I've got a general purpose southern counties accent, if anything."

Liz was determined to master the chopsticks and had managed to transfer a few grains of rice and the odd noodle to her mouth.

"Aren't you going to try them. Rob?"

"I'm not on a diet," I replied.

"Come on, don't be a spoilsport! You'll be finished ages before me otherwise."

That was true. "Okay, but if we haven't got the hang in five minutes, how about we both go back to conventional tools? Otherwise the food will be cold!"

"Fair enough."

We didn't really stand much chance in five minutes of mastering a technique for which the Chinese had had a lifetime of practice, but in the chopsticks duel I was just beginning to get the edge over Liz. Until I was distracted by the arrival of the latest customers to the restaurant which had filled up; only the corner table behind me was still free.

Kissy gave me a little wave and smile as she passed our table with her one-ball boyfriend. "Hi there, Rob. Hello, Liz. Strange we both thought of coming here, isn't it?"

"Hi," I said lamely, my attempted smile coming out more as a grimace. I'd hoped for more than a meeting of minds. A delicately poised morsel of water chestnut fell onto the tablecloth.

"Isn't that one of the Mummers?" whispered Liz, after Kissy and her companion had taken their seats.

"Uh huh." I was surprised that either girl would have recognised each other out of costume. I fell silent.

"Penny for your thoughts, Rob?" asked Liz, who couldn't have failed to notice that I'd lost interest in the food.

"Er, yes, I'm okay," I flannelled. "Something just came into my mind."

"Want to share it?"

No way! "No, it's, er … it's just something I should have done at college today." Like check where the bloody dart had gone, for instance.

I abandoned the chopsticks.

Liz continued to chat away and I suppose I must have responded in kind through the rest of meal. It was while we were waiting for our coffee order that something else entered my mind. Genuine, and just as embarrassing.

"'Scuse me a minute, Liz, just need to pop to the cloakroom."

I stumbled out and along the narrow corridor to the single unisex WC. I wasn't sure that I had enough cash on me to meet the bill. My plans, such as they were for the evening, had been more along the lines of a drink in one of the pubs with live music. I checked my wallet and found three pounds and in my pocket about eighty pence. I was pretty sure that the meal alone was at least five pounds. I also found a screwed-up dog-eared voucher for a free take-away from the Kowloon, a left-over from my freshers' pack aeons ago. I hoped the management would accept it as collateral. I wasn't fond of washing up at the best of times.

I returned to our table, where Liz was sipping her coffee.

"Are you all right, Rob?" she asked. I probably didn't look all right.

"Just a little queasy stomach. Unfamiliar food, I guess." Though it wasn't fair to blame the meal. I couldn't think of any way of approaching my predicament with the bill, which I noticed had already been placed on a dish by the coffee pot.

Seven pounds eighty five pence. There was also a fifty pence piece on the dish. I reached for my wallet with a silent prayer.

"It's okay, Rob, I've already paid."

"What!" You could have knocked me down with a chopstick.

"I'll tell you outside," Liz whispered.

"But …"

"Later!"

We left the restaurant almost immediately. I didn't know whether to be relieved, embarrassed, or just plain gobsmacked, and my confusion must have been quite obvious.

"Seems I'm not the only surprising person this evening," I managed to say, when we got outside.

"Shall we take a walk in the park?" said, Liz, slipping her arm round mine.

"Why did you…." I began.

"It's my birthday."

"Ah!"

But Liz forestalled the congratulations I was about to offer. "I owe you an apology, Rob."

"For what?" If anyone needed to apologise, it was me.

"Tell me, Rob, your airmail wasn't intended for me, was it?"

"Well, er, not exactly …er, no." There was no point in pretending otherwise.

"Who were you expecting?"

"It doesn't really matter now. You turned up, she didn't." Not in the way I'd hoped for, at least.

"I know I've taken advantage of you. I really wanted to do something special for my birthday, but I still don't really know a lot of people here in Tencastle, except my flat-mates, and they were either going home or were too busy with their boyfriends. I don't exactly get many offers of dates from boys, you know. I'd dreamt of some handsome prince whisking me off to a ball, like Cinderella. I was feeling pretty sorry for myself, really. And then this note landed on my table."

I grimaced.

"I didn't know who had sent it, honest!" she went on. "I almost didn't come. It seemed crazy, too good to be true. But I waited across the road to see who turned up, if anyone. When I saw you, and no one else joined you, I plucked up courage. You've always seemed quite a kindly person and I hoped you wouldn't tell me to bugger off!"

She seemed close to tears. Instinctively, I put my arms around her, to comfort her.

"What would you have done if nobody had turned up?"

"I don't know. Gone for a burger and a Coke at the Union, I suppose. What would you have done?"

"Probably the same," I confessed.

She looked up at me, her eyes wet. "I'm sorry, Rob, I shouldn't have done it. But I have really enjoyed this evening."

"There's no need to apologise, Liz. There would have been two lonely and disappointed people otherwise, wouldn't there?"

"Do you really mean that?"

"Yes, I do," I declared, quite sincerely.

"You're not just saying that because you feel sorry for me?"

"Not at all. I don't deny the evening has been quite a surprise in many ways, but you're good company, Liz, and that's something I've not appreciated before, even when we were involved in the mumming." I paused. "You really did well in that, you know."

"Do you think so?" Liz squeezed my hand.

"Sometimes it takes a quirk of fate to see a person in a new light." I hoped I didn't sound patronising. It wasn't my intention.

"You're very sweet. Rob. Thank you for being so ... understanding."

"Just one thing, Liz. I'm not happy about you footing the bill for the meal."

"Please, that's my treat."

"No, Liz, thank you, but that wouldn't be fair at all."

"Well, suppose we go Dutch? Half and half?"

"Is that okay with you?" It seemed a good compromise.

"If you insist."

We'd nearly reached my car.

"Can I give you a lift back to your digs?"

"I'd be very grateful, thanks."

"Where do you live?"

"Just off Dyfed Road. It's about a mile."

I explained the whimsical nature of Jessica's behaviour, which, among other things, currently required passengers to climb in via the driver's door, the lock on the passenger door having become inexplicably jammed.

"Front or back seat?"

"Front."

"Okay, but look out for the gear lever knob – else it will get caught in your dress."

Dyfed Road was in the opposite direction from the cottage, along past the station, and up the hill beyond the old Castle Brewery. Jessica, fortunately, behaved herself.

"Would you like to come in for a coffee?"

I thought about it, but didn't want to go along with possible implications of acceptance.

"Thanks very much, but I've got an early start tomorrow." For whatever.

I got the impression that Liz was also quite pleased for the evening to end there. I got out of the car and helped her negotiate the gear knob.

"Thanks very much, Rob, for a lovely evening. It will be a birthday to remember!"

"Happy Birthday, Liz." And I kissed her hand.

Dan was in conspiratorial mood next morning at breakfast. "Didn't know you had a new girlfriend."

"I don't."

"Lover's tiff, then, was it?"

"Get stuffed!"

"Ooh, touchy, aren't we. Liz Burke, wasn't it? Didn't think she'd be your bit of skirt."

"It was. She's not."

"So, why all the holding hands in the park?"

"Are you going to produce compromising photos next?" I was getting tired of this inquisition.

"Now that sounds interesting," Dan mused.

"There's nothing to compromise. It was her birthday, and she asked me yesterday if I'd like to make up a foursome. She'd booked a table but her friend had gone down with the flu. That's the truth!"

Well, half truth and nothing like the truth. I don't think Dan fully believed it either, but it cut off further speculation of my honour or reputation, not to mention that of Liz.

After all the hours I'd put in mugging up on obscure points in one hundred years of educational history and the finer points of theory and philosophy, all pretty useless at the chalk face, the examinations themselves, all three papers, were unchallenging. It was obvious that they did not intend anyone to fail, with questions verging on the banal, and, for anyone whose revision had only started the previous evening, the option to 'set and answer a question you had hoped to find on this paper'.

To celebrate their conclusion in a suitable way Jake had organised the back room of the Castle for a party. "Last time we're all likely to get together for a bash," he said, as we drove in from the cottage. "We'll soon be scattered to the four corners of the globe."

"Have you made any plans for your digs next year?" I asked. "I was wondering whether there's any possibility of us staying on at Penybont."

"I don't know. The owners are supposed to be coming back, but I haven't heard anything definite." He thought for a moment. "Would you really want to be committed to driving every day to Carrick?"

"Yeah, Jessica's not getting any younger," said Dan.

She coughed and jerked in indignation.

"Now you've hurt her feelings!" I said. "I suppose really I ought to be looking at somewhere in Carrick."

"Well, you've got two or three weeks of bugger all before the exam results come out, then another week before the grand Ceremony to check things out."

"What are you going to do with that time, Dan? Go home, like Sunny?"

"Oh I don't know, mooch around, relax. Too expensive to keep flitting back to Brighton."

"We could go out for picnics!"

I couldn't quite picture Jake perched on a tussock sipping vacuum flask tea and daintily eating cucumber sandwiches from a plastic plate.

"Seriously!" he said. "Take the bus or train out or even Jessica. A group of us, a few of the girls as well. We haven't really explored the area beyond Tencastle."

"We could go boating again." Dan said provocatively.

"Pillock!"

It seemed from the heaving mass of humanity at the Castle that Jake hadn't restricted his invitations to those who'd actual been examined. Apart from our mutual friends I'd mentioned it to Trevor, Liz and Bronwen in my tutor group. I hoped that neither Liz nor Kissy would let slip some remark about the Kowloon evening that might cause Dan to question my account. I needn't have worried.

"What's the plan?" I whispered to Jake as he led them all through to the back room.

"Drink, eat, be merry, drink, sing, drink, dance, drink … is that okay with you?"

Stupid question. I wasn't sure about the dancing bit, though, in the confined space.

A tap on my shoulder. "Hi Rob, thanks for inviting me. Hope you didn't mind me bring Gilbert along too."

"Not at all, Liz." The pair reminded me of Jack Spratt and his missus. Gilbert would have made a rake look fat. I caught sight of Min and Huw chatting. "Enjoy yourself. Excuse me."

"Rob! Good to see you!" Min reached up and gave me her usual huggy kissy greeting. She'd dispensed with her teeth brace. "Dan was just telling me about the picnics you're organising."

"I, um…that was Jake," I prevaricated.

"Great idea! We could do some dancing. It will be midsummer's day soon!"

Min had taken over as the driving force for Carpiog, ever since the trip to the inter-varsity festival in the Spring. Holly and Harry were still keen, and she'd roped in several new recruits while keeping Gron on board as foreman. They'd celebrated the first of May by dancing on the Castle mound at crack of dawn. God knows why, no one was there to watch.

"There must be some old stone circles around," Min's eyes lit up as her idea blossomed.

"I'm definitely not cavorting around naked beneath the moonlight!" I said, knowing how her mind worked.

She looked disappointed.

"Anyway, you'll soon be a respectable married woman, won't she Huw?"

"But not yet!" she grinned wickedly, punching Huw on the arm.

"But would you be up for a bit of stick bashing again if I keep her under control?" said Huw, smiling. He gave her a squeeze.

Which is how on several occasions in the following two weeks, in raggies and blackened faces, we scared the pants off several bus passengers and were forced to travel in the guard's van back to Tencastle by a stroppy stationmaster up the line. We made no pretence about collecting for charity, other than for our own liquid refreshment.

"Rob, you have got a decent suit, haven't you?"

"Yes, I have now. Did you want to borrow it?"

"Thanks, but I don't think it would fit me," said Jake. He had a full six inches height advantage over me.

"Then why …?"

"You'll need it yourself,"

"Will I?" I had a growing suspicion that there was far more to Jake's casual enquiry.

"Present for you. Sorry it's a bit late for your birthday." He handed me a plain white envelope.

Three months too late, in fact. The card in the envelope was absolutely plain. I looked at him, puzzled.

"Go on, open it up."

Two tickets fell out and drifted down to the floor. He retrieved them and passed them over.

"Bloody hell, Jake, it's for the Ball!"

"Yep, compliments of the President-elect. I was given half a dozen for myself and friends."

"Well thanks very much, that's very good of you, but why do I need ...?" My suspicions returned. "You've ruddy well set me up!"

"Would I do that?" Jake said innocently.

"Too bloody right you would!" I felt like a rabbit caught in a trap. "So you're going to pair me off with some ugly buck-toothed crone whom no-one else would look twice at!"

"Have I ever let you down?" Jake protested gently. He was getting more fun out of the exchange than I was.

"You're pretty fond of roping me into your harebrained schemes!"

"But they've always worked out well, haven't they? And you can't say we haven't had some good times as a result."

"Yes, but this is different."

"Trust me."

He knew me well enough to be pretty sure I wouldn't make a big issue of it and turn him down flat. I shrugged, accepting the inevitable. "Okay, I suppose I'll have to go along with it. Do I know the victim?"

Jake touched his nose. "Wait and see."

"Bastard! What's the plan then for tomorrow?"

"Well, I was hoping you'd drive. Dan and Sunny, they're going together, and myself. We'll meet our partners there at eight o' clock."

"Where's 'there'? Not the Thomas Hall Observatory again, surely?" By all accounts the dome had been an inspired location for last year's ball, until some drunken prat had set off the fire alarm.

"The Rivers, would you believe?"

"Really?" Distinctly up-market. "Don't rely on a lift back, will you. I might be leaving early."

"Somehow, I doubt that you will."

Jake wouldn't give me any further clues either to his date or mine, no matter how much I tried to wheedle a name from him.

Sunny looked ravishing. When you're sharing a house as four independent people, as we were, it's so easy to accept a person, as, well, just being there as a friend. She was a lovely person to be with, easy to chat to and get on with, but even in our journeys to Carrick, I'd never really thought of her in any other way. I wondered how I'd overlooked the fact that she was indeed very good-looking. Her shimmering blue dress clung to her slim, but shapely figure, and the lightest touch of lipstick and eye-shadow enhanced perfectly her olive complexion. She could have been an oriental princess. Her Prince Charming looked like Dan in a suit and bow tie, smarter than I'd seen him before, but then they'd not seen me dressed up like a suave James Bond at Monte Carlo either. God knows where Jake had acquired his penguin suit from, but with cravat and white gloves all he needed was a top hat and cane to break into a Fred Astaire routine.

Jessica had never carried such elegant passengers before.

We were a little early. I left Jessica in a nearby street as parking at the Rivers Hotel could be difficult. Not so much the parking itself as the high probability of being boxed in by latecomers and later leavers. Excluding college premises, Rivers was the only decent venue in Tencastle that was big enough to cater for full-scale formal functions, and most of the wedded folk in the area that weren't pinched for a penny had used it for their reception.

Dan and Sunny started to make their way to the hotel. Sunny then turned back to me, fishing for something in her clasp handbag.

"Rob," she said. "Sorry, I meant to give this to you earlier. It was jammed at the back of a drawer."

I recognised the lilac envelope immediately. "Thanks."

"I was making a start today on clearing out my stuff. I hope it wasn't anything important."

"Probably not." I said calmly, though inside I was fuming. If Benji had been there I would have stuffed his brushes up his backside for ruining my love life. Why on earth Mary's letter should have ended up in his room I couldn't imagine. As it was, I was standing outside a posh hotel, dressed up to the nines, waiting for someone I didn't know, and, at that moment, didn't want to.

Jake looked anxiously at his watch several times.

"Perhaps they've had second thoughts," I said, miserably.

"No, no, have faith!"

It wasn't me who seemed worried.

Jake glanced at his watch again then caught sight of someone across the park, and waved frantically. Not Fred Astaire style at all.

"Rhiannon!" he called. "Over here!"

Annie? My date or his? Quite mixed emotions were flashing through my head … anticipation … elation … reservation, even, about a possible awkward situation if he'd set up a foursome with Mary.

Someone tapped me on the arm. "Aren't you going to say hello, Rob?"

I took my eyes off Annie and turned. "Dilly!" I exclaimed, "Good to see you! You look beautiful." She did, too, those dark sparkling eyes, and black hair framing a perfectly oval face with its satin-smooth skin. I glanced back at Annie, now arm in arm with Jake. No sign of Mary.

Dilly noticed my wrinkled brow. "It is me, you know."

"Sorry?" She was smiling at me. And I blinked as the penny dropped. "You and I?"

She nodded, put her arms around my neck and gave me a quick peck on the cheek. "I think that's the plan, Rob."

"But did you know who you'd be meeting?" I was still too gobsmacked to believe what I was hearing.

"I had a pretty good idea."

"And it didn't put you off?" I couldn't believe my luck! I definitely owed Jake.

"Now why would I think that?" she said coyly. "Shall we go in?"

The ballroom was larger than I had imagined and more ornate, with cream-white hanging drapes and gilt chandeliers. On an oval-recessed stage at the far end a quartet were already in full swing, with jazzy sixties-style music on sax, clarinet, bass and drums, – the Dragonhearts, their banner incorporating the Welsh flag proclaimed. The bar at the opposite end was doing a brisk trade. Down one side plum-coloured padded chairs were grouped around tables bedecked with white cloth and candlesticks.

We joined Dan, Sunny and Rhiannon at one of the similarly furnished tables in the carpeted alcove, beyond which French windows opened onto a patio area that led onto lawns alongside the river. Jake was at the bar at the opposite end of the hall getting in a round of drinks.

"Pint, I guessed for you Rob," he said, when he returned bearing a large tray, "and Dilly, you're white wine, is that right?"

I wondered how he knew.

The remaining vacant tables were quickly filling up with beaux and debutantes magically transformed from the usual hairy scruffs and jean-and-sweater clad young females typical of Tencastle's student population. I scarcely recognised Rud, with yet another new girl in tow, nor Dicky and Sparkle, who actually looked awake for a change. I didn't know Bronwen's partner, though I guessed he was her fiancé. Kissy was with One-ball, while Sophie and Suzie radiated elegance in the company of Ivan Petrovsky and Tom Merchant respectively. Even Liz Burke with her stick man would have turned a head or two with her surprising grace on the dance floor.

"You ready?" asked Dilly, indicating the growing number of couples already swaying to the music, among them Huw and Min, absolutely stunning in the lowest cut dress that still afforded a modicum of decency.

I needed no second bidding. Without blowing my own trumpet, I'd always thought of myself as a reasonable dancer, but Dilly had that natural skill of anticipating every move I made, jiving, waltzing, tangoing – inventively – and quickstepping to whatever tempo the band played. We hardly took a rest until the buffet was served. That in itself was a feast worth every penny I hadn't had to pay for it.

"Shall we get a breath of air outside for a bit?" I suggested.

"Mmm, that would be nice." Dilly leant gently into my arms.

A number of couples had spread out onto the patio, in the warm calm summer's evening. A few, like us, strolled across the lawn to the river bank. My arms clasped softly around her waist, I stood behind her as we watched the Tene flowing gently by.

"Looks so peaceful and idyllic, doesn't it?" Dilly murmured, after several minutes.

I kissed her hair. She squeezed my hands in response.

"I shall be sorry to leave this," she said wistfully.

"Tonight?"

"That too. No, I mean Tencastle. You'll be moving on as well, I suppose?"

"Not far, only Carrick. I might even be able to stay on at the cottage. Where are you going?"

"Almost back home. Not so far away either."

"Aberystwyth?"

"Near there, Machynllech. You remembered?" She sounded surprised.

"On the eisteddfod trip. Your boyfriend met you off the coach."

She detected the hint of jealousy in my voice and laughed, "That was my brother, silly!"

I felt like a pillock. "Sorry, I thought …"

She laughed again, turned round and kissed me. "If you're thinking about competition, there isn't any."

"What about the guy who came with you to the party … wasn't he …?"

"Jeff, you mean? He used to be my dancing partner but that's all. He's not, um, interested in girls, as girls."

"Right. If only I'd have known."

"If you'd have known …?"

"I would have asked you out long ago."

"Hmm, really? Whenever I looked you seemed to be quite happy in other company."

She could have meant Sophie and me at the housewarming, or even one of my other brief and unproductive flirtations with Rhiannon or Mary Williams, for instance. But she managed to say it without a hint of reproach.

"Can we go back in, Rob, I'm getting a bit chilly. You can show me more of your skills on the dance floor."

Inside, the time for exuberant dancing had all but passed. The lighting had become more subdued, the pace of the music likewise, and couples more intimate. Only a few remained in their seats, Jake and Rhiannon among them, talking earnestly with each other. I wondered for a brief instant how I'd have been making out with her, not that I had any intention of swapping present company. Of Dan and Sunny there was no sign.

I lost track of time, of how long we clung to each other, our bodies swaying softly to the music, feet barely shuffling, conversation unnecessary as our eyes and caressing fingers said it all. Her head resting on my shoulder, her delicate perfume almost narcotic in the peace and contentment it brought me. We were hardly aware of the moment when the band finished its last set at eleven o'clock.

"Rob, it's been a magic evening." She looked up at me, eyes almost glistening, and kissed me, passionately.

"It's been my pleasure, Dilly. Truly."

We embraced and kissed again.

"You wouldn't like a coffee by any chance?" I said.

"Persuade me."

"Your place or mine?"

"Mine, I think, Rob, it's nearer, and we don't want to disturb your friends, do we."

Or them us, I thought. It was quite possible that Dan and Sunny might even be back at the cottage already.

We left the hotel, arm in arm. I started walking to where I'd left Jessica.

"No, let's walk, Rob. It's no distance."

It still took us over thirty minutes to reach the terraced cottage three streets away. There was a light in the upstairs window.

"Your flat mate still up?"

"No worries, Rob, she's staying with her boyfriend. I always leave my light on when I go out." She fumbled in her silver clasp bag and pulled out the door key. "Here, can you do it?"

I opened the door, stood back and followed her in.

"Close the door."

I did as she asked, and she flung her arms around me again, tongue probing in my mouth. We broke off the embrace, and she looked at me, smiling.

"Come with me." She took me by the hand, and led me to the stairs.

"Upstairs kitchen?"

A barely perceptible shake of her head. "Later."

Her room, very feminine, very tidy, contained beneath the window a single bed upon which she pulled me down. Her hands now were pulling at my shirt, reaching underneath caressing my stomach, mine exploring the back of her dress for a zip or catch.

From across the town the bells on the church clock rang out the midnight hour.

Graduation day!

Author's notes and acknowledgements

This novel is set in the early 1970's, before mobile phones and personal computers became part of everyday life. Had they been available many of the situations just could not have developed in the way described.

Although some incidents have been inspired by actual events, the characters in this novel are ficticious and no reference to any person living or dead is intended, even when the location is real. Tencastle and its environs exist only in my imagination; no town served by the rail link from Shrewsbury to Swansea accurately fits its description.

There is no longer an RAF search & rescue facility at Brawdy near St Davids.

I've taken a few liberties with the interior of the old college on the sea front at Aberystwyth. The Students' Union was relocated to the main campus above the town shortly before the time in which this novel is set, but the original building, still owned by the University, remains in the location described.

My fictional Carpiog Morris would have been one of the first revival Border sides, and certainly a pioneer of the many mixed teams we see today. Cecil Sharp began collecting traditional dances and songs after seeing Headington Quarry Morris Men perform on Boxing Day, 1899. The Morris Ring, formed in 1934, is the oldest of the three national Morris organisations (the others being the Morris Federation and Open Morris), and is still restricted to male dancers. The Inter Varsity Folk Dance Festival (IVFDF) has a long history continuing to the present day. There were probably very few Welsh bagpipe players in the early 1970s, though there has been a revival of interest in recent years.

I should like to record my appreciation of the professional advice received from Gary & Caroline Smailes at Bubblecow in helping me transform a raw manuscript into something presentable to my publishers,

Troubador. My thanks also goes to Michael Jecks, Mike and Wendy Gluyas, and to Mecki, John and Susie of Winkleigh Morris for their advice, reading and encouragement, to Hilary Bix for making sense out of my ideas for the cover, and to Ceri Rhys Matthews for crucial help with a Welsh phrase, I accept full responsibilty for any remaining mistakes and abuses of the Welsh language.

Colin Andrews
Morchard Bishop, May 2011

www.bonnygreen.co.uk